Barbara Howe lives on the third rock from the sun, while her imagination travels the universe and beyond.

Born in the US (North Carolina), she spent most of her adult life in New Jersey, working in the software industry, on projects ranging from low-level kernel ports to multi-million-dollar financial applications. She moved to New Zealand in 2009, gained dual citizenship, and now works as a software developer in the movie industry. She lives in Wellington, in a house overflowing with books and jigsaw puzzles, and wishes she had more time to spend universe hopping.

Reforging series by Barbara Howe available through IFWG Publishing

The Locksmith (book 1)
Engine of Lies (book 2)
The Blacksmith (book 3)
The Wordsmith (book 4)
The Forge (book 5)

Reforging: Book 5

The Forge

By Barbara Howe

The Forge

ISBN-13: 978-1-922556-37-0

Printed in Garamond and Goudy Old Style typefaces.

IFWG Publishing International
Gold Coast, Australia

www.ifwgaustralia.com

In memory of
Lamar Howe
Fire Wizard
1929-2021

Acknowledgements

I'd like to thank Gerry Huntman, who has stuck with this through all five books in the Reforging series. Thanks also to Maria Kelly, Rebecca Fraser, Catherine Archer-Wills, and everyone else at IFWG Publishing Australia who has contributed to one or more of these books, and to Letha Etzkorn, Jo Leary, Tim Jones, Caroline and John Interrante, Cindy Epsaro, and Anne Somerville who have been enthusiastic and supportive along the way.

But most of all, I have to thank my Covid bubble: husband, Art, and daughter, Lucy. If they hadn't given me time to write, or if they hadn't kept asking for more, this never would have happened.

A Warrior of Heroic Stature

Jean Rehsavvy, Frankland's retired Fire Warlock, paced the floor in his study at two in the morning. In their bedroom on the floor above, Lucinda snarled into the darkness. Drown the man and his sleepless nights.

Expending her own power to warm the bed on a frigid February morning drove sleep further away. Pulling the pillow over her head and burrowing deeper under the covers didn't help. After a quarter hour, she flung the duvet aside and pulled on a robe. Whatever was bothering him would upset her, too, but she couldn't stand not knowing.

When she walked into his study carrying two mugs and a plate piled high with jam tarts and shortbread, he greeted her with a smile. "Thank you, my dear. I hope I did not wake you."

She shrugged. "Why are you up? I thought we could finally relax. Things seem to be going so well."

"They are, and far better than we had any reason to expect last summer. Frankland is in such good shape I may turn my attention to other vital issues, such as the one raised by this report from our agent in Danzig." He nodded at an open letter lying on his desk.

Lucinda set her mug on the corner of the desk and lifted the letter. She could read nothing past the address to Warlock Quicksilver. Her gaze slid away and refused to focus on the cramped writing. "For your eyes only, I gather." She dropped it and pulled a chair towards the fire. "What does it say?"

"There are three items of interest, which, when taken together, are arresting. First, the emperor has ordered several warlocks to begin training to call down the lightning."

"Several?" Scanning the upper stories with her mind's eye reassured her that her shriek had not disturbed the baby or their staff. René rolled over in bed grumbling. She sent him a warm thought—*go back to sleep, little brother*—before returning her attention to her husband. "Several? Even one…"

"Relax, my dear. The Empire's political structure will support only one."

"You've said that before, but even one lightning wielder is frightening. They've conquered most of Europa without any. Why start now?"

Jean gave her a long, considering look over his mug's rim. If she picked up her own mug, she'd spill it. She sat on her shaking hands.

"We drove them to it," Jean said.

"You're joking. Aren't you? Please?"

"No, my love, I do not jest. The empire cannot abide their bitter rival having two, and soon four, lightning wielders. I have been expecting this ever since I began teaching you and René to call down the lightning."

René ambled out of the fireplace, rubbing his eyes. "Hey, hot chocolate." He nabbed Lucinda's mug and gulped. "Thanks."

She said, "Don't mention it."

Jean said, "Disturbed sleep is highly unusual for you, my young friend."

"I had to find out what scared Lucinda," René said. "I was sleeping fine until then."

Lucinda repeated what Jean had said. René leaned back against the wall and slid to the floor, yawning. "Is that all?"

"No," Jean said. "The emperor has quadrupled the price on your head."

René's eyes popped open. A grin spread across his face. "Wow. Nice to know what I'm worth." Jean's quelling look had no effect.

"And me?" Lucinda said. "Did they quadruple the price on my head, too?"

"No," Jean said. "That is the only surprise. The empire is broadcasting firm and clear orders that its agents are, under no circumstances, to harm you. If the necessity arises, they must protect your life with their own, as if you were the emperor himself."

René splashed hot chocolate across the hearthrug. Lucinda jammed her fist against her mouth and whimpered. "No, no…"

"Yes, the implications are obvious." Jean tapped the letter. "My correspondent reached the same conclusion, and he has not been privy to our discussions. This is serious news, indeed."

René said, "You're saying the emperor wants Lucinda around long enough to unlock the Fire Office."

"Yes, and when she does, the empire intends to throw its full arsenal at us."

"I get that. It's been nagging at me since September, when reforging the Water Office took two weeks, that we wouldn't have as much time for the Fire Office. But Beorn's seen me as Fire Warlock, and that means—"

Lucinda said, "It may mean Beorn's dead and you're Fire Warlock before we're ready to reforge the Fire Office."

"Or," Jean said, "it may mean you are Fire Warlock of a smaller Frankland. Perhaps all that will remain is a small circle around the Fortress, and our great cities will have been absorbed into the empire."

René, breathing hard, glared. "Wouldn't like that."

"So what do we do?" Lucinda said. "If we can't fix the Fire Office—"

"My dear," Jean said, "I have not said we will not fix it."

She shot to her feet. "You think I'll unlock the Fire Office with the empire waiting to pounce on us while we're defenceless? That's nuts!"

Jean's hand on her shoulder pressed her back into the chair. His voice soothed. "No, my dear, I do not expect that of you. I do expect you to someday unlock the Fire Office, but the empire will not know when to pounce, nor will we be defenceless. After all," he said, smiling at the scrawny boy sprawled on the hearth, "we will have one of Frankland's finest warlocks—a lightning wielder of heroic stature—to thwart their vainglorious aggression."

A grin flitted across René's features, but his eyes were wide and staring. "Yeah, right."

René sat cross-legged atop Storm King's highest pinnacle. On one side, the black crater yawned, all detail lost in shadow. On the other, a dim panorama of lava flows, fields, forest, town, and villages spread out into the far distance. The rising sun picked out the summit in gold, but provided little warmth on a February morning.

René sneered at the cold. Fury kept him warm. When a ragged column of flame whooshed into existence a few yards away on the ridge, he kept his glower focused on the retreating shadows, not acknowledging the Fire Warlock's presence.

Beorn watched him for a moment, before picking his way across the rocks to sit beside him. "I'd be feeling overwhelmed, too. I was when I realised I'd be Fire Warlock."

René turned his glower on Beorn. "You were already a warlock. What'd you expect?"

"I expected Jean to keep on being Fire Warlock forever, like he had been since before my granddad was born. I wanted to be *a* warlock, not *The* Warlock. Nobody in his right mind wants to live like a monk until he burns to death."

"Humph." René turned back to the black crater. "Maybe you won't have to burn."

"I'd rather burn than face the first Locksmith's 'hidden terror'."

"Humph."

"You won't have to worry about that. After it's fixed, the Fire Office will let you retire."

"Won't care. If there's nothing left of Frankland to be Fire Warlock for, I might as well kill myself and be done with it."

Beorn said, "There ought to be."

"You had a vision?"

"No, just common sense."

"Common sense, my ass. Common sense says the empire will wipe us out while our defences are down."

"Maybe not. We've got some advantages—"

"Don't tell me we'll win because they'll be fighting me. I already thought of that. It's not enough." René rolled away from the fist Beorn aimed at the side of his head.

"Cocky bastard. I was going to say that, but that's just one. Here's another: when it comes to lightning throwers, we outnumber them."

"Do now. Won't then."

"How do you figure?"

"We'll have four, you think. But after Lucinda unlocks the Fire Office, you'll be dead, or as good as." René's face scrunched tight. He scrubbed his sleeve across his nose before continuing. "Quicksilver will be too busy to fight. Who else knows enough about the Office to rebuild it? And he'll need both Lucinda and Sven's help. He won't let her fight anyway—he can't risk her getting killed while we still have the Earth and Air Offices to unlock. That leaves me. One, against the whole empire."

"Uh-huh. One against one. Don't tell me you're afraid of a fair fight."

"If it is a fair fight, no. But they have more warlocks than we do, even if they can't call down the lightning. And what makes you and Quicksilver so sure they'll have only one who can?"

"Well." Beorn lay down on the rock and contemplated the sky. "The training's dangerous for a warlock without a teacher who's been through it himself, even with the new spells. Instead of killing everybody that tries, maybe it'll only kill half. And they'll have forgotten, like we did, that once you're in your twenties it's too late to start. The more of them that try... You know how competitive us hotheads are. Once word gets out that the emperor's letting some try, others will give it a go, and he won't be able to stop them. So they'll thin their ranks for us themselves."

"Huh."

"Any trainees the lightning doesn't kill, the infighting will. When it's all over, they'll have one lightning thrower and a much smaller group of would-bes who hate his guts because he'll keep reminding them that he can, and they can't. The emperor will have his hands full managing that lot."

René said, "Do you really believe that or is that just wishful thinking?"

"Umm..."

"Oh, great."

"A warlock's wishes are powerful things."

René snorted.

Beorn raised his head and studied René. "Here's one advantage I do believe in. When was the last time Frankland's—or the empire's, either, for that matter—Fire Guild Council didn't sound like a pack of braying donkeys when they got together?"

"Uh..."

"Didn't think you'd know. As far as I can tell, and I've checked with both Jean and Lucinda, the last time we had a guild council not set on flaming each other was when the Fire Office was forged. Right after that, Fortunatus and the first Locksmith had their falling out, and never talked to each other again. Having a guild council where we actually like each other is... It's a miracle, that's what it is. The friction's even worse in the empire. It's this, more than anything else, that's convinced Mother Celeste it's time to reforge the Fire Office."

"She'll change her mind once you tell them the empire's training lightning throwers."

"Not going to tell them. Not yet anyway. Not for months, maybe not for years. Not until all four Guild Councils are committed to the rebuild. Don't want to frighten them away before we even start."

"Think you can convince Eleanor and Paul?"

Beorn sighed. "Eleanor, yes. Paul... I'd as soon argue with the empire's lightning thrower. But I was listing advantages. There are the Fortress and the traps in the tunnels. Even with the Fire Office down, we won't be defenceless. Don't forget that. Sometimes defence is easier than offence."

"Sometimes. Which sometimes, exactly?"

Beorn combed his fingers through his beard. "Good question. You've got time, years yet, to figure that out. Which reminds me, Jean and Sven have taught you a lot, but getting some other perspectives would be a good thing. You're sixteen. Soon time for you to go to university."

"And have to write essays and sit exams. Gee, thanks."

"Don't mention it."

"Why should I waste my time? Three years ago Quicksilver said Lucinda and I were reading theory at the university level, and after all we learned about the Water Office, I could teach a course on either fire or water magic."

"You're an arrogant cuss even if you are right. Read magic if you want, and have time, but I'm not sending you there for that. You're going to read history."

Sparks flew. "You're out of your frostbitten mind. I can't stand the everlasting political wrangles between this king and that Fire Warlock, and which duke married what princess, and all that rot. I need to outfight the empire's lightning wielder, and you want—"

"Hold it right there. If all you care about is outfighting a warlock, forget it, we're doomed."

René scowled. "But—"

"I don't give a rat's ass about that drivel either. You're going to read history so you can become—once Jean's gone—Frankland's foremost authority on the art of war, all the way from the continent-sweeping campaigns of the massed Greek and Roman armies to the proxy battles between back-stabbing diplomats." Beorn gave René's shoulder a hard shake. "And that's so that when you do go up against the emperor and his advisors, you can outthink them, because then, and only then, are you going to have a chance at outfighting them."

"The art of war, you say." A spark caught and flared in René's imagination. "When you put it like that, history might not be so bad, after all."

Later that day, Lucinda stood before her sitting room fire with her palms pressed together, calming her nerves. She had not attempted summoning the lightning in the six months since she had unlocked the Water Office. Jean had forbidden it before her arm was fully regrown, saying a lightning wielder must be hale and whole. Although the healers had declared her fit several weeks ago, the memories of the pain she had suffered made her reluctant to grapple with such extremes, ever again.

But she was a warlock. Duty called.

Despite the damage to her arm, she had returned to full strength faster than Jean, and he tired more quickly than he once had. After enjoying the resilience of a young and fit body for over a century, even the normal decay of ageing would have confounded him, but he seldom complained. More often, he expressed gratitude for their rapid recovery, an achievement they might never have accomplished on their own. Certainly it would have taken years, not months, if they had not had the Earth Guild's finest healers pumping life and health into them. How anyone ever reached a half-century before the Earth Guild discovered and codified the wonders of healing magic, she could not imagine.

During those six months, René had practiced with Beorn every week, but complained he was backsliding because Beorn wouldn't let him draw hard enough. Beorn balked at letting him test his limits, saying neither of them could judge those limits, and he'd rather drown than let the boy kill himself. He would hand the job over to Jean when he recovered, and the sooner the better.

Too soon, for Lucinda's taste, and for Jean's too. His tension, felt through their bond, was infecting her, but they had agreed, and it was time. She walked through the fire, and met the three male warlocks— Jean, René, and Beorn—on the caldera floor, at the opposite end from the glowing lava lake.

René said, "You said you didn't like this place."

"I never come here without good cause," Jean said, "but the caldera rim is too exposed. When we returned to Frankland from our travels, hiding our activities would have been to no purpose, as the empire already knew what we were about. Now, however, they do not know how fit Lucinda and I are, and we would rather keep them guessing."

"They'll know when somebody throws a lightning bolt."

7

"Sure they will," Beorn said, "but not who's here, or who threw which ones. We're going to let it get about that Jean's giving me lessons in better control. God knows I need that anyway. With luck they'll think you're a laggard."

"Oh." René looked pleased. "So they'll be surprised when I knock their butts to kingdom come. Gotcha."

Lucinda shivered. She wouldn't want to knock anyone's butt to kingdom come, especially not her own, but the power she would be controlling would rip her apart and scatter her ashes to the four winds if she misjudged.

Her misgivings faded as the opening exercises proved easy and painless. Soon, testing their strength in the open air became a pleasure. Jean relaxed enough to tease René about his aim being inversely proportional to the power of his attacks, and ordered him to practice the same exercises as Beorn, to increase his control. René groaned and rolled his eyes.

"You and the Fire Eaters may have free run of the practice room," Jean said. "They, too, would benefit from these exercises."

René's eyes lit. "I get to teach them?"

"Certainly."

"That's more like it!"

When it was Lucinda's turn to test her limits, Jean took her hand. "Unlocking the Water Office will have expanded your limits considerably. I will call down the lightning. Compare that with your own sense of your new limits."

She nodded. Lightning crashed. Thunder boomed. Power washed over her, but no pain. She was neither blinded nor deafened. Something wild, dormant these last few months, stirred, deep in her soul. "I can do that."

"I thought you might." He pointed. "Strike that boulder."

Still holding his hand, she took a deep breath, focused, pictured a lightning bolt as intense as the one that had almost killed her, and pulled on the inexhaustible fire in the earth beneath her feet.

Who's Next?

The lightning Lucinda had commanded, majestic and terrible, ripped through the sky and hit the target boulder dead centre. Chips flew. She lifted fists to the night sky and bayed. René whooped. Jean grabbed her and spun her around and around. He led them through the fire to the practice room in the Fortress, where they joined hands like children and danced across the flagstones, laughing and singing, until out of breath. They adjourned to the kitchen for a second supper of champagne, cold beef on warm toast, and apple tarts, and Jean's mood gradually slipped from jubilant to thoughtful, quiet.

Lucinda was relieved when René and Beorn left, headed for their beds. She sipped her wine, contemplating the rising bubbles, then refilled their glasses and beckoned for Jean to follow her back to the practice room. "It's not that easy, is it?"

He said, "No, my dear, it is not. Tell me your assessment of your ability to control the lightning."

"As lightning bolts go, mine was feeble. You've thrown some that would have blasted that boulder to pebbles. But…it'll do. I'll take another look at the lock on the Fire Office, but I expect I can unlock it without harm, given another six months to a year of steady progress."

"Good. Your assessment matches mine. Before the coven are ready to reforge the Fire Office, you will be fully fledged. Assuming…"

"Right. Assuming I survive the last step, when I have to stand on my own and not draw through you any longer. That's a big assumption, isn't it?"

He frowned into his wine. "Perhaps not as much as you fear. Calling the lightning on one's own is the most dangerous phase of the training, but you are the most cautious warlock I have ever encountered."

"Because I got burnt too many times in the kitchen before I learned how to shield."

"Perhaps so." The lines at the corners of his eyes creased into a ghost of a smile. "Your control has always been superb, and our recent trauma will reinforce your predisposition towards caution."

"Oh, God, yes."

"I am not, therefore, as worried about you surviving that last step as I am of René when his time comes."

She sighed. "Right. Well, he wouldn't be half as good as he is if he wasn't enthusiastic. Assuming we both survive our training as lightning wielders, that only solves half the problem, doesn't it?"

The hint of a smile vanished. "That is so. You will channel the force needed to unlock the office, but you must direct it somewhere."

"And that somewhere better not be the other officeholders. I understand that. But Jean, why are you so worried? I ought to be able to absorb the blast as well as control it."

"Impossible. There is no record of anyone absorbing a direct lightning strike and surviving."

"Except you."

"I survived only under extraordinary circumstances. The force of the blast was distributed between us, and you still had to drag me back to the land of the living."

"There have been mundanes who survived lightning strikes."

"Yes, but they were not attempting to contain it…to prevent it from harming others. In every documented case, the greater portion of the lightning's power was deflected, passing over their skin and around them, and even then, none survived without serious injuries."

"But we both absorbed power and not only survived, but recovered."

"With an extraordinary amount of help from the Earth Guild."

"Yes, but are you sure it's impossible to absorb the blast? How many warlocks are there who can absorb as well as channel? You and me, but no one else I've ever heard of. Maybe no one else has ever attempted to see how much they can absorb."

"Perhaps not. I never stretched my own limits in that respect until last summer, nor do I see how one can do both at once."

"I did both while destroying that wretched conspiracy."

He stopped, arrested. "So you did." After a moment, he shook his head. "In that case the power did not flow as quickly as in a lightning strike, and you could have stopped at any time. Unlocking is an explosive event. Both releasing the lock and absorbing the blast are sufficiently dangerous as to require one's full attention. Attempting to do them together could be deadly. I thank you, my love, for your attempt to spare me, but I believe I must still be the buffer between you and the officeholders."

"Then we'd better see how much you can take."

He failed to hide a yawn. "I would rather go to bed, but if you insist."

She flamed him. The flames bounced off.

"I beg your pardon, my dear. I was unprepared."

She flamed him again. The flames bounced off. "Why didn't you lower your shields?"

He looked disconcerted. "I did. Raising them was an instinctive reaction. Let us try again."

Half an hour later, she hadn't touched him. She was tired, apprehensive, and ecstatic, all at the same time. He was wide awake and furious, pacing circles around the iron table.

She said, "What did you expect? You're so good you can slam a shield into place faster than thought. You spent a century and a half honing your reflexes, and the one time you went against all that conditioning and let your shields down you nearly burned to death."

He ground out, "I expect my body and mind to obey my conscious will. What right have I to harangue you and René about control if I cannot control my own reactions?"

"Aren't reflexes by definition without conscious control? I'm glad they're so good. In our exercises you kept telling me to attack harder, but I didn't want to hit one of you men with your shields down. Now I know I can throw anything at you and it'll never hit you. I dare you ever again to call my attacks against you weak."

That sally earned a wry smile. "That was before you became a lightning wielder, my dear. I would never be so foolish as to say that now."

"If you can't let your shields down, maybe the best course is for me to absorb the blast."

He stopped pacing. "Certainly not. We will find another way."

"Wouldn't it be useful to at least see how much I can absorb now?"

He gazed at the ceiling for a long moment with his back turned before responding. "Yes, that would be instructive."

"Go ahead, flame me."

She let her shields down. The instant fire flew at her, her shields slammed into place. She hunched over, shaking and drenched in cold sweat.

Jean strode to her side and pulled her against him. "My love… My dear…"

She mumbled into his collar, "Give me a moment, before you flame me again."

"Again? My dear, are you…"

"Am I what?"

"Were you anyone else I should inquire if you are mad."

"Probably am. I'm a warlock, remember. Flame me again."

After several more attempts they gave up and went to bed, but despite having been awake half the previous night, sleep would not come. Lucinda was staring at the ceiling when Jean laughed.

She rolled against him. "What?"

"Imagine, two warlocks fretting over an inability to drop their shields. The school faculty will come for us with firearms and pitchforks, if we ever admit to such heresy."

The first thing Lucinda heard on entering the Warren's amber meeting room a few days later was Enchanter Paul saying, "Impossible. We can't do it."

Lucinda said, "What's impossible?"

Beorn muttered in her ear, "Off to a great start."

Paul and two witches—the retired and current Water Sorceresses, Lorraine and Eleanor—turned to greet the Fire Guild contingent. After the usual exchange of small compliments and pleasantries, more genuine than when Lucinda had first entered the room three years earlier, she repeated her question, "What's impossible?"

Sorceress Eleanor said, "I asked if the Air Guild could spread the news about several recent trials. Reports of Master Duncan's trial flooded the country, but since then the quarantine and the war absorbed everyone's attention, and several other important trials have gone unnoticed. Everyone in Frankland should understand that justice shall prevail in lesser cases, too."

"A worthy goal," Paul said, "but the Air Guild is hamstrung, and will take decades to recover. With the skeletal staff remaining, we are far behind on negotiations for treaties and trade agreements, and the Air Office ranks those ahead of keeping mere commoners informed. I would love to help, but if we fall any further behind, the pressure… The Air Office is already making my life a burden. I don't need any more."

Lucinda's interactions with Paul in the months leading up to the Yule War had left her disinclined to sympathise, even though she knew the events in December had come as a severe shock to him. Now, seeing his haggard face and stooped shoulders, she was ashamed of her remaining animosity. She had seen the effects of an office's pressure on Jean and Beorn, as well as Sorceress Lorraine. She could not wish that on anyone, nor could she deny he had been making a heroic effort to repair the damages.

Mother Celeste patted Paul's hand. "The Earth Guild has been able to relax since we lifted the quarantine. What can we do to help?"

Paul sighed. "Thank you, but I don't know if anyone can."

"May I suggest," Jean said, "help from mundane sources: printers, scholars…"

Lucinda's mind wandered during the discussion that followed. The past year's events had left few of them untouched. On their honeymoon travels, their hosts' surprise at Jean's apparent youth became a running joke. Now, with the beginnings of crow's feet around the eyes, and hair growing back in with a hint of silver at the temples, he seemed ageless, no longer young. When she first noticed the grey hairs, she had attempted to pluck them. He fended her off with a smile, saying he had earned them and was proud of them. Fine lines were evident in Lorraine's face, too. Still the second most beautiful woman in Frankland, after Lucinda's stepsister Claire, no one would ever again mistake her for a maiden of seventeen.

The newest officeholders looked no older, but both Beorn and Eleanor had a new gravitas about them, a sense they had been tested, and earned the right to be called Their Wisdoms.

Thanks to her friends in the Earth Guild, Lucinda's own appearance, though thinner, was little changed, but the skin on her right arm was shockingly pale compared to her left, and probably always would be. Away from home, she wore long sleeves and gloves.

The discussion of aid for the Air Guild wound down. Paul's expression was sour. Jean's was a polite mask. Had Paul's rejections of his suggestions been due to the Air Office's constraints or simple obstinacy? She would have to ask Jean later.

Beorn brought them back to his reason for calling this meeting. "When we reforge the Fire Office—"

Eleanor said, "Are you starting with a flawed assumption?"

"Eh?"

"You look well-rested, for a change."

Beorn squinted at her. "Well, yeah. I'm happy about that, believe me."

Eleanor said, "As you should be, but if the Fire Guild is in such good shape now, do we really still need to reforge the Fire Office?"

"Yes." The unequivocal answer, in unison, came from five voices. Jean, Beorn, and Lucinda swivelled to stare at the other two speakers, Sorceress Lorraine and Mother Celeste.

Lorraine tilted her head at Jean. "After you, Your Wisdom."

"It is true," Jean said, "that Frankland is once again peaceful, but this state is merely a reprieve. The empire, our old enemy, has not yet recovered from the last war, but it will, and will attack with greater force. Nor will Frankland stay free of internal strife. The last few months have demonstrated the commoners' power, and as their strength grows, they will not be content with the feudal society the four offices endeavour to uphold. We are no longer balanced on a knife's edge, but certain events—a future king evading the Great Oath, perhaps, or an alliance between the empire and an expanding state in the New World—could push us there again. We must repair the Fire Office while we can, and be grateful the mood of the populace gives us an opportunity to do so."

"I have to agree with Jean," Mother Celeste said. "You've been so focused on the Water Office, dear, you haven't seen all the problems the Fire Office causes. I can't say I've seen them all either—I suspect the Fire Guild keeps a few carefully hidden under their hats—but I've seen enough. Now that we know we can, we must."

"Very well," Eleanor said. "I'd rather not jump blindly into it if we don't have to, but I trust the more experienced officeholders' judgement."

"Well, I'm not convinced," Paul said. "The Water Office, yes, but the Fire Office…"

Lorraine said, "We have discussed this before. We cannot wait hundreds or a thousand years for another locksmith. We must repair the Fire Office, if Lucinda and Jean are able and willing to endure such a harrowing event again."

Lucinda said, "I'd really rather stick my head in a nest of vipers, but what I want doesn't have much bearing."

Beorn said, "It'll take years for the rest of us to get ready. By the time the coven's ready, they'll be ready."

"All right, I suppose," Paul said. "It is the Fire Guild's domain; I defer to them."

"Good," Beorn said. "Having everybody agree on it is a great start. Back to the point I was trying to make—reforging the Water Office took two weeks. Reforging the Fire Office has to go faster."

Heads nodded. "I know next to nothing about warfare," Eleanor said, "but even I can understand that. How long will we have?"

Beorn and Jean exchanged a glance. Jean said, "As soon as the empire realises the Fire Office is gone—and given the extent of their spy network, we must assume they will know immediately—the emperor will order all the Empire's resources diverted into a full-bore attack. They cannot bring all their firepower to bear at once, but we must count the time in hours, not days. We must assume we have no more than one day—twenty-four hours—and even that will tax our defences to the limit."

Lorraine broke the stunned silence. "Twenty-four hours to reforge an office? Is that possible? The Fire Office is the most complex of the four."

"Rebuilding the Water Office was exhausting," Eleanor said. "We had to stop and rest, or back up and fix mistakes, regularly. Doing it all in one day…"

Jean said, "Many spells the other guilds contribute should be the same, or similar, in all four offices. With one experience behind it, the Reforging Coven should find those flow more easily and rapidly on the next."

"Right," Beorn said. "Things get easier with practice. Which makes me think… It's not so hard now to unlock the Water Office. If we practice on it—"

"No!" Only Jean did not participate in the roar of protest. His lips twitched. Lucinda threw him a suspicious glance.

"Good God, no," Mother Celeste sputtered. "We're still recovering from it being broken. If we broke it again, dear God… Practicing taking an office apart and putting it back together is a good idea, but please, let's do it on one less vital. Either the Earth or Air Office would do."

Paul's head snapped up. "Speak for yourself, madam."

"You didn't think we would do the Fire Office next, did you? That's far too risky. We need at least one other experience under our belts before we tackle that one, and I, for one, think we should save it for last." Mother Celeste patted Paul's hand. He snatched it away, and glowered at her. "Don't worry," she said. "You'll have time to get ready. I volunteer the Earth Office to be next."

Beorn's moustache-stroking didn't quite hide his smile. She gave him a hard look. "That's what you wanted, wasn't it, you great dunderhead. I should have known better. Oh, never mind."

Paul said, "It is very well, madam, for you to offer the Earth Office as the next to be reforged, and yourself as the sacrificial victim, but you overstep your authority with the Air Office."

She said, "Well now, as to sacrifices… We know the first Locksmith despised the first Frost…er, sorry, the first Water Sorceress. And it's sensible to worry about destroying the Fire Office. Maybe the locks on the Earth and Air Offices aren't as barbaric?"

The three warlocks looked at each other. Lucinda frowned and shrugged. "That witch was vicious and more than a little demented. I wouldn't put it past her to have been nasty all the way around out of spite."

"Oh. Well…Let's see, shall we? Sometime in the next few weeks, when you have time, dear, you should read the lock on the Earth Office."

"Yes, ma'am."

"And even if it is as bad…" She shrugged. "I've been an officeholder for nearly forty years. Not as long as my distinguished colleagues, but long enough to be heartily tired of it at times. I wouldn't mind retiring while I still have some life left in me. And as for losing my right arm…" She smiled. "My teachers tried to beat left-handedness out of me, but never quite succeeded."

"My dear Celeste," Jean said, "it is both noble and generous of you to volunteer to be next, but is that possible? We believe we must rebuild the Fire Office within ten years."

Eleanor said, "Why ten?"

Jean hesitated. Lucinda said, "The longer we wait, the more likely it is the Reforging Coven will be disrupted—further disrupted—and we risk losing or forgetting the experience gained from reforging the Water Office."

"Well, yes, but…"

Mother Celeste eyed Jean. Lorraine eyed Lucinda. The two senior witches exchanged a glance. Celeste nodded.

16

Lorraine said, "The coven's cohesion and experience is, of itself, sufficient reason. We should not leave our plans unbounded, and a maximum of five years between each office is better than ten. The Fire Guild may have other reasons, which we do not need to question."

Celeste said, "I agree. We should reforge the Fire Office within ten years, and reforging the Earth Office in five is quite reasonable. I began investigating the spells in the Earth Office years ago when Jean first raised the idea, and got more serious about it after our locksmith appeared. The Earth Office is the least complex; most of what we do, from healing to building to farming, the Earth Guild did long before the office was created, and don't need its backing. I haven't finished training Astrid to be Earth Mother, but both she and the coven could be ready within three or four years."

"Excellent," Lorraine said. "Let us proceed with the Earth Office next, the Air Office two or three years later—"

"No." Paul, with flaring nostrils and bared teeth, looked like a fire wizard. "We just spent half an hour discussing suggestions for relieving the pressure on the Air Guild, and only came up with two strong enough to blow the seeds off a dandelion. When do you think we will have time to study the Air Office spells? I see no hope of relief in the near future. And even if we could analyse the spells, we must hope the lock on the Air Office has no 'hidden terror'. If we were to unlock it, and it rendered me unfit to serve, that would be a disaster. There is no one else fit to hold the office."

"Yes, Paul, we know, but the guild's schoolchildren—"

"You think we'll find an enchanter among the students at the school? Not likely. Having Oliver and Winifred so close to the same age was a rare occurrence. And now the Fire Warlock tells us one of Ollie's daughters will be an enchantress, but he won't tell us which one." He cast a baleful look at Beorn, who returned the glare. "Given the historical averages, we won't have another enchanter appear—appear, mind you, not be trained as my apprentice—for another twenty to thirty years. Which, of course, considering the historical averages, would be fine. I've only been Air Enchanter for fifteen years. I'm just beginning my reign."

"Fifteen years," Beorn muttered, "is more than I'm likely to get, total."

Lucinda slid her wand sideways and poked him with the tip. "Not helping," she whispered.

There was another long and uncomfortable silence.

"Very well, Paul," Lorraine said. "Truncated tenure is not sufficient reason to delay dealing with the Air Office, but lack of an apprentice is, as is satisfying the office's mandates. We will continue this discussion some other time. It is not urgent now, as the Reforging Coven can begin work on the Earth Office straightaway. You should find the leisure time you need to analyse the office's spells, once you reconsider Jean's suggestions."

The meeting ended. Paul, clearly disgruntled, bowed curtly all around and stomped away.

Mother Celeste plucked at Lucinda's sleeve without taking her eyes off Paul. "Come for dinner tomorrow, just you and Jean."

Interference

Dinner with Mother Celeste was the most relaxed meal Jean and Lucinda had had in over a year. The magic guilds had been busy for weeks after the Yule War, helping the royals restore order and put things to rights. All three relished the chance to unbend with friends, and they stayed long over their after-dinner port, Jean and Lucinda describing the wonders they had seen in their travels. Their honeymoon seemed a lifetime ago—fitting, perhaps, since they had both nearly died.

If Jean were a cat, how many of his nine lives had he already used? Seven? Eight? Lucinda shuddered, and refocused on the conversation. She had no desire to spoil his good mood, or hers.

Later, they drifted through the Warren's courtyards and cloisters, content to follow aimlessly in the Earth Mother's wake as she pointed out the earliest signs of incipient spring—signs Lucinda would never have noticed—amid the snowdrifts and bare branches. She was soon lost in the labyrinthine passages, and was startled to discover herself in the antechamber to the amber meeting room, having approached from a corridor she was unfamiliar with.

Mother Celeste held the door for them. "I hope you don't mind."

Lucinda's scalp prickled. *Jean, what...*

His brow puckered. *I do not know.* "After you," he said.

Inside the amber room, Sorceress Lorraine rose to greet them. "I trust you will forgive me for convening this private meeting."

"Of course, Your Wisdom." Lucinda attempted a curtsey, but her head spun, addled from too much wine and the sudden shift in mood. She clutched at Jean's steady arm.

His pucker had deepened. "We do not object to a private meeting, but we are surprised."

"Sorry," Celeste said, "but we wanted to talk to you without Paul, and if we came to you, well…the Fire Guild do gossip. Maybe we're two old busybodies seeing trouble where there isn't any, and maybe…"

"Nonsense," Jean said. "You are the two wisest women in the land, and we would be remiss not to listen to your concerns, whatever they may be." His voice was as urbane as ever, but the muscles in his arm were taut. Butterflies flapped in Lucinda's stomach, making her sorry she had eaten as much as she had.

Jean said, "What is of such moment that high-ranking members of three guilds must talk, but we cannot include the Air Guild?"

Celeste said, "We know there are good reasons for the prohibitions against interference in other guilds…" Lucinda's butterflies took wing. Jean went rigid. Celeste flapped a hand at him. "Oh, not you. The Fire Guild is in better shape now than I've ever seen it."

Lucinda let out a gusty breath and dropped into a chair.

Jean said, "I gather, then, your concern is regarding the Air Guild."

Lorraine said, "No. The Earth Guild lost so few in comparison to the others, I intend to stir up a hornet's nest among them." Celeste gave her a stern look. Lorraine sighed. "I beg your pardon. Yes, the Air Guild's current state disturbs us. Is it true that the Fire Office relies on the Air Guild more than on either the Water or Earth Guilds?"

"Yes, that is so."

"Practice on the Air Office, as Celeste suggested is, therefore, desirable, but will not happen. We cannot afford to wait for the Air Guild. The Air Office must come last."

"What?" Lucinda said. "Yesterday you gave Paul marching orders to be third. Why'd you change your mind?"

"I did not change my mind. Yesterday, I merely set the terms of the debate. Paul must understand the question is when, not if. Celeste and I will not allow Paul to shirk his duty to Frankland."

"Certainly, the Air Office must also be reforged," Jean said. "With the changes already begun, the Air Office will, in time, become Frankland's millstone, although it will be years before rebuilding it becomes urgent. And while practicing on the Air Office would be beneficial, I would equally well like to misdirect the empire's attention, and make them believe the Air Office will be third."

"Yes," Lorraine said, "any measures we can take to mislead them about our intentions, we should."

"That sounds like a good idea," Lucinda said, "but so does practicing on the Air Office. Why did you say we can't?"

"Because Paul is quite right. There is currently no one else who can hold the Air Office. Enchantress Carla is in failing health, and Enchanter Phillip does not have the mental capacity. This is the crux of the problem as I see it. Three ranking members of the Air Guild were engaged in reforging the Water Office, and barely coped. With only one…"

Jean said, "I share your concern, but other omens demand we reforge the Fire Office soon, or lose our best opportunity."

"I agree. The Fire Office must be reforged soon." Lorraine stretched her hand towards Lucinda. "And by soon I mean within the next decade or so."

"Yes, ma'am. I understand," Lucinda said.

"I simply want to ensure that the Fire Guild's single-minded focus on security does not blind you to this other small difficulty."

"Difficulties, you mean," Mother Celeste said. "And not so small, either. Lorraine only covered half the problem."

"Did I? The other half is…?"

"Where will the coven be during the reforging?"

Jean said, "In a secure place, of course. We must be able to work without compromising our safety."

"Where?"

"The practice room in the Fortress's depths is, by far, the best defended shelter in Frankland."

"That big cave where Lucinda had us practicing locking and unlocking? Thought so. You're thinking we need to handle the Fire Office in one long, sustained effort, don't you? The empire won't give us a chance to have recesses, and you expect them to attack anyone who comes up for air. Do you remember how edgy Paul was in that room? He was frantic to escape after only half an hour. Do you think he can cope with being forced underground a whole day and night, possibly longer?"

After a long silence, Jean said, "I had not considered location an obstacle. Enchanter Paul tolerates this amber chamber. I assumed he would tolerate the practice room when necessary."

"Particularly," Lucinda said, "when we can't guarantee his safety outside it."

"This is different," Celeste said. "That room is underground. Do you know that most of the year he beds down on a sleeping porch, in the open air? He's as afraid of being trapped as you are of drowning. How well would you cope with being forced aboard a ship in the middle of the Atlantic Ocean?"

Jean's voice had steel in it. "If necessity required it, I would set aside terror and carry out my responsibilities. Other warlocks have done so. We do not always like what fate serves us."

Mother Celeste sighed. "I should have known better than to ask a warlock to have pity. Paul isn't a warlock. He can't tolerate it for long."

Lorraine's voice was icy. "He is an officeholder. He will do his duty to Frankland."

Mother Celeste snorted. "You're thinking like warlocks, all three of you."

Lorraine's eyebrows arched. "I beg your pardon."

"Yes, you too, Lorraine. It's not a matter of will. I'm speaking now as Frankland's foremost healer, with decades of experience. Forcing him underground for an extended period will break him, driving him either violently berserk or catatonic. I can't say which."

Jean drew in a deep breath, then let it out slowly. "I see. You are saying we must explore every possible avenue to minimize our dependency on the Air Guild, even if it further alienates them and burdens the others."

"Yes."

"Enchanter Paul will be well within his rights to be offended. I would be irate if the other guilds barred the Fire Guild from participating in reforging any office."

Lorraine said, "When I suggested this meeting I did not see the full extent of the difficulties. Now I understand that we—the full membership of the four magic guilds, that is—need only be more creative and cooperative than anything in our history for the past half-millennium suggests we are capable of." She flicked her fingers. "An easily surmountable obstacle."

The fine lines around Jean's eyes deepened. "Thank you for your optimism."

"Well, Jean, I do know you enjoy a challenge."

He gave a short bark of laughter, but sobered quickly. "It would be useful to understand which spells in the Fire Office require enchanter-level magic. Since you have offered your full cooperation, you may help in that assessment."

"I may help?"

"Yes. Your experience in overseeing the Water Office's reforging has given you a broad expertise in spellcraft across all four guilds, comparable to no one else in Frankland other than myself."

"That is true," she said. "I simply had not considered all the implications of our interference."

Jean's eyes danced. "No sorceress has ever tendered her expertise in another guild's domain, therefore no sorceress will ever tender her expertise in another guild's domain. I cannot blame you for being set in your ways."

She gave him a long, cool stare. "Set in my ways? Nonsense."

"I would help," Mother Celeste said, "but I doubt I can say anything useful about Air Guild spells."

"No, I rather think not," Jean said.

"So while you and Lorraine sort through them, Lucinda could read the lock on the Earth Office."

Lucinda sighed. She wanted a nap. "Yes, let's do that."

A sea of papers—Jean's notes—covered the amber chamber's conference table. Jean and Lorraine both wore their inscrutable officeholder expressions, giving away nothing other than that the news was not good.

Fair enough. The news Lucinda had to impart wasn't encouraging either. She sank into a chair beside Lorraine and rubbed her eyes. Jean looked like he would have been better off with a nap, too.

She said, "That wretched fire witch… The lock on the Earth Office is identical to the ones on the Water and Fire Offices." She quoted the spell:

> *Earth, Air, Fire, and Water agree*
> *To let the fire within the Locksmith, me,*
> *Draw on their power that none may find,*
> *On this Token of Office, the spells that bind.*
> *Whichever power releases the lock, I swear,*
> *Shall face my hidden terror there.*

Lorraine said, "I suspected as much. At least we know what to expect."

"Do we? The lock, yes, but there's no guarantee the hidden terror is the same."

Mother Celeste said, "Did she like earth mothers as much as she liked sorceresses? Maybe I'll lose both arms. That would be…"

Jean said, "My dear Celeste…"

"Annoying. Never mind. What have you found?"

He sighed, and gathered his notes into a neat stack, a page with several columns on the top. "Many spells are sufficiently lightweight, in terms of demands on both power and mental acumen, to require only an ordinary air talent from the middle ranks."

"That's promising."

"Is it?" Lorraine said, "Will the middle ranks be more comfortable underground?"

Celeste said, "That's a good question. Indifference to being trapped would be exceptional, and more likely in schoolchildren than in the experienced guild members the coven would usually draw on. Those attitudes tend to calcify with age."

"Hmm…" Jean said, "Even if we found talented youths, our difficulties do not disappear. Some spells require either a mage's intellect or enchanter-level power, or both, to cast."

"Meaning Paul has to do them," Celeste said. "How many?"

Lorraine said, "In my opinion, too many for any one man to handle in the limited time Jean would allot. He was inclined to be optimistic, based on his own experience as an officeholder, until I reminded him that wind power is the most erratic and quickly exhausted of the four."

"Oh, dear. Well…"

Lucinda was reading Jean's notes over his shoulder. "Those spells… Does it have to be an enchanter?"

Jean hefted his notes. "My dear, we are specifically discussing Air Guild spells."

"I know that. I meant, could someone from another guild handle a few?" That drew frowns from all three. She said, "Look, we all know there's overlap. Beorn's practically a healer. He's dosed me several times with the potions his wife taught him to brew. René hears things no one else can hear. Isn't that air magic? And, Jean, you make things fly. If that isn't air magic, what is it? Couldn't you or a water mage cast some of these spells, even though you're not officially in the Air Guild?"

Lorraine's eyes lit. "Charles' expertise in weather magic certainly overlaps with the Air Guild." She reached for the paper and ran a fingernail down the list. "This spell, and this one…plus the last one. It might be possible. Your idea has merit."

"Perhaps," Jean said. "Telekinesis of small objects is, as you suggest, air magic, but within the grasp of most air talents in their early teens. The examples you gave are not mage-level magic. We do not know if crossing guild boundaries is possible at that high a level."

Mother Celeste said, "But it's worth a try, isn't it? If the Fire Guild handles a few and the Water Guild handles others, would that be enough?"

"I do not know." He frowned at his list. "In the Fire Guild, neither Beorn nor Lucinda nor Sven have demonstrated the slightest inclination towards air magic. René has. He would enjoy flying, if he could." The corners of Jean's mouth turned upwards briefly. "Although it offends him to be compared to air wizards. More to the point, he will be too busy to be useful in the reforging. That leaves Sunbeam, who shows inclination but is too old and inflexible to learn new ways, and me." He frowned down at the paper. "And I am far older than Sunbeam."

"But Jean," Lucinda said, "you can already do enchanter-level magic. When I first unlocked, you flew three people down from the aerie into Storm King's caldera. That's serious air magic."

"That was with the Fire Office's support, my dear."

"So was calling down the lightning when you became Fire Warlock, and you learned how well enough to do it without the Fire Office. Maybe you could fly, too. Have you tried?"

He looked taken aback. "No."

Mother Celeste tsked. "Stodgy."

Lorraine said, "Set in his ways." She winked at Lucinda, who covered a snicker with a cough.

Jean's glower changed quickly to chagrin. "I deserved that, I suppose."

"Study the spells with René." Lorraine's voice was honey sweet. "If you experience difficulties at your advanced age, he can help you over the hurdles."

The weak February sun was long gone; with no sunlight coming through the practice room's skylights, the ceiling was lost in the shadows. Lucinda threw flame the length of the room; the shadows retreated and danced in her peripheral vision, but did not disappear. The space had always seemed huge to her; with no bats or seeping water, she never thought of the room as a cave. She had not understood, even when Paul had been here that one time, that someone else might be keenly aware of the tons of granite poised over their heads.

"Jean, how did the Great Coven manage?"

"They were not under direct attack, and did not work underground. A lull between enemy campaigns gave them time and unsuspecting opponents, luxuries not available to us."

"Celeste and Lorraine are right, then. We have to work around the Air Guild."

"If we can. This idea that Sorcerer Charles and I can assume their responsibilities troubles me. All three of you witches seemed to hold the opinion I can do anything."

She wrapped her arms around him and nuzzled his ear. "Can't you?"

"Certainly not. I am aware of my limitations, even if you are deluded about them."

"I asked you earlier if you had tried to fly, and you said you hadn't. You should try."

"I have been trying, my love, ever since we entered this room."

"Oh." She didn't look down. The slight unevenness of the flagstone floor was evident in the pressure on the soles of her shoes. "Well."

"Yes, you see. There are difficulties."

She pulled back to see him better. "Difficulties are made to be overcome."

The skin around his eyes crinkled. "Slave driver. I will do my best. That is all I can promise."

"That'll do," she said, and kissed him.

Air Witches Underground

Irene perched on an iron chair, taking in the practice room's skylights, scorch marks, and fireproof furnishings. She kept a tight grip on her respiration rate and on Sven's hand.

"I'm not typical, remember," she said. "This room oppresses but doesn't frighten me. Oliver would have hated it—it would have terrified him."

"You have not been here long," Quicksilver said. "Imagine spending a day and a night—twenty-four hours—in this room."

"Twenty-four hours?" Her respiration rate accelerated.

Sven growled, "You're upsetting her."

Quicksilver laid a hand on her shoulder. "Relax, my dear. You need stay only a few minutes today."

Her breathing slowed. "Thank you, Your Wisdom. Today, you say. Meaning someday you will need me here for that day and night you mentioned."

"Yes. We must be well-protected when we reforge the Fire Office, and this is the safest place in Frankland."

"Yes, sir, I can understand that. Are you suggesting I spend time in here before then, attempting to become inured to it?"

"That is, indeed, what I am hoping for. We can have a tunnel cut from your apartment, so that you may slip in whenever it suits you."

"I'm willing, Your Wisdom, but that's unlikely to work for typical air talents."

"Yes, Mother Celeste suggests habituation works best if started while the subject is very young, before their talents begin to manifest."

"I have my doubts," Lucinda said. "I couldn't tolerate a ferry over the river at the age of six."

Quicksilver said, "Your father subjected you to that horror without giving you an explanation or asking your permission. If a child is appr-oached with the respect due a high talent, perhaps…"

"Maybe."

"But that begs the question, what child does one experiment on? A regimen of exposure to this room serves no purpose if we are not confident we have a latent air talent."

Irene frowned at her shoes. Sven scowled at the ceiling. The silence lengthened.

Irene said, "Warlock Arturos said one of my daughters will be an enchant-ress."

"That had occurred to me," Quicksilver said.

Sven mumbled, "You don't say."

"Please, not Miranda, Your Wisdom," Irene said. "That episode in the tunnels gave her nightmares. This room would torture her."

"I agree," Quicksilver said. "It is too late for her to start. She has already exhibited strong talent, and even if she had not… I do not approve of torturing children."

"I never imagined you did, Your Wisdom. That leaves…"

"Is there anything we can do to make this room more comfortable for air talents? I am willing to consider anything that does not compromise the room's integrity."

"Start by finding comfortable chairs." Irene released Sven's hand and paced the perimeter, studying the walls and ceiling. "Can you increase the air movement? Dead air has a dampening effect on air magic. That's probably what upset the Air Enchanter the most. Only someone supremely confident of their abilities could work air magic in here now."

Quicksilver and Lucinda exchanged a look. She reddened. "I was too optimistic, wasn't I?"

"Even indoors," Irene added, "strong air talents are always aware of air currents outside the walls, but the thickness of this ceiling would block any sense of movement. An illusion of scudding clouds across the ceiling might help. So would more light."

Quicksilver said, "If we effect those changes, will you give me permission to approach Gillian?"

Irene twisted her wedding ring, avoiding his eyes. "Have you asked Warlock Arturos about her? She's the one that will be an enchantress?"

"I did ask him, but he does not in fact know which one."

"Oh… He could have said so."

"I believe Enchanter Paul's reaction annoyed him."

"It annoyed me, too. Still…Gillian might spend many miserable hours in here and not have the power you need."

"Even a level three air witch who can withstand this room will be useful in the reforging."

"Oh, I see." She chewed her lip. "I don't like the idea of subjecting my daughter to this…experiment, but I understand the reasons. You can ask her, Your Wisdom, as long as you let her change her mind if it becomes unbearable."

"I will do so. That is a reasonable condition. I have another request, unrelated to your children."

"Yes?"

"While you are habituating yourself to this room, I would like you to coach a small team of wizards in advanced air magic."

"Wizards? Who?"

"For the nonce, assume Warlock Snorri, Sorcerer Charles, and myself."

She gaped at him. "Advanced… No one ever…"

He smiled. "And because it has never been done in Frankland, it never will be done in Frankland."

"I will be honoured to help you in any way I can, Your Wisdom, but are you trying to cut the Air Guild completely out of reforging the Fire Office?"

"Completely is impossible, but the less we require of them, the smoother it will be."

"The Air Enchanter won't like it."

"He may have no choice but to accept it. We will not put the rest of the coven in danger for his comfort."

Gillian, when asked if she would venture into the underground chamber, pressed close to Irene's side. "What for?"

"A good question." Quicksilver settled more comfortably into the sofa in the van Gelder's drawing room. "Some day—years from now, not soon—we intend to work a great feat of magic there for Frankland's benefit—a feat requiring witches and wizards from all four magic guilds. As no adult in the Air Guild will go underground for any length of time, if at all, our best healers think we will find the air talent needed in a young person, such as yourself, whose talents have not yet developed. If you can become comfortable there now, before developing into an air witch, as we have reason to hope you may, then when the time comes, the healers say, you should be able to endure long enough to work the spells needed."

"It won't look like a cave," Irene said. "The Earth Guild have made the ceiling disappear. It looks like we're outside, under heavy cloud."

"It's sunny today." Gillian sounded outraged.

Quicksilver said, "Lighting the chamber with full sunlight would require a tremendous effort—a heroic feat of magic itself. Clouds were much easier."

Gillian made a face. Irene nudged her. "Be polite, sweetheart."

Arturos said, "You wouldn't be in there by yourself. Your mum's been spending time in there, an hour or two every night after you're in bed, every night for the past fortnight. Once we understood the room was a problem for the Air Guild, it took a while to fix it."

Irene said, "'Ameliorate' would be a better description than 'fix.' But it is true, the room is less oppressive than it had been."

Quicksilver said, "We will do everything we can, within reason, to make you and your mother comfortable, because we need you. I know of no one else I could ask or trust with this undertaking. If, when you are older, you can spend the hours required in that room, and can work the spells we need, you will be hailed as one of Frankland's greatest witches. Are you willing?"

"You can back out any time," Lucinda said. "We won't hold you to a promise you can't keep."

"Don't make any promises about the future," Irene said, "before you've been in there once."

Gillian scowled with her lower lip thrust out, but nodded. "Once. I'll do that."

"Thank you." Quicksilver held out a hand. "Let us proceed."

Gillian squeaked, "Now?"

"Delay will not make it easier."

With one hand in Quicksilver's, the other in Irene's, they approached the tunnel, the other adults following. Gillian gasped as she passed through the door, held her breath for the few steps through the narrow tunnel, and gasped again on emerging. She backed against the wall, breathing through her mouth like a dog panting after a hard run.

"Slow down, sweetheart. There's air here." Irene blew air in her face with a sturdy fan. "If you breathe too fast you'll get dizzy and faint."

Gillian's panting slowed. She popped her thumb in her mouth and sucked noisily. Irene sighed. She had been delighted, earlier in the year, when it appeared Gillian had broken that habit.

"You'll feel better near the vents." Irene pointed towards a metal panel set in the wall by the near corner. "There's air blowing in."

Gillian ran, tugging Irene along, and pressed her face against the lowest vent. Her hair streamed out behind, bouncing in the breeze. "What's making it blow? There's no wind outside today."

"If you'll back up," Arturos said, "I'll show you."

Gillian scowled but inched away, and he swung the panel open, revealing a shaft cut in the rock. Near the ceiling a pair of bellows wheezed, one opening while the other closed. "Earth magic," he said. "There's another one in that corner. The vents on the other side pull the air out, so there's always a cross breeze."

"Come away from the wall," Lucinda coaxed. "Won't you feel better out in the open?"

"No," Gillian said around her thumb. "Nothing holding the rocks up."

"Rocks? What rocks?" Lucinda said. "I see clouds."

Gillian threw her a disgusted look. Irene threw a startled glance upwards. She had not considered that a seven-year-old could be immune to an illusion taking in an adult warlock.

Quicksilver said, "The Earth Mother assured us the ceiling is in no danger of falling."

That statement earned a rude noise. Irene gave Quicksilver an apologetic half-smile and a shake of her head. "It was worth a try, anyway."

"The illusion may still prove useful. Is there anything you would suggest, Miss Gillian, to make it more satisfactory?"

Gillian considered that. With a tight grip on her mother's hand, she crept further into the room, then turned in a full circle, studying the region where the walls faded into the sky. "The walls don't stop."

"Yes, that bothers me, too," Irene said. "They should have a definite boundary."

Gillian yanked at Irene's hand. "Mama, out."

"Yes, dear, it's close to suppertime anyway."

"Not supper. I want out." She was blinking hard. "Mama, please, no walls. No tunnels, either."

Quicksilver offered her a hand. "I will take you anywhere you desire, within reason of course."

"Top of Storm King?"

"Certainly."

Irene shuddered. Quicksilver smiled. "You will have to release your mother's hand."

Gillian froze. She squinted at her right fist, balled under her nose with the thumb planted in her mouth, then at her left hand gripping Irene's, then back at her right. She released Irene and grabbed for Quicksilver. Fire engulfed them.

The fire died. They stood on a ridge, with the ground dropping away thousands of feet on either side. Gillian crowed. She clapped her hands and laughed, bouncing on the balls of her feet, with her breath making mist in the thin, frigid air. She danced and threw out her arms, spinning until she collapsed in a dizzy heap at Warlock Quicksilver's feet.

"We can go home now. I'm cold."

When Quicksilver arrived at the van Gelders' suite the next morning, he found Gillian on the balcony, engulfed in a bearskin big enough to envelop the entire family. All he could see of her were two grey eyes and a pink nose lifted towards the falling snow. She'd been there some time already, judging by the accumulation on the fur.

He said, "I was concerned about you last night. Did you sleep well?"

"I dreamed about mountains and flying."

"Ah, a good sign. Better that than caves."

"What do you want me to do in that cave? Just see how long I can stand it?"

"For now, yes. When you exhibit a mastery of the basics of practical air magic, I will ask more of you, but that will not be for years yet. For now, you should merely endeavour to stay a little longer each time."

"How will I know if I've stayed longer?"

"I will move a clock in."

"How many mountains are there in Frankland?"

"Many, but I have never counted them."

"I've only seen one. I want to see more."

"Any one in particular?"

"Jungfrau."

He gave her a quizzical look. "Jungfrau is not in Frankland."

"Papa flew to the top of it."

"Your papa caused an international incident. Enchanter Paul was not pleased with the apologies he had to make."

"Oh." Gillian's nose wrinkled. "Ben Nevis?"

"Ben Nevis is in Frankland. I will be happy to take you there after your next session in that chamber. Any others?"

"I want to see them all."

"All? That will require many sessions. If I am not available to take you, one of the other warlocks will."

A small hand emerged from the folds of the fur. She spat in the palm and held it out to him. "Deal."

His slight grimace faded into a smile. He spat in his own palm and shook the proffered hand. "Deal."

"If Gillian can do it, so can I."

Irene set down her coffee cup and gave her older daughter her full attention. "You want to go underground?"

"Don't be silly, Mama. But Warlock Quicksilver wants an air witch's help. He should have asked me. I'll be one before Gillian."

"Miranda, sweetheart, I told Quicksilver not to ask you. You're already having nightmares about the tunnels."

"Alex said that after he fell off his horse and broke his collarbone his grandfather made him get back on as soon as the bone healed. He said it would be harder the longer he waited."

"I've heard others say that. It may be true for horses, but..."

"Maybe it's true for tunnels, too. You don't know. You're treating me like a baby."

Irene studied the aggrieved girl. An only child herself, she had never considered the positive aspects of a little sibling rivalry. "Gillian told you what it's like in there?"

Miranda nodded.

"All right, then. Let's talk to Warlock Quicksilver."

Quicksilver, not being a healer, sought advice from the Earth Guild.

"If she wants to, by all means, let her," Mother Astrid said. "Attitude makes a big difference."

Shortly afterwards, one determined nine-year-old and several nervous adults stood by the tunnel door in the van Gelder's apartment.

"I will lead you directly to the closest vent." Quicksilver held out a hand. "Ready?"

"Yes, sir." Miranda took Quicksilver's hand with her right, and grabbed Sven's with her left. "Let's go." Once through, she spotted the vent, released their hands, and ran.

On catching up, Irene was relieved to see Miranda breathing normally, although her face was bedewed with sweat. "If you feel up to it," Irene said, "come away from the wall. You'll like the acoustics. It's a very lively chamber."

"Lively, huh?" Arturos said.

"It echoes, Your Wisdom. All those hard surfaces."

Miranda crept a few feet from the vent and vocalised. Her eyes widened. She made a circuit of the room, singing.

"How is it?" Arturos said.

"It's as good as Airvale's concert hall. You should have told me."

The two warlocks looked bemused. Sven said, "Never noticed, did you?"

Quicksilver said, "Certainly we have noticed. We simply did not consider it sufficient inducement to overcome an air witch's aversion to being underground."

"Actually," Arturos said, "I meant, how do you feel? God-awful or just awful?"

"It hurts, here." Miranda tapped her chest. Sweat trickled down her cheeks. "But I don't mind as much as I'd expected. It's not trying to kill me—not like the tunnels. It's even sorry it's bothering me. It likes having people here, and it had been lonely and bored for so long."

Arturos squinted at the illusory clouds, then shared a long look with Quicksilver over her head.

Quicksilver said, "The tunnels are malignant, you say."

"They'd kill me if they could." Miranda's voice quavered. "How we will get in and out?"

"Your mother can escort you—"

"They put up with her now because she's in the Fire Guild, but she used to be an air witch, and they don't like that. With two of us…"

"Mistress Irene, have you experienced any animosity in the tunnel from your suite?"

"No, sir, but I'd never claim to be the most aware. Now I'll be looking over my shoulder every time."

Sven said. "I'm happy to escort you, whenever you want. Either of you."

"And if he's not around," Arturos said, "somebody else from the Fire Guild will. Count on it. Don't let some lazy wizard's grumbling put you off. We'll make this as easy for you—all three of you—as we can."

Quicksilver said, "Miranda, do you share your sister's desire to dance atop every mountain peak in Frankland?"

"No, sir. Can you take me to the music room now, please?"

Tea and a Tournament

Brilliant May sunshine illuminating the sole undamaged wing of the Royal Palace could not dispel Irene's nightmare memories from the previous year's Yule War. She stuck close to Lucinda's side as they crossed the courtyard, started when spoken to, and flinched at the butler's booming announcement: "The Warlock Locksmith. Countess Irene Matheson. Misses Miranda and Gillian van Gelder."

The butler needed a resonant voice to be heard in the vast reception room he had ushered them into. The ceiling sported a fine example of rococo art—a blue and gold allegory of flying cherubs and enraptured worshipers—but she was too nervous to take it in. The girls gawked.

Irene prodded them, murmuring reminders of their manners. They crossed an ocean of blue-patterned carpet and exchanged formal greetings with the waiting royals. Irene noted Miranda's supple curtsey, Gillian's and Lucinda's awkward ones. The Queen Regent was graceful and gracious, but the boy king seemed a bit stiff. Protocol satisfied, the girls resumed their gawking.

The queen, amused, played docent, pointing out hidden symbols and giving the visitors time to absorb the splendour of their surroundings before turning their attention to the table. The tension in King Brendan's shoulders eased.

Over tea, Irene's nerves steadied as the queen made polite enquiries about life in the Fortress. The children tucked into the food. Irene kept a stern eye on the girls but they acquitted themselves well, and she avoided dribbling clotted cream on her new spring-green silk. She suspected Lucinda had eaten at home beforehand, otherwise she would have been too busy wolfing down everything in sight to make conversation.

Their hunger satisfied, the children began exchanging news. The king said, "My favourite hound just had puppies. Would you like to see them?"

The girls' faces lit. "Yes!" "Mother, could we?"

"I don't see why not."

Gillian ran for the door. The king would have followed at a dignified pace, but Miranda grabbed his hand and tugged him along. Hurrying after them, he looked more like a normal boy than an underage and overburdened ruler, smothering under the court's stultifying routine and rigid protocol.

The queen watched him go with a smile. "Your children are good for him. He seems more comfortable with them than with any of his cousins or courtiers' children."

Irene said, "When they met him they didn't know he was royal."

"But now they do, and they still treat him as if they want nothing more from him than companionship. That is what I find remarkable. I hope they will continue to show such kindness. Even a king needs friends."

"Do you mind that they call him Alexander?"

"Not at all. It is one of his names, and I think he prefers it." Queen Marguerite signalled to the servants. They cleared the table, then retreated out of earshot. She said, "I hope you will not take it amiss that I did not invite you here today simply because we enjoy your company, although we do. I need womanly advice."

Lucinda shrugged. "Not at all, Your Majesty. How can we help?"

Irene nodded agreement. She doubted her own judgement on matters of national importance, but trusted the noblewomen's advice less. Generations had passed since the royals had consulted with anyone outside their limited circles. When the invitations had arrived, the two witches had speculated on the purpose. The queen had been having discussions with officeholders and mages on governance and policy, but this was the first time she had summoned two witches, and no wizards.

Queen Marguerite stared out the window, wearing a slight frown. "Frankland will need years to fully recover from the Yule War."

"Decades," Lucinda murmured.

Centuries, Irene thought. Even with the most troublesome nobles gone, commoners and the remaining nobles were struggling to adapt to the changes forced on them. Frankland would need a steady hand on the tiller for a long time.

"Which makes it all the more important that we not ignore long term issues forever," the queen said. "My son is too young to worry about the succession, but the question of a match for him has troubled me since he was a small child. His grandfather was adamant that Brendan should not marry a cousin. He claimed Frankland's nobility are too inbred for our own good, and I cannot refute that."

Lucinda's head bobbed. "Yes, ma'am."

The queen's smile was brief. "Europa's other royal families intermarry, but no Frankish king has ever married foreign royalty, other than from recent immigrants such as my family. My father thought he could convince the Fire Warlock of the need for fresh blood, but..."

Lucinda coughed. "I wouldn't advise that, ma'am."

"To be honest, I'd rather not attempt it. But if neither our own nobility nor an external match will do, then who?"

"A Frankish witch."

Irene added, "The highest-ranking witch that will have him."

Queen Marguerite looked taken aback.

Lucinda said, "Marrying a powerful common-born witch will deepen the commoners' affection for him. They'll view it as further proof he's serious about reinvigorating the nobility."

"And," Irene said, "That he's determined to be fair, by not picking one or other of the noble factions always fighting for dominance."

"Oh," the queen said. "Perhaps... I had not considered... You said, 'high ranking.' Wouldn't a strong witch frighten them?"

"Why? They wouldn't be living with her."

"But if they should think he's ruled by his wife..."

"King Brendan, henpecked?" Lucinda snorted. "Not possible. The magic behind the Great Oath won't let that happen."

"It has always appeared to me," Irene said, "that weak men choose women they can dominate, and that the strongest men are further strengthened by powerful helpmates. No one imagines that Warlock Quicksilver was diminished by marrying Lucinda."

"Or that Enchanter Oliver and Master Sven were...are...er..."

Irene's eyes widened. "Pardon? I'm not..."

"Sure you're not," Lucinda said. "Don't worry about that, Your Majesty. They'll respect him for it."

"Of course, the witch's guild will matter," Irene said. "Most Franks won't react well to a water witch."

"Er, no. But that's not likely, since he has an affinity for the Fire Guild."

Irene glanced sideways at Lucinda. "Umm…"

"Right, then, perhaps not a fire witch either. But an air or earth witch… Either of those. An air witch wouldn't hurt him with the aristocracy. Might even help."

Shouts outside the open window attracted their attention. Several hounds bounded across the lawn, followed by three running children: one royal boy and two fledgling air witches. Irene's fingers tightened on her teacup.

"An air witch," the queen mused. "Having a trusted advisor who understands treaties and contracts would help with international relations, too."

Irene scowled at Lucinda from behind the queen's turned head.

Lucinda mouthed, "Sorry," and coughed.

The queen turned towards her with raised eyebrows.

Lucinda said, "Maybe we shouldn't have gone on so much about rank and guild. His choices, even among the talented, may be slim."

"Why?"

"Because there can't be many high-ranking witches who would give up their independence for such a cramped…" Lucinda blushed. "Er, sorry, Your Majesty."

Irene said, "That's Lucinda's opinion. She doesn't speak for all witches."

The queen's colour had risen, but she kept her voice under control. "It is a difficult position at times. I can understand why someone might feel that way. I will keep that in mind."

The conversation moved on to other topics, but Irene was distracted, watching the children outside at play. Had she and Lucinda just doomed one of her daughters to life in a golden straitjacket? And if so, which one?

Where in the palace's immaculate lawn had Gillian found a loose stick? Alexander sighed when her throw sent it only a few feet away. The dogs whirled, pounced before he could reach it, and returned it to her, knocking her down with their enthusiasm. He flinched, but she didn't cry. She wrapped an arm around one dog's neck, pulled herself to her feet, and gave the stick another feeble toss.

He shoved between her and the dogs, grabbed the stick, and flung it into the middle of the lawn.

The dogs ran. Gillian ran after them. He groaned.

"Alex," Miranda said. "What's wrong?"

He waved at the dogs bounding around the little girl. "They'll knock her down again."

"That's all right. She bounces. I meant at tea. You didn't look happy."

"Nothing's wrong."

"Something is wrong." She frowned at him. "Now, you have to tell."

He returned the frown. "It's nothing really. It's just…" The dogs and Gillian returned. He threw the stick again, and grabbed the back of Gillian's dress. "I heard some of Mother's ladies-in-waiting talking about the succession. That's why she asked your mother and Mrs Rehsavvy to tea today, to ask their advice about who I should marry."

Miranda gawked. "How old are you?"

"Thirteen."

"That's too young to think about getting married."

"Is not. In the empire they start making alliances for their princes and princesses as soon as they find out which sex the baby is. If I'm not married and fathering children by sixteen, they'd say I'm not doing my duty." He fended off the returning dogs and threw the stick. "I don't think I'd mind that, if it was with a pleasant girl. It's just that the girls the court keeps shoving at me annoy me."

Miranda cocked her head and considered. "Do you have to marry one of them?"

"The queen always comes from a noble family at court. That's the way it's always been. If not one of them, then who?"

"Marry a witch."

"A witch?"

"The best stories always end with the hero marrying the good witch. We know you're a hero, but they—" She flung out an arm. "They don't. If you marry a witch, they'll know you're a hero."

He chewed his lip. "There's a flaw in your logic, but… All right. You're a witch. Will you marry me? When you're old enough, I mean."

"No." A tail was beating a rhythm on her skirt. She shoved the dog away. "I'm tired of these dogs. May we see your music room? You do have a music room, don't you?"

Alexander led Miranda and Gillian in offended silence to the music room. Miranda brightened at the treasure trove of instruments. She ran to the pianoforte and played a lively folk dance. Gillian poked through a shelf of music. When Miranda finished the dance her audience applauded. She gave them a brilliant smile. Gillian handed her a songbook.

"Are these any good?"

Miranda flipped through the pages. "They might be fun." She propped the book on the music stand and began sight-reading.

Gillian pulled Alexander towards a sofa at the far side of the room. He listened in brooding silence as Miranda picked her way through the song. Gillian kicked off her shoes and tucked her feet underneath her, turning so she could watch Alexander.

Miranda finished the first read-through, then began playing the song again with more confidence.

Gillian said, "We can talk now."

Alexander said, "That wouldn't be polite."

"Why not? She won't mind. She won't even notice as long as we don't shout. She's not playing for us."

"Oh."

"You should tell her you're sorry."

He turned an outraged glare on her. "Apologise? For what?"

"You upset her. That's why we came here."

"I asked her to be my queen. She turned me down. I'm the one that should be offended."

Gillian made a rude noise. He brooded a bit longer, then said, "I thought girls want to be royal. Aren't lots of fairy tales about princesses?"

She shrugged. "You said queen. That's different."

"They're both royal."

"Princesses are spoiled girls who get to do whatever they want."

"No, they don't."

"Queens have to behave like grownups. Who wants that?"

"Humph. The nobles' daughters do."

"But you don't want them because they want it too much. You want somebody who doesn't want it. You're stuck."

He eyed her sideways. She drew back. "Don't look at me. I don't want it either."

"I wasn't thinking that. I thought the Air Guild were supposed to be diplomatic."

She frowned for a moment, then grinned. "I don't know what that means, so it's not my fault I'm not."

On their honeymoon, Lucinda had marvelled at Jean's ability to jump for long distances with a dozen people in tow. Her respect for that feat had grown as she came into her full powers as a warlock, and understood her limitations.

Walking through the fire to anywhere within a radius of ten miles is almost instantaneous, but a jump the length of Frankland requires a warlock's full attention and will to hold both shields and flames at full roar while the seconds pass. Unlike calling down the lightning, which requires the ability to channel rapid bursts of raw power, traveling through the fire for long distances requires stamina. Few warlocks have the self-discipline to acquire both.

The drain on the warlock's reserves is even heavier crossing open water. An alert warlock can cope with flames failing over land. One alights somewhere safe, rests for a bit, then carries on. But over water…

As they made plans to return to Thule for that summer's triennial tournament, the five hundred miles of ocean between the Faroe Islands and Thule loomed in Lucinda's imagination like an infinite, terrifying void. The gift of cold water had given her more stamina than the average warlock, but Jean's offhand observation that she had the stamina to jump on her own gave her cold sweats. When they did jump, with her hand in his, she counted seconds, forty-six of them. Perhaps she could do it on her own, but was grateful she didn't have to.

Once in Thule, Lucinda revelled in their holiday as guests of the old lightning-thrower, Mjöllnir. His flame-haired granddaughter Hildur at fifteen was a level three fire witch, and Jean recognised signs that her talent would continue to develop. For the few days before the tournament started, Lucinda, Katie, and Hildur trailed along in the wake of René and the Fire Eaters, participating in their pranks when it suited them, and enjoying girl talk when it didn't. As Lucinda had never become close to any of Frankland's few level-four fire witches—they had spurned her during the siege while her talent was hidden, and the fawning about-faces afterwards had not inspired trust—she welcomed a burgeoning friendship with another strong-minded, intelligent fire witch.

Lucinda expected Hildur to be an enthusiastic spectator at the tournament, as she had been three years before, so was miffed when play began and she didn't appear. Lucinda's ability to follow the action had improved, but she couldn't distinguish the minor combatants, and missed Hildur's running commentary.

An hour in, with smoke billowing across the valley and waves of power confounding her mind's eye, Lucinda was grumbling about Hildur's absence when Katie grabbed her sleeve.

"Ma'am, look, is that her?"

Lucinda followed her pointing finger. "What? Of course not." She turned back towards René, halfway across the valley, then snapped around for another look as she realised her mind's eye and her physical eyes didn't agree. Yes, that was Hildur slipping onto the field, dressed in trousers and her hair tucked under a man's hat.

Lucinda gathered her skirts, and with Katie following, jogged along the sidelines for a closer look. Hildur lasted less than a quarter-hour, but her removal from the field was not due to lack of ability. Warlock Hrafn, Thule's younger lightning wielder and Hildur's father's cousin—a stubborn, narrow-minded man who reminded Lucinda uncomfortably of Warlock Flint—dragged her from the field by the ear. The two of them had a shouting match in Norse, spitting fire at each other. A pair of Thule's earth witches edged away.

Hrafn gave her an order Lucinda understood, even without translation, to be, 'Go home and hang your head in shame.' He lifted a hand as if to strike her, glanced at Lucinda frowning over her shoulder, and gave the girl's ear another hard yank instead before sprinting onto the field. She spat something after him, but he was already out of hearing range.

"What was that?" Lucinda said.

Hildur reddened. "I called him a poxed wet sheep." She turned towards Lucinda. "You said Warlock Quicksilver insisted you must learn to fight although you didn't want to. I want to learn. I know how, in theory, but they won't let me practice. I'd be better at it than half those foolish men out there."

"And they don't want you showing them up. I was watching. You can throw flame as well any untrained level-three male, but your shields need work. You're lucky you weren't burnt."

"If war comes to Thule, everyone in the Fire Guild will have to fight. We don't have enough men, and being a girl won't protect me."

"Protect you, my arse," Katie said. "Makes you a target, more like. Everybody should know how to defend themselves."

"Did they teach you?" Hildur said.

"Not much." Katie shrugged. "My attacks are no good, but I can raise a shield as fast as Mrs Rehsavvy. I learned when the Fire Eaters were torturing her. They don't all have good aim."

"Your attacks are no good? You need practice, too."

The two young women shared a glance, then turned their gazes on Lucinda. She looked out across the valley at the fighting wizards, then back at Katie and Hildur.

She said, "Think we can find trousers to fit me?"

The room in the Thule Fire Guildhall was cramped and poorly lit, but it was sheltered, out of sight of prying eyes. Katie danced across the floor, exulting in the freedom of movement the men's clothing gave her. Lucinda was still in skirts; the only trousers they found that would fit over her hips were far too long in the leg.

"Hildur, mirror shield," she snapped, and threw flame.

How many times had Jean said that to acquire mastery of a subject, one should teach it? Both Hildur and Katie were apt students, and without the pressure of proving themselves to critical male judges, laughed at the pleasure of exercising their talents. The day sped by, but Lucinda kept part of an eye on the tournament action, and they were bathed and clad in their party frocks when the men finally stumbled off the field.

René had acquitted himself well, and never let an attack get through his shields. Lucinda went to sleep that night with an easy mind, grateful she didn't need to watch him as closely as she had three years earlier, and eager to resume sparring with the other women. She was shocked when she woke the next morning with tension crawling down her spine and worry hovering like vultures. She nudged Jean awake and told him what she was feeling.

He sighed. "Your gift has proven trustworthy in the past. We must take this warning seriously, but without specifics to direct our attention, there is little we can do other than be alert and cautious."

"We could cancel the tournament."

He gave her a sardonic glance and didn't bother replying. He did warn the other players. Mjöllnir took the warnings to heart, but they made no dent in the Fire Eaters' enthusiasm. Play began.

The three women slipped away to the guildhall, but Lucinda couldn't focus on their training. By midday, with a pounding headache, she abandoned the other two and returned to prowling the tournament sidelines.

Most players, with the notable exception of René, were more cautious, and though the action was vigorous, few burns were reported, even among the new recruits in the Fire Eaters. The lack of injuries did not soothe her nerves; if anything, it deepened the dread for the coming storm, whatever it might be.

The day's play ended. The players offered her backhanded compliments, teasing her for her unwarranted concerns but crediting her with ensuring no one got badly hurt. She brushed aside their comments and went in to supper with no appetite and a still-throbbing head.

Hildur glowered. Lucinda couldn't fault her for being angry. She was frustrated, too, over the lost day.

After supper, the Fire Eaters got into a loud argument over the details of some historical tournament. Lucinda ignored the increasing volume, continuing to scry in the fire for dangers, until René said, "I'll prove it."

Lucinda's head snapped up as he passed her. "Where are you going?"

"There's a book I want. Back in a few."

For several heartbeats the world seemed to darken. She crouched by the fire, frozen. Then Jean's thundered command, "Stop, fool!" spurred her to action.

Too late, René had disappeared. She beat Jean to the fire by inches. *The pearls—I can't drown.*

Fine. Go.

She counted seconds with the flames roaring in her ears as she tracked René's progress. Ten seconds…Twenty… If she caught him before he fell, they'd have a chance. Twenty-five…

His panic beat at her. *I jumped too far.*

Keep going. You're too far to turn back.

At thirty-nine seconds, his flames died, and he dropped into the immensity of the Atlantic Ocean.

Drowning Warlocks

Lucinda dove towards René. They fell over mile-deep water, leagues from the nearest land. She grabbed a sleeve, but he was tumbling and it was jerked from her grasp. She caught his foot as they hit the surface.

Whoever knew water could be so hard?

They plummeted. She lost her grip. Saltwater filled her head. Nerves screamed from cold more bitter than any she had ever imagined. Her skirts billowed around her head. She fought through them and grappled with René's limp form. She wrapped her arms around him and kicked.

Jean, help!

Coming, love.

She was disoriented, unable to tell down from up except by the dragging of her clothes and hair. Their descent slowed, stopped, reversed. The pearls' magic must be at work; her feeble kicks couldn't account for it. Her lungs burned.

I won't drown. I can't drown. My pearls won't let me. I won't drown. I won't.

Hold on, love. Help is coming.

She broke the surface, gasped, choked, and breathed in salt spray. René was inert, his weight pulling them down. She couldn't lift his head out of the water.

The sea surged. She looked up. They were in a valley, with a mountainous wave rolling towards them.

Jeeeeeeaaaaaaan!

Something grabbed them, pulling them under. She screamed, and breathed water. She kicked and floundered and fought through a confusion of water and fire and flailing bodies, and then suddenly she was in Jean's arms, and he was lowering her to lie on flagstones before a fire.

47

For a brief moment, she was warm. She coughed and wheezed and vomited salt water. Someone nearby swore like a fishwife. Sorcerer Charles?

Jean left her, and the stabbing cold returned.

Jean!

I must warm René, love.

She couldn't lift her head. Her mind's eye glimpsed René lying face down on a divan, with Jean, Sorcerer Charles, and an earth wizard she didn't recognise at work on him. She had never heard Charles swear, but he was in full flow, cursing imaginatively without repeating himself.

Jean shot her a worried glance. She should have been belching saltwater, but she was too cold to move, too cold to shiver. If she lost any more heat she'd die.

But it wasn't her body that had nearly succumbed to the frigid water. As Jean pumped heat into René, the grip of the bond between her and the boy loosened, the bitter cold faded, and other sensations returned: saltwater filling her sinuses, aching muscles, shoulder and hip throbbing from the contact with the water's surface. She coughed and wheezed and bawled.

The healer's assistant squatted beside her, pinched her nose, and, when she opened her mouth, shoved in a spoonful of brown powder. She swallowed, and expelled buckets of watery bile.

"Good, good," the assistant said, and shoved another spoonful in Lucinda's mouth. "All out. All." She conveyed in broken Frankish that the powder, tasting of sun-baked laundry and dry autumn leaves, remedied the saltwater Lucinda had taken in. Another less violent spew followed. A third spoonful caught in her throat. Her mouth was a desert. The powder wouldn't go up or down. She choked.

"Good, good. All done." The assistant patted her on the shoulder and beamed, then left her coughing with a sore throat.

Jean knelt beside her. She buried her face in his shirt and sobbed.

She had regained control, despite aching everywhere, by the time Charles said, "He'll be fine, in a week or two."

The sorcerer staggered to the settle. "What were you doing, screaming underwater? Did you lose your mind? The pearls have limits. They can't save a person *trying* to drown."

Lucinda glared. "Of course they have limits. How could they save René? Or me with something pulling us under?"

Charles voice rose. "Something? Somebody, you mean. Me. And next time don't kick the person trying to rescue you."

Jean's hands gripped her. "Calm yourself, my dear."

She shook him off and yelled, "How was I supposed to know—"

The healer stepped between them and cuffed her on the ear. "No yelling." Charles got a slap. "Patients sleeping."

Jean's "Enough," was quiet but biting. "There will be no more raised voices, or violence." Under his scorching glare the healer backed into the wall, but stayed there with crossed arms and thrust-out chin.

Jean said, "The past few minutes have been trying for all of us. We must make allowances for each other. Lucinda was panicking when you reached her, Charles. Pulling her under intensified her fright."

Charles huffed, "That's how the magic works. You can't travel through the water without getting all in."

"I understand, but imagine yourself in a burning building with an unseen assailant dragging you into the fire. You would experience visceral terror, too."

Lucinda said, "I thought you were the kraken."

Charles goggled, then laughed. "I've never been mistaken for a sea monster before. All right, I can see why you would be kicking and screaming." His expression hardened. "But you'll have to forgive me for being angry about needing to drag you out of the North Atlantic."

Jean said, "Save your anger for the true culprit. Lucinda was chasing Snorri, attempting to reach him before he fell into the sea."

The healer's assistant shoved a mug of some herbal tea into Charles's hands. Slumped against the corner of the settle, he was haggard and shaking. Lucinda knew what traveling through fire cost a warlock. She had never considered what traveling through water would cost a sorcerer. Her face burned.

She shuffled across the flagstones on her hands and knees and laid a hand on his arm. "This was hard on you, too, wasn't it? I'm sorry I fought you. I'm very glad you came when you did."

His pinched look eased. He patted her hand. "Fifty miles is a long swim. I shouldn't have yelled at you; it wasn't your fault. What in the name of all that's holy was that halfwit boy doing?"

"We were in Thule for tournament, and he wanted a book from home."

Charles's jaw dropped. "He nearly killed himself for a book? That's a new one."

Jean said, "He appears to be regaining consciousness."

Lucinda lurched towards the divan. René thrashed and moaned. He opened dark, empty eyes, then recognition flooded in and he reached for her. She gave him her hand and he clutched it with both of his, strangling her fingers. He closed his eyes and screwed up his face, shuddering.

She stroked his hair with her other hand and projected warm, comforting thoughts—*It's all right. It'll be all right*—over and over as he fought down the urge to cry. She cried for him. Jean watched with a stony expression.

When René's tremors had eased, Jean rasped, "You are a very fortunate young man. Be grateful I have not compounded your injuries by flaming you for your foolishness. Have you taken leave of your senses? You ignored everything I ever taught you about control, and the need for caution and forethought when jumping through the fire."

"Sorry," René mumbled. "You make it look so easy. I'd helped you, remember? I never thought it would be so hard on my own."

"I would ask you if you have learned your lesson from this near disaster, but as you were unconscious while in the water, Lucinda and I will suffer the nightmares that should rightfully be yours."

She said, "He'll get his share. That's the beauty of these bonds. Every time I wake you screaming he'll be jolted awake, too."

René groaned.

Charles snickered into his tea. "Serve him right," he muttered.

"A fitting punishment," Jean said. "That and the amusement the Fire Eaters will find in his forfeiting the remainder of the tournament."

"What?" René scrambled to sit up and fell off the divan. "You can't do that to me."

"Not I. You have done that to yourself. Your reserves are empty. If I asked you to prove your membership in the Fire Guild, you could not warm a cup of tea, much less light a candle. Days will pass before you can hold a shield, or conjure a feeble attack you would have jeered at Lucinda for."

"You're joking." René held out an empty palm and glared. Nothing happened. His eyes widened. "Nooooo."

"You'll recover," Lucinda snapped. "But in the meantime, I'll have to babysit you."

"You and the Fire Eaters," Jean said. "Babysit is the appropriate word."

Setting out again from the Orkney Islands, where the closest healer had been, they walked through the fire, Jean and Lucinda on either side of René, propping up the swaying boy. They walked into a ring of sombre faces in the Thule guest hall. Along with Frankland's Fire Eaters, the entire Thule Fire Guild was packed in, awaiting word of the feared drowning. A brief burst of exuberant joy pivoted into boisterous ragging. With both Fire Guilds in full roar, he laid his head down on the table and slept. The hall cleared soon after, the exhausted witches and wizards heading home or falling into bed in the guest hall.

Lucinda slept late the next morning; René slept later. With the tournament already in play, she and Katie rolled him onto a pallet, dragged him into the guildhall, and left him asleep in the corner while they resumed their training.

He was ravenous when he awoke. They broke for dinner and ate in silence, too busy to waste time talking. On his third bowl of stew, René's movements slowed. He lifted a chunk of bread, bit, and chewed with his eyes glazing over. He swallowed, hefted the bread halfway, and let it drop. Lucinda walked him, half asleep, back to his pallet. He was comatose as soon as he was flat.

Halfway through the afternoon, she became aware that he was awake and watching. After a while he began offering advice. Soon he was on his feet, coaching Hildur. He ventured out into the room, got burnt from a blast reflected off Katie's mirror shield, and retreated to a corner. He cheered them on from there.

After that René and Hildur were inseparable. Mjöllnir and his wife hosted a banquet the last night of their stay. Hildur and René didn't say a word to each other all day. She glared at him throughout dinner. He turned away every time she caught his eye. Lucinda smiled into her wine and forbore from offering advice.

They returned to Frankland and within an hour everyone in Blazes and the Fortress heard the story of René's near drowning. Lucinda had expected non-stop teasing, but the urge petered out when met with his cheerful acceptance. He turned aside even the most vindictive thrust with a grin, saying, "Go on. You're not saying anything the Fire Warlock didn't already say, twice as loud with three times as many curses."

He didn't add, "You couldn't do it either." There was no point. He had failed, but would someday succeed, at a feat none of them could even attempt.

Two weeks after their return to Frankland, René was failing again. Gasping and dripping sweat under thick padding, he gave ground under his shorter opponent's relentless barrage. His responses were slowing, his arm tiring. Alexander feinted, bypassed his defences, and dealt him a hard blow with the flat of his blunted sword.

"Ow!"

He was a warlock, drown it! Warlocks never lost to mundanes, but no self-respecting warlock, even as far back as Fortunatus, ever admitted using mundane weapons. The Yule War had shown him how vulnerable wizards were to arrows. Maybe avoiding sword fights was caution, not self-confidence. Heresy. He flicked a glance at the two spectators, and caught another bruising blow to the ribs.

Alexander pressed the attack. René backed, backed again, caught the heel of his shoe on uneven flagstones, fell, and made a half-hearted attempt to rise.

Alexander brought his sword to rest against René's chest. "You are dead."

René went limp, wheezing. "If the floor were level…"

"No excuses. Outdoors, the battlefield may be littered with fallen branches, loose stones, rabbit holes. Indoors, footstools and carpets that slither out from underfoot. If you stumble, you must regain your balance. If you fall, you must roll to avoid your opponent's thrust and rise to continue the fight. In a tournament, yes, your opponent will wait for you to rise. Honour demands the same in a duel, but rage has led men into dishonour." Alexander lowered his sword and gave René a hand. "In a clash of armies, with men killing and dying shoulder to shoulder, a fallen man will find no mercy."

René dropped into a chair and sprawled, still gasping. "Point conceded."

Alexander made a dignified descent into another chair, his erect posture perfect. "Nor will a swordsman who tires as quickly as you survive long."

René groaned. "I know what that means. Exercise, and a bloody lot of it."

Quicksilver said, "Increasing your physical stamina will pay dividends in many ways, including undergirding your control of magical power. If you had taken my advice to regularly climb the Fortress stairs, you would have made a better showing today, and in traveling across the ocean."

"Is it true," Alexander said, "that you can run up the stairs from the main gate all the way to the ballroom?"

Quicksilver's eyebrows rose. "As Fire Warlock, I could, but usually late at night when the Fortress slept. Who told you that?"

"The guards, when I was serving there. I was impressed. If Snorri could do that…"

René groaned.

Beorn clapped him on the shoulder. "Great idea. Let's see you do it."

René gave him a dark look. "Bet you can't either."

Beorn leaned back in his chair with his hands clasped behind his head. "We're not talking about me."

Quicksilver said, "We have not been, but perhaps we should. The exercise would be beneficial to you, too, my friend."

Beorn's grin vanished. "Damn."

Alexander smiled. "A competition, that's what they need. Who will be first to accomplish this worthy goal?"

Beorn and René looked at each other. In unison, they said, "You win."

Quicksilver laughed. "You two cannot evade so easily. If King Brendan is to teach Snorri swordsmanship, Snorri must be fit to learn."

Alexander's brows drew together. "If I am to teach him? I hadn't expected you would take seriously my suggestion that he should learn." He reddened. "In fact, I thought you would laugh at it."

"It's a great idea," Beorn said.

"Want to know why I didn't laugh?" René said. "Because the empire's warlocks would. Anything I know that they don't could give me an edge."

"If you do want to learn, my fencing master should teach you."

The three warlocks exchanged glances. Quicksilver surveyed the practice room. "While your suggestion has merit, Your Majesty, our intent is that Snorri will glean what knowledge he can from several alternative methods of combat, not necessarily becoming adept with any other than the one he is already skilled in, nor do we want knowledge of either his training or this practice room to spread. We would rather not bring your fencing master here."

Beorn said, "We'd rather you taught him. How about it?"

"Sure. It'll be fun."

René groaned.

Alexander grinned. "For me, anyway."

The king and the two older warlocks had gone. René remained at the iron table, scowling at a pile of downy feathers. The table stood parallel to the practice room's rear wall, several feet away. At one end, an empty chair sat in the draft from the corner vent. A page of Irene's notes, held down by a reference book on air magic, fluttered in the edge of the breeze. Away from the draft at the other end, the insubstantial bits of fluff refused to budge.

He, Quicksilver, and Sorcerer Charles had begun their exploration of air magic in March, and it was now July. His magic was fully restored, and he'd made good progress, Irene had said, on training his mind's ear, but if he couldn't do this simple thing, how could he do the harder bits? A level one fresher at the Air Guild School could make a feather float. René's scowl deepened.

"You're trying too hard," Irene had said. "Relax. It's supposed to be easy."

René snorted. Easy for some, sure. Quicksilver could do this in his sleep.

In his sleep… Maybe there was something to that. René never fully relaxed in these frostbitten chairs with their decorative iron leaves poking him in the kidneys. He, for one, would be delighted when Master Duncan delivered the promised new ones. He didn't like the illusion of clouds, either. This room used to be a safe refuge but now seemed dangerously exposed, and the constant threat of rain unnerved him.

He left, returning a few minutes later with an armful of pillows and a large umbrella, which he wedged against a chair back. After arranging the pillows to his satisfaction he draped his arms over the chair arms with hands dangling, rested his feet on another chair's seat, and rolled his head, shoulders, wrists, and ankles.

Katie escorted Irene and the two girls in while he was working the tension out of his shoulders. Miranda ran to the nearest vent. Gillian, her nose level with the tabletop, looked at the umbrella and snorted. She paused for a moment to watch his contortions, then sprinted after her sister.

Irene claimed the chair in the draft. "They will need to leave in about fifteen minutes. Will you escort them out?"

"Sure." He closed his eyes, took a deep breath, held it for a count of ten, then let it out over the same interval. Repeated that several times, while letting his mind wander. He had done well on his single day in the tournament. Only the other warlocks had scored on him, and they hadn't done it often. Even Hrafn had said not bad for a sixteen-year-old. At the next tournament, three years away, nobody would score on him, not even Quicksilver. He smiled, pleased with himself. Compared to what he could do as a warlock, making down float was nothing.

A feather floated inches above the table. He crowed. "I did that!"

Irene said, "Congratulations. I knew you could."

The feather rose over his head.

He goggled. "I didn't do that."

A giggle came from the corner. Snorri's head snapped around.

Irene said, "Miranda?"

"No, Mama, that was Gillian."

Gillian said, "I want to play with feathers, too."

"Precocious, aren't you," René said.

Her nose wrinkled. "I know what that means. You think I'm a baby."

As tempting as it was to agree, he couldn't, even without her mum and sister frowning at him. His dunking had scared him witless; at nine and seven years old, the nerve and self-discipline these two girls displayed in subjecting themselves to the Air Guild's greatest terror left him speechless. Besides, he'd learned his lesson with Alexander. Never dismiss someone just because they were younger than he was.

"No, it means you're more grown up than some adults I've met. I'm precocious, too, you know. Oddballs like us have to stick up for each other." He slid the basket of down the length of the table. "Let's play."

That autumn, René left for Oxford. The void his departure created in the Rehsavvy's house was soon filled by two more babies in rapid succession—both boys, to Lucinda's mild disappointment. René was still in her head, eager to share and argue with her over his studies. She learned things, too.

They met twice a week in the caldera. Lucinda would test her limits with her hand in Jean's, then still under his watchful eye, stand on her own and practice with less forceful draws, becoming confident in her ability to gauge the amount of power needed. Then it would be René's turn, each exercise stretching his limits a hair's breadth. With feeble draws compared to Lucinda's, he was years away yet from standing on his own.

Jean and Beorn took turns drilling the Fire Eaters in his absence. In between the men's longer and more heated sessions, Lucinda drilled a few fire witches Katie recruited for the new Women's Auxiliaries. Most treated it as a lark; only Katie took it seriously. Irene and her two girls spent increasingly longer periods in the practice room. Irene surprised them all, herself included, by kissing Master Duncan when he delivered the new metal chairs.

Whenever René was home between terms, the library became off limits to the children, with the library table serving as the stage for lead soldier re-enactments of famous battles. Jean, his eyes alight, presided as the Fire Eaters, Sven, Lucinda, and Katie all clustered around, picking apart the mistakes and second-guessing the real commanders. Alexander joined in the fun whenever he had time.

Hildur wrote that she had reached level four. René had several short-lived romances with girls he met while at university. None impressed Lucinda; with each new one she sighed and wished Hildur was a Frank.

With the unlocking long past, Lucinda felt stronger than ever before and overflowing with vitality. Not even the rigours of pregnancy and childbirth had much effect. She was back on her feet within hours of each delivery.

Jean's crow's feet and the silver at his temples became more pronounced, but he was healthy and content. With the pressure on the Fire Guild reduced, he divided his time between the duty of preparing for the reforging and the pleasures of home, family, and writing a history of the Great Coven. With a self-discipline that awed their already-devoted staff, he slowly and painfully regained the fitness he had enjoyed as Fire Warlock.

They recruited additional staff who could tolerate the aversion spell on their house, and Lucinda established an uneasy truce with the cook, a level-two earth witch, over control of the kitchen. With help from Mother Celeste involving spells for self-mesmerisation and relaxation potions, first Lucinda and then Jean succeeded in letting down their shields long enough to thrust their hands into a light candle flame. After that it became easier to control their shields as they worked up to hotter fires, becoming comfortable at absorbing each new level under their own control before flaming each other.

René's final year at university overlapped Miranda's first year at the Air Guild school. To neither the Rehsavvys' nor the Mathesons' surprise, she was invited to stay for the summer term's intensive work with the school's concert master, the only first form student to receive that honour. That same summer, René graduated with a double first in history and magic. Beorn officially named him his apprentice—replacing Lucinda, to her relief—and began training him in earnest. Lucinda's sense of prescience, quiescent in the three years since René's near drowning, began to blow cold air on the back of her neck.

Gunther Introduces Himself

"If I had any hint what will go wrong, I'd tell you." Lucinda glared at Beorn. "I don't keep secrets like that. I trust in 'forewarned is forearmed.' Unlike some people I know."

The big wizard held up a hand, palm out. "All right, I hear you. But sometimes you have dreams that drop clues, even if you don't understand them."

"I have three small children, and a boss who keeps me hopping when they're not tugging at my skirts. I don't have time to dream. Or if I do, I don't remember them. I thought about that, mind you, and racked my memory for anything recent. Not a thing."

"Huh." He chewed his moustache. The other men seated around the Guild Council's polished cherrywood conference table showed similar symptoms of concern.

Sunbeam said, "Under normal circumstances, I would say you are imagining things, my dear, and that you have nothing to worry about, but this proposal to reforge the Earth Office is appalling. You nearly suffered an untimely end in unlocking the Water Office. I cannot for the life of me understand why you are willing to do it again. You would be mad not to worry."

"Thank you." She spoke through clenched teeth. "But we're in better shape to handle unlocking the Earth Office. I'm not worried about myself or Jean—"

Beorn said "Eh? But you said—"

"If I, or someone in my immediate family were in danger, my skin would be crawling and I would see black death around me. The Rehsavvys aren't dying; I can tell that much."

"See, you could tell us something."

"Well… Fine. But that's all."

"Is anybody else dying?"

"I told you, I don't know."

"It isn't necessarily magic at all," Sven said. "You could be falling ill, and misreading the symptoms."

"That's no good. I've had these sensations for a week now, and Granny Hazel says I'm as strong as a horse."

"In the past, Lucinda's sense of prescience has proven to be astonishingly accurate," Jean said. "I do not care for prophecies and oracles, but her history has convinced me to take her warning in this matter seriously. That does not mean that the danger, whatever it is, arises from the plans to reforge the Earth Office."

"What else could it be?" Sunbeam said. "You said the empire won't be a threat again for years yet. The biggest danger to Frankland right now comes from inside, and the wizard entrusted with ferreting out and punishing traitors twiddles his thumbs and does nothing to save us." He gave Beorn a pointed glare.

Beorn rolled his eyes. "Sorry, old man, but we're never going to agree on that. I'd guess the threat comes from the empire, even if they're not ready to act on it yet."

Jean said, "That does seem the most likely avenue. Frankland is calmer now than at any previous period in my life. I do not sense treachery at work, and we know the empire cannot rest while we remain unconquered. I infer you have not seen anything to justify Lucinda's sense of disquiet."

"No, but maybe I haven't been looking hard enough. I'll look again. The rest of you, do your own digging. Keep your eyes open. And as for visions…" He shrugged. "Haven't had any since becoming Fire Warlock. Thank God."

"What's the news from the empire?" René said. "When will they be ready?"

"Good question," Beorn said. "Like we expected, their warlocks are doing a fine job of weeding themselves out. The emperor sanctioned three to start training as lightning throwers. The oldest killed himself. Four others tried without being sanctioned. Two killed themselves, and the emperor had the other two executed for treason. They were already short-handed after the last war with us. Now, they've got only two ordinary warlocks—"

René snorted. "Oxymoron."

"—a couple more underage possibles, and the two half-trained lightning throwers: the emperor's second son and a half-cousin twice removed. Jean and I have a dozen franks riding on them. He's betting the son is the last one standing; I'm betting on the cousin."

"Care for a side bet?"

"Check 'em out first."

René grinned. "Yes, sir."

The clock chimed the hour; time for the children's tea. The Rehsavvys' house sighed and settled down to enjoy the lull, but before the clock chimed a quarter past, a howl broke the quiet. "Mama! Mama! Mamamamamamama…" The wailing child rocketed through Lucinda's sitting room door and into her lap. The flustered nursemaid followed, waving a wet facecloth.

"I'm sorry, ma'am. I know you're not to be disturbed, but he got away from me."

"It's all right." Lucinda kissed the top of Drew's head and peeled sticky hands from around her neck. "What happened?"

The nursemaid scrubbed the dirty hands with the facecloth. Drew fought and screamed. His palms were scrapped and bleeding.

She said, "I was feeding little Robbie. Master Eddie had finished his tea and was playing with the dog. Drew ran to join in the fun while my back was turned. I think he fell against the stack of firewood and skinned his hands on it."

Lucinda examined the small hand. "Fetch the tweezers. He's got splinters."

The clock chimed half past before she finished extracting slivers of wood. Drew's tears had reduced to an occasional sniffle, and his head was lolling. He was asleep when the nursemaid came back for him.

She eyed her mistress's collar. "I'm sorry, ma'am."

Lucinda tugged the collar and twisted her neck to see. The bloody handprint was impossible to miss. She sighed. She should have known better than to wear a white blouse at home. He'd left marmalade in her hair, too. It wasn't the nursemaid's fault the now-cherubic boy was a firecracker; she sent them away without complaint.

She turned back to the fire, but it was merely burning logs. The thread of information she had been following had snapped, and she couldn't remember what had seemed worth pursuing. Three days of diligent search by everyone on the guild council, with the exception of Sunbeam, had turned up nothing to account for the cold prickles running down her spine.

It hadn't been a wasted effort, having exposed several small but festering problems that could become bonfires if left alone for too long. Beorn had been pleased, and mumbled about doing this exercise again in six months. Lucinda had not been pleased, and went on doggedly searching on her own after he called off the team effort, but all she found were molehills and blind alleys.

Unsure what to do next, she sat cross-legged on the hearth rug to give her back and neck a break, and let herself be mesmerised, for a while, by the flickering flames licking the charred wood.

The clock chimed three quarters. Her skin crawled. Someone was watching her.

Without taking her eyes off the burning log, or giving any sign she'd come out of her trance, she sifted through a store of spells, found the one she wanted, and snapped it into place.

The fire roared. On the other side, a man jerked backwards, but she had hooks in him and wouldn't let go. "Gotcha," she said.

He fought her. She noted regular features, dark eyes, a short brown beard, and lavish clothing. She had no more attention to spare. *Jean! René!*

Yes, my love?

What's up, big sister?

Watch.

For several minutes she and the intruder struggled in a silent battle of wills. His strength astonished her. Another lightning thrower? Not quite, or she could not have held him over such a distance. He could be one of only two men, but which one?

The struggle was exhausting. If he kept fighting, she would lose him.

He stopped struggling and smiled, but the smile didn't reach his eyes. "Indeed, Madam Locksmith, you have 'got me,' as you so gracelessly phrased it." His Frankish, though heavily accented, was clear and unhesitating. "Allow me to introduce myself." He made an elegant bow. "Warlock Sturmmeister, at your service."

"Who?"

His eyes sparked. "You should heed your stepsister's advice, madam, and acquaint yourself with Europa's noble families."

"Right, I remember now. Prince Sigismund's the heir, and you're Prince Gunther, the spare."

A snarl flashed across his features, followed by a polite mask. "A spare, madam? Hardly. I am, after the emperor, Europa's highest-ranking warlock. When I am emperor, I shall be the continent's supreme wizard."

Yeah, right.

Quiet, little brother.

She was talking to an Emperor's son, and her hair was coming down on the side where Drew had grabbed with marmalade-sticky fingers, but be damned if she would primp for this dandy. She cursed her darling cherub, and kept her hands locked together in her lap.

"A little arrogant, aren't you? You have Prince Sigismund to contend with. I don't imagine he'd be happy hearing you say that."

He leaned back, relaxed now, and dismissed her objection with a graceful flick of the wrist. "His happiness is not my concern. He is merely a level-four earth wizard. Europa will not tolerate an emperor who is less than a warlock."

"She has before."

"She need not do so again. Unlike Frankland, my dear Locksmith, the Europan Empire adapts as times change. It disturbs you, doesn't it, that Frankland cannot. That your aristocrats are slavering degenerates, your witches and wizards are more fit to rule than your rulers, and your offices prevent you and your companions from exercising your rightful authority. That's why you are willing to endure an inferno to unlock those offices. When the Fire Office is rebuilt to your satisfaction, you will claim your rightful place as Frankland's queen."

Sweat trickled down her neck. "That's nonsense."

"Not at all. That is as it should be. Your Marguerite is no witch. She is not eligible for the title 'queen.' But you..." He leaned forward, eyes gleaming, close enough to reach through the fire and touch her. "You fascinate me. You are the most powerful woman in Europa, if not the world. You cannot be satisfied with the throne of a country as unimportant as Frankland."

"I don't want—"

"Not when you can have more."

Her jaw hung open. "I...what?"

"Leave the narrow confines of your domestic prison in Frankland behind." His eyes flicked to the handprint on her collar. "You need not concern yourself with mewling, puking infants, or the querulous demands of an ancient, fading husband. You cannot imagine he will long continue to satisfy you. Come to me and together we shall fulfil Europa's destiny. Together we shall unite Europa; all of Europa, from east of the Urals to the Atlantic Ocean and the colonies beyond shall be ours."

She let go, but now he held on.

"Consider my offer, my dear."

She shoved him away and broke the contact, but not before she heard him promise, "We shall meet again."

"Drink up. You need it."

Lucinda clutched the cup Beorn shoved at her, but even with both hands her trembling sloshed the milky green liquid out of the bowl.

"Here," he said, and cupped his hands around hers, holding the cup steady while she gulped. The Earth Guild tonic's questing tendrils spread through her, strengthening muscles and shoring up bones.

Her hands steadied. "Thanks."

"No problem." He let go and corked the bottle. "I've been keeping more of this on hand since the Water Office went pear-shaped."

She leaned back against Jean's shoulder and gazed at the practice room's clouds. The last few minutes, after she collapsed in her sitting room, had left her confused. "Why are we here? Why was I so weak?"

"I brought you here, my love," Jean said, "because I am quite sure no one can spy on us here. You are exhausted because you fought a battle with a strong and determined opponent across the breadth of Europa. In such a battle, holding on is harder than breaking free. No one other than a fully-fledged lightning wielder could have done what you did. I do believe you have given Prince Gunther a nasty shock."

She set the cup down and smoothed her skirts. "It wasn't just holding him to the fire. He scared me."

"You didn't act like it." René sat on the iron table, swinging his legs and grinning. "Saying 'Who?' was brilliant. He didn't like that at all."

"Maybe not, but I felt like an idiot. He threw me. I was expecting him to say Prince Gunther or Lord Wilhelm. What did he call himself? Master of something?"

"Sturmmeister," Jean said. "Storm master."

"You usually call foreign wizards by their war names. Why not Prince Gunther?"

Beorn grinned. "Because it pisses him off."

"Oh. Right. But as I was saying, he scared me, knowing so much about me. He'd been spying on my conversations with Claire. I'd thought for weeks someone was watching me, but this must have been going on for months."

"Years, my love," Jean said gently. "You forget that you are the most powerful witch on this continent, and one with unusual talents. By now, both our enemies and our allies will have reviewed and analysed your entire life."

Her face burned. "Frostbite."

René laughed. Beorn patted her arm. "You've got nothing to be ashamed of."

René said, "You can't really get angry at them for it. We do the same to them."

"Indeed," Jean said. "We must. If we do not understand our enemies they will always surprise us."

She swallowed another sip of Beorn's tonic. "Just because you're right doesn't mean I have to like it. But I don't understand. If they know so much about me, wouldn't they know about our bonds? Why would he make such a disgusting proposal when he should have known you would be listening in?"

"Bonds are not easily identifiable. Perhaps they do not recognise that we have one."

"Or maybe," René said, "they do, and he said what he did because of it, not despite. To sow suspicion, you know."

"That would be in character," Beorn said, "but the way I see it, our friend Gunther can't grasp what a bond means. He's the type that would never let somebody else inside his head, and can't understand why anybody would ever want to. He'd think that as powerful as you are, Lucinda, you'd never stand for it."

He pushed his chair out of striking distance. "Don't flame me for this, but, you know, I'd almost like to see you take him up on his offer."

She screeched, "You what?"

"Whoa. I said don't flame me. I don't mean it. But I'd love to see him grappling with somebody he can't bully. I'd laugh myself silly, watching.

If he really thought there was any chance you'd take him up on it, and understood what you'd do to him when he gave you orders, he'd never have offered."

Jean's voice had a hint of fire in it. "While that might be amusing, it would not be fair to the parties involved, nor is it fair to spy on a wedded couple in the sanctuary of their marriage bed." Her face burned again. His grip on her shoulder tightened. "Lucinda, my dear, have you recovered sufficiently to return home on your own?"

"Sure. You're not coming?" She twisted around to look at him. His expression was grim.

"Not immediately. While I am not surprised the empire knows what your stepsister said to you in a public house, I had believed our home was shielded from prying ears and eyes."

Beorn said, "Far as I knew, it should be."

"But apparently it is not." Jean rose and began pacing. "My dear, you said you have felt as if you were being watched. Where in the house have you experienced that sensation?"

"Usually in the sitting room. Sometimes in the dining room."

"In our bedroom?"

"No."

"And you, René?"

René frowned. "Mostly in my bedroom. Once or twice, like Lucinda said, in the dining room or her sitting room."

"But not in the library? Either of you? No. The kitchen? The nursery? The hall? The conservatory? Only those three rooms, then, and nowhere else? René, I believe you do most of your spellcasting from your bedroom."

"Yes, sir."

Lucinda said, "I do mine from the sitting room, although last summer I also did some from the blue guest room."

Jean nodded. "I suspect the Air Guild spells we have been using for seeking out trouble at a distance may have opened channels that a determined interloper could exploit."

"Uh-oh." Beorn's face had gone grey. "The Fire Warlock's study. We have meetings there all the time. A hole there…"

"Would be most unfortunate." Jean paced tight circles, snapping orders. "Lucinda, go about your daily routine, but do not use those spells. Read or write or talk to the children in those rooms, but avoid magic. René, bring

Master Sven and Mistress Irene here and explain the situation. Beorn, fetch Enchanter Paul and meet me in the Warren's amber chamber. We have work to do."

He vanished into the fireplace, with Beorn hard on his heels.

Security Breach

"Nothing ever changes in Frankland." Sorcerer Charles shook his head in quiet bemusement. "And yet change happens. Ten years ago I would never have believed this possible."

Lucinda wasn't sure she believed it yet. Charles and the two Sorceresses, Lorraine and Eleanor, sat at the table in the practice room, side-by-side with most of the Fire Guild Council. They all looked grey and lifeless in the dim light filtering through the clouds, but began to come alive as Lucinda circled the table, pouring coffee. She was the only one who had slept that night. René yawned, stretched, shook kinks out of his back and neck, and began unloading the trolley she had brought from the kitchen.

She said, "Where's Irene?"

Beorn said, "She was chewing her nails by midnight. I sent her to bed."

Sven said, "She'll be ready when the time comes."

Beorn lifted his mug and chugged the scalding coffee. Sorceress Lorraine shuddered. Her back was straight, but she looked ghastly, pasty white with blue bags under her eyes.

Lucinda said, "You'll feel better after you've had breakfast."

Lorraine looked askance at the steaming bowl of porridge René set on the table. "I fear I am too tired to eat."

Lucinda said, "Scrambled eggs might be easier. No? Strawberry jam on white bread?"

She smiled. "Thank you, Mother Hen. Perhaps I can manage that."

Jean scratched at dark stubble. "The Fire and Earth Guilds have often collaborated. As a young man, I dreamed we might forge such a relationship with the Air Guild, but my attempts in that direction came to naught. In my wildest dreams, I never imagined I should ask the Water

Guild for aid in dealing with the Air Guild."

Lorraine said, "It would have been futile to turn to the Earth Guild for help with this problem, and when we cannot trust the Air Guild…" She nibbled at the jam and bread Lucinda handed her. "I am glad we were able to help."

Lucinda said, "What did you find?"

"That my initial terror was unfounded," Jean said. "There was no treachery intended, and our security breach is not as large as I feared."

"That's good news. The Fire Warlock's study is still secure?"

"So it would seem. The Air Guild spells for seeking trouble open a channel from one location to another. What we discovered is that those channels are inherently bi-directional. That is, a sufficiently powerful witch or wizard in the far location may, under some circumstances, turn the channel to their own ends, and use them to spy on us."

"But you said…"

"That there was no treachery involved. Yes. The Air Guild did not hide the nature of these channels. The Great Coven knew their properties and went to some lengths to prevent them from being suborned. Additional Air Guild spells reduce the risk by preventing creation of incoming channels, and by destroying all channels immediately after we are done with them. Those spells protect the Fortress and the other seats of power—"

"The Crystal Palace, the Warren, and the Hall of the Winds?"

"Yes, plus the royal family's older domiciles. We have not given away any secrets from our conversations in those places. Our house, however, is not so well protected. The spell to prevent incoming channels is simple and covers the entire house, but the one to detect and close unused channels is more intricate, and therefore expensive for private citizens. I had probed the spells on the library, identified that one, and assumed, more fool me, that it covered the house rather than just the library. Even so, it is unlikely the channels originating in other rooms would have been discovered had not Prince Gunther taken an interest in you, my dear."

"Frostb—Sorry, Your Wisdoms."

"No offence taken." Lorraine finished her bread and jam and reached for the eggs.

Eleanor said, "It appears that in spying on you, he stumbled onto a channel originating in your dining room. A methodical search led him to channels originating in your sitting room and Snorri's bedroom."

"That doesn't make sense. I've felt someone watching me off and on for over a week, but I hadn't gone looking for trouble outside Frankland until four days ago, and I've never used the dining room fireplace for that. I'd focused on problems inside Frankland and left the foreign search to Jean and Beorn."

"And me," René said. "It's my fault. I've used the fire in your sitting room or the dining room sometimes when I was waiting for dinner and too lazy to go upstairs."

"I guess that explains it all, then. How much have we given away?"

"As far as we can determine," Eleanor said, "nothing."

Beorn said, "We got really lucky. He got lots and lots of history lessons, family and staff squabbles, and Blazes gossip."

Lorraine added, "Plus a surfeit of mewling, puking infants."

Beorn grinned. "Yeah. Enough to make him bored out of his mind. If he paid attention, he got a pretty good idea what sort of people you are, and how well you get along together, but none of that's secret. You haven't dropped any hints about strategy, or what we're planning on doing with the Fire Office."

Lucinda sank into a chair, limp with relief. "That really is good news. So we'll pay the Air Guild to cover the entire house and we'll be fine, right?"

There was a long silence. She leaned forward and clenched her teeth. "I don't like being spied on. Why would we not fix this problem?"

Beorn tugged at his beard. "We've been arguing about this for the past hour. Yeah, we could put those spells on the house and you'd not have to worry about Gunther spying, but…"

"But?"

"And for sure we want to block him from your sitting room, but…"

Jean said, "If we do not block the other channels, he may infer we did not find them. René suggested that if he continues to use those to spy on us, we could perhaps use them to feed him misleading information about our intentions."

"And you agreed to this lame-brained idea?"

"It has merit. Advantage in war is often a matter of keeping your opponent unbalanced."

"But if we can't be free to talk even in our own dining room…"

"You and René are already well-trained never to discuss state secrets

71

outside of a few safe places. When we discuss strategy, we retire to the library or adjourn to the Fortress. I do not foresee that much needs change."

"The idea of letting him watch us eat dinner makes my skin crawl."

Beorn said, "Too bad. Deal with it."

She subsided, grumbling. The others finished their breakfasts and left, leaving Lucinda alone with Jean.

She said, "There's something else I don't understand."

"Yes, my dear?"

"I pushed myself as hard as possible the first two years after starting training to call down the lightning, and then, since I lived through it, unlocking the Water Office pushed me further along. Prince Gunther started training nearly three years after I did, but he almost won that battle of wills. How did he get to be so strong?"

Jean's expression hardened. He beckoned for her to join him at the fireplace. "The empire has employed a training technique neither we nor Thule's warlocks have ever considered. Watch."

A fire sprang to life in the grate. Within it, an image grew of Prince Gunther hurling fire on a mountain ridge. Two terrified mundanes flanked him with their hands on his shoulders. A fire wizard and an earth wizard with burn cloths over their arms watched from a safe distance. Further away, a small group of courtiers huddled next to a tunnel entrance.

Lucinda said, "What are those men doing? Standing that close to a lightning wielder in training is dangerous."

"Indeed. That is rather the point. Look closely."

She leaned in, then jerked backwards. "Jean, there are ropes. Those men are tied to him. Whatever are—"

Gunther miscalculated. The three men were knocked off their feet. Moisture on their bodies vaporised, sending gloves, hats, and boots shooting away. In an instant, flames engulfed all three. Lucinda clapped her hands over her ears to block the men's screams, and cursed the fire wizard for being slow to extinguish the flames.

The two wizards ran to the prince and rolled him in the burn cloths. The courtiers followed with a stretcher, lifted him onto it, and carried him away. Lucinda's jaw hung open as the stretcher bearers vanished into the tunnel, followed by the two wizards, leaving the two badly burned mundanes screaming in the snow.

The image in the fire disappeared. Jean's face was a grim mask. "If the force of that mistake had not been distributed among three men, Prince Gunther would have died. Instead, he survived, though badly injured, and emerged with his capacity significantly expanded."

She croaked, "Did the—" She swallowed, and tried again. "Did the other men…"

Jean shook his head. "They died of their injuries."

"Were they guards? Volunteers?"

"No. They were felons." He nodded towards the fire. "That was the second time he overdrew."

"Second! How many men has he killed?"

"Three. He now works with four men tied to him as sacrificial victims."

"No wonder Beorn called him a bastard."

"This use of human shields was his idea. He is ruthless, and brave enough to return to his training after being injured. Do not ever forget, my love, that this man is dangerous."

René went hunting, but his prey turned on him.

Prince Gunther sneered, "This is Frankland's next great warrior? You look like an apothecary's apprentice."

"And Warlock Quicksilver looks like a scribe, but your armies couldn't beat him."

"What wars has he fought since retiring? None. He could not survive against us without your infernal Fire Office's backing. When your foolish Fire Guild Council destroys it, you will face me alone. Surrender now; you cannot hope to win."

"What makes you think I'll be alone?"

The prince laughed. It wasn't a pleasant sound. "Thank you for confirming our supposition that you intend to destroy your Fire Office."

Frostbite.

I told you this was a bad idea, little brother.

"Reforge it, you mean."

The prince waved a lazy hand. "Words. Call it what you will. I call it our opportunity to unite all Europa."

"Yeah? Well, if or when the time comes, I'll be looking forward to kicking your cousin's butt all the way back to Danzig."

The prince's eyes sparked. "Yes, I imagine you could 'kick his butt', as you so crudely suggest. But not mine, you laggard. I began training to call down the lightning after you, but I am farther along now than you are, nor am I so weak I must steal power from an old, has-been warlock to call down the lightning. I stand on my own. You are no match for me."

Don't respond to that, little brother.

René opened his mouth, closed it again, and glowered. "Arrogant bastard."

"No, simpleton, I am the legitimate son of a legitimate emperor. An itinerant peddler's by-blow is not my equal, and never can be. When we meet in person, I will teach you to regret your upstart effrontery. Until then…" His smile was malicious. "Continue to exercise caution. I will be disappointed if you kill yourself, and deny me the pleasure."

The prince's image vanished, and the flames with it, leaving behind a cold, half-burned log.

René stood in the library door, looking like a puppy expecting a reprimand.

"That went well," Lucinda said.

He made a rude noise and dropped onto the hearthrug, pulling his knees up to rest his chin on them.

"We did warn you," Jean said, "that Prince Gunther is dangerous. You assumed he was no more of a match for your wit than the average Frankish nobleman. You met clever aristocrats on our travels. You should have known better."

"Yes, sir," René mumbled. "I shouldn't have let that slip."

Jean's stern voice softened. "Frankland will not fall because of today's confrontation. Admitting we intend to reforge the Fire Office shall cost us little. The empire has already gambled heavily on that eventuality, to the point the emperor has effectively signed the death warrant of his favoured son, Prince Sigismund."

Lucinda said, "You don't think there's any chance Sigismund could win a power struggle?"

"I give that outcome small odds. Sigismund is a level-four earth wizard of average intelligence with scruples. Gunther is a brilliant warlock with none. The Empire's political climate has always favoured ruthless warlocks. This seems unlikely to be an exception."

René glared. "Especially when the ruthless warlock can call down the lightning. Everybody around him will be too scared to stand against him. I want to know, was he deluded? Or was he telling the truth?" His voice rose. "You've kept me from going as fast as Lucinda all along, and it pisses me off. I can believe he's ahead of me. Why the hell did you let that happen?"

Jean regarded the seething youth for a moment before responding, without raising his own voice. "I have kept you on a tight rein since we began your training because Frankland cannot afford to lose you, aside from my personal conviction that I would be overcome with grief and remorse were I to misjudge and allow your untimely demise. Is he ahead of you? How does one measure 'ahead'? Can he launch a lightning bolt with more power in it than you can? Yes, but he cannot throw it where he wants it, nor can he throw more than a few before he exhausts himself. Our training has focused on developing your stamina. You can make draw after draw without tiring, and your aim is better than his."

"Meaning," Lucinda said, "you can do more damage to them than he can to us."

Jean's eyes danced. "Particularly as his aim is so bad he is as likely to kill his own men as his opponent's."

The rigid set of René's shoulders relaxed. "That's not so bad then."

"Of course not," Jean said. "He is also less skilled than you at estimating the power needed, and is more likely to kill himself. We can still hope he may do so. If you must confront him again, either of you, remember this: he is a master at manipulating the truth. He knows better than to lie to a warlock, but the truth he tells will be a selective, incomplete truth. Whether that is deliberate, he is deluded, or he does not know the whole truth himself will often not be obvious."

Lucinda said, "I'd really rather not ever talk to him again."

René said, "You're going to tell me not to."

Jean said, "I do advise against it, but if you must tweak his nose… please, be more effective at it."

Lucinda lay in bed, watching Jean sleep in the dim moonlight. His arm lay across her, his hand warm on her thigh. Six years ago, at their wedding, he had appeared a young man of twenty-seven. He now looked like a mature and distinguished man in his early forties. The peacetime since the Yule War had been good to him. He had even put on a little weight. He was still slim, but no longer emaciated, like a man whose wife could burn water.

She marvelled at how handsome he was. Why had she ever thought him plain? What a fool she'd been at nineteen.

And what a fool she was, still, not to know he would age faster, once freed from the Fire Office. She had recognised the rapid ageing in Lorraine; she hadn't wanted to admit it in Jean.

Lucinda's heart quailed. Enchantress Winifred's words—drown that woman!—filled her head.

Do you think you and your husband will live into old age together? You may not have another Yule.

Was this why Lorraine and Mother Celeste had agreed, three years ago, that the Fire Office must be rebuilt within ten years? Had they known? She remembered the searching looks the two witches had given him while talking about the timing. Of course they had known. Drown them, both of them.

He had known, too. She was sure of that. He would have known his time was limited, even before they married. She felt cheated, but not by him. She would have been hurt and angry if he had played the martyr and refused to marry her.

Jean stirred. The rhythm of his breathing changed, indicating he was waking. They could do nothing now, other than make the best of what time they had left. She nuzzled his neck. As the saying went, she had made her bed, she should enjoy lying in it.

A Wish Granted

The stragglers were taking their time, inspecting the creatures washed ashore, as they gathered at the water's edge on Frankland's northern tip. Lucinda did not chivvy them along. She was not eager for this venture.

With three children under the age of five at home, she would have preferred to skip this year's tournament in Thule, but she had promised Hildur she would return to drill Thule's fire witches while the men were otherwise occupied. Her children were in capable hands, and she would not stay long. She had no excuse not to go.

Her immediate concern was the challenge of carrying Katie and a half-dozen Fire Eaters through the fire across five hundred miles of ocean. She had no qualms about jumping that far on her own, but taking responsibility for other lives made her heart race. Not that she would let them know she was nervous. They were already giving René doubtful looks; they didn't need her further unnerving them.

Lucinda's party were to go first. Jean was coming, too, at her insistence, but would step in only if she faltered. Then he would return, and come again with René, but René was to do all the work. Jean and Lucinda believed he could do it—three years of an exercise regimen under the king's supervision had done wonders for his stamina—but René was sweating in the chilly breeze.

He turned away from the Fire Eaters and kicked at clumps of seaweed. *Hurry up, big sister. I can't stand them staring at me.*

"Right, then," she said. "Are we ready? Let's go."

The last straggler jogged across the beach, they joined hands, and Lucinda called up the fire. She counted seconds. In less than a minute, they stood before the Fire Guildhall in Reykjavik. Warlock Mjöllnir and

Hildur emerged to welcome them.

Lucinda stared. "You're a warlock." As if Hildur didn't already know that.

"Yes, Warlock Staðfastur. Steadfast, that is. For three months now," she said.

Lucinda's fantasies of matchmaking for René evaporated. The Fire Office would never let a foreign warlock into Frankland, and rightly so—a warlock's first duty was to their country. "You didn't tell me," she said.

"Why should I?" Hildur turned away. "I might as well not be one."

Jean and René arrived, both wearing broad smiles, and Lucinda had no opportunity to speak to Hildur alone during the bustle of preparations for the tournament. The Thule witch performed her duties as hostess with smouldering eyes in an expressionless mask. Even after the tournament began, she was tight-lipped and ferocious in her attacks in the women's drill. When they stopped for dinner, Lucinda drew her aside.

"What's wrong?" Lucinda asked.

Hildur gestured for Lucinda to follow, and led her down a rocky path through a pasture. Lucinda waited until they were out of earshot of the other women, their voices muffled under the splash and babble of a nearby waterfall, before trying again. "What's wrong? Why did you say you might as well not be a warlock?"

"Thule is small," Hildur said. "But our Fire Guild is strong. Our warlocks are strong. We teach our warlocks to call down the lightning. Because we are small, all our warlocks must learn. All except me. I am a warlock, but they will not teach me."

"Because you're a girl?"

"No." Hildur tossed her head. "I am the daughter of warriors. Thule does not expect the daughter of warriors to be weak and cowardly, as Frankland does." She clambered onto a boulder and sat with her arms hugging her knees. "Grandfather and Warlock Hrafn say they will not teach me because I am a woman, and women should not call the lightning. That is a lie. You are a lightning thrower. Other women in Thule's past have thrown the lightning. Grandfather and Hrafn delude themselves, inventing excuses for why they should not teach me, but the truth is they cannot teach me."

"Oh?"

"Grandfather was already past his prime when my father was born.

Grandfather taught Hrafn to call down the lightning, and when my father was old enough, Grandfather began to teach him. But Grandfather was already old, and losing faith in his judgement of how much a young man can control. When my father was twenty-four and approaching the end of his training, Grandfather lost his nerve, and asked Hrafn to complete the training. Hrafn is a skilled warrior, but he is hard-headed and impatient. He is not, and never should be, a teacher. We have had warlocks like him before—men whose impatience kills the students they are trying to teach."

"And that's what happened to your father?"

"Yes. Hrafn pushed him too hard. He overreached, and died. And now I am old enough to learn, but Grandfather and Hrafn are both afraid to teach me." She stared across the pasture, the fire in her eyes a stark contrast with the placidly munching sheep. "And in truth I am afraid to learn from either man. I do not argue as I should. Thule will suffer because of their stubbornness and my cowardice."

The two women sat, side by side, in silence. Lucinda had no advice to offer. She agreed with Hildur's assessment of Thule's male warlocks as teachers, but could not offer to teach her in their stead. Drilling fire witches in self-defence was one thing, but teaching a foreign warlock to call down the lightning was another. The Fire Office would never let her.

Hildur stirred. "One thing has come out of this predicament. Have you ever used a firearm?"

"What? No! Of course not." Firearms were for the lower ranks. No ranking fire wizard in Europa would admit to the impotence implied by shouldering one.

Hildur bared her teeth. "I am not so proud. Grandfather has given permission for me to learn. Even if I can't throw the lightning, I can still throw death. Would you like to try?"

Lucinda considered the offer. She had no desire to become adept with an instrument whose only purpose was to kill, but knowledge was power, and she could afford to trade a little status for it. She nodded. That evening, Hildur, Lucinda, and Katie had a lesson in loading and firing a musket.

Lucinda went home directly after the tournament, nursing a bruised shoulder from the musket fire. Jean and the Fire Eaters returned a few days later, without René. She was not altogether surprised.

"Mjöllnir offered to teach René a few techniques he has developed,"

Jean said, "and having a different teacher would be good for the boy. I let him stay, since he has proven he can cross the ocean on his own."

They both knew René had another, redheaded reason for an extended sojourn. Lucinda wondered if letting him stay in Thule was wise, but she felt no hint of trouble, and the few glimpses she had into René's mind, tenuous over such a long distance, suggested he was happy. She went on with her work and gave him little thought over the next month.

She was in the kitchen, icing a cake for Jean's birthday, when she had the first indication René's latest escapade might have serious consequences.

Lucinda, get your ass up here now, Beorn roared in her head, *before I throw your damn-fool little brother into the Irish Sea and drown him.*

The cake was ruined; she'd dropped the icing bowl on it. She told the cook to bake another, yanked off her apron, and walked through the fire into the Fire Warlock's study. Jean arrived right behind her.

The ruby in the Fire Warlock's ring pulsed a bright, angry red. She shaded her eyes to look at him. His face was a darker red than his beard. He was leaning against his desk, arms crossed, feet spread wide apart, glowering at René and Hildur.

Hildur? Lucinda's jaw dropped.

They stood by the door, hand in hand, with nervous smiles fixed on their faces, like thieves trying to explain away the queen's jewels found up their sleeves.

"What did they do?"

"What did they do?" Beorn roared. His face got redder. He slammed a fist on his desk. "You tell them."

"Uh, it's like this…" René said.

"It's my fault," Hildur said.

"Is not," René said. "If Mjöllnir and Hrafn weren't such asses—"

Her eyes flashed. "They are not asses. They do the best they can."

"Do what?" Jean said.

René and Hildur looked at each other. "Please, let me tell it," she said.

He shrugged. "Go ahead."

"As I have told Lucinda, all warlocks in Thule must learn to wield the lightning, but Grandfather and Warlock Hrafn refuse to teach me. So I ask René for help, and René says Frankland will teach me."

"Oh, dear," Lucinda said.

"Yes, this is difficult." Jean took a long breath, held it, and let it out.

"René cannot make such promises on behalf of Frankland."

Beorn rumbled, "You haven't heard the whole story yet."

"Oh? Let us sit and talk this through." Jean gestured towards the sofas by the fireplace. "Come and sit, please. Our discussion will be easier if we are all comfortable."

Beorn snorted. He stomped away, and dropped into a chair on the opposite side of the room, still with his arms crossed and glaring. Jean shot him a dark look before turning back to Hildur.

"My dear Hildur, you do not know what you ask of us. I confess I am in agreement with your grandfather, and will do everything I can to avoid putting such a burden—and it is a burden, not a privilege—on a woman. I approached teaching Lucinda with great trepidation, and only because Frankland was in extremis, and could not have survived without a locksmith able to handle locks of great power. Thule is not in such dire straits."

"Not now, no, but we will be. If I do not learn, who will pass on the knowledge? We have no other warlock. Grandmother read the runes, and they say if I do not learn, and teach the ones who come after me, Thule's defence will die with Hrafn." She extended her hands in entreaty. Jean held his out and she clasped them. "Please, Your Wisdom, teach me."

Jean shook his head. "I regret that I cannot. It is not simply my choice." Jean gave René a glare that would have scorched wood. René returned the glare with a set jaw. "As René should have known, the Fire Office will not permit us to impart a skill of such magnitude to a foreigner."

René said, "I do know that. I also know there's a loophole." Hildur released Jean's hands and brought hers back to clasp René's.

Jean said, "I do not recall a loophole."

"Didn't think you would. Before Lucinda, how often have two warlocks gotten married? Married to a Frank, she's not a foreigner any longer."

"If you seek permission—"

"So we did."

Hildur Rocks the Boat

There was a mind-cracking silence. Jean and Lucinda stared at René and Hildur. They stared back, defiant, hand in white-knuckled hand.

Eventually Lucinda found her voice. "You did what?"

"Got married," René said. "She's eighteen, I'm nineteen. We're old enough. And I learned years ago it's easier to get forgiveness than permission."

"I understand now why the Fire Warlock is angry." Jean's voice seared. "You think the Fire Office will accept a foreign warlock brought in by marriage—"

"I know it will. It let her into the Fortress, didn't it? It wouldn't work for a Frankish witch to marry a foreign warlock, because the Fire Office assumes girls are blithering idiots, and their loyalties always follow their husband's. That's how they did things a thousand years ago, and that's why this will work. According to the Fire Office, she's a Frank now."

Jean rose and stalked across the room to stand beside Beorn at the window. He leaned against the window frame with his eyes closed, pinching the bridge of his nose between thumb and forefinger.

René said, "You can't tell us the marriage is no good, and we have to get an annulment or whatever. I already checked; there's no grounds. We haven't lied about anything, we're not related, or any of the other problems." They were both blushing. "And we consummated it, so that's no grounds either."

Beorn snorted, but his face had lost its red hue. "You know, he may be right. I popped a cork because I was sure the Fire Office would make me fry them both, but it's not. It seems more confused than anything else. All I'm getting for certain is that she can't ever be Fire Warlock—"

Jean said, "I should certainly think not!"

"And before we say anything else, we need to probe her. Sorry, Hildur."

She paled, but neither voice nor spine wavered. "René warned me. I am ready."

"Jean, you're better at that than I am."

Jean turned away from the window with a sigh, and another glare at René. "Yes. Let us proceed."

He and Beorn took her away, leaving René in the study with orders not to go anywhere.

He flopped down on the sofa with a groan. "God, that was even worse than I thought it'd be. I've pissed both of them off enough times, but not usually both at the same time."

Lucinda said, "If Beorn had flamed you, you would have deserved it, you knucklehead. You think you're pretty clever for finding this loophole, but what good will it do? If the Fire Office does accept her as a Frank, it won't let her teach anyone else in Thule."

"Won't now. But passing on what she knows won't happen for years, and when we reforge it, we can tweak it a bit to let her. Quicksilver's been saying we need to make it more flexible in how we treat allies, and that fits right in."

"Argh." Lucinda fought down the urge to wrap her hands around his neck and throttle him, and instead stalked over to the window, as Jean had done.

René trailed her. "Look, Lucinda, I know it's a shock, but look at it this way: it'll be good for Thule, but it'll be good for Frankland, too. Having another warlock on hand when we reforge the Fire Office, especially another lightning thrower, will be a big help."

She perched on the window seat and glared. "Is that what this is all about? You took advantage of her crush on you to rope a girl—a girl!—into fighting in a war her country has no part in?"

"Oh, for the love of…" He sat on the other end of the window seat. They were knee to knee, and eye to eye. "She's a warlock, for God's sake. Could anyone take advantage of you when you were eighteen? You didn't even know you were a warlock then."

"Whose idea was it to marry?"

He reddened. "Mine. She just asked for help in talking Quicksilver into teaching her, but I didn't have to argue her into it. When I suggested it, she jumped at it."

"I'm not surprised. She went starry-eyed over you six years ago, when we first went to Thule. I admit I like her, and had thought before she became a warlock that she'd be a good match for you. But how do you feel about her? Are you in love with her?"

He turned away and leaned forward with his elbows on his knees, frowning at the floor. "In love? Drowned if I know. I like her a lot and will be glad to have her around. I already knew I'd have a wife some day, and I'd rather have her than any Frankish girl I've met. Who else but another warlock will understand what I have to do? All I've done for the past five years is get ready for a war with the empire, and we still have, what, another five years to go?"

"Wait, you told her about our plans to reforge the Fire Office?"

"Don't screech at me. Mjöllnir guessed. So, yeah, she has an idea what's coming, and that just seemed to make her more determined to marry me. Enjoy the time we have, she said. Sounds like a good idea, to me."

Lucinda sighed and leaned her face against the cool glass. "I can't argue with that. I can't argue with the benefits of having another lightning thrower on hand, either. But whatever happened to that confident warrior who wanted to take on the Empire's lightning thrower single-handedly?"

He turned his head and grinned at her. "I'm still here. I just want to make sure that when it comes, I can fight him without having to fight the rest of his army single-handedly, too. Don't you see? I'm working on building up our army, and the Fire Eaters are only part of it. So if Prince Gunther and Lord Wilhelm whittle down the Empire's army for us before the fight even starts…" His grin widened. "Then more fools, them."

Jean and Beorn returned with Hildur, nearly an hour later, supporting the dazed and quivering girl between them. The ruby had stopped throbbing, although it still dazzled Lucinda's eyes.

Beorn shoved Hildur into René's arms. "Just because she's a gem doesn't mean you aren't still on the hot seat. You're moving into the Fortress, where I can keep an eye on both of you. Put her to bed and hold her hand while she rides out the nightmares. Mrs Cole's waiting for you in the kitchen. Scram!" They scrammed.

Lucinda said, "The Fire Office is happy with her?"

"With her, yes. The whole situation, no." He dropped into a chair, threw back his head, and stretched out arms and legs. "God, I hate that.

Going to have to teach you to do it—you ought to be as good as Jean. But I am sort of glad I did. I'd be proud to have a daughter like her. I'd like to know why so many of us male warlocks are such asses, and you two females come along and you're both jewels. We could use a few more like you."

Jean, brooding by the window, said, "Your sample is too small, my friend."

Lucinda said, "Don't forget the first Locksmith was a woman."

"Uh, right," Beorn said. "Forget that, then."

"So what do we do with her?"

"Keep her," Beorn said. "Put her to work in the school assisting Emma Johnson. We need a second Practical Arts teacher and she'll be good at it. She'll be good for that fool boy, too. Calm him down a bit."

"Does she get a spot on the guild council?" The great ruby blazed. "I guess that's a no."

"Right. No dice." The light dimmed and returned to its usual random flashes.

Jean said, "If she can tolerate the aversion spell on our house and swears the oath for membership in the Fire Guild, then yes, I agree, we have no grounds to reject her."

Lucinda said, "The aversion spell? How could…"

"The spell filters for attitudes, courage, and loyalty. From what we know of her so far, I believe she will give her adopted country her all, as long as Frankland does not go to war with Thule. Even then, she would be candid about her choices; she would be neither spy nor traitor."

"If you say so. And will the Fire Office let us teach her to call down the lightning?"

The ruby did not react. "Huh," Beorn said. "Funny, that."

Jean shrugged. "The Fire Office is not always transparent in its decision making, but I assure you, even if we were to teach her, the office will not let us hand such a potent weapon to another nation, not even an old ally. Allegiances change, you understand."

"But Thule already has this weapon," Lucinda said. "We'd just be helping them keep it."

"True."

"And if they lose it, Thule's likely to end up in enemy hands."

"Also true. I do not deny the idea has merit, but…"

"We might be able to help them." She recounted her conversation with René. "And we don't have to decide now. We could start training her, and if the Fire Office gets agitated, we could stop. Even three or four years from now, she wouldn't be far enough along to train anyone else."

"That is true. Those are not, however, the only considerations."

"What else?"

There was a long pause before he answered. "I am feeling my age more often these days, my dear. Teaching you and René has been draining. The idea of taking on another beginner is...daunting."

It would be years before she reached the most dangerous phase of the training. If his control began to slip... Lucinda's fists bunched the fabric of her skirt. "Fine. I'll teach her."

Jean's head snapped around. "My dear..."

"You always say that to know a subject thoroughly, one has to teach it to someone else. I have the control and the patience. This is my opportunity. You do want me to improve, don't you?"

A small circle of warlocks gathered on the floor of Storm King's caldera in the early morning chill. Lucinda raised her head and stared at the rim far above. She ought to be nervous. She wasn't. Why not?

Jean had been an excellent teacher. All she had to do was follow his example and pass on what she had learned from him. Was her lack of nerves earned self-confidence or arrogance? Time would tell.

It helped that her student was a woman with good sense and a strong streak of caution despite a fiery temperament. Teaching a risk-loving adolescent male would be a different story.

She lowered her gaze to the young woman facing her. "We'll start with me calling down the lightning and letting you feel its power. Raise your own shields." Hildur nodded. "Ready?"

Hildur rubbed her palms on her skirt and swallowed hard, but held out a hand. "Ready."

CRASH!

"Yeow!" Hildur snatched her hand away and hugged her arm tight across her chest.

Lucinda said, "We won't do that again for a long time. Months. Years, maybe."

"Good."

When Hildur stopped massaging her arm, Lucinda said, "All we'll be doing here for many, many months is simply testing and expanding your limits. We'll work on control in our exercises in the practice room. When you're ready, we'll start. Draw as much power through me as you can control, as fast as you can."

Hildur muttered something in Norse. She rubbed her hands together, again wiped them on her skirt, and reached for Lucinda's hand.

Lucinda said, "Whenever you're ready."

Hildur nodded and pulled.

"You can pull harder than that."

Hildur blinked at her, then pursed her lips and pulled.

Lucinda said, "You've not had anyone telling you to push yourself, have you?"

"Not since I reached level four. They warned me to keep it under control, so I wouldn't hurt anyone."

"I'm a lightning thrower. You won't hurt me. Remember that. Pull harder. Faster, too."

Hildur screwed up her face, clasped Lucinda's hand with both of hers, and pulled hard enough to leave her gasping and off balance.

Lucinda said, "Now that was a respectable draw."

Beorn said, "Not bad for a beginner."

Hildur threw back her head and laughed. Smiles all around answered her.

Jean said, "Controlled power is exhilarating. You will experience that surge many times over the course of your training."

"Yes, sir," she said, "but that wasn't... Well, it was, but... You're not treating me like a girl. You're treating me like a warlock."

Hildur's smile lasted until the afternoon. The Fire Eaters' meeting in the practice room dissolved in the onslaught of angry responses to René's announcement that Katie and Warlock Staðfastur would be joining them.

"We won't want to stop play because a girl gets hurt and cries about it."

"Thomas Russell," Lucinda snapped. "You won't touch Katie. Her shields are better than yours."

René grinned. "Hers are better than mine, and none of you can touch me." That earned him a few glowers.

Lucinda continued, "And could you stand in Storm King's caldera with your hand in mine while I call down the lightning and not scream? Staðfastur did."

"Maybe she did, but it still hurt, didn't it?"

"It did, but—"

"Come on, Snorri. What'll you do when she gets burnt?"

"Send her off for treatment and try not to let my guilty conscience make me lose my concentration and get burnt myself." All traces of levity had vanished from René's face. "I don't want her to get hurt. She's my wife, frost it! But I'll put up with it for the same reason Quicksilver gave us permission years ago to torture Lucinda. Anything we do to her won't be as bad as what the empire's warlocks would do. Staðfastur's a warlock. She has to be able to protect herself against battle-hardened enemy wizards."

"Does she? With the Fire Warlock looking out for—"

The Fire Warlock emerged from the fireplace and leaned over the objecting Fire Eater. "I can't be everywhere at once. Staðfastur is going to learn to fight like a warlock, and you lot are going to help. Shut up and get on with it."

"I pity you," Prince Gunther said. "How fearful you must be, that you must recruit women to fight your battles for you. Do not pin your hopes on her. Your foreign bride will turn tail and flee when she sees Frankland overrun."

"You wish," René said. "She's no coward."

"Coward or not, you cannot believe she will fight for you. Her loyalties lie with Thule, not with Frankland. You certainly don't think your great hero, Warlock Quicksilver, will agree to teach a foreigner to call down the lightning, do you?"

Don't answer that, little brother.

René steamed, but didn't respond.

"No, I didn't think so," Prince Gunther said. "Even if he were willing, you wouldn't dare live with a fire witch who could fry your genitals when you make her angry."

René glowered. "That's funny. You made an offer to a lightning thrower."

Prince Gunther showed pearly white teeth. "I will be stronger than your Locksmith. I will enjoy teaching her who is her new lord and master."

René hooted. "I thought you were a warlock, not an airhead."

Gunther snarled, "She is stronger now, but I will surpass her because I am a man. And I am stronger than you or Warlock Quicksilver because I do not dilute my strength with water or air magic."

René stiffened. "What?"

"Surely you did not imagine you could hide your ridiculous interests." Gunther's voice dripped contempt. "Warlock Quicksilver sends his brats flying through the air as if he is an enchanter. I have seen your university essays on air and water magic. Fah. What drivel. You can never be a true warlock like me when you waste your time pretending to be an airhead or fish monger."

"Look, Gunther, a real warlock—"

"You forget yourself, bastard. I do not tolerate familiarity from common dirt."

René grinned. "Too bad, Gunther. I'm not your subject. I can call you anything I like."

Gunther was livid. "I will not kill you in battle. I will capture you and display your execution before my court, and all of Europa will know how I treat insubordinate mongrel curs."

René's grin widened. "And let them all hear me call you Gunther. Good move, chum. Oh, and Gunther…have a nice day."

Had It With Paul

The concert was over, the applause diminishing. The audience seated under the stars on the lawn below the Hall of the Winds was dispersing, happily debating the merits of the evening's entertainment and the talent of the student soloists. The small orchestra were packing up, giddy with their success and the end of the summer term.

Gillian wove through them, dodging swinging trombones and falling music stands. No one was trying to hit her, but she was short for ten, and the taller teens in the orchestra never saw her. Miranda had just latched her viola case when Gillian rocketed into her, almost knocking her over. "That was lovely. Miranda, you're the best."

Miranda laughed. "It wasn't a contest, Gillian."

"I know, but I was listening for you. I heard other people make mistakes, but I didn't hear you make any."

"I made a few. You just didn't hear."

"That's what I said."

"Did Mama and Papa like it?"

"Of course they did. Papa clapped harder than anyone else around."

"He's a fire wizard. Where are they?"

"They said they'd wait at the stairs. Less crowded there."

Miranda slung her viola case over her shoulder. "Let's go."

Gillian's smile dimmed. "Uh-oh."

Miranda turned. The school's concertmaster was leading a stranger towards them. Enchanter Paul approached from another direction, frowning at the concertmaster and trapping the two girls between the three men. The concertmaster performed introductions. Miranda caught "Master Antoine of the Royal Orchestra..." and for a moment everything else was noise. He asked a question, she responded automatically, but must have said something appropriate, because he was still smiling as he turned to Gillian.

"Bless me, another van Gelder. Are you a musician, too?"

"I can play, sir, but not like—"

"No," Enchanter Paul said, "Miranda is a much stronger talent."

"It would be miraculous," the concertmaster said, with an apologetic glance at Gillian, "for even the van Gelders to produce two such talents. Miranda is one of the finest young musicians I've ever had the pleasure of working with. It would be a crime against humanity to stifle that talent under the Guild Council's dry and dusty duties."

Paul's brows lowered. He squeezed Miranda's shoulder so hard she gasped. He didn't notice. "Nonsense. I'm proud of my granddaughter, and naturally I'm glad she has such a useful talent to occupy her spare time, but with the Air Guild depleted we cannot afford to indulge an enchantress's avocation."

He and the concertmaster walked away arguing. Master Antoine hesitated, bowed to the girls, murmured, "I hope to hear more from both of you soon," and trotted after the other two men.

Paul called over his shoulder, "Tomorrow, Miranda, we must discuss your course of studies for the fall term."

The two simmering girls watched him go with identical sullen expressions.

Gillian said, "He never even looked at me."

Miranda said, "I should be so lucky."

That September Mother Celeste and her apprentice, Mother Astrid, began a series of visits to every Earth Guildhall in Frankland. By the time they finished, nearly a year later, they had depleted the guild's supply of potion for overused voices, and amazed the other coven members with their endurance.

"What made it particularly tiring," Mother Celeste said to the other women gathered around the Queen Regent's tea table in early August, "was that we couldn't give satisfactory answers to the most common questions. 'We'd rather not draw attention to the office's worst deficiencies right now' is not an answer I'd like to hear to the question, 'What problems are you trying to solve?' I would mention a few, but they weren't enough by themselves to justify all the trouble."

Astrid said, "Or 'What are the plans for the Air and Fire Offices?' We'd smile politely and say we could only speak for the Earth Guild. They should direct their other questions to the Fire Warlock. I doubt many did."

Lucinda laughed. "Not many, no. But there have been a few. We recruited two more Fire Warlock's agents from it."

"Oh, good. I'm glad that was useful."

The queen said, "The Earth Guild is ready, then?"

"Yes," Mother Celeste said. "The fifteenth of October, rain or shine, we'll begin reforging the Earth Office."

Lucinda's teacup rattled against its saucer, startling the other women. "Sorry." She envied Mother Celeste's composure; the Earth Mother sounded almost cheerful. "It's just... Now that we've set the date, I'd rather it was tomorrow, instead of two months away. I want to get it over with."

"No one can fault you for nerves," Mother Astrid said, "considering what you went through the last time."

Lucinda shrugged. "No one does, except for me. Jean and I are ready. Have been for more than a year. We can handle it."

Then why did every mention of unlocking the Earth Office make her scalp prickle? She didn't sense death tapping her shoulder, but she couldn't shake the creeping dread. Was it prescience or her fervid imagination telling her it would hurt? What had they overlooked?

Mother Celeste patted her hand. "You'll be fine."

Lucinda's nerves steadied. "Everyone else is much calmer than before the Water Office reforging."

"That one worked out well, and we've had more time to get ready," Celeste said. "We haven't needed to keep as many secrets, either."

"Except for the actual spells," Irene said. "But ordinary Franks don't have the education to understand them anyway. Most of those who do are in the Reforging Coven."

"Who are ready, of course." The queen paused with her teacup halfway to her lips, noting the glance shared between the two earth mothers, Eleanor and Irene's stiffened posture, and Lucinda's thinned lips. Her brow puckered. "But you've had years to prepare."

"We're ready for this office," Mother Celeste said. "We're more concerned about the other two. Let's say it's a good thing the Earth Office relies so little on Air Guild spells."

"Oh? Oh, dear."

"Mother Celeste was being diplomatic," Eleanor said. "But if we can't talk freely here, what's the point? And I've had it up to here with Paul." She waved her teaspoon over her head. "Every time we ask about reforging the Air Office, he says it may be decades before another enchanter comes along who is fit to hold the office."

Lucinda resisted the urge to glance over her shoulder. As the queen's teas with her female advisors had expanded in scope, they had long since settled on a twice-monthly gathering in a smaller, less ornate chamber that was easier to shield against eavesdroppers than the palace's enormous reception room. The servants had been dismissed. Confidences shared stayed with the six women in the room. Lucinda still tensed whenever discussing any officeholder's shortcomings. They could not hide from the Fire Office.

Eleanor went on, "It's been five years since Warlock Arturos let slip that one of Paul's granddaughters will be an enchantress, but he ignores recommendations to train a female apprentice. I ask you—" She caught sight of Irene's stricken expression. "Oh, dear. What's wrong?"

"I hadn't realised…" Irene said.

Lucinda said, "We haven't discussed reforging the Air Office outside the officeholders' strategy meetings. It's no secret, but with the Earth Office coming next, it hasn't gotten much attention yet. I hadn't mentioned the succession issue because it had seemed pretty obvious."

"Now that Eleanor raised it, it is," Irene said. "Stupid of me not to have realised, because I know there are no promising boys at the school. I just assumed… It's always been a man."

"And this is Frankland, and nothing ever changes in Frankland," the queen said.

"Exactly."

"Wouldn't you want your daughter to hold the Air Office if she could? It's quite an honour."

"Well, yes, it is." Irene set her fork down and stared at her suddenly unappetising slice of cake. "I suppose if the one who becomes an enchantress can cope with the hardships of being an officeholder—and don't tell me there aren't any—then I shall be proud and happy for her. But…tell me she will endure a decade-long apprenticeship to Enchanter

Paul without heartache, and I'll celebrate now."

"Please forgive my ignorance. He has always been perfectly charming to me. What is the difficulty?"

"Charming, I'm sure, but does he take your advice? As for the children… He wishes they were boys. They know that, and resent it. They haven't fully forgiven him, either, for the disrespect the guild showed Sven and me. Even if they had… He's a Europan-wide authority on contract magic, but otherwise he's not much of a mage."

"Oh?"

Irene looked to the other women for help.

Lucinda crossed her fingers. "He mistakes position for ability, and ignores or condescends to anyone who isn't already knowledgeable or who is striving to prove themselves. He can't, or won't, help them get there."

Eleanor said, "Questions irritate him."

Mother Celeste said, "He's not a good judge of people."

"And he plays favourites," Irene said. "He sees Miranda regularly, and ignores Gillian. Maybe that will change with Gillian at the guild school this autumn, but I'm not optimistic."

Eleanor said, "Irene, I'm so sorry. I didn't realise…"

Irene made a helpless gesture. "Why should you? No apology necessary. I'm glad I found out now rather than later."

The queen said, "Is there anything we can do to help? Invite him to our next meeting for a gentle discussion of his relationship with his granddaughters?"

Mother Celeste laughed. "To be harangued by six women over teacakes? Won't work. He regards most of us as uncouth, irritating nags and busybodies, rather than as real people he should respect."

"Who does he respect?"

"Warlock Quicksilver," Eleanor said.

"Sometimes," Lucinda said. "And Sorceress Lorraine. As far as I can tell, she's the only woman he ever listens to. If she and Jean approached him together, he would know they meant business."

The queen said, "Would it help if I joined them? No, I suppose not. Perhaps Brendan?"

"Too young. Inexperienced." Lucinda waved a fork at Irene. "Back up a moment. You said he's been paying attention to Miranda. Isn't that an improvement?"

"It might be," she said, "if I could believe he values a fine musician more than a strong seer."

Mother Celeste snorted and mumbled under her breath.

"I'd forgotten that," Lucinda said. "Too bad. You once told me he pushed Oliver to marry Winifred so he could found a dynasty. Seems ironic he can't recognise now that he could have one."

"Ironic, yes." Irene shrugged. "I doubt he has ever heard Eleanor's suggestion, because it simply wouldn't make sense to him. As I said, everyone assumes the Air Officeholder will always be a man, as the Fire Warlock has always been a man."

"That's not so," Lucinda said. "A few have been women."

Several shocked voices said, "Really?"

"Really. Of necessity during the Scorching Times. But otherwise, you're right. The Air Officeholder has always been a man, and the Earth and Water Officeholders have always been women."

The queen hid a smile behind her teacup. "An Earth Father might be acceptable, but the Water Office clearly has to be held by a woman. Whatever would they call a man? Frost Maiden simply wouldn't do."

Eleanor's jaw went slack. She stared at the queen for a moment, then a brilliant smile lit her face. "Wouldn't do at all."

Dressed as usual in solid black, Warlock Quicksilver was as conspicuous against the white and aquamarine furnishings of the Crystal Palace's reception room as an inkblot on an otherwise pristine page. Enchanter Paul hesitated on the threshold, taking in the warlock's wineglass and relaxed posture. Paul's bulging eyes were comical, but neither Quicksilver nor Sorceress Lorraine betrayed any amusement.

"Please, come in." Lorraine gestured towards a bottle-laden side table. "May I offer you refreshment?"

Paul's glance slid over the array. "Thank you, but no, I—" His eyebrows rose and he took a closer, longer look at the labels. "On second thought, given the quality of the offerings…"

"Jean, would you do the honours?"

"Certainly." Quicksilver poured Paul a generous glass of a deep ruby wine. "Come, sit. Enjoy."

"Haven't we some business to attend to? I wasn't expecting to see you here, Your Wisdom."

"My presence here is an unusual occurrence," Jean said, "but Sorceress Lorraine asked us old-timers here to address a concern our younger colleagues have raised."

She said, "Surely business may wait a few minutes. Jean was telling me stories from his travels. I recall you passed through Constantinople when you were a young man. What was your impression of the city, Paul?"

Paul's glass had been emptied and replenished before she steered the conversation towards Frankland's present problems. "It is clear Frankland benefited from your youthful travels. We must hope your successor will also have a few years to experience life outside of Frankland before assuming the Air Office."

Paul's contented look dissolved, briefly replaced by the mulish expression that appeared whenever the topic of his retirement came up, then he smiled. "Well, yes. Personal knowledge of our trading partners is invaluable, and takes time to acquire. We can't hurry that along without leaving him ill-prepared."

"Now as to that…" Quicksilver refilled Paul's glass. "We are concerned that you have not noticed the other officeholders' recommendations concerning that difficulty."

"I have?" Paul frowned. "What recommendation?"

"That the next Air Officeholder be a witch. Specifically, one of your granddaughters."

Paul's head snapped back. "You can't be serious. They're too young…"

"They will grow," Lorraine said. "Children do. If you wait for an enchanter, he will be younger, and you will have less time to train him."

"And mercurial…"

"Again, they are children, and neither is as impetuous as many others their age."

"The Air Office requires a high capacity for scholarship and logical reasoning.…"

"Their father, mother, and stepfather are among their generation's intellectual lights. Through a combination of innate ability, familial expectations, and access to a well-rounded education, either girl is more likely to fit the needs of the office than any random boy plucked from the guild school."

Quicksilver said, "Similarly, there can be few boys at the school who will have been as steeped from babyhood in the ideas of personal responsibility and duty to one's country."

Lorraine said, "Nor will you find any children elsewhere with as many connections among not one, but two magic guilds and the aristocracy."

"Well, yes," Paul said, "but… There's the issue of balance. It won't do to have three of four offices held by women."

"Why not?" Quicksilver's eyebrows arched. "It has happened before."

"During the Scorching Times, you mean. Those female warlocks didn't last long. The Fire Office always reverted to a man in short order."

"If the Air Office is held by an enchantress," Sorceress Lorraine said, "Frankland will not be unbalanced long. Indeed, we will need a witch in either the Fire or Air Office to restore the balance."

"I beg your pardon?"

"You have not heard the news? The Water Guild Council has approved Sorceress Eleanor's proposal that the next holder of the Water Office should be a sorcerer."

Paul blinked at her. "What? Why?"

"Because it seems the surest way to drown that contemptible title, Frost Maiden. Further, Eleanor does not want to serve as long as her predecessors have. She intends to begin looking for a suitable replacement after she has been in office only some thirty to forty years. The period with three female officeholders will be a generation, perhaps two. Scarcely the blink of an eye in Frankland's history."

Quicksilver added, "Nor do I believe even three strong witches could sway King Brendan and Warlock Snorri when they are in agreement."

"But…but…," Paul spluttered. "We've never had a Water Sorcerer or an Air Enchantress."

"I cannot see why not," Sorceress Lorraine said. "I only regret I will not live to see them."

"You talk as if it's obvious one of the girls will be fit to hold the office. It isn't obvious to me. Even if, as Warlock Arturos said, one of them will be an enchantress, we don't know which one. Or rather, I don't know. Arturos knows, but he won't tell me." Quicksilver countered Paul's glare with a bland expression and a shrug.

Paul continued, "We may end up with one having the talent and the other having the temperament. Or neither having the temperament. What then? I'll have wasted my time."

"Nonsense, Paul," Lorraine said. "One, possibly both, will be on the

Air Guild Council. The sooner she assumes her duties, the sooner you may share the burden of your responsibilities. Unless I am mistaken, and you want to hoard them all for yourself?"

Paul flushed. "Of course I want assistance."

"The better she understands the office's demands, the more help she will be to you on the Guild Council."

"Well…yes, that is a good argument. Guiding them towards being contributing members of the Guild Council will be worth my time. I will undertake to do that."

Lorraine favoured him with a dazzling smile.

Quicksilver said, "Thank you, Your Wisdom. That will do for now. We may postpone any further decisions until the children have begun to develop their talents."

Paul humphed, and took refuge in his wineglass. The conversation drifted into less controversial topics. Paul finished his wine and left. Lorraine watched with a thoughtful expression as he sailed away on the wind.

She said. "You should suggest to Lucinda that she begin training those two girls, while they are still very young, to let her draw stands of power from them."

Quicksilver said, "She has already been doing so, with considerable success."

"Good." She turned away from the window. "You do realise that nothing we said today addressed his primary objection."

"Indeed so."

"He has good reason to be afraid."

"I should hope that I have never taken anyone to task for his or her fears." Quicksilver's eyes travelled over her empty right sleeve. "I can only judge a person by how he or she chooses to respond to those fears."

With none of the drama that had infected the Water Office's unlocking, the small group involved in unlocking the Earth Office gathered in the Warren on the fifteenth of October. A riot of eye-popping yellows and reds covered the hillsides and a sharp nip in the air made Lucinda want to tramp for miles in anticipation of coming home to a warm fire and a steaming mug of hot chocolate. It was a shame the icy fingers crawling down her spine blunted her enjoyment of the glorious autumn morning.

She clutched at Jean's arm. "Are you sure we're ready?"

He drew in a deep breath, held it, and let it out slowly. "No, my love, I am not sure, but I do not know what else we can do, nor would it be wise to postpone this event for long."

"Right. Let's get it over with."

The youngest earth father, Pierre, led them through the Warren to a barn-like pavilion on the far edge. Mother Celeste stepped out to greet them. Lucinda goggled. The Earth Mother was covered from shoulder to toe in chain mail. Only her right hand was exposed.

She laughed at Lucinda's surprise. "You didn't think I would give that madwoman a go at me if I could avoid it, did you? I may be an old biddy but I don't see why I shouldn't protect myself."

Jean said, "You used the spells I suggested, I trust."

"Those, and a few others."

Beorn poked at her shoulder. His finger stopped an inch short of the mail. "Looks good. Got a helmet?"

"Think I'm a fool?"

"No. Just double checking."

They followed her inside the rustic building. Tiers of seats, all empty, circled a sand-covered arena.

"What is this?" Lucinda asked.

"It's usually for equestrian competitions. If we're going to have a bloody mess, better here than in my parlour."

"Can't argue with that."

They sat on stone benches in the arena's centre. Father Pierre helped Mother Celeste with her helmet. Lucinda set a lock to hold her shields down, and thanked Mother Celeste for taming the wild heartbeat and shortness of breath accompanying that exposure. As with the Water Office, the other officeholders laid down protective spells while she followed Mother Celeste's guiding green lamp through the thicket of spells to the lock on the Earth Office.

"Ready," she said.

Jean slid into place on the bench beside her and slipped his hand between hers and Mother Celeste's, ensuring she touched only the emerald in the ring. Beorn laid his hand on her shoulder. Sorceress Eleanor and Enchanter Paul laid theirs on Jean's shoulders. Father Martin draped another layer of mail over Mother Celeste's head, leaving only a small gap for air.

Lucinda reached through Jean's lighthouse beacon and wrapped her fist around cords of power plucked from the four officeholders. Her lock holding her shields down was still in place. So was Jean's. Her mouth was as dry as if she'd been eating the arena's sand.

"Ready?"

"Ready," Jean said.

"Ready." Mother Celeste's voice was muffled but steady. Lucinda called up the words of the lock, gathered her courage, and shoved. Lightning raced across the words of the lock spell. A miniature sun exploded in her face, washed across her, and sank into her soul. She was alive, dazzled but unharmed, and ablaze with power.

Jean sprawled in the sand. Blue flame, nearly invisible, rippled over him.

She pounced on him. "Jean!"

He groaned. Father Pierre crouched beside her. The healer reached for Jean, snatched his blistered hand away, and swore. Lucinda put out the flames. Jean opened his eyes and mouthed 'Thank you.' His eyes rolled back and his head lolled.

The healer eyed her. "I'm not touching you."

"What?" She held out her arms. Her skin glowed. Sparks danced across her fingertips. Bright threads, like minuscule lightning, arced from her hands to the floor.

Her right hand was sticky with blood.

She whirled. The others in the arena were statues in a frozen tableau. The two earth fathers knelt beside Mother Celeste, their eyes wide and staring. Sorceress Eleanor choked, stumbled away, and vomited. A spreading pool of blood lapped Lucinda's skirts.

The Earth Office

Big sister, what happened? I know you're there, Lucinda. Talk to me.
She raised her head. She was sitting on slate steps alongside the stream running through the Warren. She didn't remember going there. The wooden pavilion was not in sight. Drying drops of blood behind her indicated she'd come down the stairs. She pushed a lock of hair out of her eyes before remembering the blood on her hands. She wiped them on her skirts. Her dress was already ruined.

Big sister?

I'm here, little brother.

Mother Celeste is dead. Quicksilver's not answering. Beorn's on Storm King, making noise like the Fire Office has gone berserk. The Warren's acting like a kicked anthill. What happened?

I'd rather not have to remember.

Tough. Tell me.

It was awful. Father Martin said the black magic spell adapted to circumvent the chain mail. Instead of operating like a cleaver that the mail could turn aside, it became spikes that slipped through the rings. One pierced her heart. Death was instantaneous.

Lucinda wiped her eyes on her sleeve. She had not been crying before, but now, once started, the tears poured.

I should have known. I'd had that prickly feeling for months. I thought it meant Jean or I would be hurt, but I was wrong. It wasn't for us. She was bawling now. *I should have warned Mother Celeste.*

Don't be an ass, Lucinda. What could you have said? Don't die on us? What good would that have done? Chain mail seemed like a good idea. Could you have known it wasn't?

No. I thought it was brilliant.

Then don't beat yourself up. How's Quicksilver?

Father Pierre says he'll be fine. He took it harder than I did because he's older. Less adaptable, Pierre said.

Is there anything I can do?

A cloud blocked the sun, muting the morning's brilliant autumn colours. Her skirt fluttered in a freshening breeze. The woman Lucinda had once been would have been chilled, but she was hot. She wasn't sure she would ever again feel the cold.

That bothered her. Even for a warlock, that wasn't normal.

She wiped blood from the slate with her sleeve. *Tell Katie to meet me at the bath. I need help.*

As a dry run for rebuilding the Fire Office, it was a disaster. Lucinda browbeat Mother Astrid and the three shocked officeholders into giving her their attention long enough to throw a temporary and less drastic lock on the Earth Office, then they all returned to their guild strongholds to spread the news and prepare for the state funeral.

No one suggested they begin rebuilding the Earth Office.

Jean moved through the next three days like a sleepwalker. Lucinda could not recall him saying a single world to their staff or to her, either out loud or through their bond. She was too numb to care.

The Warren's Great Hall, that she remembered as being thronged with noisy people, either boisterous, as for their wedding, or frantic, as for the Yule War, was eerily silent, despite being packed to the rafters. The service made no impression, neither the eulogy nor the internment nor the dignitaries she spoke to. Hours later hunger pangs brought her out of her daze. Glad for a reason to be busy and refocus on the living, she dove into the kitchen, gave the cook the evening off, and fixed a supper of her family's simple favourites: bangers and mash, fried onions, baked apples with cinnamon.

The children wolfed it down. Jean didn't appear. Her efforts to call him met a blank wall.

After supper she went looking for him. He wasn't in Blazes or the Fortress, or any of a dozen other places she considered. On a second and more thorough scan of the Warren, she found him in the mortuary chapel. He was kneeling in the first pew with his hands clasped and his arms resting on the rail before him. His head was bowed, but his back was straight, his shoulders tense. Half a dozen other men and women scattered about the ancient chapel, all members of the Earth Guild, prayed in the dim light.

The mortuary chapel was not a place Lucinda would have chosen to seek spiritual comfort. The chapel had been gloomy the day before, despite dozens of candles, with an endless line of sniffling mourners shuffling past Mother Celeste's bier. Without a body lying in state, the barrel-vaulted, thick-walled room still smelled of dank decay.

Lucinda shuddered. The Fire Guild's open air funeral pyre, lit at nightfall on the day of death, was more to her liking.

She slid into the pew beside Jean. He acknowledged her presence with the slightest motion of his head, but did not otherwise move. She waited. After several minutes, in which she had rejected every idea from touching his arm with a finger to giving his shoulder a good, hard shake, he lifted a knee, and winced. She gave him a hand up onto the pew and pushed the kneeler out of the way. He grimaced as he stretched and massaged unresponsive calves.

"Tomorrow," she whispered, "let's talk to Mother Astrid about resuming the work on the Earth Office."

"Yes, I suppose we must, sometime, but there is no need to hurry."

"The sooner we get started, the sooner everyone involved will be forced to get past this and back to dealing with the living."

"That is not wise. Those who loved her must be given time to mourn."

"Those who love Beorn won't have time to mourn him, if he dies when we unlock the Fire Office."

Jean stared straight ahead. A muscle in his face twitched. "Perhaps the cost is, as others have said, too high. Perhaps we should reconsider—"

"What?" Heads turned towards them.

"Keep your voice down."

She clenched her fist on the rail. The muscle in his cheek twitched twice more before he spoke again, in a low tone to avoid disturbing the other mourners. "Mother Celeste's death has reminded me, once again, of my own mortality. I have been reviewing my sins, and pride is chief among them. I have been guilty of hubris in daring to rebuild the Fire Office. With the royals now understanding the power of the Great Oath, and the Water Office functioning correctly, perhaps we need not repair the Fire Office."

Lucinda surged to her feet, banging her knee on the rail. She shouted, "You've been telling me for eight years we have to, and now suddenly you think we don't?"

He turned towards her with blazing eyes. "I am willing to admit I might be mistaken."

An earth wizard scurried towards them, flapping his hands. Jean grabbed her arm and pulled her from the pew. He made a sketchy bow towards the wizard and the other shocked mourners. "My apologies." Fire engulfed them.

When the flames died, some part of Lucinda's mind noted a harvest moon and other lights, below and far away, but her attention was focused on her dear husband. "Might be mistaken? Well, you sure fooled me. And René and Beorn. Not to mention Lorraine and Celeste. Do you think all the work we've done has been wasted?"

"No, not—"

"Or that the problems have vanished just because things are better than they have been?"

"Certainly not, but perhaps we should re-examine the calculus that has informed our decision-making. Perhaps Frankland can live with the remaining problems if the human cost is too high. I now have an Earth Mother's—an officeholder's—blood on my hands. I—"

"On your hands," she shrieked. "You think this is your fault?"

He scowled at her with his hands on his hips. They circled each other like sparring pugilists. "Yes."

She made a rude noise. He flushed. She said, "You are guilty of hubris if you think that. Blame that wretched Locksmith from a thousand years ago with her obsession over black magic, and the Great Coven for not giving us a way to fix their mistakes. You're not to blame for trying to fix them."

"You have on more than one occasion accused me of paranoia, but as Fire Warlock it is my responsibility—"

"Was, you mean."

He grimaced. "A habit of more than one hundred years standing is difficult to break. Yes, as Fire Warlock it was and as a member of the Fire Guild Council it still is my responsibility to ensure the safety of Frankland's citizens, including and most especially the safety of the royal family and the officeholders. In that I have singularly failed."

"She knew it was risky. You didn't make her do it. And if we don't rebuild the Fire Office... The Fire Warlock can't retire, remember. Do you want me and René and all the rest that come after us to burn to death on the Fire Office's whim?"

He flinched. "No."

"Then you'll feel guilty if we do or if we don't. Take your pick."

His shoulders sagged. His head drooped. "I am sorry, my love. I cannot make a rational decision on that question today, nor for some time to come."

She stopped yelling. "If we don't rebuild the Fire Office, Mother Celeste's death will have been for nothing." She glanced down. They were at the Aerie, the small flat surface atop Storm King's broken cone. A black void yawned at her feet. She dropped to the ground and grabbed handholds of rock. "Jean, help! Walls. Please!"

Illusory walls closed around them. He came nearer. She relaxed her grip on the rocks and leaned against his thigh. "Thank you."

He stroked her hair. "I am sorry, my love, for upsetting you, but it is never wise to make plans so rigid we cannot adapt them to changed circumstances."

She hugged his leg. "Maybe so, but I think you're wrong. I am sorry I yelled at you."

"Don't know that you should be," a deeper voice said. She turned. Beorn sprawled on a sofa on the opposite side of the cold fire pit. He grinned at her. "Seems like pissing him off was just what he needed to pull him out of his misery."

"Indeed," Jean said. "I am, after all, a warlock."

"I could have stuck my oar in when you two started yelling at each other, because you've both forgotten something, but I wanted to see how you'd work it out."

"Oh? What have we forgotten?"

"Lucinda, you've forgotten that Celeste was his closest friend for half a century, and he expected her to outlive him. You've got to give him time to grieve."

She scrambled to her feet. "I had not forgotten that. When we unlock the Fire Office we won't have the luxury of..." She swallowed and looked away.

"You won't have time to grieve over me, you mean, because we'll be at war, and you'll do what you have to, to survive. You'll have to wait till it's all over, and then you'll grieve. But we're not at war now. Give him and Astrid time. And, Lucinda… You've got three little boys. Which two don't you love?"

"Are you nuts?" She spat sparks. "I love them all."

"Right. So don't give Jean any guff about not needing Celeste now that he's got you. Don't even think about it."

She studied the floor with her face on fire. "Yes, sir," she mumbled.

Jean sounded amused. "What words of advice do you have for me, Your Wisdom?"

Lucinda looked up. "Yes, what has he forgotten?"

Beorn grinned. "That whether or not we unlock the Fire Office isn't his decision. It's mine."

Jean went very still. Beorn's grin widened. "Don't like me pulling rank on you, eh? I don't do it often, but I will if I have to, and you'd best not forget it."

Sven Confounds Gillian's Teacher

"What have we here?"

Gillian started, and slammed the book shut. The teacher snatched the volume from her grasp.

"You thought you could use magic to hide this from me, didn't you? I've been teaching longer than you've been alive. I know all the tricks, young lady. Let's see what trashy novel you'd rather read than your assignment."

The teacher opened the captive book to the title page. Her face went blank. The other students cast furtive glances at her. In a moment, she was dragging Gillian by the arm out of the classroom and into the first form supervisor's office.

The supervisor paged through Gillian's book. "What is this?"

Gillian said, "*Introduction to Contract Magic.*"

"I can see that. I meant, why? This is a fourth form textbook. What can you possibly want with this? You'll get confused reading this now, before you've mastered the fundamentals, which is what you are supposed to be reading now, young lady."

"The class is reading about using the wind to enhance your senses. What does that have to do with contracts? Besides, it's baby magic. I could do that as long as I remember. The teacher hasn't talked about anything the whole term that Mama and Papa didn't talk about at home years ago."

"That's all very well for you, but your classmates have not had the benefit of a mage's attention at dinnertime."

"Then why haven't you let me join the class where they're studying stuff I don't know? Stuff that would be useful. Like contract magic."

"And skip you ahead of your older sister? That would never do."

"Why not? Miranda wouldn't mind. As long as she has music lessons, she's happy. She teaches me everything she learns anyway."

"You can't possibly understand the theory when you don't have the magic yet to work the spells."

"That's wrong. You have to know what you're doing first."

The supervisor gave a long-suffering sigh. "More precisely, theory and practice go hand in hand and feed on each other. Practice needs theory to inform and direct it, and theory needs to see results to correct misunderstandings. Each is useless on its own."

"My mama writes spells without being able to test them."

"Oh, sure, and they're fine examples of mage-level erudition." The supervisor threw up her hands. "Arguing pedagogy with a first-form student is ridiculous. Go back to your classroom and do your assignment."

But the supervisor's sarcasm had pushed Gillian past caution. "They are. The mages said so."

"They are what?"

"Mage level spells."

The supervisor leaned back in her chair and stared at Gillian. "That's absurd. Next you'll be saying that vicious rumour is true, and your mother wrote Enchanter Oliver's spellbook."

Gillian drew herself up to her full four feet two inches and looked the supervisor straight in the eye. "She did. And he was proud of her."

The supervisor ignored the offended stares as she stalked through the library with a howling girl by the ear. She didn't stop twisting the ear until she found Maximilian Silver's *Life of Enchanter Oliver van Gelder* on the biography shelves.

"You have spent too much time with the Fire Guild."

Her captive rubbed her ear. The supervisor sounded like a fire witch rather than a cool air witch, but Gillian chose not to say so. She didn't need injury inflicted on other body parts.

The supervisor lectured as she searched the table of contents. "I don't know what your mother told you about your father, but it is clear we can't count on her to tell you the full story. She is obviously an embittered woman. It is high time you learned the facts for yourself. Read this, especially this chapter, and write a report by the end of term."

She thrust the book, opened to the chapter titled *The Spellbook*, into Gillian's face.

Gillian folded her arms across her chest and refused to take it. "Papa Sven said I shouldn't waste my time reading trash."

Being locked in an airless room is an excruciating punishment for any normal member of the Air Guild, but Gillian was not normal. She thanked her lucky stars she had accepted Warlock Quicksilver's request and had already spent many hours conditioning herself to tolerate windowless spaces. This closet was at least above ground. She could endure a week's detention, maybe even two, and then the term would be over.

The detention probably would stretch to two weeks, because she would not beg for relief or write 'I shall not lie to my teachers' one hundred times each afternoon.

"No cheating," the supervisor had said. "I have a spell to tell me if you used magic to make the copies."

Gillian was offended. She would never dream of cheating. If she had earned a punishment, she would take it like a man.

The table and chair crammed into the closet were adult size, too big for her. She dropped Silver's book on the floor and propped her feet on it, getting as comfortable as she could before she started writing.

Dear Papa Sven,

I will not go back to the Air Guild School next term. You can't make me...

An hour later, her letter done, she stretched her cramped fingers before turning to a fresh sheet. Her teachers wanted a factual account of Papa's life, did they? She tucked her tongue into the corner of her mouth and started writing. She would give them one. If it upset her grandfather, that was just too bad.

"It's a pleasure, sir," the first-form supervisor said, "to have this opportunity to talk to such a distinguished teacher. I'm sure I don't need to waste your time explaining the necessity for maintaining discipline and order in the classroom."

A pleasure was not the term Sven would have chosen for this conversation, or the dash he had made through a downpour to get here. It was unlikely the supervisor would still be pleased when they were done,

111

but he held his fire. "Yes, the discipline issue is what brought me here, but I would like to review her academics before we get into that."

"Certainly." The supervisor spread a sheaf of papers across the Air Guild School's conference table. "Gillian regularly complains about our focus on fundamentals, but she hasn't done half the work we've assigned her, and her marks on the work she has done are not outstanding."

Sven chose an essay at random and held it up to the window, but gave up and summoned his mental flame for illumination. The conference room's feeble fire did little to dispel the December gloom. "Explain to me why this received the marks it did."

"Her argument was correct but too terse. None of her classmates would be able to follow her logic."

"She wasn't writing for them. She was writing for an adult already familiar with the subject."

"But how can we be sure she understands the material if she doesn't show us? The examples she provided to support the argument are inadequate. She should have given us four pages with a full example, rather than a summary and two pages of citations."

"The citations show she's read a good deal more than required, and the summary shows she understood what she read. I'd rather see that than one regurgitated example."

The supervisor's smile faltered. "But that wasn't what we asked for, and we can't let the students cut corners."

"Has Enchanter Paul commented on her work?"

The supervisor preened. "He agreed with us that her laziness and rejection of authority are her two biggest shortcomings, and commended me for providing the steady guidance and discipline she needs to develop good habits."

Sven sighed. "She's not lazy. She's bored."

"How can she be bored, when she hasn't done half her assignments?"

Sven rubbed a hand across his face. He was not going to raise his voice. He had to deal with close-minded staff at the Fire Guild School, too, and shouting never helped. "Perhaps you could explain these other demerits?"

The supervisor peered at the paper. "Oh, yes, those are for her penmanship."

"What's wrong with that? It's legible, more so than the florid style in fashion these days."

The supervisor frowned. "Legible, yes, but that florid style, as you call it, is more suitable for a young lady. Gillian writes like a man."

"I wasn't aware that handwriting was sexed, but now that you point it out, she does write like a man—a specific man: her father. Her handwriting is almost identical to Enchanter Oliver's."

"See?"

"They both write like they're in a tearing hurry. Her sex doesn't have anything to do with it."

"It's not proper for any young lady, witch or no, to be in such a hurry."

Sven sighed again. Had the supervisor never experienced the sense of urgency a true scholar feels on realising how little of the full breadth of human knowledge one can encompass in a single lifetime? Probably not.

He skimmed the other papers. The marks were consistent. She had been criticised for things unrelated to her mastery of the subject, and given no recognition when she'd gone beyond what was asked for. No wonder she hadn't bothered doing half of them.

"By the way," he said, "you will return to her the book you confiscated—*Introduction to Contract Magic*. That copy was her own, not your library's."

"How did she come by—"

"I gave it to her."

"Whatever for?"

He shrugged. "She said she wanted it."

"But…"

That should have been sufficient reason. He didn't intend to share his suspicion—his hope—that Gillian would someday be the supervisor's superior, either as Air Enchantress or simply on the guild council. The Reforging Coven needed Gillian's passion for magic. If Miranda, whose passion was for music, turned out to be the enchantress…

That was a problem for another day. He wrenched his attention back to this day's problem.

"Tell me your view of the disciplinary issue."

He was pleased with how non-confrontational his request sounded. The Air Guild didn't have a monopoly on diplomacy, after all.

The supervisor said, "We have been concerned from the start of term over Gillian's tendency to fabricate stories, and equally on her insistence on sticking to her fabrications after being confronted with the truth. She has been punished several times for lying."

"What is the nature of these alleged lies?"

"Mostly casting aspersions on the character of Frankland's most notable men and women. For example, a few weeks ago she insisted that Warlock Quicksilver can do air magic."

"He can. He does. Anyone who has spent any time with him has seen him make small objects fly." Taking in the supervisor's stricken expression, Sven added gently. "It's not the end of the world, you know. Many talented people have a foot in more than one guild."

"I know, but for an officeholder...a great one at that... Officeholders should be pure, exemplars of the qualities that make their guild unique."

Sven snorted. "Rubbish. You don't want a pure fire wizard holding the Fire Office. Trust me. The pure ones are the ones who bring on the Scorching Times because they can't control their tempers. The other guilds have their own character flaws that make the purest individuals troublesome."

The supervisor bridled. "Enchanter Paul is a pure air wizard, and an impeccable Air Enchanter."

Sven's jaw tightened. He was here on Gillian's behalf. This was not the time to alienate the Air Guild by expressing his opinion of their guild head. "How does this relate to the current issue, which appears to be concerning her opinion of Silver's book on Enchanter Oliver?"

"Her opinion was clearly unjustified. She called it a piece of trash."

Sven winced. He owed Gillian an apology for getting her into trouble. "She was quoting my opinion of it. It wasn't a work of sufficient scholarship to earn the title 'biography.' I wouldn't have been as harsh if it had been labelled a memoir or collection of anecdotes."

"But, sir, Mr Silver interviewed dozens of people."

"Yes, and as far as I can tell, every one was in the Air Guild. His coverage of the first eighteen years of Ollie's life seems reasonably complete, though tending towards the hagiographic and skimping on his conflicts with his father, but the last third of his life—the years after he left Airvale, the period that makes him worthy of having a biography written—is largely fiction. Ollie's professors and peers at the university would not recognise him. I was Ollie's constant companion for most of his time as an undergraduate, and corresponded regularly with him for years afterwards. Silver never approached Irene or me. We did not know a so-called biography was in the works, and were astonished to see it in print."

Sven didn't enjoy destroying people's illusions, but Enchanter Paul shouldn't have let the book be published as it was. There had been heated words—not only Sven's—over it at the last meeting of the Company of Mages.

He said, "Even if Silver's work had been adequate, the punishment inflicted for expressing her opinion seems unduly harsh."

"I'm sorry, sir, to have given you a mistaken impression. Her major fault was another lie."

"What lie?"

The supervisor seemed to have become fascinated with her wedding ring, twisting it around and around, watching it and not him. "I understand, sir, that having married Enchanter Oliver's widow, you would naturally want to think highly of her talents and intellect."

Sven's face tightened. "You have it backwards. It's because I think highly of her talents and intellect that I married her. Should I gather from this that Gillian said Irene wrote the spells attributed to Ollie?"

Startled, the supervisor looked up. "Yes, sir."

"I see." Sven crossed his arms and stared at the ceiling. "Enchanter Oliver was one of Frankland's finest men. I am proud he called me friend. He earned the title hero, and he earned his place in the Company of Mages, but the story of that book of spells is more complicated than it seems, and you are not in a position to judge the facts." He brought his gaze down to meet the supervisor's staring eyes. "Especially if you consider Silver's *Life* an authority."

The supervisor blushed and looked away.

Sven said, "Even before my stepdaughter was involved, I thought locking an air witch or wizard in a closet seemed unduly harsh."

"Locking a child in the closet is the punishment of last resort. We always post a listener outside, to let the child out when he or she gives in. Nearly always, half an hour, or three quarters at most, is enough to make even the most recalcitrant offender submit to authority."

"And how long did it take before Gillian submitted?"

The supervisor wouldn't meet his eyes. "She hasn't yet."

"What?"

"She's been in detention three hours every afternoon—"

"It's been a week," he shouted. "She's an air witch. My God, that's barbaric."

The supervisor flinched. "Yes, sir, but—"

He roared, "She's in detention now? Let her out. At once."

"Sir, we—"

His fist banged on the table. "Now!"

Sunbeam Takes a Stand

The first-form supervisor fled. The door slammed behind her. Gillian submit? Sven should have known better. Miranda would have given in the first day, but Gillian, like her father, had a foot in the Fire Guild. She would fight back.

Sven put his head down in his hands. He should have come as soon as he'd gotten the girls' letters, but he hadn't wanted to derail the second rebuild of the Earth Office. He had never considered this cruelty. He should have come...

The supervisor returned with a sullen, glassy-eyed girl, clutching a sheaf of papers to her chest.

"Papa Sven!" The papers tumbled to the ground, forgotten, as she hurtled into his arms.

He gave her one brief squeeze before pushing her towards the door. "Outside with you. I'll follow shortly. Go."

She ran.

Sven turned to the supervisor. "What did—" The supervisor flinched. Sven closed his eyes and took a deep breath. Several deep breaths. When he had his voice under control he started again. "What did Enchanter Paul say about this?"

"I believe the dean reported that Gillian was lying again, but not what the actual lie, er, statement was. The Air Enchanter said he was tired of hearing that she lies, and we must break her of that vile habit once and for all. He ordered repeated detentions until she retracts her, um..."

"I see." Sven spoke through clenched teeth. "Well. Thank you for an enlightening discussion." He gathered the papers Gillian had spilled across the floor. "What was she writing?"

117

"It certainly wasn't the lines she was supposed to be copying." The supervisor gulped and retreated when he turned a glare on her. "I beg your pardon, sir. I believe she was writing what she called Enchanter Oliver's 'true story.'"

"Which you wouldn't have approved of had she finished. Not," he said, holding up a hand to forestall the supervisor's objection, "that she would say anything defamatory about him, but the reputations of some current residents of Airvale might take a beating."

"Sir… I don't want to offend you, sir, but perhaps you're not the final authority on Enchanter Oliver's life either." She paled, but held her ground. "They're air witches, sir. They should know how the Air Guild sees him."

The supervisor had more nerve than he would have credited a mid-level air witch with. Among the many things he had learned from Warlock Quicksilver was that anyone willing to confront an angry fire wizard deserved a hearing.

"I admit I am not a neutral party in this matter." He straightened the papers, thumping them into a neat stack. "Sorcerer Charles—the Senior Water Mage—is, and has taken an interest in the girls. I will ask him to read Silver's book with them, and guide them in separating fact from fiction. Will that satisfy you?"

The supervisor blinked at him. "Yes, sir. Of course, sir."

"Good." He stirred the conference room's fire. "Warlock Snorri, I need a favour. I don't dare take Gillian through the tunnels…"

Sven and Snorri, with Miranda between them, trudged along the muddy path to the headland overlooking Airvale, where Gillian danced along the cliff's edge. Sven pulled his hat brim further down to keep the rain out of his eyes. It ran down the back of his neck instead.

Snorri said, "Frostbite. What did they do to the poor kid? How can anybody be happy in this weather?"

"She'd better not get too close to the edge," Sven said. "If she falls…"

"She won't," Miranda said. "She never does."

"How do they treat you? I thought you were happy here."

"I am. The music teachers are amazing. The rest…" She shrugged. "It's not bad. When they talk about Mama or Papa or Enchanter Paul, I don't listen. If they insist on me paying attention, I nod and say 'yes, ma'am,' and they leave me alone. I tell Gillie not to argue, but it doesn't do any good."

"I'm not surprised. She's Ollie all over again. We had concerns over sending her here, but we didn't expect so much trouble so soon."

"Where will you put her when you take her home?"

"Where?" Sven turned a puzzled frown on Miranda. "What do you mean, where?"

"She's been sneaking out of the dormitory and sleeping on the porch all week. She won't be happy indoors for a while. A long time, maybe."

"That could be a problem…"

Gillian saw them, and ran to meet them. She would have hugged Snorri but he held the sodden girl at arm's length. "You're not touching me like that. You look like a mermaid fished out of the deep."

A few minutes later, after a wet and tearful goodbye between the two sisters, Gillian and the two wizards stood atop a mountain under clear skies, all three warm and dry, thanks to a little fire power.

"When you've had enough here, we'll go to the Warren," Sven said, "and have a healer work you over."

"I don't need a healer."

"If I take you home now, your mother will need one."

"Why?"

Sven knelt and laid a gentle hand on her head. "You've been pulling your hair out, haven't you? You look like you're going bald on one side."

Snorri added, "Your eyebrows are almost gone, too."

"You've lost weight, you have bags under your eyes, and what are these?" Sven pulled her wrist up and out, and ran a finger along the underside of her arm. "Bite marks?"

She spread her fingers. "I didn't have any fingernails left."

"Right. The Warren, definitely."

She pulled her arm away and thrust out her chin. "I'm not going back to Airvale next term. You can't make me."

"So you said in your letter, but remember, young lady, you are still a minor. You don't have the final say."

"Just because you're old doesn't mean you're always right," she flared.

"Of course not. But I don't have the final say either."

The haunted look in her eyes deepened. "Enchanter Paul?"

"No, your mother."

She spun around and around, giddy in her relief. "She won't make me go back."

"No, I wouldn't think so, especially since I agree with you. None of us need the heartache sending you back would cause. But I want something in return."

She came to a halt facing him. "What?"

"I want you to become a world-wide authority on a subject in the Air Guild's domain."

"What subject?"

"Communication spells."

Gillian grinned. "Oh, those are easy."

Gillian's first few days home in the Fortress coincided with a rare warm spell, letting her sleep in a tent on the family's balcony. After that, with winter bearing down on them in earnest, she camped a few feet inside the glass doors of the infrequently used ballroom. The Fortress staff carried a desk into the conservatory for her to let her do her lessons without her fingers freezing, and she commandeered the spot in the dining room closest to the windows. No one argued with her for it; that end of the table was notoriously chilly during the winter months. She exercised on the parapets, unnerving the guards, and slipped between ballroom, dining room, conservatory, and library on the outer walkways, gradually easing her way further inside the walls, and never venturing far from a window.

No one pressed her to return to the practice room. Her parents and the warlocks watched, and worried.

"Ma'am?"

"What is it, Katie?" Lucinda replied, without glancing her way. Drew was demanding her attention. His little arms went everywhere other than where she wanted them to go, but she would not let him out into the snow-covered garden clad only in his nappy.

"It's Sunbeam, ma'am."

"What about Sunbeam?"

"He's in the square, acting odd."

Lucinda looked up. Katie was at the window, peeking around the frame. The moment's inattention was all Drew needed. He bolted. The nursemaid grabbed him. Together they wrestled him into his clothes, then the nursemaid led her three charges down the stairs.

Despite the cold weather, Drew would undoubtedly succeed in shedding his clothes sometime during their outdoor excursion, but the neighbourhood gossips wouldn't blame that on his mother. The conventions had been preserved. Three little fireballs were too much for one mundane minder, but the Rehsavvy's choice of servants who could tolerate the aversion spell on their house was limited.

Usually Lucinda didn't mind the lean staff. Spells on the house kept it clean and handled most menial chores, and she didn't approve of the usual upper class abandonment of children to servants' supervision—care that wobbled between excess indulgence and not-at-all-tender mercies. Her children didn't run to their nursemaid for comfort instead of their mother.

Still, they were a handful, and the oldest was already showing signs of nascent talent. The Fire Guild's repertoire of spells did not include many to help with raising children. Send them cowering under their beds, more likely.

"Sunbeam, ma'am."

"Oh, right." Her mind's eye focused. Sunbeam was pacing back and forth on the square with his hands tucked behind his back and his head lowered. With every turn he glanced at the Rehsavvy's house and muttered to himself.

Katie said, "He's been doing that for several minutes now."

"Like he's working up the nerve to knock on our door? But the aversion spell doesn't spill over. We have tradespeople and messengers come to the house all the time."

"Yes, ma'am, but they don't come in. Everybody in Blazes knows that."

Sunbeam stopped, straightened, squared his shoulders, took two firm steps toward the house, then pivoted and shuffled a dozen paces in the opposite direction. He paced towards them and away twice more before coming to a halt. He stood with his fists on his hips, scowling.

Sunbeam, scowling? Lucinda sucked in her breath, casting about for a new spell on the house, but before she had time to begin, he marched across the street and hammered on the door with his walking stick.

She ran for the hall and reached the top of the stairs, with Katie right behind, as Tom ushered Sunbeam into Jean's study. She leaned over the bannister and beckoned to Tom.

"He doesn't look good," she whispered.

"No, ma'am, he doesn't," Tom said. "Should I fetch Granny?"

"Please."

Tom ran for the door, and Lucinda sat on the stairs to watch the action in Jean's study with her mind's eye.

Jean's eyes widened when Sunbeam entered his study. He dropped his pen and rose, holding out his hand. "Welcome, Gilbert. I had not expected a visit."

"No, of course you didn't." Sunbeam ignored Jean's outstretched hand, instead clutching at his left side with his right hand. Pain distorted his features.

"Are you ill? Please, sit, and I will send for the healer."

"No, I shan't sit. I shan't be here long. I am not here on a social call."

"I see." Jean's hand fell to his side. "Nevertheless, I would advise you to take a seat while you are here. You appear to be under some strain."

"I am. It's not easy to hold off your abominable aversion spell."

"I beg your pardon. A stroll in the garden might be easier." Jean waved towards the door, but Sunbeam didn't budge.

"Your aversion spell, by the way, is deplorable. To suggest the few inhabitants of this house are the only ones in the whole country who care what happens to Frankland is outrageous. An insult to us all."

Jean's lips tightened. "That is not the intent of the spell, I assure you, nor how it works. Allow me to explain—"

"Some other time." Sunbeam's complexion had turned grey. Sweat beaded his forehead and upper lip. "That's not why I'm here."

"Please, enlighten me."

"You are aware, I am sure, that I have not approved of either attempt at the so-called 'reforging' of the offices."

"I could not avoid being aware of your opinion, but I had been under the impression you acknowledged reforging the Water Office was a success."

"It did turn out better than I had believed possible. Yes, I admit that, but only because it was clearly badly damaged from the start. I sill think you mad to let your wife risk her life in that endeavour."

Jean's eyes glittered, but he didn't respond.

Sunbeam continued, "But no one has claimed the Earth Office's problems are of the same magnitude. Mother Celeste's death was unnecessary." He shook a finger in Jean's face. "And I hold you responsible, sir."

122

Jean flinched and retreated before the shaking finger. Sunbeam pursued him, thundering, "And if you continue with this madness, sir, and destroy the Fire Office, Frankland's shield, I personally shall charge you with treason, sir." He gasped and clutched at his heart. He croaked, "And with our friend Beorn's murder."

He folded like a marionette whose strings have been snipped. Jean caught him and lowered him to the floor.

"Murder," Sunbeam gasped. His eyes rolled up. "Treason," he whispered. Another gasp, and he lay still.

Jean Rehsavvy, Frankland's retired Fire Warlock, paced the floor in his study at two in the morning.

Lucinda lay awake, staring at the dark ceiling. She considered going downstairs, but there was no point. She had no comfort to offer.

In her mind's eye, she reviewed the events of that awful day: the healer's undiplomatic assertion that the aversion spell had driven Sunbeam's soul from his body the instant his heart stopped, his death worsening the growing animosity in the town between the Fire Eaters and everyone else driven away by the aversion spell, and finally, the scene at the funeral pyre, where Sunbeam's widow had spat in Jean's face.

Lucinda's fists clenched. How dare that woman show the Fire Warlock Emeritus such disrespect? He was still flagellating himself over Mother Celeste. Sunbeam's death had heaped burning coals on his conscience.

She forced her hands open, took a deep breath, and held it while counting to ten. Then she rolled out of bed and pulled on a robe. How could she comfort Jean when she needed comfort herself? She couldn't really blame Sunbeam's widow. She would want revenge if Jean died from someone else's spellcasting. The widow deserved sympathy. Shame over her anger aggravated Lucinda's physical unease.

She stomped into the kitchen and flicked her fingers at the wood in the fireplace, laid ready for the morning. A bonfire roared to life.

Great, just great. Lack of control over her temper was something else to feel bad about. She brought the fire under control and rummaged through the pantry.

Beorn had offered to withdraw the aversion spell, but she had rejected the offer. It was too late, the damage was already done, and if tensions in Blazes were growing, she preferred having the extra assurance the spell gave her. The chill in her relations with the townsfolk had been gnawing at her for some time, but she had only become conscious of it after Mother Celeste's death, when they had gotten downright frosty. She couldn't do much about that, and she preferred getting the cold shoulder—a fine thing from the Fire Guild!—to either duplicitous fawning or open hostilities.

Lucinda slammed her rolling pin onto the kitchen table. She had expected reforging the offices to take a toll, but this aspect of it had surprised her. She should have known better. Nothing ever changed in Frankland, and when change happened anyway, Franks went berserk, even when they benefited from the change.

She should be grateful Blazes wasn't burning. Yet. She shuddered, imagining a mob attacking her house while she and Jean were in the Fortress, rebuilding the Fire Office.

The divisions in the Fire Guild were harder on Jean than on her. She'd spent more than half her life with her talents hidden, never quite fitting in. Never quite at home in her home village. She had more close friends now, among Frankland's other heroes, than she'd had then. But Jean had been Fire Warlock for over a hundred years, and despite frequent clashes with other warlocks, he had expected and received deference from the lower ranks. Sunbeam's widow had shocked him to the core.

Lucinda shoved trays of elephant ears into the oven, slammed the oven door, frowned at it for a moment, then backed into her husband's arms.

"Jean, what are you doing here?"

"I came to thank you, my love, for bringing me a measure of solace."

"You can thank me after they come out."

His arms tightened around her waist. "I was not referring to the pastries, however delectable they may be. I value more highly your willingness to share my sleepless nights."

As if she had a choice. She smiled and didn't comment as he nuzzled her hair.

Tomorrow, she would bake for Sunbeam's family. Even if they spurned the gift, she would feel better for having offered.

Irene Disturbs Quicksilver

On a blustery day in early March, Irene was in the conservatory, watching Gillian chat with empty air. She started when Warlock Arturos leaned over her shoulder.

He whispered, "What's going on?"

"Warlock Quicksilver is telling my other students a story. He's at home in Blazes. Snorri is in the practice room, and Sorcerer Charles is in the Crystal Palace."

"Ewww." Gillian scrambled away from her desk.

Irene said, "Snorri has been providing sensory input to assist with the story."

"Yeah?" Arturos strolled over, got a whiff, and retreated. "Tell Snorri to put his shoes back on. We don't need to smell his stinky feet."

"They're not his feet," Gillian said. "The old man in the story took his shoes off, getting ready for bed."

"Huh. Some assistance, that is. What else can he do along that line?"

Irene said, "Oranges, bacon, peaches… Mostly food."

"Figures."

She smiled. "He's rather good at it."

He grunted. "Making their stomachs rumble won't defeat the empire's army."

Her smile faltered. "Well, no."

"When the story's over, give Gillie something else to do and come up to my study. We need to talk."

When Irene reached the Fire Warlock's study, Sorcerer Charles was already there. The two warlocks filed in shortly after.

Arturos said, "Either Irene's a terrific teacher, or you're top-notch students, or both. You three have done things with air magic I'd never have believed anybody outside the Air Guild could do. Lucinda had a good idea there."

Charles smiled. Snorri grinned. Quicksilver's face was expressionless. "But…" he said.

"Yeah, there's a but coming. All three of you walked through the tunnels. No jumping through the fire, or swimming. Why not?"

Snorri yawned. "It's exhausting. A couple hours doing level three Air Guild spells and I'm ready for bed."

"Right. One enchanter-level spell will lay you up for a week. If you ever get there. At the rate you're going, you might not. You're all spending too much time on this for too little payoff."

"Agreed," Quicksilver said.

Charles nodded. "It's been an interesting challenge, but when the time comes, we can't afford to exhaust ourselves with one air spell apiece."

"Right," Arturos said. "Not when we need you full of pep for the work you're best at. Especially you, old man. We need you on fire magic."

Quicksilver sighed. "Very well. I cannot say I am surprised. I am too old for air magic to come easily."

"Me, too, I'm afraid," Charles said.

"Don't blame it on age," Snorri said. "It's hard. Let's forget about the higher-level spells, and keep on with the level two and three spells."

Arturos frowned at him. Snorri shifted his feet. "I meant in my spare time. Gillian needs somebody to practice with."

Arturos's frown deepened into a glower.

Snorri backed a step. "And it's fun."

Arturos's expression lightened. "Uh-huh. Thought so. You can keep going as long as you don't wear yourself out and neglect the Fire Guild. Now push off, the lot of you, and get some sleep before you die on your feet."

The three wizards left. Irene lingered.

"It wasn't a complete waste of time," she said.

"Never said it was," Arturos said. "If it gives Snorri a surprise or two to spring on the empire, that's all to the good."

"I meant it's been beneficial for Miranda and Gillian. Either one could sail through the school's practicals for their current power levels, and they will be well-prepared as their powers develop."

126

"Not surprised. Miranda's doing well there, but she's lost ground on spending time in the practice room."

Irene sighed. "Yes. She had gotten as far as spending three hours in a stretch there, but she can't do that now. Her summer holidays aren't long enough for her to regain what she loses. She likes school well enough, so don't even think of asking her to spend time in their punishment closet."

"What do you take me for? I'm here to protect women and children, not give you nightmares."

"Really? Who suggested they spend time in the practice room?"

"Quicksilver, not me, and he didn't make them do it, remember. Miranda volunteered."

"That's true, and those who knew praised her for it. The school wouldn't understand. Her friends would think her mad, and the staff would try to cure her."

Arturos shuddered. "And leave her as bad off as Gillian. Drown them. Drown them all and their insufferable head, too. Your girls are champs, Irene. It's not their fault they've been undermined by a bunch of asses." He raked his fingers through his beard, and sighed. "We didn't have much of a chance anyway. I'm calling a council meeting tomorrow. You're invited."

From the Fire Warlock's study, Irene went directly to Sven's and closed the door behind her. "The Fire Warlock has stopped my older students' studies."

"I'd been expecting that for six months or more," Sven said.

"It's time, Sven."

He wouldn't meet her eyes. "Warlock Quicksilver won't like it."

"He won't like it any better next week or next month. He won't like it either if the Fire Warlock calls a halt to the whole endeavour."

Sven was silent for a few seconds, clenching and unclenching his jaw. "You're right. It's time."

Irene's formal schooling had ended at seventeen. She had not sat an exam in a decade and a half, but she sometimes still dreamed of writing nonsensical answers to test questions she didn't understand, or of discovering herself in the exam room for a class she hadn't realised she was enrolled in, and had never attended. She experienced the same panic now, in waking life, as she waited for the Fire Guild Council members to settle down at the conference room's gleaming cherrywood table.

The solidity of the leather satchel leaning against her feet, reminding her she had been studying this subject for six years and was an acknowledged expert, brought little comfort. Mistakes in this exam would have consequences far more disastrous than a failing grade.

Warlock Arturos dropped into the armchair at the head of the table. "Reforging the Earth Office took too long."

Warlock Quicksilver, head bowed, stared at his clasped hands resting on the table. Lucinda chewed her lip. Snorri glowered and made thick slashing lines with his charcoal pencil, ruining the sketch he'd started of Sven in profile. No one disputed this simple statement of fact.

Arturos said, "You've rebuilt it five times now, and got it down to two twelve-hour days, which isn't bad, but it's not near good enough. The Earth Office is the easiest. The Fire Office is the hardest, and you won't get a chance to practice on it. I'd like to know how long that'll take."

Sven said, "At least four sixteen-hour days, perhaps five, assuming we follow the same procedures, and we make no major mistakes in spellcasting, or uncover any unpleasant surprises during the unlocking. Also assuming we sleep well enough every night to function the next day. That much heavy magic use is exhausting."

"Right." Arturos tugged at his beard and stared at the ceiling. "Unless somebody has a better idea, there's no point. I don't like it, but I'd like giving Frankland away to the empire even less. I'm calling a halt."

A muscle in Quicksilver's face twitched. Snorri and Lucinda stared at the wall.

Sven looked at Irene. She nodded. He cleared his throat. "There's another way."

Heads turned, focusing on him. He flushed. "Irene and I have a proposal for a radically different approach."

Snorri nudged Irene. "Don't forget to breathe."

She gasped. She hadn't realised she was holding her breath.

"All right," Arturos said. "Let's hear it."

Sven said, "We've been talking about other options ever since Irene was given permission to read the Fire Office spells, but we thought we might be overly pessimistic about the time the reforging would take. We wanted to see—"

"Skip it, Sven," Snorri said. "Get to the point."

"Fine. We can restructure the Fire Office. Divide the spells into two tiers: the ones essential for defence, and everything else. Postpone everything else until Frankland's security has been re-established. We can then spend as much time as we need on the everything else to ensure we don't make mistakes due to fatigue or being rushed. We've already sorted the spells into what's necessary and what's not. There will still be serious spellcasting required, but we think the core spells can be handled in Quicksilver's twenty-four hour limit."

Snorri's eyes blazed. "Yeah. Let's do it."

Arturos gave his shoulder a hard shake. "Keep a rein on it. We haven't heard details yet." But Arturos's own expression had lightened, as had Lucinda's. Only Quicksilver appeared unmoved, his eyes hooded, his face blank.

"Here are the details." Irene dredged papers from her satchel. "The first tier of spells, the ones essential for defence, centre around the Fire Guild spells securing Frankland's borders and controlling the lightning, the Earth Guild spells channelling invaders towards the Fortress, and the Air Guild spells for communication and scrying external threats." She handed out copies of a single page to the four warlocks. "The second tier includes everything else." This list consisted of several pages, closely written. "The nobilities' shields, the Fire Warlock's extended life, guild management, riot control, internal threats, the challenge path, etc."

For a few minutes, the only sounds were rustling papers. Then Arturos mumbled, "The king won't be happy about the nobles not having their shields."

Sven shrugged. "If we don't do this, they'll be without their shields anyway for the four or five days it takes to rebuild. If the empire overruns us in that time, they'll lose a lot more than their shields."

"Agreed," Quicksilver said. "Whether or not we restore their shields at all is a minor quibble compared to the drastic nature of the changes you are suggesting." He frowned at the papers Irene had given him, then lifted his eyes and frowned at Sven. "The most notable characteristic of the spells in each office is their entwined nature, creating one seamless whole. If I understand you, your proposal would require rewriting many, if not most, to work in isolation."

"Not in isolation, no, but in several smaller groupings."

"Would that be bad?" Lucinda asked. "Repairs would be easier."

"Indeed, they would." Quicksilver scanned the lists again. "Some years ago I had considered such alterations, but could not see how to pull the whole apart without breaking it, and rejected the idea in favour of making changes in the spells only where we knew problems existed. This structure works. The suggestion of replacing it with an untested structure distresses me. If we had time and opportunity to experiment that would be reassuring, but we do not."

"We can experiment with the structure of the Earth Office," Sven said. "Some spells in both tiers are used in all four offices. We can test them out there."

"Yes, that would be a necessary first step, but not sufficient. I have understood the intertwined nature of the spells to be a factor in what gives the offices their strength. This restructure you propose will make the Fire Office itself more vulnerable to attack."

Sven took a deep breath. "I disagree, Your Wisdom."

"Explain, please."

"Yes, sir. The spells in the second tier aren't the ones giving the office its strength. We aren't proposing to change the intertwined nature of the Fire and Earth Guild spells in the first tier, but we do want to separate them from the Air Guild spells with their inherent vulnerabilities. By focusing on a smaller, more cohesive core, we should produce a Fire Office at least as strong as the one we have now. Maybe even stronger."

"Sounds to me like it's worth considering," Arturos said.

"Yeah," Snorri said.

"I agree," Lucinda said.

Quicksilver smiled. "I see I am outnumbered." His smile faded. "Perhaps my sense of disquiet stems from being an old man, too long familiar with the existing Fire Office, and younger minds were needed to imagine a new one." He frowned again at the list of spells. "My first impression is that your selection of spells for the first tier is by and large correct, but I will need time to digest these lists. If only you had found a way to avoid these dependencies on Air Guild spells in your first tier."

Irene shifted and coughed. Quicksilver focused an intense stare on her. "Have you?"

She said, "They have to be there, Your Wisdom. The Fire Office would be blind and deaf without them. But there might be a way to reduce the demands on the Air Guild during the reforging."

"Pray, continue."

"The Air Guild spells in the first tier could be built up as a separate corpus bound to a different object—another ring, for instance. That could be done beforehand. During the reforging, they would be moved onto the Fire Warlock's Token of Office and tied in with the other tier one spells. Moving enchantments from one object to another has been done, although not on such a large scale. The tricky part would be connecting them to the other Fire Office spells. We've never done that before, but we think it's possible. If it worked, it would slice the support needed from the Air Guild during the actual reforging down to three spells, but if it went wrong…"

"Yes?"

"The corpus of Air Guild spells could collapse."

"That body of Air Guild spells, you say. Not the entire Fire Office?" She hesitated. He said, "You think it possible the entire collection could collapse, forcing us to start over, losing hours of work."

"It is unlikely, Your Wisdom, but I can't rule it out."

Quicksilver leaned back, his arms crossed, his eyes hooded. "Young lady, you have no idea the extent to which you are frightening me. With one hand you are offering hope for a solution to a thorny problem troubling my sleep for years, while with the other raising yet another weapon to add to those already arrayed against us. The risk of disaster…"

Sven said, "Remains, whether we try a different way or not. With this, Snorri could use those spells for the defence, until it's time to move them."

Snorri's eyes lit. "We'd be nuts not to try it."

Arturos said, "What do you say, old man?"

Quicksilver brooded and didn't answer.

Arturos clapped him on the shoulder. "Get used to it, because we're going to run with it. Irene, let's see those rewritten spells."

Putting off a nasty problem doesn't make it easier to deal with, and you make yourself sick waiting.

Gillian had heard Mrs Rehsavvy say that, and she believed it. She'd had headaches and tummy aches for months now, once the joy of being free of the school had worn off, but she had been afraid to do what she knew was needed. Then when she'd finally screwed up her courage, there'd been no opportunity for more than a fortnight. When had that big, lonely cave gotten so busy? Every time she looked, somebody was there:

131

the noisy Fire Eaters, Mama and Papa quietly doing spellwork, Snorri and Alex fencing… She would rather die than turn into a whimpering baby with somebody watching.

Today, with Mama, Papa, and all the warlocks at the council meeting, the practice room was empty. She had checked, sending her mind's eye through the tunnel, but even that was hard. The tunnel hated her, no question.

She didn't want to do this, but she had to, and it had to be today. Her parents had talked about the council meeting last night, after they thought she was asleep. If the Fire Warlock called a halt, she didn't want it to be because she'd failed.

The tunnel from the Matheson's suite to the practice room started in her parent's bedroom, with a door indistinguishable from an ordinary closet. She dragged Papa Sven's favourite armchair over and wedged the door open; the door at the other end was closed. She chewed on her lip while studying the short passage. If she couldn't open the far door, the tunnel would swallow her and squeeze all the breath out of her like an anaconda.

She thrust out her lip, crept closer, edged her head in, and jerked back. After two more vain attempts, she retreated to the bedroom's far wall and, on the count of three, threw herself through the tunnel mouth.

She crashed into the far door. It didn't open. The door behind her slammed shut. She experienced a moment of sheer, blind terror before her fumbling hands found the latch. The door didn't budge.

She shrilled, "The Fire Warlock will burn you if you hurt me."

The door creaked open far enough for a skinny child to squirm through. She fell into the practice room, scraping her palms on the flagstones, then fled towards the far corner, putting air between her and that hideous tunnel.

She was in, and she was stuck. She couldn't face that tunnel again. She sucked on the torn heel of her hand and twitched. No one knew she was here. She would starve. No, she'd go mad before then. They would find her body with bloody fingers where she'd torn at the walls…

The Fire Warlock emerged from the fireplace with a damp cloth and a tub of ointment. She flew into him hard enough to make him grunt.

"When you go, take me with you," she said. "Through the fire."

"You bet," he said. "Let's see those hands."

With her palms cleaned and bandaged, and a firm grip on the Fire Warlock's hand, she calmed enough to venture into the centre of the room, where she examined the illusion of an overcast sky. "There's more light."

"Thank Sorcerer Charles for that," he said. "He suggested putting prisms and mirrors in places to capture more sunlight."

"It's warmer, too."

"The Fire Eaters' practices heat the place up."

"If you put in more vents, it might not even make me hurt."

"If we put in more vents, it would spook the Earth Guild, and blow our papers away while we're trying to read the spells."

"Oh."

"It hurts, eh? Tell me about that."

"Not now, but it will. It gets worse the longer I stay here. It'll hurt here." She rubbed her face. "Like someone with hands bigger than yours squeezing my head. And here, like a bulldog sitting on my chest. After a few hours it feels like an ox."

"Ugh. If it hurts, why are you here?"

She glared at him. "Quicksilver and I made a deal."

"I know, but I thought you wanted out. After that closet."

"It's funny. After that closet, this cave doesn't scare me any more. As long as I can leave before it hurts too much." If an air witch could blush, she would have, remembering her panic from a few minutes earlier. There was always somebody from the Fire Guild here. "The cave doesn't want to hurt me, but that tunnel…" Her voice quavered. She clamped her lips shut.

The Fire Warlock gave the tunnel a dark look. "Tell Sven about that— he'll be real interested—but don't tell your mama. Wouldn't want her to worry. And when you need help getting in or out, and can't find anybody, yell for me. I'll hear. That's a promise."

A brisk fire drove the April chill from Alexander's small morning room. The yolks in the eggs were runny, just the way he liked them. He mopped up the last of the eggs with toast, savouring both his breakfast and the peace of the breakfast hour, his time alone before the daily influx of courtiers, diplomats, and citizens all clamouring for his attention.

His father had never been alone. Servants had been within arm's reach at all hours, courtiers had dressed him, entertained him, even wiped his

133

arse for him. From Alexander's infancy, people had surrounded him, too, but he had learned to appreciate the benefits of occasional solitude during his sojourn with the Rehsavvys.

He rested his left hand on the table, the unadorned walnut as smooth as satin under his fingers. Several small Frankish landscape paintings in unadorned frames hung on the room's linden panelling. A glass-fronted bookcase against one wall held scholarly works on Frankland's history, popular tales of Frankish heroes, and atlases dating back centuries showing how Frankland's cities and towns had changed over time. A chessboard in the corner held an unfinished game, awaiting an hour or two of Warlock Snorri's time.

There was no gilt anywhere in the room. He had no need for show here in this private room, populated only with objects that brought him pleasure and comfort. Besides, gilt could not compete with the splendour on display outside the windows, where a line of flowering cherry trees glowed in the slanting morning light. He watched, mesmerised, as a light breeze fanned the blossoms, then realising he still held his fork, speared a bite of sausage.

He stopped with the fork halfway to his mouth. The fireback was gone. Beyond the fire, another young man watched him.

The King's Temper

The room beyond the fire was larger and more sumptuously appointed than Alexander's morning room. With his chin resting on his hand, his elbow on the chair arm, and one leg crossed over the other knee, the room's occupant looked quite at ease.

Alexander lowered his fork, rose, and bowed. "Good morning, sir. Prince Gunther, we presume. Or do you prefer Warlock Sturmmeister? To what do we owe the honour of this visit?"

The other man tilted his head without rising. "Good morning, and yes, I am Warlock Sturmmeister. I wished to see for myself this mundane boy styling himself king of Frankland. I am surprised you haven't screamed for your guards."

The eighteen-year-old king had stiffened. After a few seconds he lowered himself into his chair. "We became inured to warlocks appearing in the fire during the Yule War. We have no need for guards. We are confident the Fire Warlock is watching and will intervene should the need arise."

"Should the need arise. Ha! I could step through the fire and drag you back to Danzig with me before your Fire Warlock could react, and he could do nothing in retaliation. He cannot step outside Frankland's borders."

The emerald hanging on the gold chain inside Alexander's shirt did not vibrate or prickle his skin. His lips thinned.

Gunther said, "You did not know this? Tsk, tsk. Such a small thing, but so significant. Would Frankland pay a heavy ransom for your return, or would your Fire Guild abandon their mundane king and install another puppet? I am almost inclined to do it for the entertainment value."

"How diplomatic of you," Alexander murmured.

"Diplomacy, pah." Gunther waved a lazy hand. "Diplomacy is for cowards and underlings and rulers of countries without the strength to enforce their demands. Diplomacy is for kings like you who are happy to be dictated to by greater men. Or women. Your Locksmith is a greater man than you."

Alexander's eyebrows rose. He spread marmalade on the last piece of toast before saying, "Although they sometimes appear in the same person, the qualities that make a good warrior are not the same qualities that make a good ruler. Frankland's warlocks understand that."

Gunther laughed. "Do they? You cannot believe Warlock Snorri will let you cling to your throne once your Fire Office is rebuilt. I will be kinder than he. Once we have conquered Frankland I will keep you alive for my amusement. You will have daily lessons in how a truly great emperor rules."

Alexander had been eating his toast while Gunther talked. He swallowed, licked his lips, and sipped his tea. "If you are trying to intimidate us, or make us angry, you are not succeeding."

Gunther shifted his weight forward, nearly coming out of his armchair, but fell back into a rigid facsimile of his initial relaxed position. "You are too stupid to know when you've been insulted, or you'd be raging."

Alexander dusted crumbs from his hands. "You, sir, have been extraordinarily well blessed. You are among the wealthiest and most powerful individuals in the Western world, and yet the things driving you are pride, greed, arrogance, and envy. We can feel only one emotion towards a man in your position who cannot enjoy what he has been given." He leaned forward, locking eyes with Gunther. "That emotion is pity."

Gunther lunged towards the fire, snarling, "I'll teach you to—"

A bang and bright flash sent Alexander rocking backwards. When his vision cleared, the fireback had returned. Gunther was gone. He blinked at Warlock Arturos bending over him. "What happened?"

"Our pal Gunther hit the Fire Office's shields. I reckon he hurt himself pretty bad. Maybe even killed himself, if we should be so lucky. You all right?"

"Yes. Uh, maybe." Alexander rubbed his eyes, shook his head, and blinked a few times. "Yes, I'm fine."

"You weren't worried that he really could reach through the fire and grab you, were you?"

"He wasn't lying when he said he could."

"Just means he didn't know any better. More fool him, he should have. Hold on—how do you…? Never mind, let's go someplace where it's safe to talk."

Shortly afterwards, Alexander was in the Fire Warlock's study, watching the Fire Guild Council as they crowded around the fireplace, reviewing his confrontation with Prince Gunther. When the images faded, Arturos said, "There's a couple of things I want to know. First, how do you know he wasn't lying?"

Alexander pulled the gold chain from under his shirt, and showed them the be-spelled emerald. "The Earth Mother gave this to Mother when she assumed the regency, saying it would help. Mother passed it on to me when I reached my majority."

Arturos grunted. "Did she now?" Under his breath he added, "Should've said something to me."

Alexander gave him a regal stare. "You disapprove?"

Arturos spread his palms. "Hey, not saying it's a bad idea. I just need to know what's going on, that's all."

"Humph. Is it true you can't leave Frankland?"

"Yep. That's something we want to fix. Even going just a couple miles over the border would make some things easier."

Alexander nodded. "Your second question?"

Arturos tugged at his moustache while eyeing him. "I know you've got a temper. Why weren't you angry?"

Alexander shrugged. "Gunther doesn't matter."

Snorri yelped, "Doesn't matter! That bastard's threatening Frankland and you think he doesn't matter? That's nuts."

Alexander stared him down. "He doesn't matter."

Quicksilver laid a hand on Snorri's shoulder. "Relax. In the sense relevant to the king, he is correct. Which man rules the empire when we reforge the Fire Office will not matter. The empire will attack; there is no question about that. Any emperor who did not pursue the opportunity would not survive the bloodbath following that failure, and all the contestants for the throne understand that, nor would they consider that option. They are all ruthless, ambitious men who do not spare any regret for the lives lost in their wars. Whether he intended it or not, King Brendan's goading Prince Gunther into a rage has done Frankland no harm."

Alexander said, "I didn't really mean to make him angry. He was obviously trying to enrage me, and it wouldn't have been right to give a scoundrel like that—a man who intends to usurp his own brother! That's disgusting!—any power over a rightful king."

"You spoke to him from your authority as king. The magic in the Great Oath shielded your emotions from his taunts, as it would not consider him your social equal."

"He isn't. He may be a superb warlock, but he's deluded about anything else. Er, will it consider him my equal if he becomes emperor?"

"If he does usurp his brother…possibly. Probably. Clearly, if his brother dies of natural causes without issue and he inherits the crown legitimately, then yes, it will consider him your equal."

Alexander gulped. "Oh. Lovely. I'd really rather not have to talk to him again."

Arturos grunted. "You won't have to. The Fire Office is on the alert now. He won't get anywhere near you."

"Thank you." Alexander gave Snorri a sideways glance. "Is there any way to share that shield against taunts?"

Snorri glowered.

Quicksilver sighed, shook his head, and began pacing. "None that I am aware of. It is inherent in the king's authority."

"Ah, well," Alexander said. "Despite their aggressive stance, we are not currently at war with the empire. The Fire Warlock should inform the emperor of Prince Gunther's plans to usurp his brother."

Arturos grunted. "Already did. Got a 'thanks, but mind your own business' in response."

"You did what you could. Thank you."

They watched Quicksilver pace. Into the silence, Mrs Rehsavvy mused, "Whoever is emperor when we reforge the Fire Office will be in a nasty spot. He can't not attack, but he can't win either. If they lose, he won't survive a coup. If they won, they'd still take a lot of damage, and Frankland wouldn't be easy to digest. Their other captive states will grab the opportunity to turn on them. It could be the end of the empire whether they win or lose. Talk about pyrrhic victories."

Alexander's chest tightened as she talked. "If? Tell us you are confident you can repel an invasion."

Snorri's eyes went to the emerald dangling against the king's chest. "Uh…"

Alexander sighed, clutched the emerald, and settled back in the leather armchair. "Now, you must tell us everything."

Alexander listened in silence, his shock deepening, as Quicksilver described the time limits they expected to have for the Fire Office, the lack of Air Guild talent, the proposed restructure that was currently consuming the Guild Council's time, and finally the difficulties they were having in recruiting additional Fire Eaters.

When he finished, Alexander said, "How many air and water and earth wizards are you training? How many mundanes?"

Quicksilver hesitated. Snorri jumped in. "They'll be reporting to the Fire Eaters. We won't start recruiting them until we've sorted out the Fire Guild."

"His Wisdom said you had a dozen Fire Eaters. You can't hope to cover all of Frankland with so few, when they can't jump through the fire."

"Well, yeah, that's a problem, but—"

"There are many people in Frankland that could—that would—help, but they're not fire wizards. That's not a problem. The problem is you're too narrow-minded to consider them."

Snorri spat sparks. "I'm not narrow-minded. I bet we couldn't find a dozen people outside the Fire Eaters who don't go berserk near that aversion spell."

They turned on him, all speaking at once. "Irene, Miranda, and Gillian—"

"Granny Hazel and Master Duncan—"

"Sorceress Lorraine and Sorcerer Charles," Quicksilver said.

"Really?" Mrs Rehsavvy said. "When have they been to our house?"

"They have not. I used the spell elsewhere."

Snorri said, "Fine. I'm off by a few. Still—"

"And we haven't searched outside the Fire Guild," Sven said. "The king is right. The Fire Guild is too stodgy. We're having trouble imagining a war where there's no Fire Warlock. Hopelessly old-fashioned, dull, and stodgy, that's what we are." Snorri glowered.

Alexander said, "What's this about an aversion spell?"

"If you will recall, Your Majesty," Quicksilver said, "my explanation of the protection spells on our house in Blazes included a description of an aversion spell. The terms, grossly over-simplified for a non-technical audience, are that it will repel anyone who, in an emergency, will value their own comfort over Frankland's good health."

Alexander gawked. He had lived for months in the Rehsavvy's house and never noticed. Who else...? Later. He focused on the current problem. "Am I to understand you are using this spell to decide who belongs in the Fire Eaters?"

"Yes. Every Fire Eater passed through this filter. I began recruiting them with this war against the empire in mind soon after I realised we had a capable locksmith."

Mrs Rehsavvy said, "You what? When? You mean before our wedding?"

Quicksilver's eyebrows rose. "Certainly, my dear. Immediately after the end of the siege and my release from the Fire Office."

"Oh. Then that first tournament in Thule..."

"Began their training, yes. The timing was most fortuitous. Does this really surprise you, my dear?"

Arturos was grinning. Snorri smirked. Sven patted her shoulder. She subsided, grumbling.

Alexander turned back to Quicksilver. "What does 'Frankland's good health' mean? The Water Office working? Good roads? Postal system? Enforced contracts? All that other stuff you and Grandfather taught me about civil society?"

"Not in this respect. Soundness of the infrastructure is not as important as love of Frankland and a desire for equitable dealings across all levels of society."

He rubbed his nose and considered this. "That's the root problem. Drop that spell and you'll find enough recruits to cover every corner of Frankland."

They gaped at him. His face heated. "Look at you. Tell me you're not set in your ways."

Snorri sputtered, "What are we supposed to do instead? Ask for volunteers and take whoever comes? That'll work out well. Half of them will be spies for the empire, and the other half will run away screaming the first time a fire wizard throws flame at them."

"We understand, you need a filter of some kind, but the one you're using is too restrictive. If you can create one that sophisticated, then surely you can create one that will sort out the spies and cowards."

"That's exactly what this one does—"

Alexander's voice rose. "Nonsense. His Wisdom said it repelled people who didn't agree with him about Frankland's good health. There are legions of ordinary Franks who don't understand, or wouldn't agree with his ideas about 'good health,' but who love Frankland in their own way. Who would be willing to give their all to protect Frankland." He leaned forward, gesturing. "Who would stand their ground to protect their homes and their families, even if it meant dying to do it. Would you deny them the right to defend their homeland?" He must stop shouting. Shouting was undignified. "It's not fair. Not to them. Not to Frankland."

Arturos grinned. "See, I knew he had a temper."

He glared. "Gunther doesn't matter. This does matter. 'Good health,' you say. Losing Frankland to the empire would not be 'good health.'"

Quicksilver had listened to this tirade with his head bowed, wearing a pained expression. "That is certainly true, Your Majesty, as is everything else you have said. Thank you for taking us to task. I will ask the Earth Mother's advice in creating a different aversion spell, one based on an individual's willingness to face pain and death in defence of home and family."

Alexander's anger dissipated. "Thank you. The aversion spell you're using may still be useful for selecting the core officers, if you open the Fire Eaters to members from the other magic guilds."

Snorri snarled, "Drown me if I'll turn command over to a gaggle of cold fish and mud brains."

Alexander slammed his fist on the chair arm and shouted, "You will not talk about our people that way."

"I'll talk about them however they deserve."

He and Snorri were on their feet, nose to nose. Arturos grabbed Snorri by the shoulders and shoved him onto the sofa. The wooden framework cracked.

"Sit down and shut up," Arturos roared, "before I throw your sorry arse in the North Sea."

Quicksilver, his face like stone, stepped between Alexander and Snorri. "They deserve our respect. Demeaning any of Frankland's true sons and daughters, even from the lowest ranks of mundanes, tarnishes the Fire Guild."

Arturos said, "We've never needed to call on the other guilds for help with defence, Your Majesty. Sometimes it takes a while for a new idea to percolate through our own muddy brains. I won't make any promises, other than that we'll talk it over after we've had time to calm down."

Alexander forced his fists open. "We will expect a report when you have done so."

Snorri said, "Are we done here? I'm ready for my second breakfast." He dove into the fire and vanished.

Sven said, "What's the matter with him? He's not usually that much of an ass."

Arturos rolled his eyes. "Gunther's needling got to him. I threw up a barrier so they can't get to each other, but he can't seem to let it go, and he won't talk to anybody about it, not even Lucinda." He ducked into the fireplace. "I hadn't finished my first breakfast. See you later."

Sven was next, offering to escort Alexander back to the palace.

His chin rose. "Thank you, but no. We will speak to Warlock Quicksilver alone."

Beorn and Lucinda Contemplate Jean

Lucinda hesitated on the hearth in the Fire Warlock's study, reluctant to leave Jean alone with the king after his use of the royal *we*.

Jean said, "May my wife stay, Your Majesty? With our bond, it is difficult to keep anything from her."

Alexander nodded without taking his eyes off Jean. "We don't mind if you stay, Mrs Rehsavvy."

"Thank you," she said.

Jean pulled an armchair around to face the king, and sat leaning forward with his forearms on his knees. Alexander pulled his own chair closer, until they were almost knee to knee.

Jean looked down at his hands. "If you intend to berate me for being stodgy and set in my ways, let me save you the trouble. Lucinda and several others have already done so, and it is quite true. I do not like being reminded of my shortcomings—no one does—but the reminders are necessary." He looked up, meeting Alexander's gaze. "Your suggestions are helpful. We should have consulted with you earlier."

"Thank you," Alexander said. "We trust you will keep us better informed in the future."

"Yes, Your Majesty."

"But that wasn't why we asked to speak to you alone."

"Oh?"

"Warlock Sturmmeister wasn't just trying to rile us. He was trying to sow discord between the Fire Guild and us. We don't want his insinuations to poison our relationship."

Jean's expression was bleak. "Indeed."

"You remember, you have promised to tell us what we need to know,

Your Wisdom." Alexander clutched his emerald. "Tell us your plans for the monarchy after the Fire Office's reforging."

Jean, equally serious, straightened. Watching them, Lucinda was struck, once again, by the similarities between the old man and the young one. They might have been father and son, although the younger man was a head taller, with an athlete's physique instead of the underpaid, undernourished scholar Jean presented as, an impression reinforced by the fraying scholar's robe she had been unable to persuade him to relinquish.

"That is a fair question, Your Majesty," Jean said. "Prince Gunther's statements about usurpation are nonsense. Neither I, nor Warlock Snorri, nor anyone currently on the Fire Guild Council, is under the delusion we have the talents or temperament to rule. Nor would we usurp a king who has taken the Great Oath—a king the people love. That way lies madness and self-destruction. Neither the people nor the other officeholders would stand for it."

A faint smile played on the king's lips, but neither his posture nor his grip on the emerald relaxed. "Thank you for that reassurance, but we never thought we were in danger. That wasn't what we meant."

"Oh?"

"We and you and Warlock Snorri are players in the short term. Our question is about the long term. When we are gone, will the new Fire Office destroy the monarchy?"

"Where does the greatest threat to the monarchy come from?"

Alexander frowned. "Our father believed it came from the Fire Office."

"Your father was…mistaken. As long as you and your descendants are fair and just, the new Fire Office will continue to support them. That, I admit, was not what I intended years ago when reforging first became a possibility and not just a pipe dream, but events and others whose judgement I trust, including Sorceress Lorraine and the Company of Mages, have convinced me continuity is necessary. It is, however, my intention to make the Fire Office more responsive to change. If the monarchy collapses, the Fire Office will support another method of choosing the ruler."

"What other method? Why would the monarchy collapse if the Fire Office supports it?"

"I told you the conditions for the Fire Office's continued support."

"You said…Oh… You think our grandson or great-grandson will forget the lessons we have learned and will refuse to take the Great Oath."

"Not as soon as that, no. Failure to remember may not come for centuries, but it will come. History says such failures are inevitable. Wise men and women are far fewer than the weak, the cowardly, the greedy, and the foolish. All dynasties eventually fail. They all either wither or rot."

"That's what you meant. The greatest threat to the monarchy comes from within."

"Yes."

"I see." Alexander was silent, his hands resting on the chair arms, the emerald forgotten. After a bit, he said, "What's fair? It isn't fair to leave Frankland without rules for clear and orderly successions. That leads to civil war. If the monarchy does fail, how will the Fire Office choose the next ruler?"

"The Fire Office will not choose."

Alexander's eyes widened. "But…"

"Much experimentation is taking place elsewhere in the world, my young friend. I do not believe we can now foresee what the best method for choosing a ruler will be, nor should it be the Fire Guild's decree. The other officeholders must be involved, as well as the best and wisest men and women of their time. Our intention is that the Fire Office shall support any method that is decent and orderly, as long as the officeholders agree and the ruler so chosen takes the Great Oath. That will be a requirement henceforth for any ruler to assume command."

Alexander's pinched expression relaxed. "Yes, we agree." He was thoughtful for a few moments longer, then gave a decisive nod. "Yes, that will be fair. We can support that."

The tension in Jean's shoulders eased. "Thank you."

"You asked Father's permission to reforge the Water Office, and Mother's permission to reforge the Earth Office, but you haven't asked for approval to reforge the Fire Office."

"True. I had not asked the Queen Regent because I thought it best to wait until you were of age and firmly in control."

"And now, after Mother Celeste's death, you're afraid we won't give it."

"Perhaps. Emotions—yours, mine, the whole country's—have been raw. I thought it best to wait for some time to heal the wounds."

"And to give the Great Oath more time work on me." Alexander smiled. "Don't look so surprised. We know what it's doing. We feel it pushing us. We don't mind. It pushes us in directions we approve of, but we do have some idea what living with the Fire Office must be like. We've been thinking over the reasons you've given us for rebuilding the Fire Office, and thought they were sufficient, but we had assumed Frankland would win the war. Now…"

He pulled the gold chain over his head and turned the emerald over and over in his hands. "I…we…we think you haven't told us all your reasons for reforging the Fire Office." He gave Jean a penetrating stare. "We think you have kept some secrets from us."

Jean's face was a blank mask. "Secrets, Your Majesty?"

Alexander's mouth was a thin line. "Secrets, Your Wisdom." He turned his intense stare on Lucinda. "Mrs Rehsavvy, what would happen to my sister if we pursued my father's plans to marry her to Prince Sigismund? We order you, tell us."

She opened her mouth. Her jaw and tongue worked, but nothing came out, not even a protest. Jean seemed frozen.

Sweat rolled down her nose. Her stomach threatened to heave itself up her throat. She saw double then triple. Flames danced in her peripheral vision.

Jean, help!

Jean barked, "Rescind that order," but the king was already shouting, "Stop! Keep your secrets."

She slumped against the sofa back with her hand over her mouth, fighting down nausea. Jean dabbed her face with a handkerchief. The room spun. Beorn and René swam into view. Beorn shouldered Jean and Alexander aside and shoved a cup of Earth Guild restorative under her nose.

She rocked forward, grabbed, gulped, and poured half of it over her chin or up her nose.

"Whoa, whoa, easy now." Beorn wrapped his hand around the back of her head and held her still while René dribbled the potion into her mouth.

The world steadied; the multiple images coalesced into Jean and René on her left, horror in their eyes. On her right, the prematurely serious and self-confidant monarch had dissolved into a frightened teenager. Straight ahead and inches away, Beorn scowled. He let go and straightened. "Still queasy?"

"Yes. No. I don't know."

"Let's hope it'll do." He turned the empty bottle upside down over the cup. Two drops fell. "Hadn't gotten around to brewing a new batch."

She wiped up the mess. "If I need any more I'll suck on the handkerchief."

"Ugh."

Alexander said, "Mrs Rehsavvy, we're very sorry. We don't like making people suffer."

She waved the limp cloth at him. "I'll be fine."

Jean sank onto the sofa beside her, and put his face down in his hands. "You will be. I am unsure I will. Let me advise you, young man, not to send Princess Sophie to the empire."

"Don't be ridiculous." Alexander glared, affronted. "I like my sister. I wouldn't send even Lady Susan into that nest of vipers."

Beorn snarled, "Then why'd you ask such a damn-fool question? And why'd you pick on her and not him?"

Alexander stammered, "I...I'm sorry. I didn't know what would happen. I thought he'd had a lot more practice at bluffing and evading than she had, and would wriggle out of answering."

"It is true," Jean said, "that I am more experienced, but I am no longer Fire Warlock, and you have far more power available to you than your father had. Given such an order, I do not know that even I..."

"Hmmm, well, let's not find out. Father was right about one thing at least." Alexander looped the chain over his head and tucked the emerald under his shirt. "The Fire Office does keep secrets from the king."

Beorn crossed his arms and glowered, breathing heavily. His mouth worked without sound. His face reddened until it was the same shade as his hair. Alexander's alarmed glance at Jean was met with a stony stare.

"No," Beorn snarled, "the Fire Office would never do that." The tension drained away. He put his head in his hands and mumbled curses.

"No, of course not." Alexander's expression was as stony as Jean's. "We hereby give you permission to reforge the Fire Office."

Jean breathed a long sigh, followed by a heartfelt, "Thank you, Your Majesty."

"More than that, we command you—"

"Watch it!" René waved the empty bottle. "Be careful what you say."

Alexander frowned. "Yes, but...that's exactly the point. We don't want that happening again."

Jean said, "I have pondered this problem for many years. With your approval, I will write wording for an order I trust will resolve the issue. Before issuing the order, you may discuss it with others whose judgement you value: Enchanter Paul, Mistress Irene, Father Jerome, your mother…"

Alexander's expression lightened. "Yes, do that. Thank you."

While Jean went to the Fire Warlock's desk for pen and paper, Beorn said, "I've got to give you a warning."

Alexander looked wary. "What warning?"

"I liked the way you handled Gunther. I've got folk like you and them"—he waved at René—"to cut me down to size when my head gets too big, but our pal Gunther doesn't get it nearly often enough. So when somebody does…" Beorn jerked a thumb at Jean. "He said you didn't do Frankland any harm, and he's right. But that youngster, Brendan Alexander, now, that's a different matter. If Gunther's in power and if we lose—two big if's there—Gunther's 'amusement' and, er, 'kindness' could make you wish he'd just killed you and been done with it."

Alexander had turned chalk white. His eyes swept the four warlocks. "We gave our permission, and we won't withdraw it. We believe reforging the Fire Office is necessary for Frankland's 'good health.' But when you do…" He flashed a momentary smile. "We command you, do not let Frankland fall."

On a bright morning in late June, Lucinda stood in the shadows in the practice room, watching three wizards and one witch engage in an energetic argument around the iron table.

Jean and René were occupied, as they had been for nearly three months, in making Sven and Irene sweat, defending the new spell structure as they picked it apart. Jean had convinced himself within a fortnight that Irene and Sven's spellcraft was sound, and that the Air Guild spells could be isolated, cast ahead of time, and moved. It had taken him two months to reach the shocking conclusion that restructuring the Fire Office was not only feasible, but prudent.

That conclusion was an intellectual one. For decades his had been the strongest voice in Frankland advocating change, but he too was infected with the idea that because nothing ever changed in Frankland, nothing ever would change, and he had reached the limit of change his emotions could tolerate. Lucinda was heartily sick of sharing his dreams. She had banned soufflés from their house, lest a collapse be taken as a bad omen.

René, the little beast, enjoyed the exercise of imagining all the possible ways the reforging could fail. Jean didn't. His headache hammered at her own skull.

Beorn loomed over her shoulder. "What are they arguing about now?"

"The sturdiness of the Air Guild spells."

"Should've known. They keep coming back to that one. When do you think Jean will be ready to present it to the full coven?"

"Not soon. Intellectually, he agrees with Sven and Irene, but the emotional hurdle... The sheer amount of change terrifies him."

"Scares me, too, to be honest. René's the only one it doesn't seem to bother."

"He's too cocky to know when to be scared."

"Uh-huh. It'll make the other officeholders nervous, too."

"Especially those most resistant to change of any sort."

"Uh-huh."

"Speaking of Paul, when will you tell him the Fire Office reforging will be underground?"

"Uh..."

"Come on, Beorn. We've been talking about this for years now. Putting off a nasty problem doesn't make it any easier to deal with."

"Yeah, I know, but it never seems like a good time."

"Chicken."

"You could tell him."

"Gee, thanks."

"Look, Lucinda, you remember Duncan's trial, when I lost my temper and got into a pissing contest with Lorraine? I don't want to do that again, ever. I've been working real hard at keeping my temper around the king and the other officeholders, but Paul rubs me raw."

"He does that to all of us. I take back calling you chicken... The new spell structure does have one big argument in its favour, from his point of view. He can do all the hard work on the Air Guild spells beforehand, and only have to be here in the practice room for the unlocking and moving the spells. Neither of those will take long. He can be in and out again without too much fuss."

"Won't help that much. Moving the spells comes late in the rebuild, and once the empire attacks, the Fortress will shut tight. Won't let anybody in or out. He'll have to stay in the Fortress, inside the closed shutters, for the duration."

"Oh. You're right. He won't like that either. Drown it."

At the iron table, Sven snapped out an answer before René had completed his question. When the guild council had first dug into the proposed structure, Sven and Irene had been nervous: Sven blushed and drummed on the table, Irene hyperventilated or didn't breathe at all. Now they exhibited no trace of nerves.

Beorn rumbled, "Not soon, you say... He's not looking too good."

Lucinda's automatic protest died on her lips. She had noticed the dark circles developing under his eyes, and the salt-and-pepper hair, gone silver at the temples. His hair had been dark brown, once. The crow's feet around his eyes were evident even from a distance, and other lines in his face had not been there when she first saw him, nine years ago.

Beorn said, "We won't have long between René throwing the lightning on his own and Jean..."

Lucinda's throat tightened. "And Jean losing the ability to handle the reforging. A couple of years at most."

Beorn squeezed her shoulder. "Sorry, Lucinda."

She grimaced. "I'm a warlock. I have to face facts. And one fact is we've been fools to think we can convince the empire the Air Office will be next. The empire's wizards can see the effects of accelerated ageing on him. They aren't idiots."

Beorn blew out through his moustache. "Yeah."

"Time to light a few fires."

"Starting with...?"

For answer, Lucinda marched across the room and interrupted Sven in the middle of a lecture on the influence of fire elements in air spells. "Sven, this isn't working."

Sven blinked at her. "What?"

"When we discussed presenting this proposal, months ago, I agreed with you that the rest of the coven would treat it with more respect if it came from the senior Flame Mage, but it won't work. He can't do it."

Jean said, "My dear—"

She stopped him with a hand on his shoulder. "He's losing sleep worrying about it. He can't argue for it with the enthusiasm it needs. His head likes it, but his heart clings to the old, safe structure he's known for a hundred and fifty years. Sven, you have to present it."

Both men's colour had risen. Jean stared at the papers spread out before him with his jaw clenched and his lips tight. Sven glanced at him, then met Lucinda's eyes and nodded.

Beorn said, "How soon can you be ready?"

"Gather the coven," Sven said. "We're ready."

Gillian Confounds René

Lucinda surveyed the men and women gathered in the Earth Mother's amber chamber. With a solid night's sleep behind him, Jean looked better than he had in weeks. Alert and smiling, he nodded as Sven began his presentation. Enchanter Paul's sour expression deepened the longer Sven talked.

Why was Paul always so inflexible? She had asked Jean, but he couldn't explain the enchanter's obstinacy. He, at one hundred fifty-six, nearly twice Paul's age, was more open to new ideas. If people became more set in their ways as they aged, it should have been the other way around. The Air Guild in general was reputed to be indecisive and easily led. Were there earth and fire spells built into the Air Office to counter those tendencies? If so, the Great Coven had overdone them, and the spells had still not protected Paul from Enchantress Winifred's manipulation.

She would love to see just what had gone into the Air Office, but five years after Sorceress Lorraine had given Paul his marching orders, he had not produced a catalogue of spells. Had he done any analysis at all? How could she set his tail on fire if he hadn't listened to Lorraine?

Sven's presentation touched on and rebutted all the objections the warlocks had raised. Their relentless scrutiny had given his and Irene's arguments the force of a hardened steel blade. He finished the first part of the presentation and invited questions. In the discussion that followed, the mood coalesced around cautious optimism, with Mother Astrid and Sorceress Eleanor wholeheartedly endorsing testing the structural changes in the Earth Office. The Fire Guild had not been the only ones worried.

Paul was the only dissenter.

Then Sven described the proposal's second part: to isolate and build the Air Guild spells beforehand, and use them for defence until needed in the reforging. Paul's reaction was, "Impossible."

Sven said. "Why? Moving enchantments from one object to another is straightforward. The scale of the task is unusual, but not infeasible."

Paul flicked a hand. "I didn't mean that. You're right; we could do that. And you're right, too, that we could isolate those spells from the others, although I can never condone basing Frankland's defences on something untried and untestable when we already have a structure we know works. What I meant was that we can't enchant an object with that large a body of Air Guild spells."

René said, "That's not nearly as many spells as are bound to the Fire Warlock's ring."

"That's not the point. The Air Office won't allow enchanting another object."

"Why not?"

"Why not? Because it would be too dangerous, that's why not. Those spells are the Fire Warlock's eyes, ears, and voice. Imagine what would happen if such an enchanted object fell into the wrong hands. A spy with those powers could learn all of Frankland's secrets. Not enough to destroy the offices, but enough to wreak havoc. They could undermine our alliances, destroy our trade, assassinate the royal family…" Paul shook his head. "I'm not nasty-minded enough to imagine all the consequences. The Fire Guild would know those better than I." He shot a baleful look at Jean. "I'm surprised you haven't crushed this nonsense, Your Wisdom. You at least should have thought this through."

Lucinda steamed. They had considered it from all angles. The dangers had given everyone of the Fire Guild Council, even René, sleepless nights.

Jean was expressionless. "I am confidant Master Sven and Mistress Irene have provided a complete analysis."

Sven's cheeks and neck were tinged red, but his voice was calm and even. "We do understand the dangers such an object represents. Precautions would be taken to destroy it from afar if it was stolen, or if the spells could not be moved in the reforging. It would have to be guarded most carefully until then."

"Guarded most carefully." Paul snorted. "It's better to avoid the potential for problems altogether. That's why the Air Office won't allow it."

Eleanor said, "Is that stricture against the use of these enchantments common knowledge among the Air Guild? Or did you discover that during your analysis of the spells in the Air Office?"

"It's not common knowledge, no. I discovered it about halfway through the analysis."

"You're more than halfway done then. Excellent. Sorceress Lorraine and I have been speculating on your progress. When may the Coven expect to see transcripts of those spells?"

"Not for several years yet, madam. I have little time for it."

"Make time, Paul. Now, as to the Fire Guild's suggestion, despite the obvious danger in binding the spells to a ring, the idea has merit, not least because it will give the defenders an advantage during the reforging. Can you suggest an alternative that the Air Office would support?"

"No, madam, I cannot."

Without lifting his eyes from his sketching, René said, "How about this? Spells can be bound to anything, not just inanimate objects. If the spells were bound to a specific person, even if he were captured the empire couldn't use them, and they would dissolve when he died."

Paul frowned. "A person? What person?"

René laid down his pen and faced Paul. "The Fire Warlock's apprentice. Me, that is, when the time comes. I'll use the spells when I'm Fire Warlock, so what's the difference? We wouldn't have to move the spells at all. The Coven would just bind the core fire and earth spells to the Token of Office to start with. After we defeat the Empire, we would add the air spells. Call it tier one-and-a-half. We wouldn't have to hurry."

Paul flapped a hand. "That idea is…"

"Rather clever." Sorcerer Charles smiled. "Sometimes young eyes can find solutions their elders are too conventional to see."

Jean's expression was quite bland. "True. As an old man I sometimes must stop myself from rejecting my young friends' opinions out of hand, but the exercise is always worthwhile."

Beorn's moustache twitched. Lucinda hid a smile behind her hand.

Paul glowered. "The exercise would be worthwhile only if the idea actually worked, and this one won't. If the Air Office does permit the spells to be bound to a living being, and I'll have to investigate to see if it is possible, that being will have to be an authorised individual. I am quite sure the key term here is 'authorised.' The Fire Warlock's apprentice might or might not be authorised, but once the Fire Office is torn down, that authorisation would cease to exist. The spells would collapse."

René deflated. He mumbled something that might have been a curse. Faces that had been wearing smiles turned sombre.

Mother Astrid said, "Perhaps another authorised individual? I understand why the Fire Guild wants these spells available during the reforging. Could someone else use them and feed Snorri information?"

Paul snorted. "Who, madam? Few individuals would be qualified, and they will be busy spellcasting. Nor do I think anyone from the Earth Guild could use them."

"No, probably not," she admitted.

Jean frowned. "To be useful during battle, the connection between the two would have to be very close. Nothing short of a bond would work, I expect."

Paul said, "The Water Guild could use them, and there are few water spells in your tier one."

René went rigid. Sorceress Eleanor blanched.

Lucinda sucked in her breath. The suggestion was almost obscene. Or was it? Some members of the Fire Guild did have the ballast of cold water in their souls. Paul's chuckle interrupted her train of thought.

He said, "Now there's an idea even an old man can appreciate."

René shot upright, shouting. "Think that's funny, do you? You ought to help figure out how to make this work, if you don't want me laughing at you when you're twitching underground."

Jean's sharp command, "René, be quiet and compose yourself," crossed Paul's snarled, "Underground? What is this nonsense?"

René fell back into his chair and gave Jean a dark look. Beorn rolled his eyes at the ceiling and cursed.

Jean said, "My young friend has a valid argument. A movable corpus of air spells is to your benefit as much as ours. We can guarantee the coven's safety during the reforging only in the Fortress's isolated practice chamber, deep underground."

For a moment, Paul stared at Jean with a slack jaw, then he barked, "Safety?" The cords stood out on his neck. "Safety, in that torture chamber? This entire endeavour is risky from start to finish. There is nothing safe about it, and I refuse to have anything more to do with it." He strode out, slamming the door behind him hard enough to shake the walls.

René beat his fists together and glowered at the iron table, pointedly ignoring the other dispirited men and women trickling into the practice room. None of them looked at him. They stared at the wall, the table, the illusory clouds, anywhere but at him. Gillian, fanning herself by the vent, watched with questions in her eyes. He ignored her, too. She didn't bother him. The others, however...

He had known for years that reforging the Fire Office would be costly, but he had never imagined it might turn him into a murderer. Or—he had to be honest—a murder victim. A fight with an officeholder for dominance wasn't one he should win, even if he could.

"Your idea was brilliant, René." Sven gazed at the wall a foot over René's head. "It's a shame Enchanter Paul said it wouldn't fly."

René clenched his hands together. "He didn't say it was impossible. It would just be...difficult."

They did look at him then, in varying degrees of sympathy, consternation, and annoyance. Beorn said, "You think we'd let you bond with a sorceress? Don't be an ass."

"It is out of the question," Quicksilver said. "For her sake as well as yours. We need you both. Enchanter Paul's suggestion is unbecoming of an officeholder."

René slumped into the chair, letting his hands dangle, fingers loose. "I thought..."

Beorn cuffed him. "Dimwit."

René grinned at him, but Beorn had gone back to staring at the clouds and pulling on his beard. "We've been working on this thing for five years, and we're still stuck on those frost...sorry, damned Air Guild spells. God, I wish somebody would think of something that could work."

A hand on René's elbow startled him into banging his knee on the table leg. He rubbed it and glared at Gillian. "Don't sneak up on me like that."

"You knew I was here."

"I forgot."

She gave him the disgusted look she always wore when he acted like an airhead. "What's your idea?"

He explained. She said, "What's so bad about a bond with the Water Sorceress?"

Quicksilver answered. "A bond strong enough to permit the level of communication useful during battle will not work between two strong talents from opposing guilds. Their talents would continually vie for control, irrespective of their conscious attempts at suppression. His magic would burn her, or hers would drown him, whichever proved stronger."

"Oh." She chewed her lip. "The only thing Enchanter Paul said was wrong with it was that Snorri's not authorised?"

"Yes."

"Then bind them to Alex."

René gaped at her, then turned to Quicksilver. The old warlock looked flummoxed, too, but Beorn had opened his eyes and stopped tugging his beard. The others at the table brightened.

Lucinda said, "He does have an affinity for the Fire Guild."

René scowled at her. "He's a mundane."

Gillian said, "Mama said the Air Guild spells would work even for a Fire Warlock who didn't have any air magic at all. How's that different?"

"That's true," Irene said. "Their structure would allow even a true mundane to use them, given the proper authorisation and sufficient training."

René slid down in his seat, grappling with the absurdity of a future where the Fire Warlock and the king were closer than brothers. They hadn't always been enemies, but not even Charles Magnus and Warlock Fortunatus had been close.

René had walked the Fire Guild's challenge path in search of family, though he hadn't known then what he wanted, and would have been too embarrassed to voice such a wish. Warlock Quicksilver had seen through him, and had helped him piece together an adopted family, better than the ones most people were born into. He had a wife, sister, surrogate father, grandfather, even a wise old uncle, but he didn't have a brother.

He had hoped to find a kindred spirit in the Fire Eaters, but he was their captain, and they never let him forget they took orders from him. Nor had they forgiven him for making them include women, and their lives were not tied, day in and day out, to the Fire Office. They went on holidays and forgot, for a while, the challenges Frankland faced. He never could.

Neither could Alex. René grimaced. The revelation that he had more in common with a frostbitten royal than with an ordinary fire wizard rattled him.

Beorn nudged him. "Pay attention."

He snarled, "What?"

"I was saying I like the idea. We know you can handle a bond, and it would do the royals good to understand better the threats the Fire Office deals with. See what we actually do for Frankland."

"The suggestion has merit." Quicksilver's scowl belied his stated opinion. "But this has no precedence in Frankland's history, and I cannot say I am comfortable with the idea."

Beorn clapped him on the back. "Get used to it, old man. You'll have to look a lot happier about it when we talk to Paul."

"You are assuming he will recover from his fit of temper and be willing to revisit the subject."

Sven said, "We should approach the king first. There's no point in raising the question with the Air Enchanter if the king rejects it."

René steamed. "He will."

Beorn said, "No, he won't."

"It may not be diplomatic, either," Irene said, "to present this as the Fire Guild's idea."

"It's not," Beorn said. "It's Gillian's."

Gillian said, "Enchanter Paul never listened to Mama and he never listens to me, either."

"The Water Guild, then." Beorn reached around René and ruffled Gillian's hair. "Sorry, kid."

She shrugged. "Not your fault."

Sven said, "If the senior Water Mage presents it and the Company of Mages backs it, Paul will be less likely to disparage it, or drag his feet."

Beorn said, "You want to talk to Charles?"

Sven rose. "Happy to."

Lucinda followed him. "I'll go with you, Sven, and run it by Eleanor."

Beorn rose, too. "The mages are going to ask how those spells work for a mundane. Irene, you'd better write something up."

"Yes, sir."

René said, "But…"

Beorn clapped him on the shoulder. "I haven't forgotten you and Hildur are heading off to Thule. I'll talk to the king. Relax. Enjoy your holiday."

The practice room emptied, except for René and Quicksilver. They exchanged dismayed stares.

"I thought I was the troublemaker here," René said. "Why do I feel like a juggernaut rolled over me?"

Family Ties

When Alexander emerged from the tunnels the next morning, The Fire Warlock greeted him with "Court life getting to you already?"

"I don't know why you would think that."

"You always look cheerful coming here."

"Oh. Yes, the constant jockeying for position, particularly among the women, does bore me, although I can't fault them for it." Alexander settled into an armchair by a window in the Fire Warlock's study. He hoped he would never get so jaded he would fail to enjoy the view. "With Frankland's noblemen decimated in the Yule War, many noblewomen are destined for a life of involuntary spinsterhood."

"And Frankland's most sought-after young bachelor having an eye on a girl that's not one of them ruffles their feathers. There'll be hard feelings if you marry a witch."

"Any choice I make will leave hard feelings. I might as well marry someone I have an attachment to."

"If you can convince her. A free songbird won't like a gilded cage."

Alexander frowned. "We doubt you asked us here to discuss Miss van Gelder, Your Wisdom."

The Fire Warlock chuckled. "No, but I do enjoy poking you. You're one of the few who'll tell me to mind my own business and expect me to do it."

"Hope, yes. Expect, no. We are still waiting to hear today's problem."

"Maybe a solution for once, and a way for you to help with the Fire Office reforging, instead of a new problem." The Fire Warlock described the proposed spell structure, the previous day's meeting, and Gillian's suggestion.

As soon as he caught the gist of the proposal, Alexander's head spun, thoughts scattering in a dozen directions. What he could do with that...

The Fire Warlock was stroking his moustache, waiting for him to respond. Alexander refocused with an effort. "Can this really work? A mundane can, in effect, become an air wizard?"

"That's what Sven and Irene say, and they know this stuff inside and out. The biggest question is whether the Air Office considers you authorised."

His fingers tightened on the chair arms. "Of course we are."

The Fire Warlock held up a hand. "Not saying you aren't. I'm saying there's lots about the Air Office nobody knows, not even Paul, and we all know the Great Coven made mistakes."

Alexander doubted the Great Coven could have been that incompetent, but... "We understand." He consciously relaxed his grip. "This is astonishing news. Our role as king will be easier if we, too, can identify threats to Frankland. If we can see which courtiers are working against us..."

"Sure you want that?"

"Pardon?"

"The Fire Office focuses on external threats. It doesn't poke its nose into conversations between nobles unless there's good reason. If you start listening too close to your courtiers, you'll hear them say unflattering things about you—things they may not even mean when they're trying to flatter or get a rise out of somebody else."

"Oh."

"Spies and eavesdroppers are distrustful by nature, and distrustful people don't tend to have close friends."

"We are a king. Kings—and, we imagine, Fire Warlocks—tend not to have many close friends either."

The Fire Warlock shrugged. "Comes with the job. I can't argue those spells wouldn't be useful, as long as you remember they have drawbacks and how to work with them. You wouldn't get to use them for long anyway. You'd have to give them up when we reforge the Fire Office."

"Oh."

"That's the point. They're the Fire Office's eyes and ears. The Fire Warlock would be blind without them."

"Yes, of course." He chewed his lip. "If the Air Guild did it once, they could do it again. After the Fire Office is reforged, they could rebuild the body of spells on us for our use."

The Fire Warlock tugged at his beard. "Ummm...."

"But this is Frankland, and nothing ever changes in Frankland. We are tired of hearing that."

"Uh-huh. Did you hear what I said about Snorri?"

"Snorri? We confess our mind wandered."

"Moving the Air Guild spells to the Fire Office would come pretty late in the reforging. It would give Snorri a big leg up over the emperor if you could feed him information while the fight's on about where their wizards are and what they're up to."

"Yes, we see."

"But you'd have to have a bond with Snorri."

"A bond. Like a brother?" Alexander heard the dismay in his voice. He recoiled under the Fire Warlock's knowing stare.

"Closer than," the Fire Warlock said. "You'd be in each other's heads a lot. Snorri can tell you more about that than I can—he already has bonds with the Locksmith and Quicksilver."

"Why isn't he here discussing it?"

"He and Staðfastur just left for a holiday in Thule. She's homesick."

Alexander frowned at the Fire Warlock. After an uncomfortable interval the Fire Warlock added, "And he's having some trouble getting used to the idea, too. Bonding with another warlock—even one that's a girl—didn't bother him as much as the idea of bonding with you."

Alexander's lips thinned. "Because we are mundane."

"Partly." The Fire Warlock combed through his beard with his fingers. "Besides that, he's been conditioned to dislike the upper crust on principle, and there's your blue blood attitude towards class and lineage—or lack thereof. Gunther takes pokes at him over it, and it upsets him. Anything that stirs up a strong emotional reaction will bleed across a bond. You'll have to be honest with each other about your feelings and willing to change, or you'll end up tearing each other's throat out."

"Why are you suggesting it if you are also advising against it?"

"I'm not. If you two can get past your knee-jerk reactions, a bond might be a good thing."

"Why?"

"Looking over your shoulder, so to speak, while you're learning how to use the spells will help him later. They take some getting used to, even for a wizard. But more important… A bond will help both of you temper your views on class, and you'll understand each other better. Warlocks and kings have been at odds for far too long."

Alexander said, "So long that any attempt to reduce that friction seems like a good idea."

"Thought you'd see the wisdom of that."

But a bond with Snorri? His father would have called Snorri common—as common as dirt. Merely thinking that phrase sent a pulse of pain through his skull. Nausea surged.

Sometimes he wished he'd never taken that frostbitten oath.

He pressed his fingers to his temples and reflected on the quiet dignity his kennel master possessed and on the innate intelligence that must be scattered throughout the labouring classes to produce at random an individual like Snorri. His headache and nausea subsided.

He said, "Yes, Your Wisdom. We do see merit in this proposal. Does Snorri?"

René's mood was as black as the lava-laden sand beneath his feet. He had jumped to this remote beach—so remote there were no rats within miles, or so he'd heard—to work off some of his fury, but blasting boulders had brought him no relief.

Since it wasn't a tournament year, Hildur and he had come to Thule by themselves, to celebrate Midsummer with her old friends. He'd been looking forward to it. His affection for the old warlock, Mjöllnir, increased on every visit. But Mjöllnir hadn't been first in line to greet them when they arrived. That had been his mother-in-law, a low-ranking air witch.

He hadn't been eager to see her. He was still angry with Enchanter Paul, and by extension the whole Air Guild, over the previous day's confrontation. He yearned for the easy, if rather volatile, camaraderie of fire wizards, not the tense atmosphere around easily offended airheads.

Hildur's mother met her with open arms and motherly warmth. He had gotten singed.

"How dare you show your face here, after stealing my girl away. You're no member of *my* family. Never will be."

Naturally, he'd lost his temper. He'd shouted. Hildur had shouted. The mother, a dozen aunties, and assorted cousins had shouted.

Mjöllnir had stepped in, shouted them all down, chewed out his daughter-in-law, professed he was proud to call Snorri his grandson, and sent them all away in different directions to cool down.

René wasn't sure he ever would. He stripped off his shoes and socks to walk across the sand and meet the incoming tide, but the line of steaming footprints in his wake failed to amuse him. A rope of seaweed reduced to ashes in his hand. He hurled it over the waves.

"Poor, miserable creature. Can't even throw a proper tantrum."

René spun. There was no one in sight. He had already checked; there was no other human within miles. "Who the hell are you?"

The light, unaccented voice floated on the breeze from offshore. "You can hear me and reply, too? How utterly delightful. Warlock Sturmmeister was right. You are one of us."

"I am not an airhead."

"Tsk, tsk, name calling is so undiplomatic, but I will excuse your bad manners. I can expect little else from someone exposed to the Fire Guild for so long. Otherwise... I have been watching you, you know. If you can control that temper, your Air Guild might be convinced to let you in."

René searched the horizon. The Thule Fire Guild would never let a foreign enchanter set foot here. The voice must be coming from a ship.

"After all, where else will you go? Your uncouth behaviour has made enemies for you in Frankland's other guilds, and once your Fire Eaters reject you—"

René froze.

"Not a happy idea, is it? I'm so sorry. But you should have thought of that before you wasted so much time on air and water magic. Do your Fire Eaters know you never did a single paper on fire magic at university? What will they say when they learn?"

René snarled, "They'll say I'm following Warlock Quicksilver's good example. He's written about magic from all four guilds."

"Ah, but he was desperate to be recognized as a mage, and you aren't. Or if you are, the signs have escaped me. Warlock Quicksilver's broad interests earned him no love in the Fire Guild. Why do you think your Guild Council hated him so much?"

René stood motionless, gazing out to sea, with his hands hanging slack by his sides.

"Come, come, you're usually faster with a retort than this. You are having a bad day, aren't you? Didn't you realise your Fire Guild Council has always been filled with men who are pure fire? Men like Warlock Sturmmeister. Men who resented Quicksilver's unnatural domination of their guild, and he only demonstrated talent for one other guild. How much more will they hate you when they realise you have affinities for two other guilds, one your old enemy the Water Guild, and both so much weaker than the Fire Guild?

"It's a pity, knowing your wife will abandon you, and your Fire Eaters will turn on you. That's not just my opinion; that's fact. A seer in Frankfurt had a vision of your most trusted friends flaming you when your reserves are so exhausted you can't even hold a shield. Shocking. Such a sad betrayal. Just warning you.

"Well, I must be going. Ta-ta. It's been a pleasure."

René located the ship, leagues out to sea. He clenched his fists. He could easily jump that far, fire the ship, and sink the bloody air wizard.

That would be an act of war. His hot temper turned icy cold. A war now would likely leave Beorn dead. He wasn't ready for that. Not now. Not ever.

Lucinda Asks a Favour

After the Yule War, Lorraine had abandoned the Crystal Palace, and moved into a cottage in the Outer Hebrides. She took little part now in the magic guilds' day-to-day business. Jean and Lucinda corresponded with her regularly, but did not see her often. The last time had been two years earlier in the Fortress's practice room, during their emergency investigation of a security breach. Lucinda knew both Jean and Lorraine were experiencing accelerated ageing. Jean looked middle aged. She expected the same of Lorraine.

But in the six years since the Yule War, Lorraine had aged sixty. Lines webbed corners of her eyes and mouth and the back of her hand; the flesh on her upper arm sagged and jiggled; her hair, once silver-blond, was white. Lucinda tried to hide her shock, but Lorraine noticed and wasn't offended.

"Without help from the Water Office or the Earth Guild, I cannot postpone the inevitable." Clad in paint-spattered linen, with her hair in a loose braid and a scarf over her right shoulder, she embodied contented retirement. "Think what you will, but my mirror tells me I look very well for a woman of eight score years."

"You'd look exceptionally well for a woman half that," Lucinda said. "What are you painting?"

Lorraine turned the work so Lucinda could see. It was a delicate line drawing of creatures in a tide pool, overlaid with a faint wash of colours.

"This is lovely," Lucinda said. "How do you do such fine work left-handed?"

"With magic, of course, so that I may continue to work right-handed. I have had to abandon sculpture; anything beyond a light brush or pen exhausts me. I have no idea how mundanes who have lost a limb manage."

While Lorraine washed up for tea, Lucinda surveyed the spells on the cottage, and was satisfied on finding Lorraine's home as secure against eavesdroppers as hers. A woman who had spent her entire life studying others' secrets would have a keen appreciation of privacy.

They talked over tea about Lorraine's quiet retreat into art, and Lucinda's noisy family in the nexus of Frankland's public life, soon to be further enlivened by a fourth arrival. Lucinda absentmindedly rubbed her growing baby bump and waited until the tea tray was cleared away to broach the reason for her visit. "The gift of cold water... You gave it to Jean, too, years ago."

"He promised me he would never tell."

"He didn't. I guessed. He can absorb power, too, and I've seen the ice in his soul. It's what's kept him alive for so long, isn't it? If you hadn't, he'd have flamed out in a war or provoked the Fire Office to kill him, like every other Fire Warlock before him."

"I have pondered that, many times. There can be no proof, but yes, I believe it was a factor—major or minor, I cannot tell—in his longevity."

"A major one, I think. And he gave you fire."

Lorraine cocked her head. "Why do you say that?"

"I've seen fire in you. Before the unlocking, when you talked about the Water Office's injustices, you were as passionate as a fire witch."

Lorraine stared into the distance. "Perhaps. I do not deny the fire, but it was already there. Without it, I would not have interested him." She refocused on Lucinda. "Why does this matter to you?"

"You know, don't you, that Beorn has foreseen René as Fire Warlock? He's been training with Jean and Beorn for years. If he burns out before he's had time to train his own apprentice, we'll be back to where we were before Jean, with every Fire Warlock burning out because they've not had adequate training. So much of what they need to know will be lost—again—and we'll have incompetents like Sunbeam or criminals like Old Brimstone holding the office."

The crow's feet around Lorraine's eyes had become more pronounced. "I see. No, I agree. Frequent turnover of Fire Warlocks is not good for Frankland."

"And knowing René will be Fire Warlock doesn't tell us much about the outcome of reforging the Fire Office. The empire will attack as soon as the

Fire Office is taken down; we're certain of that. If they destroy any of our cities, or if what's left of Frankland afterwards is a fraction of its current size, then we will have failed. René will be leading the defence, and it will be difficult."

"How difficult will it be? Charles has kept me informed of the Reforging Coven's discussions, but I suspect your guild council has not shared all its concerns."

"Well…" Lucinda had not gotten permission to share guild council secrets with Lorraine, but she hadn't asked for it either. She crossed her fingers and summarised the challenges facing them. Little of what she said about either the Fire Guild or the empire surprised the older woman. "And so, Your Wisdom," she concluded, "any weapon we can give René, we should."

"I see." There was no discernible change in Lorraine's posture, but the persona of relaxed artist had been shed like a pair of house slippers. The witch sitting across the table from Lucinda was alert and engaged, a Water Sorceress capable of facing down a howling mob. "And if one of those weapons is the gift of cold water, it would be irresponsible, for Frankland's sake, not to use it."

Lucinda let out a long sigh. "Thank you, Your Wisdom. I thought about approaching Sorceress Eleanor first, since she is the current officeholder, but there is the history of bad blood between the two guilds, and Paul's suggestion at last week's meeting didn't help."

The corners of Lorraine's mouth lifted. "You fear a request for the gift coming from a warlock—even from one the Water Guild acknowledges a debt to—would be rejected out of hand."

"I didn't mean that, quite. Eleanor would listen to me, but…"

"But she would take your request to the guild council, and they are not all as judicious as they should be, nor would they understand what the gift has already done for Frankland, as I have never disclosed that I have given it to two warlocks. They would be astonished that you know of the gift, appalled at my reckless liberality, and offended at your audacity in asking for such an undeserved honour for Warlock Snorri."

"Exactly. I can understand that. The Fire Guild have our own secret honours. What could René do to earn it?"

Lorraine's smile deepened. "Nothing."

Lucinda echoed, "Nothing?"

"The gift of cold water is never earned. It is given in anticipation of what the recipient will do with it. The giver always expects something in return, and it has never yet failed to return far more than it cost the giver."

"So will you give it to René?"

Lorraine went to the window and gazed out a long time. "Warlock Snorri would make good use of the gift. If he serves even a third as long as Jean that will be well. But the gift is not without cost to the giver. A cost an officeholder could easily bear; a retired witch, perhaps not so well."

Lucinda's face burned. "I'm sorry, Your Wisdom. I shouldn't have asked if you would do it. I meant to ask if you could persuade Eleanor."

"I understand, but Eleanor is not a good choice for the giver. I must think this over before I give you an answer. Come, let us take a walk."

They walked along the shore, talking about the loss of Mother Celeste, Jean's battered conscience, and other subjects that could never be adequately conveyed in a letter. Much later, on returning to the cottage, Lucinda said, "Why did you say Eleanor shouldn't give René the gift?"

Lorraine sorted through items on her table, laying out pen and paper, before answering. "Because the gift is, in some ways, similar to a bond. It entangles the lives of giver and receiver in ways that are not obvious. I did not fully comprehend how entangled until after you lifted that cursed lock on the Water Office. We have survived the exchanges because we three all have both fire and ice in our souls. Had we not... After more than a century, either I would have succumbed to Jean's fire, or his flame would have been drowned, whichever of us proved the stronger."

"And Eleanor?"

"Even with the Water Office's support, a decades-long entanglement with a warlock would not be healthy for her. She has no fire in her soul. As you say, I do. For Frankland's sake, I will give it to René."

Lucinda sighed. "Thank you, Your Wisdom."

Lorraine patted her shoulder. "Do not worry for the future. That spark is not as uncommon among the Water Guild as the Fire Guild would assume. There will always be someone who can give a Fire Warlock's new apprentice the gift, if that candidate can benefit from it."

"You'll tell your guild council they should give it to his successors, too? That would be wonderful! Much more than I hoped for."

"If, as we both assume, it has been beneficial, we must assume it will continue to be beneficial. The council members do not understand the gift, no more than I did in my twenties, and revealing that I have given it to both you and Jean will educate them in its uses."

Lucinda's nose wrinkled. "Maybe. I hope it doesn't get you in trouble with your guild council."

"At my age? Bah. The revelation will do me no harm. The worst I have to fear from them is the tedium of making the same explanation a dozen times over."

"There are only seven on your guild council."

"And two of them are mages." Lorraine's eyes twinkled. "I stand corrected. Two dozen times."

Spending his holiday in an icy truce, with Hildur's mother and aunts ostentatiously ignoring him, had not improved René's temper. On their return to Blazes, he settled onto the sofa in Quicksilver's study and responded to Lucinda's questions about their visit to Thule with one-word answers. After a few sallies, she gave up and recounted her conversation with Lorraine.

René's voice rose. "You want her to give me the gift of cold water? Are you nuts?"

Quicksilver frowned at him. "She is certainly not 'nuts,' as you say. This is excellent news."

"Excellent, my arse. I don't want it."

Quicksilver and Lucinda regarded him in silence for a moment. His face heated. "Don't you remember what Lucinda looked like after Lorraine gave it to her? We thought she was one of them. I don't want the Fire Eaters thinking I'm a cold fish."

Lucinda said, "I could put my lock on your talents until the outer manifestations have worn off. They wouldn't even notice. You need this to be the best Fire Warlock you can be."

René yelled, "I don't need that to be a good Fire Warlock."

Jean's frown deepened. "My dear René, your behaviour seems irrational." He reached for René's arm. "Whatever—"

René shook him off. "I won't have it and you can't make me." He dove into the fireplace and emerged in the Fire Warlock's study.

Beorn greeted him with a curt, "What's got into you?"

"That's a fine way to greet a returning traveller."

"The returning traveller wasn't doing a fine job of greeting the stay-at-homes. Think I wasn't watching? You ought to know better."

"Then you heard what Lucinda said."

"I did. It's a great idea."

René bristled. "If it's such a great idea, why don't you get Her Iciness to do it to you?"

"I would if the Fire Office would let me, and if I thought it would work on me. I don't have whatever it is you and Jean and Lucinda have."

"I'm not a cold fish," René yelled, "or an icicle. Stop trying to make me one."

Beorn grabbed his shoulder and gave it a hard shake. "We've been trying to teach you about control and using your head for half your life now. When are you going to learn? Sorceress Lorraine is offering you something that'll help you with control. You said you'd be nuts to take it. I say you're nuts to turn down any kind of power when it's offered." He shoved René towards the fireplace. "Get out of here and don't bother coming back until you've either taken it, or come up with a reason I can understand why you shouldn't."

René strode into Sorceress Lorraine's studio. "I'm here. I—"
She held up her hand for silence. The pen floating above the paper dipped, made three short strokes and one long, graceful curve.

He steamed. If he hadn't known the Fire Warlock would be watching him, he would have turned on heel and walked out.

The pen dropped into its stand. She turned to stare. "I was expecting Warlock Snorri. Who are you?"

"I am Snorri. Who do you—oh." He grimaced. "I forgot. Lucinda put her lock on me to hide my talents."

"Why?"

He clenched his jaw and bowed stiffly over the hand she held out to him. "Because... Look, Your Wisdom, wait a bit while I cast some spells against eavesdroppers." She waited. When he finished, he said, "Quicksilver doesn't want the empire's spies knowing why I'm here. If they see someone looking like a warlock arriving and like a sorcerer leaving, they'll figure it out."

"A sensible precaution. If, as he suggests, the empire's intrigues are many and various, you will not be offended that I must ascertain you are who you say you are."

His jaw tightened. "No, ma'am. Better you should."

"Perhaps you remember an incident during the preparations for reforging the Water Office when the Air Enchanter embarrassed himself."

René snorted. "Which one?"

"This incident pertained to your attendance and Lucinda's. Do you recall what he accused you of, and what came after?"

"Whatever it was, I didn't do it. I didn't want to piss off Quicksilver. I didn't play any of the tricks on Paul he deserved. Oh! I remember. He said I wasn't paying attention, and I was. I said Father Jerome was winning the argument because he answered Lucinda's questions, and I was about to call him—Paul—an airdick when you interrupted."

Lorraine's eyebrows rose. "Ah, yes, the refreshing honesty of the Fire Guild. I will not enquire as to what you call me behind my back. Besides your recall of this incident, you have a warlock's warm hands. For the moment, I may trust you are indeed Warlock Snorri. I had not expected you directly after your return from Thule, but it has been several days, and I had begun to wonder."

René's face heated. "I wasn't happy about it when Lucinda told me. I'm still not happy, but I'm here."

She gave him a cold blue stare. "Not happy is, I dare say, an understatement. Why do you find the suggestion offensive?"

The heat in his face spread to his ears. "Hey, look, I didn't say..."

"Why are you here? Why do you want the gift of cold water? To please Lucinda?"

"Her and Quicksilver and Beorn and Hildur... They think I'll need it to fight off the empire when the Fire Office is out of commission. They told me I'd be stupid to turn it down."

"But you resent that you must."

"Look, can we just get this over with?"

She shook her head. "In your present mood, it would be unwise. I must consider... In the meantime, I understand you play chess. Visitors are rare, and I would enjoy the diversion."

René's longstanding interest in chess warred with his impulse to say no. Playing would be better than this cold water nonsense, and he could afford to indulge an old woman. Still, it was only fair to warn her. "I'm pretty good."

"So I have heard. There is a board in the next room." She moved her drawing aside. "Bring it."

They played. She beat him, easily. He glowered at the board. "Best two out of three?" He changed tactics, played a defensive game, and lost. He changed tactics again, and played a recklessly aggressive third game. She took his queen straightaway, and he never recovered.

She said, "You have let emotion cloud your judgement, and your level of play has diminished accordingly. Your emotions are also in conflict with your need for the gift of cold water. As long as you resent the necessity, you will not make good use of it."

He spat out, "What do you expect me to do about it? Frankland needs me to do all I can to keep the empire from swallowing us."

"I applaud your sense of duty, but duty alone is insufficient. I will not give it to you."

He bounced out of his chair and smacked the table with his fist. Chess pieces danced. "So, I have to tell Lucinda you've broken your promise."

He turned away from her cold stare. She said, "As I told Lucinda, the gift must be given freely, but the recipient must also be open to receiving it. In your present state of mind, it would be wasted on you. Go home, and do not return unless you can find a reason for wanting it."

The War's First Casualty

"**Y**ou cretin!" Lucinda's blast knocked René off his feet. "You pathetic juvenile imbecile!"

He rolled into the practice room's fireplace and came up slinging live coals at her. "Stop telling me what to do!"

"Grow up and I might!"

"Drown it, Lucinda—"

"I stuck my neck out for you and begged Lorraine for a favour. She wasn't thrilled, but she was willing. But did you appreciate it? No. You not only turned it down, you did it in the worst possible way. Who do you think you are, Warlock Flint?"

She blasted him without letup. He was on the defensive, and sweating. He glanced over his shoulder at the corner she was pushing him towards. "Frost it, Lucinda. I don't want—"

"I don't care what you want. This isn't about what you want. This is about what Frankland needs and if you can't see that, you're a disgrace." Her pulse pounded. Her chest heaved. Screaming was tearing her vocal cords. She would pay for that later, but she was too angry to care. Jean watched without interfering, his eyes torches, his mouth an iron bar.

She punched through a shield and set René's sleeve on fire. Her own skirt smouldered. She ignored it. "Why that aversion spell on our house lets you in is beyond me. Putting Frankland first, my foot."

"Frostbite. I am thinking about Frankland. I've been wasting too much time with the other guilds. How can I win a war with the empire if I'm not focused on being a pure warlock?"

Lucinda stopped mid-stroke, wand raised. Jean barked, "What nonsense is this?"

René's anger beat back at them. "She just proved she can beat me and she doesn't even want to be a Fire Eater. You think it's fine to have that ice or cold water or whatever it is in you, but you had the office backing you when you fought your wars. How can I beat another lightning-thrower if I'm not as much of a warlock as he is? I ought to burn out everything in me that's not fire magic."

"René, you are a first-class frostbitten fool." Lucinda hit him with a blast that threw him against the wall. "That's the most ridiculous idea I've ever heard."

"Stop." Jean caught her arm. "Hush. René, why do you think that?"

"Well, uh, I heard…"

Lucinda said, "You didn't hear it from Beorn or Sven or us. Where did you hear it?"

He fumbled. "I don't remember… I must've… Oh." The livid colour drained from his face, leaving it grey. He leaned against the wall and slid down to the floor. "You're right; I'm an idiot."

She lowered her wand and snuffed the fire in her skirt. She and Jean waited.

René drew his knees up to his chin. "That's what Gunther said."

Jean said, "You agreed not to confront him again."

"I haven't. Couldn't even if I wanted to; the Fire Warlock won't let me… But the things he said before that… That my affinity for the Air Guild makes me weak and I'll never be strong enough on my own to be a lightning thrower. They've been eating at me. And then there was an airhead in Thule…"

Lucinda sank to the floor and sat cross-legged, facing him. "Talk."

René reddened. "He called me an airhead."

"And?"

He wouldn't look at her. "And that the Fire Eaters will hate me, like the guild councils have hated him—" He waved a hand at Jean. "—when they realise how strong my affinities for the Air and Water Guilds are."

Lucinda looked up at Jean. His fury had left him; he looked tired and bleak.

He said, "You should have been flattered that the empire fears you, not taken in by their thrusts."

She said, "Gunther's proud of being a pure fire wizard. He ought to be ashamed."

René said, "What?"

Jean said, "Of all the warlocks you have known or read about, which had the least affinity for any other guild?"

René frowned, and shrugged.

"The two purest fire wizards in Frankland's history were Old Brimstone, curse his evil memory, and Warlock Flint."

René raised his head and stared. "Flint? You hated Flint."

"Flint was—pardon my language—a frostbitten reprobate, and a bloody-minded, undisciplined disgrace to his guild. Much as I love the Fire Guild, I know our faults. Disregard for the hurt we inflict on others in our single-minded drive to have our way is the worst. The historical records are quite clear; if a warlock does not have counterbalance from another guild, he—or she—takes unwarranted risks and indulges in egotistical behaviour, bringing dishonour, not glory, to the Fire Guild."

"Oh, yeah? Prove it."

By the middle of the afternoon, with Gibson's *History of the Office of the Fire Warlock* and several other histories open on the table, and a tally sheet in front of him, René admitted defeat.

Lucinda said, "Jean's right. The worst Fire Warlocks were nothing but Fire Guild. Most didn't live long enough to cause much trouble. That Old Brimstone survived as long as he did was, well, not a miracle. Devil's work, more like. The better ones, like Beorn, all had some overlap with another guild. The ones spanning three guilds were the great ones: Fortunatus and Jean."

"And, we were hoping," Jean said, "you."

René hung his head. "Guess I've blown that."

"So it would appear. Until Lucinda made her request, I had not considered the gift essential, but she has convinced me of its necessity. Further, with the Air Guild crippled and obdurate, we must have the Water Guild's good will and cooperation."

"Burn it. What do we do now?"

"We? You, my young friend, must limit the damages."

Warlocks don't walk. Warlocks jump through the fire, or if they've exhausted their magic in the Fire Warlock's service, they'll commandeer a carriage or wagon to take them to the nearest Earth Guild tunnel. Warlocks never just walk.

Except for warlocks in disguise with their talents hidden under a lock because they don't want the news spread of who they are and where they are going.

René had already walked the four miles between the tunnel mouth and Sorceress Lorraine's cottage twice that day and he would have to do it twice more. His muscles ached, he had blisters on both heels and the ball of his left foot, and the skin on his thighs was being rubbed raw where his cheap labourer's trousers didn't fit well. If the lowering clouds turned to rain, that would be the last straw.

For God's sake, big sister—

Don't cry to me, little brother. Do your penance like a man.

René pulled his collar tighter, thrust his hands in his pockets, and walked. Over the next hour and a half, he went through annoyance, resentment, and rage—it did rain on him—until agony focused on his feet crowded out everything else.

The rain stopped and the clouds lifted, but the pink and blue vista brought him no joy. He needed to step up the pace or he'd be walking in the dark.

Sorceress Lorraine perched on a rock among the tide pools, admiring the sunset. She rose and came to meet him as he limped towards her. He went down on his knees at her feet.

"I'm sorry," he mumbled. Cleared his throat and said it again, louder. "I'm sorry. Lucinda and Quicksilver were right, I was wrong, and I acted like a jerk. I don't blame you for being pissed off at me." He stopped and rubbed his nose. The folds of her gown rippled in the breeze, but she was a statue. "I know I've ruined my chances of you ever doing me any favours, but you know them, and you know we're not all obnoxious hotheads." He risked a glance. Her face was unreadable. He dropped his gaze to her feet. "I hope you're not so pissed off at me you won't tell the Water Guild Council what you told Lucinda."

She said, "Why does that matter to you?"

He twisted, turning his head a full circle, scanning the shoreline. There were no other people in sight. He eyed the birds and chewed on his lip. They'd been used as spies before. Did he dare?

"You fear eavesdroppers? Come." She walked away. He sighed and struggled to his feet.

Guess I'll be walking back in the dark.

178

If you fall and bloody your nose, remember it's your own fault.

Lorraine waved René into a chair in the corner of her studio and took a seat in the opposite corner before summoning a servant. "Prepare the guest room for my visitor."

He said, "You don't have to, uh... You don't have to..."

"You have so few blisters you want more?" He winced. She said, "I did not think so. No more nonsense from you tonight, young man." To the maid, who was staring curiously at René, she said, "When I am done with him, he will also need supper, a bath, and salve for his injuries." She dismissed the maid and turned back to René. "You will wait until the bath is ready to remove your shoes. You already stink of smoke and sweat, and I would rather not further contaminate my studio. Can you remove Lucinda's lock on your talents?"

"No, but she can do it from Blazes."

"Have her do so. I would be sure to whom I am talking... Now, pray continue."

He checked that the spells he had cast earlier were still intact. They were. "Lucinda's right, I guess. In saying it was your gift that kept Quicksilver alive so long, I mean. She said you weren't thrilled about offering me the gift of cold water, and I was a jerk to turn it down. They made me go through the whole roster of Fire Warlocks, and they were right—the worst of the lot were the ones who were all pure fire. I hate to say it, but it's so. For Frankland's sake, we need Fire Warlocks who aren't one-sided." He scrubbed a hand over his face, and winced. "For Frankland's sake, I hope you'll still tell the Water Guild Council giving a warlock the gift is a good idea."

Drown it, little brother, she'll think you're trying to sweet-talk her into still giving you the gift.

He blurted, "Not for me. I probably won't last long as Fire Warlock, and whoever comes after me will be awfully young. He'll need all the help he can get."

"Why do you reject the gift for yourself with such venom?"

"Did. Don't anymore. If you offered it now, I'd take it and be glad— mostly. But before Lucinda beat some sense into me..."

They say confession is good for the soul. To René's amazement, a heavy burden he had not known he was carrying lifted from his shoulders

179

as he recounted his psychological battles with the empire. Freed from the blinkers of rage and resentment, his clear-eyed assessment of his own behaviour was damning. Lorraine listened with no overt emotion, rather than the flamboyant histrionics the Fire Guild is prone to.

When he finished, she said, "I see. The Battle for Frankland has already begun, and your sense of self-worth was the first casualty."

René snorted. "My sense of self-worth was pretty inflated. Gunther cut it down to size fast enough."

"Take heart. He fears you."

"That's what Quicksilver said, but he's such an arrogant prick—Gunther, not Quicksilver—that I don't see it."

"I had wondered what influence was at work on you. The eager young warlock I developed a fondness for six years ago would not have turned down an offer of powerful magic, as long as the offer did not sully his honour."

René's face burned. "I know. I guess I was angry mostly because I'd let him convince me I didn't want something I really did. Water magic ought to be fun. Air magic is, and I hated the prospect of giving it up. I was stupid to listen to him."

"Stupid? I would not call it that. Whose good opinion matters more to you, your guild council's or the Fire Eaters'?"

"Guild council," he replied with no hesitation.

"As I suspected. Your closest friends, other than King Brendan, are warlocks and mages. Other warlocks' opinions matter to you. You are still young. Older and supposedly wiser men than you have fallen victim to such tactics."

She regarded him in silence until he squirmed under her gaze. He said, "Will you still talk to the Water Guild Council?"

"Of course. I never considered not doing so."

He rolled his head back with his eyes closed and sighed. "Thank you."

"My only question has been whether you would still benefit from the gift."

His eyes flew open. "Me? But I thought you…"

"That I was angry? I was, but less so than worried. I am not convinced you are yet in the appropriate state of mind. Before I am willing to give you the gift of cold water, you must promise you will honour a request I will make regarding the conduct of the war."

"What request?"

"I will tell you after you promise."

"Nuts! That's not fair."

She smiled. "War rarely is." She closed her eyes. "I am tired. Go. Give me your answer in the morning."

René eyed the bath's tiled walls while undressing. He'd have laughed at the Water Guild's eccentricities if he hadn't been the person about to step into a tub large enough to get lost in. With dark blue on the walls and lighter blue overhead, the colourful fish scattered here and there seemed to swim in an oil lamp's flickering light. Whatever sadist had designed it had meant to give the impression of the entire room being underwater.

He held his breath and slipped into the hot water. He dangled his arms outside the tub and wedged his feet against the sides. He'd not go sliding in over his head, not him.

He leaned against the back with his eyes closed, waiting for sore muscles to unknot. A foot slipped. His eyes popped open. Fish swam by at eye level. He levered himself upright, swearing, and sent water sloshing overboard. He grimaced and settled back, watching the water spread across the floor. He couldn't even take a bath without causing trouble. No wonder the Water Guild thought the Fire Guild were uncouth.

Big sister, you there?

I'm here.

What should I do? About that promise she wants, I mean.

You have to ask? I remember Sven giving you grief, six years ago, about making rash promises.

Well, yeah, but you were the one asking. Should I trust her?

Yes.

Come on, big sister. She's a water witch.

If you've already made up your mind not to, why ask me? So that I can remind you that you're the one who's been acting like a jerk? She must be wondering if she can trust you. Whatever it takes—do it.

Some time later, *Your Wisdom?*

Yes?

René recounted Lorraine's request. *Should I trust her? Would you trust her?*

I do not appreciate unguarded promises, and for most of my life I have distrusted the Water Guild, but... Quicksilver was quiet for a long time. *If we are to survive the coming war, we cannot afford to reject help offered by Frankland's other true sons and daughters. Tell me what spells you have detected on her house.*

René's chest tightened. *Sorry, Your Wisdom. I know I should've checked the place out already, but I just... Never mind. I'll do it now... Spells against theft, fire, flood... the usual. Against eavesdroppers... Oh hell! the whole house is airtight. I really have been an ass. Aversion spells...*

His jaw dropped. *That's your aversion spell, Your Wisdom. The same one as on your house in Blazes. How did...*

I told the officeholders of it, before the Yule War, to reassure them regarding Prince Brendan's safety, and she asked me to safeguard her house, too. I was pleased to do so.

Is this your way of saying you think I should trust her?

You are chest deep in water, but you could not be bothered performing the basic security checks I have been drilling into you for eight years. I should say you already do.

René roused from a dream of Gunther shaking his fist and flailing as he drowned in a whirlpool of flying cod and soaring trout, submerged quail and diving canaries.

Your Wisdom?

My dear René, it is half-past four in the morning.

Sorry, Your Wisdom.

Since you have awoken me, what is it?

You and Lorraine both said Gunther's afraid of me. Why?

Perhaps he does not like having his sleep disturbed either.

Ha, ha.

Very well then, I will give you a more serious answer. You have fenced with him on several occasions. He would not have rejoined the battle—would not have considered you worth his time—if he were not apprehensive.

René snorted. *I doubt that. He's a thug. The more people he hurts, the more fun he has.*

But he has many other more compliant victims. You have returned taunt for taunt. Have not some of your barbs struck home? You do not bend to his will. And are you not drained after these incidents? How much more drained must he be after each one, as he is the one reaching halfway across Europa to strike. I should be surprised if he can rise from his bed the next morning, and he is in a far more precarious position than you, my young friend. The empire's court is governed by fear, with numerous factions plotting to take advantage of any sign of weakness. Those sessions are dangerous for him, and he would not indulge in them if he did not have to, but he must. He must see for himself what sort of a man you are, and what sort of a woman Lucinda is, because he does not understand you. Either of you.

He sure seems to know what to say to make us pop our corks.

He is skilled at finding other's weaknesses, true. That is how he maintains control over his lieutenants. But he is not skilled at understanding others' strengths, and he does not grasp yours. There you have the advantage. Tell me how you became captain of the Fire Eaters.

I'm a warlock...

Being a warlock does not guarantee anyone will follow your leadership.

I don't know, Your Wisdom. I don't often order them around, except when the Fire Warlock's giving me orders. Usually I just see something that needs doing, or have some idea that would be fun, and they come along. And then I sort out the bits so everybody gets something he's good at, because it's easier that way.

Quicksilver laughed. *Exactly. You play to their strengths, and call out the best in them.*

I do?

You have done so, very well, in limited circumstances. If you continue as you have begun, and expand your leadership capabilities to encompass wizards from all four guilds, how can he not be afraid of you?

If I do, the Fire Eaters will get pissed off at me.

For not playing favourites, yes. That is an unpleasant possibility, but they will come through for you in battle, when it matters.

You think? The air wizard said they would turn on me.

Tell me.

After René repeated the wizard's words, there was a long silence, then, *Remember, my young friend, all prophecies are ambiguous.*

Yeah, right.

The sun was halfway up the sky before René roused again. He breakfasted alone; Lorraine had been at work for hours. When he was ready to face her, he stopped in the doorway to her studio, watching. She nodded to him, but continued with her work. He rummaged through her supply cabinet, found paper and charcoal, and sat down across the table from her. She painted. He sketched.

When at last she finished, and asked to see what he had drawn, he hesitated, but then shrugged and handed her the paper—a sketch of her in profile. "It isn't any good. Not like what you do."

"Your hand is untrained, but you have an observant eye. If you have time, take lessons." She set the paper down. "Last night I asked you for a promise."

"Yes, ma'am. I'll do whatever you want. I promise."

Her eyebrows rose. "You surprise me."

His face heated. "I'm not always an ass...I hope."

"No, you are not. Sometimes even a warlock thinks a matter through and acts rationally, and sometimes even a sorceress gives in to her emotions. I realised this morning that I had done so last night. Your complaint was justified. What I asked was not fair, and I intended to withdraw my demand."

He laughed. "Burn it. I should have waited."

"You have already shown more patience this morning than I have given you credit for. I have only one other concern."

"What's that?"

"Yesterday evening you said you would accept the gift of cold water and be glad. Why? What reasons have you for wanting the gift?"

"I want to protect Frankland."

"And?"

"That isn't enough?"

"It is truly a worthy endeavour, but that is not all, is it?"

"I don't want to disappoint Lucinda and Their Wisdoms."

"And?"

His face, even his ears, burned, but he met her gaze and held it. "I want to beat you at chess."

She laughed. "Spoken like a true warlock. Very well." Smiling, she held out her hands, water glimmering in her cupped palms. "Drink your fill."

He had not known he was parched. He drank long and deep, paused, and then drank again, finding refreshment for years lived at a fevered pace. When his thirst was quenched, he raised his head, and his heart dropped to his toes.

Big sister, help!

What—

Something's wrong with Lorraine.

Lorraine had aged a dozen years. One side of her face had gone slack. She reached for her table, missed, and staggered. He tried to steer her towards a chair. She collapsed in his arms.

Get a healer, fast.

Chess

With the healer that Lucinda brought working on Lorraine, there was nothing further she could do. She and René retreated to Lorraine's studio, out of the way of frantic servants and worried members of the Water Guild. While they waited, René frowned over the chessboard. Lucinda eyed him and chewed her nails.

"What?" he said.

"You looked like a sorcerer. Before I put the lock back on you, I mean."

"What'd you expect? You looked like a water witch when she did it to you."

"I understand now why everyone was upset."

At length the house quieted. The Water Guild visitors dispersed. Sorcerer Charles walked into the studio. René and Lucinda stared at him mutely. 'Sorry' seemed so inadequate.

Charles snorted. "You two look like guilty prisoners on their way to the courtroom."

René said, "Don't know why she does. It's my fault."

Lucinda said, "It's our fault. How is she?"

"She had a stroke." Charles sank into a chair and rubbed his face. "She was alert and speaking clearly before the healer ordered her to sleep. The healer said to thank you for your quick thinking. She'll be fine."

René met Lucinda's eyes and grimaced. She didn't believe it either.

"For now," Charles added. "Until she has another stroke, and another. It's only a matter of time."

René mumbled, "I'm sorry."

"You're sorry she's a hundred and fifty-seven years old? Or that she wanted to pay a debt she still felt she owed the Fire Guild? Don't be. We talked it over, the two of us, and I offered to do it myself, but she said the gift needed the backing of the Water Office to be effective on a lightning thrower, even a half-baked one, which meant either the current or retired Water Sorceress. We knew the cost would be high."

Lucinda said, "If I had known how high…" She faltered under Charles's frosty stare.

He said, "If you had known, then what?"

The polite fiction stuck in her throat. It was a lie, and he would know it. She would have trusted Lorraine, like herself, to put Frankland's needs over her own. Her face burned.

Charles was waiting for an answer. She blurted, "I would have asked anyway."

He thawed. "Good."

"Good?"

"I'd hate to think she suffered this for something you didn't consider necessary." Charles's eyes widened. "Oh, for God's sake, I hope it was enough. Take your lock off him so I can see."

"One moment…"

Charles peered at René. "Good. You look respectable for a change."

Lucinda shuddered and threw the lock back on.

Charles said, "Where will you go until you're more yourself again?"

René frowned and shrugged. "Home."

"I wouldn't advise it. Your Fire Guild friends will want to know what you're hiding, and you won't act like yourself for a while either. You might as well stay here for a few days." Charles jerked a thumb in the direction of Lorraine's bedroom. "She'll want to talk to you, and I can teach you a few things to make good use of it."

René's eyes lit. "That'll be flaming awesome."

Charles winced. "Flaming awesome… Think you can keep your mouth shut while you're here?"

Lorraine slept, ate, played chess, and slept again. While she rested, René spent his time with Charles, practicing calming techniques the mage demonstrated, playing chess, or listening to advice on opening gambits and end games. He kept a hard rein on his tongue, waiting for Lorraine to raise the subject of the promise he had given.

After three days, she had recovered enough to move the chess pieces herself, rather than telling him where to move them. After the day's second game, she said, "Your play has improved."

"I'm still losing," he said.

"Yes, but you have lost your anger over that fact. You are now more interested in learning from a better player and improving your game than in beating me. You are thinking more clearly because you are not letting emotion rule."

"Right. Quicksilver's been harping on control for half my life now. When he started on it, I didn't see the point. I can now, sometimes, but he's so much better at it than I am. I keep planning to do better the next time, but something will set me off and I'll forget."

"Control of one's emotions does not come easily to any warlock, not even Quicksilver. You have been striving for control for a few years; he has been for a century and a half, and at times still cannot. Do not berate yourself. You are doing very well for a young fire wizard."

René grinned. "All right then, I won't. I know I'm better at it than Gunther. He has to come up with something new each time to make me lose my temper, but he falls for the same jab every time."

"Ah, yes, Warlock Sturmmeister, who will, if I am not mistaken, soon be Emperor Sturmmeister. You remember I asked for a promise."

"And I gave it."

She studied the board. He waited. She said, "Chess, you know, is a balanced game. A match between two equally skilled players should, in theory, always end in a draw. Among the grandmasters, there should, in theory, be no winners or losers."

"But there are."

"Indeed there are. Chess, like warfare, is often a matter of unbalancing one's opponent. Of doing the unexpected, to sow doubt, confusion, and fear. Of convincing one's opponent he is beaten. The one who gives in to emotion usually loses."

He frowned. "Tell me what this has to do with that promise."

"My request is simple: whatever happens, you must not seek revenge."

His frown deepened. "You want to make sure I don't lose my temper and do something stupid."

"Giving in to anger could be your, and Frankland's, undoing. You have assured me your goal is to ensure Frankland's survival. That must remain your goal. All personal concerns are trivial in comparison. And please, if you do defeat him, and not merely expel him and his legions from Frankland's borders, do not gloat."

"Hey, come on. You can't expect me not to celebrate."

"I did not say that. Celebrate your victory, certainly, with your friends, after Frankland is restored to order, but do not exult over the emperor's loss. Gloating is not becoming for a hero, for one thing, and a waste of time. But more importantly, he has been driving you to hate him. Confound his expectations."

He glowered at the board. He understood what she was asking for, but it would be hard. Real hard. If he weren't under the influence of her gift, he'd be yelling and waving his arms. He would love to rub Gunther's nose in a Frankish victory. "You were right to make me promise first." He gave her a crooked smile. "You should play chess. You'd be good at it."

After René had been there a week, Lorraine said, "You will leave soon. The outer manifestations will have worn off by tomorrow."

René said, "Good. I'm ready to go home. Hildur's not happy with me for being gone so long. But tell me something... If war, like chess, is a matter of unsettling your opponent..."

"Yes?"

He frowned at the chessboard. "Gunther keeps needling me about not being pure fire. I ought to go full tilt the other way. I can make better use of the other guilds than he does."

"Yes, while still letting him think you are purging yourself of the other guilds' influences. That will be a difficult tightrope to walk."

"That second part's the easy one. The hard one will be getting friendlier with the air heads, and... Uh, I mean, air and water wizards."

"Earth wizards, also."

He thumped a fist on his thigh. "I can't even talk about it without making an ass of myself. I was wondering..."

"Yes?"

"About 'As fair as the king.'"

"You are considering an oath similar to the king's Great Oath for Fire Warlocks and their apprentices? Splendid idea."

"Well, yeah, but no. Can't. Uh, I mean, we'll have one after the reforging, but can't now. Uh..."

"I accept as true your statement you cannot. You need not explain why."

"Thanks."

"What did you mean then?"

"The guild council are talking about me having a bond with the king."

"Yes, Miss van Gelder's suggestion. Charles told me."

"That's to give me the benefit of the Air Guild spells during the Empire's invasion. But I was wondering if…if that would let me piggyback, so to speak, on his oath."

She paused with a rook in the air. "What an intriguing idea." She finished her move. "It has merit. Bonds fail between people with dissimilar views and goals. You and King Brendan are walking the same path, towards what is best for Frankland. If either of you stray from that narrow path, a bond will help the other pull him back in line. You would be less vulnerable to Prince Gunther's taunts."

His throat tightened. "And I'd be even less like a normal fire wizard than I already am."

"Perhaps, and I understand your distress, but the Fire Eaters are not your equals. King Brendan is."

René scowled. "You say that, but he's a royal. He'll never admit that."

"You are mistaken. If he did not hold you in high regard, he would have rejected the proposal outright. Instead, he has conditionally agreed."

"You're joking."

"I am not."

"What're the conditions?"

She smiled. "Charles was quite amused. You must agree to never again use, or permit anyone around you to use, the derogatory terms airhead, mud brain, or cold fish."

The van Gelder sisters had begun calling the practice room the Forge, much to the Fire Eater's amusement, as Gillian had been doing everything in her power to make the room less of a dark cave. Miranda, home for the weekend, had offered to help. She sat at the table with her back towards Snorri and Alexander, but kept her mind's eye on the two fencers.

Gillian, bored with their swordplay, prodded her. "If it rains outside, the floor ought to look wet. How do we do that?"

"I don't know." She shoved a book at Gillian. "There might be something in there."

Gillian buried her nose in the text. Miranda leaned back and considered the work they had already done.

An awning hung from one of the long walls, providing the comfort of shelter for the rain-dreading Fire Guild. The illusory clouds were higher and brighter, more closely matching the outside weather. When it rained outside, they heard the patter on the awning. A fading shower nearly always produced a rainbow; Gillian was proud of that touch.

Miranda didn't care about wet flagstones. She wanted the walls to appear further away, but couldn't concentrate on her textbook. What fun were illusions compared to watching Frankland's finest swordsman?

The two swordsmen were almost evenly matched. Alexander's longer reach countered Snorri's lightning reflexes; his cool, dogged determination met the warlock's competitive fire. They circled, clashed, thrust and parried, and broke apart, panting, before coming back together and re-engaging.

At length they halted to towel off sweat, chug the flagons of small beer they had brought along, and talk over the news of the empire's latest political intrigues. Alexander conversed with half his mind on the subject. The other half was on the fifteen-year-old girl at the other end of the room. He was miffed. The women at court told him he cut a fine figure, but she had never looked at him. Was illusion magic really that interesting?

Snorri broached the subject they had danced around ever since meeting for their workout. "I'll agree to your condition if you agree to mine."

Alexander set down his flagon and wrenched his attention away from Miranda. "What condition?"

"We'll do the bond now—today—without finding out from Enchanter Paul if putting the Air Guild spells on you will work."

"Why?"

"I've got mixed feelings about this bond. I figure you do, too, but we both stand to gain from it. I just don't want to do it if all you think you'll get out of it is the use of those spells."

"And you? Tell us what other benefit you expect to receive from it."

"I will, after the bond is in place."

"You are asking us to gamble on your trustworthiness."

"If we can't trust each other, the bond will fail anyway."

"Oh."

"Besides, I just spent a week with the Water Guild. Let's do this before their influence dries up and I get pissed off again about needing to."

Alexander laughed. "Ah, the Fire Guild's invigorating candour. Such a pleasant change from court."

"And another thing... You don't get to use that royal we on me anymore."

Alexander stiffened. "If we can't—"

"Look, you're constrained by the Great Oath. I'll be constrained by the Fire Office. The only chance we have of avoiding the old pattern of perpetual feuding is to chuck the everlasting dominance games and actually work together. I figure this is part of why Arturos is keen on the idea. God knows I don't like losing, but watching Gunther turn everything into a contest where he stomps on the loser makes me ill. The best deals are the ones where everybody wins. What'd'ya say, Alex?"

Alexander considered the Snorri's extended hand. When he had first seen the wizard, charging through black chaos with a burning wand to save Earl and Lady Eddensford, Alexander had wanted the other boy as a friend and ally. His opinion had put him at odds with his father, but his opinion had not changed.

He gripped the other man's hand. "We agree to your terms, René."

René's momentary affront dissolved into a grin. "Touché."

Alexander's grouchiness and sudden fits of temper over the next two months drove the court into a state of near panic. A courtier who overstepped the bounds of familiarity by calling him Alex suffered a public humiliation. Wild rumours circulated, but they never suspected his bond with Warlock Snorri. The idea that King Brendan would welcome a closer connection with the warlocks his father had despised was beyond their imagination.

The one rumour that did have a basis in fact—that the king had proposed to one of those common-born van Gelder girls and been turned down—died a swift death by ridicule. If the king himself had assured them that it was true, and the second time she had turned him down, they would not have believed it.

The frustrated king could not quite believe that Miranda had walked away from him with snapping eyes and her nose in the air either. A tension headache aggravated his temper as he rode the Fortress stairs. Finding the

Fire Warlock lounging against the tunnel door, blocking his escape, did not improve his mood.

He growled, "Have we no privacy, sir?"

"Nope," the Fire Warlock said. "None. Not on this subject, at least. You didn't ask my advice, but I'm going to give it anyway."

"Thank you so much."

The Fire Warlock ignored the sarcasm. "We all know you have a duty to secure the succession, but if Miranda turns into an enchantress she'll have a lifetime of duty of a different sort—one she's not a bit happy about. It's not fair to ask her to do both."

"Oh!" Alexander deflated. "We… Yes, I suppose you are right. But if Gillian should be the enchantress…"

"Tell me why women get married."

"What? Er, female commoners marry for security—physical or financial, or so I've been told—but aristocratic women marry for duty."

The Fire Warlock snorted. "Ambition more often, either their father's or their own. What about witches?"

"Er, I think… I don't know."

"Witches get to marry for love, and they're proud of that privilege. You should've talked about love, not duty."

The Fire Warlock giving romantic advice? Laughable, on the face of it, but Arturos, widower, had been married to an earth witch. Alexander swallowed and admitted, "I'm not sure I even know what that means."

"Figure it out, because she won't have you if you don't. And if you blow your third opportunity, she's not likely to give you a fourth."

Sorceress Lorraine's health faded with the last of the summer heat. The presence of the entire Fire Guild Council at the state funeral in October was much remarked upon, as the Fire Guild had never before deigned to acknowledge the departure of a retired Water Sorceress. Afterwards, Lucinda spent the afternoon in quiet contemplation of both past and future while rocking her three-week-old baby, the long-awaited daughter that she had, with Jean's dazed concurrence, named Lorraine.

King Brendan's and Warlock Snorri's tempers cooled along with the weather, to the relief of the court and the Fortress inhabitants. By November the king had returned to his normal, unflappable self. Only his mother suspected how much the friction had polished the self-confidant and highly opinionated young man. The Fire Eaters attributed their captain's bad temper over the summer to his conflict with his mother-in-law; they didn't notice afterwards the unusually long intervals between outbursts.

Enchanter Paul's temper cooled, too, enough to let him hear Sorcerer Charles' proposal. He agreed that building the body of Air Guild spells on the king's person should—ahem, might—work, and the Reforging Coven hammered out an agreement satisfactory to most parties involved. Starting early in the new year, Paul would build the corpus of air spells twice: once on the king for practice and for Snorri's use during the reforging, and again on Sorceress Eleanor. This second collection would be the one moved during the reforging—who would move them was still an open question—with the first available for damage control if the move failed and the corpus collapsed. With that settled, the coven began the hard labour of testing and becoming comfortable with the new spell structure. King Brendan, with his fresh eyes, and Snorri, relieved of the intense focus on spellwork that had occupied him for months, together turned their attention to recruiting an army of wizards.

Recruits

From the rear of a meeting room in the Warren, Lucinda watched a young earth wizard stride into the Warren's Dolphin Fountain Courtyard. He brightened when he spotted Katie Underwood.

He said, "The call for volunteers said 'willing to work with the Fire Guild.' I guess I'm in the right place."

Katie gave him a brilliant smile. "That you are, and you're the first one. Take the first door on the left and help yourself to refreshments. When everyone's here, the Guild Council will explain."

"Very good," he said, and walked down the corridor she indicated. He passed the conference room's first open door and turned in at the second. Beorn greeted him with a warm smile and firm handshake.

Two more volunteers followed suit, none appearing to notice the first door. Then Father Pierre turned in at the first door, and beamed under Beorn's enthusiastic greeting.

"Look at this one," René murmured. "I'll bet you a gold frank he passes both doors."

The bulging eyes and overlarge ears of the middle-aged wizard now following Katie's direction gave him the air of a nervous rabbit. He entered the corridor, and hesitated.

Lucinda said, "Don't be a snot."

Jean said, "I accept your bet."

"Burn it," René said. "You don't gamble, do you, Your Wisdom?"

Jean chuckled. "Say, rather, I do not take unnecessary risks."

The earth wizard walked past the first door, stopped before reaching the second. His head swivelled between them. He then peeked around the first door, relaxed, and walked through.

Jean strolled over to greet him. "Good day, Grandfather Ernest. I am glad to see you."

"Wouldn't miss it, Your Wisdom." He jerked a thumb at the door. "What are those spells for?"

Jean raised an eyebrow. "Spells? Perhaps you should tell me."

The wizard sighed. "Should've known better than to ask a mage that. All right, I will."

He sat in the last row of chairs and went quiet, eyes unfocused. Lucinda wrote his name on the list she was keeping of those who came through the first door.

Jean pocketed René's frank. "Consider the loss of a coin an easy lesson, my young friend. Appearances can be deceiving, and Granddad Ernest's caution will give our Fire Eaters some valuable ballast."

A stream of earth wizards flowed through the corridor. The spells filtering the candidates were masterpieces of spellcraft, merging some characteristics of Jean's aversion spell with other criteria the Company of Mages suggested. The senior water and earth mages, Sorcerer Charles and Father Jerome, had quivered like puppies being thrown a new chew toy when offered this challenge, and were deservedly proud of the work they'd done.

Someday, Lucinda hoped, she would understand the details.

When the stream of volunteers dried up, more than five score earth wizards gathered in little clumps abuzz with speculation over the Earth Mother's call for volunteers. The hint of danger seemed to have piqued their curiosity rather than dampening their enthusiasm. Lucinda wondered how well that would work with the Water Guild.

Mother Astrid ushered in King Brendan. The wide-eyed volunteers discretely smoothed waistcoats and performed other primping while she led him around the room, introducing her flock.

Lucinda snagged a teacake from the refreshment table, slipped out the rear, and walked down the hall to the third door, leading to a different room. The handful of volunteers gathered there had come out of curiosity, lacking both the courage and the conviction to pass either set of filters. After introductions, she laid out the cover story the Fire Guild wanted spread—a cover story that was true, just not the whole truth.

"As unlikely as another civil war is now, King Brendan wants to ensure that the carnage the magic guilds suffered never happens again. He has ordered us to strengthen the defences on all guildhalls and to ensure they all have escape routes in case of attack. Obviously your own Earth Guildhalls have those, but the others don't. That's what we need you for. We want you to help make the guildhalls more defensible, and to dig tunnels from them to the Warren or the Crystal Palace."

"The Yule War was years ago." A wizard with a strong resemblance to a pit bull seemed to have appointed himself spokesman. "Why are you doing this now?"

"Because Queen Marguerite was regent and she didn't see the need. The king started prodding when he came of age."

"Good for him, I guess."

"Besides the tunnels," she said, "we will test the guildhalls' defences. Warlock Flint started on that before the Water Office reforging, but he didn't do a great job, and most of what he found never got fixed. We'll do it again, with a greater variety of attacks, and we'll fix the problems we find."

"Attacks?" Alarm showed in their eyes.

"Relax. You're not the only volunteers."

"I thought I saw Granddad Ernest on the way here," one said, "and I did wonder…"

"Right. We've divided you into three groups: attackers, defenders, and builders. This group are the builders."

Their relief was evident. "How will that work?"

"The attackers and defenders will test the guildhall defences. This group will dig tunnels and fix whatever problems they find. You shouldn't be in any danger."

They exchanged glances. Heads nodded. The spokesman said, "Sounds easy enough. We're in."

"Thank you." They talked for a while longer, making plans and developing a roster. When the meeting ended, Lucinda cautioned them not to talk about the project outside the group of volunteers. "We don't want to alarm the mundanes, but conspiracy magic gives me the creeps. It would be a shame to have to create one to hide what we're doing."

They assured her they wouldn't talk, and she let them go, satisfied that word would spread. She slipped back into the rear of the other conference room, where the discussion had not yet begun. The king was chatting with the last few to be introduced. The others, still basking in the pleasure of being recognized, were making a contented hum over the refreshments.

Mother Astrid clapped her hands and called them to order. A brief scurry followed as they found seats, then the king began his prepared speech.

"We are delighted to meet with you this afternoon. You are all, each and every one of you, men of heart, with courage and a love of our homeland. If you were not, you would not have responded to the Earth Mother's request as you did. While Mother Astrid was making introductions, she and Their Wisdoms, Fire Warlock Arturos and Fire Warlock Emeritus Quicksilver, were inducting you into a grand conspiracy to protect Frankland. We trust that when you have heard our reasons you will forgive them for doing so without your knowledge or consent."

His audience's eyes darted around the room, taking in Mother Astrid's nod, Jean's sober expression and military stance by the fireplace, and each other's questioning looks. They responded in murmurs. "Of course, Your Majesty."

"Many of you have wondered why Mother Celeste insisted on rebuilding the Earth Office when it was not as obviously in need of repairs as the Water Office had been. You may have given credence to the rumours that the Earth Office was a trial run for reforging the Fire Office. With the Fire Warlock's blessing, we confess to you now that those rumours are true. Mother Celeste, out of her generosity and love for Frankland, volunteered the Earth Office for the Reforging Coven to experiment with and get the practice needed to avoid catastrophic failures when rebuilding the Fire Office. Because, you see, when the Reforging Coven unlocks and deconstructs the Fire Office, we fully expect the Europan Empire to launch an attack while our defences are weak."

Heads nodded. No one appeared surprised, but a sense of unease percolated through the room.

"What do the rumours say about how Frankland will defend herself when the empire attacks?"

The uneasiness sharpened. The wizards shifted in their seats and eyed each other. One offered, "The Fire Guild…"

"Ah, yes, The Fire Guild." The king looked over their heads at Jean. "What does the Fire Guild say?"

"The Fire Guild will defend Frankland with our lives," Jean said. "With every last man, woman, and child in the guild, if need be."

The king said, "What use are children in battle? What can a witch who can light a candle but little else do against a warlock? Pride is said to be a deadly sin, and the Fire Guild's pride has made them reluctant to admit the truth: that they, by themselves, cannot guarantee Frankland's security without the Fire Office intact."

Jean inclined his head. René scowled. The audience absorbed this in shocked silence, then broke into a hubbub of voices.

The king held up a hand, and continued when they had quieted. "You may wonder why we did not forbid the Fire Guild from reforging the Fire Office. We considered this, but do not believe that would be wise. The Fire Office's failings are better hidden than the Water Office's were, but they exist, and will eventually become the gravest threat to Frankland's wellbeing if not fixed. We cannot tell you all the reasons why, but we have given the Fire Guild our blessing in reforging the Fire Office, despite the dangers.

"That is why we are here today, my friends, to ask for your aid in defending Frankland when the time comes. It would be unforgivable of us and of the Fire Guild to threaten Frankland's security by denying you your right to defend your homes and families.

"For centuries few outside the Fire Guild have had to consider risking their lives in Frankland's defence. We are asking for volunteers only, and even if you agree today to join in this effort, you will have time to reconsider, and may withdraw or rejoin at any time without prejudice. Further, we have charged the Fire Guild to not behave as the empire does, with its caste of warrior warlocks at the top coercing all other resentful and neglected talents into doing their bidding. Your officers will be drawn from those in this room today.

"The most powerful healers among you will be exempt from the corps of defenders, as those talents are too valuable to risk, but your engagement during the planning and defensive training will be beneficial.

"Now we are sure you have questions. The Fire Guild Council will do their best to address your concerns."

The room did not explode with raised voices, as a Fire Guild meeting would have, but the atmosphere was thick with roiling emotions. One wizard's grip strangled his wand, a muscle in his neighbour's cheek twitched, the next wizard's face was flushed, his breath rapid and shallow. The only other time Lucinda had seen so many members of the Earth Guild in such distress was at Mother Celeste's funeral.

"Explain to us, please, Your Wisdoms," one of the ranking wizards asked, "why you say you have to rebuild the Fire Office?"

Lucinda sighed. The Fire Office would not let them give an adequate answer to that question. Only Jean, and perhaps Beorn, given his insistence on it despite the surety that he would be the reforging's first victim, knew the full extent of the Fire Office's inadequacies. Even the other officeholders knew only parts of the full story. Like them, the Earth Guild would have to take on faith that it was necessary.

Jean evaded the question with an answer that would almost have seemed adequate, if one didn't realise it was content free. Beorn called in Sorceress Eleanor and Enchanter Paul to substantiate the claims that all four officeholders and the Company of Mages had agreed to fixing the Fire Office. Their assurances seemed to do little to ease the gathering's agitation.

One grizzled veterinarian claimed the floor. "Pardon my language, but you're scaring us shitless. You know that, don't you? I don't care if all Your Wisdoms agree, you won't convince me it isn't an abysmally stupid idea."

Beorn grinned. "Never could stand people beating around the bush. And no, I don't expect to convince you. You'll just have to make up your mind if you'll help or not, regardless of whether or not you think it's a good idea. The king said we're looking for volunteers, and we mean that, but we're not asking you to make a decision today. We're going to start training on a project the king wanted us to do anyway, and we'll see how that goes."

He described the Guildhall Defence Project. "That'll give you a taste of what we need. If, in six months, you want to join the Fire Eaters, we'll be glad to have you. If you don't want to join, we won't make you."

"Stop right there," someone said. "Frost me if I ever want to be called a Fire Eater."

"What do you want to be called?"

"I haven't said I'd join…"

"If you did, what would you want?"

"Uh…I don't know. Something earthy, of course. Rock walls, maybe?"

"I disagree," Granddad Ernest said. "If we are attempting to work with the other three guilds, we shouldn't have names that set us apart from each other. No Rock Walls, no Fire Eaters. One name for all of us."

A murmur rose. Some heads bobbed. Other ideas were tossed out.

While they talked, Lucinda went through the room, tapping on a few shoulders and whispering in their ears.

A consensus was reached in favour of the name Frankland's Unconquered: never been conquered, never will be.

Jean winked at Lucinda. *They do not know it yet, but they are hooked.*

The meeting ended with no clear resolution other than nearly all agreeing to participate in the Guildhall Defence Project. The organisers were pleased; once engaged in that it would be easier to reel them in the rest of the way.

The few whose shoulders Lucinda had tapped lingered. When everyone else had gone, leaving the Fire Guild representatives, the king, Mother Astrid, and the nine earth wizards who had entered through the first door, René closed the doors again and Mother Astrid invited them to pull their chairs into a circle.

Nodding at the king, Beorn said, "He said we'd pull the officers from among you, remember. Well, you're them."

Jean coughed. "Or rather, we hope you will agree to be officers. We will not compel anyone."

Lucinda kept a straight face at the half-truth. The Fire Guild wouldn't compel them; their own dispositions would.

Eight of the nine looked dismayed. Grandfather Ernest looked almost gleeful. "That's what the spells on the doors were about."

Jean smiled. "Exactly."

René shifted from foot to foot inside the first door to the Crystal Palace's ballroom. Beorn chewed his moustache. None of the Fire Guild felt comfortable in this castle, frigid on a bleak November morning, but Quicksilver and Lucinda were hiding their nerves. René's anxiety had a firmer basis than theirs. He deserved the frosty stares several members of the Water Guild Council had given him at Sorceress Lorraine's funeral. He had overheard Mother Astrid telling the Queen Mum that Lorraine had never really recovered from the damage unlocking the Water Office had inflicted on her, but René knew, and the Water Guild Council knew, that she might have had another year left if she hadn't given him the gift of cold water. He had no business being here, asking for their help, when he was already deep in their debt.

If the Guild Council had spread the word, which he doubted, the volunteers would start arriving any minute now.

Sorcerer Charles walked through the Officer's door. René's jaw dropped.

"Eleanor won't need my help in the first tier," Charles said. "I might as well make myself useful elsewhere. I hope I'm not so old you'll turn me away."

René pumped his hand. "Charles, don't be an ass."

Other recruits trickled in. When there were about four dozen, more than he had allowed for in his best-case imaginings, Sorceress Eleanor ushered in the king and began the introductions. The meeting itself was short. They were already disbursing when Lucinda returned from briefing the three who had come out of curiosity alone.

She said, "What happened? Did they turn us down?"

René, bemused, was watching the stragglers talking in twos and threes. "No. It was weird. They didn't argue. We didn't have to call in Astrid or Paul. When Eleanor said the Fire Guild had secrets but we had convinced her, they just nodded, and that was it."

"The Water Guild have had their own secrets," Quicksilver said. "Surely you have not forgotten the conspiracy you took a hand in unravelling. Their history, far more than that of the forthright and transparent Earth Guild, has conditioned them to understand the damage such secrets can cause, and to accept that repairs are necessary. They have seen that change is possible, and they do not want the conditions leading to the Yule War to return. Most of those here today were either themselves attacked during the war, or had friends and family who were."

"I thought I recognized a few," Lucinda said. "One was in the guildhall Sven defended."

"Yes," Quicksilver said. "The Water Guild are, by and large, honourable people, who have not forgotten they owe a debt to the Fire Guild. We may have a few others join our new corps as word spreads of the Guildhall Defence Project."

René said, "Think we'll get any recruits from the Air Guild that way?"

Quicksilver's smile slipped. "Given that their guild head has declared they will not participate, I doubt it."

L ate at night on the tenth of May, Lucinda lay in bed drowsing over a book. After failing to grasp a paragraph on the third reading, she tossed the book aside and snuggled into the pillow. She'd rather snuggle with Jean. If only he'd come to bed so she could sleep.

My love...

She sat up, startled awake. *Jean?*

Come. You will want to see this.

A quick survey of the house while she scrambled into a robe showed him in his study, his intent gaze fixed on the fire. René emerged from the dining room fireplace in a nightshirt and flapping robe, and ran across the hall to join Jean. Lucinda followed.

In the fire, they watched a firefight blaze through Danzig, half a continent away.

The emperor was among the first to die. Lord Wilhelm, Prince Gunther's remote cousin and the empire's other lightning wielder in training, led his men on a murderous rampage through the city, searching for Crown Prince Sigismund, who had gone to earth at the first sign of trouble.

"Wilhelm, huh?" René said. "You were betting on Gunther."

"The coup is not over," Jean said. "The odds are still in Gunther's favour."

Both defenders and attackers had taken heavy losses before Lord Wilhelm's spies found Prince Sigismund. Only after his brother was dead did Gunther and his supporters step in, burning through Lord Wilhelm's weakened forces. By dawn, with a quarter of the city in smouldering ruins, Prince Gunther was being hailed as the Empire's saviour, having squashed the insurrection.

They watched in grim and horrified fascination the start of Lord Wilhelm's public execution in a glass-walled tank. The slow drip, drip of water into the tank still had hours to go when Jean waved the image away. None of them had an appetite for breakfast.

"You realise, of course," Jean said, "that Gunther's goading drove Lord Wilhelm to take the risks for him."

"Clever," Lucinda said. "Now he's seen as legitimate and it didn't cost him much to get rid of his rivals."

"Yeah, real convenient," René said. "Although I'd expected the bastard to want the fun of committing his own murders."

Jean said, "Gunther is not without self-discipline. Do not forget that."

René Confounds the Fire Eaters

The first of June brought the eagerly anticipated invitations to the triennial tournament in Thule. Two weeks later, the Fire Guildhall in Blazes was a hornets' nest, swarming with Fire Eaters and well-wishers come to see them off. Two warlocks watched the activity through a small, quiet fire in their bedroom's fireplace.

René said, "Ready?"

"No," Hildur said. "Last summer was horrible. I don't want to fight with my mother again."

"Then don't."

Hildur turned to him with questions in her eyes.

He said. "You stay with your mother. I'll stay in the guesthouse with the Fire Eaters."

"You think that will help. We'll still fight."

"You shouldn't." He shoved his hands in his pockets and hunched his shoulders. "Family's important. If I had a mum…"

"If you had a mum and dad and brothers and sisters you'd know that the people closest to you hurt you the most."

Your foreign bride will turn tail and flee… Gunther's prediction popped unbidden into his head. René turned away and glowered blindly out the window. Hildur wasn't a coward. He didn't believe that prediction. Wouldn't believe it.

That enchanter's prediction, though… *It's a pity, knowing your Fire Eaters will turn on you.* The Fire Eaters had been angry with him even before he'd welcomed the air wizard volunteers that had trickled in, despite Enchanter Paul's non-support. Frankland's Unconquered needed the communication spells those wizards brought, and they were sincere in wanting to rehabilitate their guild's reputation. The Fire Eaters saw only lying, traitorous airheads.

Another decision he had made would offend and humiliate the Fire Eaters more deeply. They might never forgive him. That announcement could wait until they returned to Frankland. He wanted to enjoy the tournament.

"What you said is true," he said. "And we hurt your mum by eloping, and running off to Frankland. She has a right to be angry with me. You'll get along better with me out of the way."

"René, don't be an idiot. She yelled at you because she won't admit how angry she is at me."

"What for?"

"For being a warlock. For growing up and making decisions without her help." Hildur threw up her hands. "Who knows? Mostly, I think, for not being the dutiful, self-sacrificing daughter she thinks she deserves. By blaming you, she treats me like a little girl, not a warlock. If you stay at the guesthouse, it will be obvious the problem is between her and me, and not her and you." Hildur's head drooped. "But she will never admit that."

René reached out and pulled her close. She leaned into him. He nuzzled her hair. "Hotheads, who'll tell you to your face how and why you've pissed them off, are so much easier to deal with."

She laughed against his shoulder. "So you're looking forward to a fight with the combined fire guilds of Thule and Frankland over changing the tournament rules?"

"You bet. It'll be the highlight of the trip."

She pulled back to look at him. He gave her a crooked smile. "I'm only partly sarcastic. By the time we've dealt with your mum and aunties, I figure I'll be spoiling for a good, fair fight. If I can't win one of those, what good am I? The tournament itself will be easy. Fun."

She snorted. "So you say." She pulled away from him and reached for her bags. "Keep that in mind. Don't let the Fire Eaters think you're nervous."

"Right. Hold on a moment." He stretched, rolled his shoulders, straightened his spine, and raised his chin. "This'll be my fourth tournament in Thule and I'm almost a lightning thrower. Nobody'll score on me except maybe one of the other lightning-throwers." He shouldered a hefty roll of burn cloths and picked up his own baggage. "As long as you keep your shields up, it will be fun. Let's go."

They walked through the fire to the Blazes guildhall. René thumped a wizard on the back. "Hey, Michael, look what I have." He nodded at the roll of burn cloths. "All for you."

Michael Abernathy grinned. No Fire Eater had gotten past his shields in months. He wasn't worried.

Another wizard earned a ribbing for over packing. Hildur watched René thread through the crowd, speaking to each Fire Eater, counting heads, offering encouragement to the nervous, teasing the confident. How could he project enthusiasm so effortlessly when he'd been glum so few minutes ago? She couldn't. All she could hope for was to endure.

She suffered stoically through the clash between her new family and her old. Neither she nor René raised their voices. The shouts came from her mother and aunts when she announced their plans for the tournament. She didn't raise her voice, either, in the meeting of the two Fire Guilds to review the tournament rules, even during the uproar over René's proposed rule change.

Support came from an unexpected source: the Fire Eaters.

"Girls don't belong there." Carl directed a pointed glare at René. "But if someone insists on them training with us then they have to take part in the tournament, too. We don't need anybody who's not serious wasting our time. Let them in, I say. It's not fair, otherwise. If they get hurt and cry and drop out, that'll be too bad, but it'll stop them whining about not getting a chance."

"My shields are better than yours, Carl Miller," Katie said.

No one but Hildur heard her amid the roar. The Thule fire wizards wouldn't have believed her anyway. Hildur listened a little longer, but heard nothing new. The same arguments had been thrashed out when the women had been admitted to the Fire Eaters' training sessions. When the volume rose to eardrum-damaging levels, she left the smoky guest hall and sat on the wall of a nearby sheepfold, alone in the cool, bright summer night.

Before long Mjöllnir joined her. "Boy's doing a lot of talking. You're not saying anything, girl."

"What's the point? Hrafn, and the ones like him, wouldn't listen. They wouldn't even hear me. They only hear wizards who've won their respect in the tournaments. Without playing, I can't earn their respect. I can't win."

"Umph. You want to play?"

"Doesn't matter what I want. I need to. I'll be a lightning thrower in a few years. The empire will try to kill me."

"Umph." Mjöllnir folded his arms across his chest and stared out into the distance. "That girl—the Locksmith... She's teaching you well?"

"Yes, sir. She and Quicksilver are teaching me how to teach. I'll be better at it than either you or Hrafn."

"Cocky."

"No, sir. I've been working at the guild school for three years. It's what I'm good for."

They talked a little longer, then Mjöllnir walked back to the guest hall where the debate was still in full roar. Hildur followed.

A blast of flame singeing their whiskers silenced the arguing wizards. Mjöllnir said, "Let the women in."

With Mjöllnir's verdict, the defence collapsed. Hrafn and a few others voted against, more abstained, but enough voted in favour for the motion to pass.

"See?" René grinned at Hildur. "Told you we'd win."

Hildur let him enjoy his victory. She didn't tell him the promise she'd given Mjöllnir in exchange for his support.

René stood on the tournament sidelines, absentmindedly fingering the burn cloth on his arm. Hildur was doing better than he had in his first tournament. She had taken a minor burn, retreated to the sidelines for treatment, and returned to the fray. God, he was proud of her.

He wasn't so proud of himself. He'd been watching her instead of his own opponents, and had let flame slip through his shields. When she had gotten burnt it had happened so fast he couldn't prevent it, and she would have resented his interference if he had. He shouldn't have gotten distracted. He didn't need to watch over her here, where the combatants weren't trying to kill each other. When the war came and he had to fight Gunther, he couldn't afford to get distracted. Frankland's Unconquered— his wife, his friends—would have to fend for themselves. Not all of them would. He wiped his eyes with his sleeve.

A light voice tickled his ear. "So sentimental. How touching."

He stiffened. "What do you want?"

"Is that any way to speak to an old friend? I merely want to convey the emperor's compliments on your Guildhall Defence Project. He is finding the exposed faults entertaining, and he thanks you for helping his generals plan their attacks."

René snarled.

The voice continued, "Your efforts to make the four guilds work together are quite amusing. Any day now I expect your earth wizards to throw rocks at the air wizards. Have your fire wizards flamed your water wizards yet? They will, you know. And as for your wife… You're worried about her, aren't you? Don't be. While you are engaged in your futile attacks on the emperor, she won't be in Frankland.

"Well, it's been a lovely chat, but I must be going. Ta-ta."

On their return to Frankland, the Fire Eaters gathered for a critique of their performance at the tournament. Each had their turn under scrutiny. The volume rose as they ragged on each other. After the tournament had been picked apart to René's satisfaction with teasing, encouragement, mild goading, and suggestions for improvement where needed, he gestured for them to stay seated.

"Several of you," he said, "have been telling me our command structure isn't working. You're right. I know you are. I can't keep an eye on everything going on in Frankland and fight the emperor, too. I've been talking to Quicksilver and Arturos, and came up with a structure they approved of. I'm telling you Fire Eaters before I tell all the Unconquered that I'm going to divide the Unconquered into two armies, North and South, with our best officers in charge."

The Fire Eaters nodded and eyed each other. René counted smug looks before delivering the punch line. "The South Frankland army will be under Granddad Ernest, the North under Sorcerer Charles."

Smoke stung Gillian's eyes and irritated her nose. She blew at a thread drifting past. Mrs Rehsavvy claimed the smoke in the Forge dissipated faster with the better ventilation, but Gillian still found a little magical push helped. Imagining what it must have been like before was enough to send her into a coughing fit.

The Fire Eaters were gone, but the room still seemed to ring with angry shouts. Snorri stalked towards the women gathered around the iron table.

"You survived," Hildur said.

Snorri grunted and threw himself into a chair.

Gillian said, "We did wonder if you might not."

"Why'd you come?" Snorri said. "If they really had gone berserk, there's nothing you could have done to help."

"I wasn't here to help. I came to watch the fireworks."

He glared. "Your sister has more sense."

"She came, too, but the noise drove her away."

Mrs Rehsavvy said, "Hildur and I would have stepped in to keep them from killing you, but I'm glad we didn't have to. Their reactions did, however, prove your point—that we need cooler heads in command."

Snorri snarled, "What I proved is I'm not one of them. You think any of them will give me the time of day after this? Not likely."

"They will, eventually. After they've cooled off. Someday they'll understand that you have to do what's best for Frankland, and when you're Fire Warlock, they'll respect you for it."

"Yeah, fine." He pushed away from the table, making the iron scrape on the flagstones. Gillian winced.

He said, "Quicksilver got respect, but how many friends does he...did he have in the Fire Guild. Except for Beorn, none that I know of until we came along." Flames rose. He vanished.

"We don't count?" Hildur said.

"Of course we do," Mrs Rehsavvy said. "But the Fire Eaters were the first male friends he had in the Fire Guild. Maybe the first male friends he had, ever. He needs us, too, but it's not the same."

<hr />

A few days later, Lucinda led Father Pierre and four mundane volunteers through the fire into Storm King's caldera. They goggled at the alien, scarred landscape.

"Have a look around," she said. "Just don't step outside this boundary." She drew their attention to the lines she and Hildur had painted on the ground, marking the safe zone. "We don't want anyone falling into boiling water."

The four guards eyed the line like it was a venomous serpent. She turned her attention to the two arguing male warlocks.

"I don't like it," René said. "I didn't like it weeks ago when Lucinda suggested it, and I don't like it now. I don't see why I—"

"You know perfectly well why the other members of the guild council agreed upon this safety measure," Jean said. "Your knowledge of your own future makes you careless. We trust you will be more considerate of others' safety than of your own."

"They'll be a distraction."

"A distraction?" Jean's eyebrows rose. "My dear René, if you cannot handle this mild hindrance under controlled circumstances, you will have no hope of calling down the lightning amidst the chaos of a battlefield without killing yourself."

René glowered, but made no rejoinder.

"All right then," Lucinda said. "Let's get on with it. Father Pierre?"

The earth father, leaning perilously far over the painted boundary, started. "Oh, yes, of course." He reached into his satchel and pulled out a pouch of earplugs.

"We could have used these years ago," Lucinda said, as he handed her a pair.

Jean said, "Yes, I should have thought of this, but I am not a healer, and I am as trapped as anyone else in Frankland's sometimes stultifying lack of innovation."

Father Pierre said, "We've been trying a lot of new things recently. Like these." He pulled dark spectacles from his satchel.

"Closer collaboration between the guilds has helped immensely, as has you youngsters' willingness to borrow from external sources, including our enemies, although I would not have approved this idea without the humane adaptations."

"I wouldn't have suggested it without them!" Lucinda said. "I'm glad the Earth Guild figured out how to protect their arms. They'd never do it more than once, otherwise."

The four guards were pulling on leather gauntlets, bespelled to dissipate the shock of the power flowing through the lightning-wielding warlock.

"We're ready," the sergeant said. They took their places, two on either side of René, with their gauntleted hands on the next man's shoulder.

"If I hurt you, I'm sorry," René said. "I don't want to do this."

"We're not worried," the sergeant said. "Are we, boys?"

"No, sir."

He gave René's shoulder a hard shake. "Stop grumbling and do what His Wisdom says."

"Proceed when ready," Jean said. "Aim for that outcrop."

"Right," René said. He scowled and lifted his wand. Lightning licked the target.

René whooped and pumped a fist in the air. The guards cheered and pounded him on the back. Lucinda's knees went weak. She grabbed Jean to keep from falling over.

"Well done, men." Jean gave them a broad smile. "We must repeat this exercise many times over the coming months, but for today let us return to the Fortress and drink a toast to the health of Frankland's newest lightning wielder."

In the dining room later, Lucinda, giddy after her second glass of champagne on an empty stomach, asked Jean a question she had avoided for months. "We're aiming to have a few surprises to spring on the empire. What surprises will they spring on us?"

Jean, despite his empty glass, appeared quite sober. He smiled indulgently at her. "My dear, if we knew, then by definition they would not be surprises."

"I meant, we have trouble changing our ways because this is Frankland…"

"And nothing ever changes in Frankland. Pray continue."

"Is innovation easier in the empire? Will they dream up things we couldn't?"

"That is certainly possible, although militarily they have done nothing new in decades. They have had no need as sheer brute force has served them well for so long. Further, their magic guilds will not—nay, cannot—collaborate."

"That's true." She knew the stories. With ultimate power alternating between the Earth and Fire Guilds, and their constant making and breaking alliances with the Water and Air Guilds, the enmity among the empire's magic guilds was worse than the friction between Frankland's Fire and Water Guilds had ever been.

Jean said, "There are, however, indications that Gunther has inspired some new thinking."

"What indications?"

Jean poured himself a second glass and contemplated the rising bubbles. "For one, they have begun stockpiling along their western border barrels of black powder."

"Black powder?" Lucinda's head snapped up. The room spun. She grabbed the table for support. "How mundane."

Jean's eyes danced. "Mundane? Black powder is a Fire Guild secret."

"But anyone can make it."

"Never let anyone outside the Fire Guild hear you say that. But, yes, I understand your point. Because mundanes can make and use it, most fire wizards—particularly those in the empire, with its contempt of all things mundane—would never consider it."

"What do they want with it?"

"I expect they will sap the walls of the Fortress, if they can get close enough."

The wine's warm flush vanished as if she'd been doused in ice water. "That's... That's frightening."

"Indeed." Jean drained his glass. "That prospect frightens even me."

Valhalla, We Are Coming

Two years after Sven and Irene made their proposal, the coven reforged the Earth Office using the new tiered structure. Several weeks later, they reconvened in the Warren's amber chamber for an assessment of the rebuilt office's performance. The coven was in high spirits, confidant the new Earth Office was more solid and useful than it had ever been.

On their way home, Jean and Lucinda dropped by the practice room where a small team of wizards were engaged in a post-mortem on an attack on a water guildhall. They listened for a while then left with Jean smiling, satisfied with their work. On arriving home, he stretched out on the sofa in the library with a book of poetry.

Watching him nap, with the book open on his chest, Lucinda thought her heart would break. His face was lined, his white hair thinning, and he had liver spots. Only his eyes—when he was awake—still shone with undiminished vitality.

Several days later, at the Queen Mother's tea, she focused on those eyes—that feature that had first captivated her—to keep her own brimming ones from spilling over. "We're running out of time." She set down her teacup and laced her fingers together. "Jean's old, and the ageing is accelerating. He can't last much longer. If we don't reforge the Fire Office soon, we may not be able to do it at all."

Mother Astrid reached across the table and laid a hand on Lucinda's arm. "Relax. His age won't stop the reforging."

"But..."

"The Earth Guild Council have been concerned about him, too. We've kept an eye on him for years. He's good for a few more months before we need to step in. We can't give him back his youth, but we can stop his decline until after the reforging."

"But that's…"

"Expensive, yes. Two years we can manage easily, four will be difficult, more than five will cost us dearly."

Lucinda dabbed at tears with her handkerchief. "Thank you."

"You fire talents… I've always thought… You either look unpleasant facts full in the face, or you ignore them completely. There's no middle ground with you, is there?"

The Queen Mother said, "But why delay so long? I thought everyone was nearly ready."

"The coven and the Unconquered are close," Lucinda said. "The Air Guild isn't. Paul agreed, under protest, to come to the Fortress's underground chamber for the unlocking, and to retreat to the safety of the Crystal Palace afterwards instead of returning to the Hall of the Winds. But we need someone in the coven—in the Fortress, that is—to move the Air Guild spells from the king to the Fire Office. Paul can't stay in the Fortress; with the shutters closed he'd go berserk. He categorically refuses to travel through the tunnels from the Crystal Palace to the Fortress, saying those spells can be moved after the rest are done and the Fire Office is active—"

"He's wrong," Irene said. "The Fire Office would be crippled without them."

"Right. Paul's the only one arguing for that, because he hates being underground. It doesn't matter anyway, because we can't open a tunnel out of the Fortress during a battle."

The Queen Mother said, "Can't anyone besides Enchanter Paul do what's needed?"

"For now, no, Your Majesty," Irene said. "It isn't a matter of power or skill. Miranda and Gillian have been practicing moving enchantments until either could do it in her sleep. The sticking point is authorization. It has to be either the Air Enchanter or his apprentice with full delegation, and he doesn't have an apprentice—yet."

"I see." The queen turned to the window. Outside, the two sisters and the king romped in the snow with a pack of dogs. "You are waiting for one of those two darling girls to develop into an enchantress."

"Yes, ma'am," Irene said.

Behind the queen's back, the other women exchanged worried glances.

Whichever one it was, there would be trouble.

Fire Eater Tom Russell fumed as Warlock Snorri, with Granddad Ernest looking on, hauled the Unconquered over the coals for their lack of teamwork. They deserved it, he had to admit. The day's practice—one of the irregularly scheduled events where all the South Frankland Unconquered, with the exception of the three air wizards, gathered in the practice room in a vain attempt to work together—had been a disaster. Water wizards gave fire wizards the cold shoulder, earth wizards stonewalled water wizards, and fire wizards were snubbing each other.

Some weren't listening to Snorri either. Tom had heard grumbling that a few recruits had expected to train with the Fire Warlock or Warlock Quicksilver, and didn't like taking orders from someone younger than themselves.

Tom could sympathise with that. Snorri looked closer to sixteen than twenty-three and not at all like a warlock. It was easy to slip back into calling the scrawny kid by his given name rather than by the war name he deserved. Burn it, Snorri was a full-fledged lightning wielder! The guild council was keeping quiet about that. Tom wasn't sure why, but knew better than to talk out of turn.

Ten years ago René—oops, Snorri—had been everywhere, poking his nose into everything and showing off every chance he could get, but something had changed after the Yule War. He'd become so focused on getting ready for war with the empire that he didn't have time for his old friends, the Fire Eaters. Tom missed those days. Snorri wasn't much fun now, and never showed off. Some younger recruits had never seen him do anything flashy—anything they would consider worthy of a warlock—and didn't believe the stories the older Fire Eaters told. He didn't lose his temper often either. No wonder they doubted him.

Tom muttered under his breath, wishing Snorri would do something flashy, just to remind these frostbitten Unconquered he was a real, honest-to-God warlock.

Snorri was wrapping up his harangue, backing off from the sarcasm, and ending with an earnest plea for them to do better next time, because he knew they had it in them.

The knot in Tom's stomach began to unwind. He looked around to see how his squad had taken it, and his mouth went dry. Jimmy Ferguson, a late recruit who had even less chance of getting through the Rehsavvy's front door than an air witch had of being a good cook, was on the verge of going berserk. Tom knew the signs: the lowered brow, the clenched jaw, the staring eyes, and the twitching fingers. He knew the object of Jimmy's wrath, too: Clarence Hawkins, water wizard.

If only Clarence would stop making suggestions to improve their fighting abilities. He was trying to be helpful, and the damnable thing was his ideas were often good ones, but he offered his suggestions in a cool, supercilious manner that drove the flammable Jimmy nuts. He annoyed Tom, too, for that matter. Why didn't he bother Snorri? He even encouraged the cold fish, for God's sake.

Snorri and Ernest walked through the muttering wizards. Tom edged towards Jimmy, groping for some distraction.

The heavy tunnel door closed behind the two officers. Jimmy flamed Clarence. Tom yelled and lunged, but the water wizard's tunic was ablaze before he got between them. Clarence screamed.

The tunnel door crashed against the wall. Clarence's flames went out. Jimmy blazed like a torch. Snorri stomped through scattering wizards. Jimmy rolled across the flagstones. A pair of fire wizards trying and failing to douse the flames scrambled away from the livid, fire-spitting warlock.

Snorri jabbed the burning wizard with his wand. The flames vanished. The screams continued. "Sleep, drown you," Snorri barked. "What are you waiting for? You—" He jabbed another fire wizard. "Grab the burn cloths. Treat Clarence. This one, too." He made another stab at Jimmy. "And when this bastard wakes up, tell him—" Tom reeled backwards as the jabbing wand swung towards him. "Tell him not to ever show his ugly face here again. He doesn't deserve the title 'Unconquered.'"

"And if any of the rest of you self-centred whiners—" Snorri's voice rose to a roar, echoing off the walls. "—would rather settle stupid halfpenny grudges than pull together to save your homes and families, you shouldn't bother coming back either." He nudged Jimmy with his toe. "This traitor's still alive. Don't count on me keeping my temper in check next time."

A wave of blast-furnace heat rolled across the Unconquered. Blindingly bright flame filled the air. When Tom could see again, Snorri was gone.

Tom had Jimmy rolled in burn cloths before most of the Unconquered had recovered from the shock. The earth wizards with healing talent rushed to help. Only after both injured men had been treated did Tom give in to the shakes that threatened to overwhelm him. He sat on the floor with his chin on his knees and reflected on the wisdom of the old adage, "Be careful what you wish for…"

For the members of the Reforging Coven, months passed in a firestorm of experimentation and innovation, with impacts on existing spellcraft that would keep scholars busy for decades. Meeting quarterly to tear down and rebuild the Earth Office, they fused into a cohesive team, with only one exception. The Mathesons never let the simmering animosity between them and Enchanter Paul boil over, and in tacit agreement the rest of the coven hid their scepticism towards Paul's suggestions.

Their innovations weren't confined to just the offices. "These badges will shift the odds in our favour." René traced a semicircle with a palm-sized silver shield held at arm's length, letting every member of the officers corps gathered in the practice room see it. "They serve a dual purpose: the Locksmith's spell will hide the bearer from the empire's wizards, and the Air Guild spells will let us communicate with each other during battle. We've already practiced with orders relayed through the king and down. These will let you pass questions and new intelligence back up, or sideways, to help each other out.

"Quiet. Let me finish," he said, as an excited chatter rose. "Questions later. We only have a few so far, but as they make more, everybody will have a chance to practice with them."

As he described the badges' capabilities in detail, Sorcerer Charles, watching with Warlock Quicksilver from some distance away, inspected a sample badge. "What an extraordinary device. Can they really replicate this for all Frankland's Unconquered?"

Quicksilver said, "Master Sven is confident that they will have badges within a few months for all officers, which is what really matters. He was unwilling to speculate on coverage for the rank and file, but I expect they will speed up production as they become more comfortable with the spells."

"And potentially make more mistakes, if they get bored with it."

"There is that."

"Could other members of the Air Guild help with production?"

"I think not. The spells' tight coupling depends upon a close collaboration difficult to ensure in a non-familial context."

"Yes, I see. Except for the Locksmith's contributions, the van Gelder-Matheson's did it all?"

"Yes. The badges were their idea, the spells their inventions."

"This Sven-Irene coupling is turning out to be as fruitful as the Oliver-Irene one was."

"In many ways, but that comparison highlights another reason why enlisting others would not help. Aside from Enchanter Paul, who as we know is always overworked, and these two extraordinary young women, I doubt anyone else in the Air Guild is capable of handling these spells."

Charles studied Quicksilver for a moment before turning his attention back to the badge. "You're saying this is mage-quality work."

"Yes. Unequivocally."

"I'm not overly surprised. Will the Company of Mages get to see the spellwork?"

Quicksilver grimaced. "Unfortunately, those are the spells we most want to keep hidden. If they should ever fall into the empire's hands…"

"Quite. Shame, though. Having to prove one's worth twice over can be discouraging."

"Indeed. Miranda's heart is in her music, and she may never receive the recognition she deserves for her spellcraft, but her sister would continue her studies in advanced air magic for sheer delight in the subject. I have no doubt she will continue to do impressive work, and the Company of Mages will acknowledge it eventually."

"The Company, yes. Will the Air Guild?"

Snorri was too busy to pay much attention to the passage of time. He was taken by surprise on June first when the Fire Guild received its invitation to participate in the triennial tournament in Thule. Where had three years gone? He paused to consider what they had accomplished.

He was proud of Frankland's Unconquered; they had become an army. He, Charles, and Ernest had spent many hours sorting out teams with personalities that could work together. Endless hours of drills had turned the practice room from chilly to subtropical, and everyone who spent time there was now calling it the Forge. They had cheered when the Fire Warlock reluctantly let the Earth Guild cut more cooling vents.

Alex had learned to use the Fire Office's Air Guild spells, with a little coaching from Enchanter Paul and a lot from the van Gelder sisters. The girls had also discovered that supporting him with magic mirrors reduced the strain on his mind's eye. He was nowhere near as fast at spotting trouble as the Fire Warlock, but René conceded he was doing shockingly well for a mundane.

And as for himself... At twenty-five, he had spent half his life training for the coming war. He had no doubt that the gift of cold water was one of the best things anyone had ever done for him. Without it, he would have killed himself or a guard in throwing lightning; he was certain of that. He had practiced with the guards for a year, then Quicksilver had at last cut him loose. He could now match Lucinda bolt for bolt, the two of them creating a continuous rolling barrage that exhilarated them and frayed nerves down in Blazes.

Hildur could draw a weak blast. She would not stand on her own for many months yet, but she could punch through any non-warlock's shields as easy as breathing. Even Michael Abernathy was afraid of her.

To balance their gains, the empire had two young, freshly hatched warlocks, and Gunther had laughed at their attempts to spread rumours saying the Air Office would be next. Warlock Quicksilver had physically aged no further, but the strain on the Earth Guild was starting to show, and with the Guildhall Defence Project over, the Unconquered were restless. Before long, they would either lose their fighting trim or their cohesion, and start fighting among themselves.

That realisation horrified him. *How much longer can we wait, big sister? If nothing happens soon...*

It will, little brother. I feel it in my bones. Soon.

Tea with the Queen Mother on Miranda's eighteenth birthday was an unusually festive affair. Given a gentle nudge by Queen Marguerite, the palace's kitchen staff had outdone themselves in fixing delicacies to please visiting air witches. Both girls were in high spirits. Alexander had nothing to add to the conversation; he was absorbed in watching Miranda's sparkling eyes and smiling lips.

The girls were laughing over some story Sorceress Eleanor was telling when his mother, as she often did, steered her side conversation with Mrs Rehsavvy towards the reforging plans, asking for any information the Fire Guild was willing to share.

Alexander used his magically enhanced hearing to listen from the other end of the table. "Even if everything goes perfectly," Mrs Rehsavvy said, "—and we know it won't—it will be exhausting."

The tone of the laughter changed. Gillian was still laughing, but Miranda had gone quiet, pale, and still. Her pupils dilated until her blue eyes seemed almost black. Alexander's heart dropped to his toes.

Across the table, Countess Irene grabbed Mrs Rehsavvy's arm. "That night," Mrs Rehsavvy said, turning, and froze.

"That night," Miranda intoned, "a great warrior shall feast in Valhalla."

Elegy

The birthday party was in ruins. A clamour arose, with women talking over one another. Miranda stared through Alexander as if looking into the void between the stars.

Mrs Rehsavvy shoved her chair backwards. "Your Majesty, I'm sorry. Please forgive me."

Mother Astrid reached for her, but she evaded the outstretched hand, stumbled towards the fireplace with her sleeve pressed against her eyes, ducked under the mantle, and vanished.

Miranda came back to life. She hunched over with her face in her hands, stammering, "I'm sorry, I'm sorry."

Bright red letters hung in the air: Please be quiet. The clamour died.

"It's a shame about your tea, Your Majesty." Countess Irene rounded the table and gripped her daughter's shaking shoulders. "But she needs fresh air."

"By all means." Queen Marguerite fluttered a hand at the pair. "Do what you think best."

"Come along, sweetheart."

"Wait." Alexander, half out of his chair, reached across the table, knocking over a pyramid of petit fours, and clamped a hand on Miranda's wrist. "Which warrior?"

Miranda turned enormous blue eyes to him. "I don't know," she whispered. "Words come to me, I don't see visions."

Her mother said, "Does it matter? Whichever warlock it is, his death will break Lucinda's heart."

It mattered to him. If Snorri died, his own heart would be ripped open, but he said nothing and let the countess draw Miranda out of his grip. The countess steered her unresisting, anguished daughter out into the sunshine. Alexander waited for them outside the music room with Gillian, silent and sober, clinging to his arm. Fifteen minutes brisk walk through the gardens restored the colour to Miranda's cheeks, but did little to lessen her hangdog look. Alexander's heart bled for her.

He said, "Warlock Quicksilver called precognition a heavy burden. I believe that is true."

Miranda said, "It is. I don't want to be a seer. I don't want to ever hurt anyone else like that again. Mama, why didn't you tell the Locksmith to make her lock on that talent last until I was fifty?"

Countess Irene sighed. "Because you're an adult now. No one, not even the Fire Warlock, has the right to impose a restriction of that magnitude on another law-abiding adult without good cause. You have to choose how to use it, and you can't make that choice without being aware of the consequences, good and bad. I will introduce you to someone in the Water Guild who is proud of being a seer. Talk it over with her, and with other people whose opinions you value. If you then still want that lock, I'm sure Lucinda will be happy to oblige."

Miranda shrank. "She won't want to even be in the same room with me."

"Nonsense. Don't be melodramatic." The countess turned Miranda around, facing her. "Look at me. Are you angry with Warlock Arturos for letting slip that one of you girls would be an enchantress?"

"No… Well, yes." Miranda held up thumb and forefinger an inch apart. "About this much. I'm angrier with Enchanter Paul for being such a jerk about it."

Gillian said, "If Mrs Rehsavvy puts a lock lasting years on that talent, he'll be furious."

Miranda gave her a sardonic glance. "And your point is?"

"All the more reason to do it."

Countess Irene frowned. "Children…"

Gillian, unrepentant, ducked behind Alexander.

The countess rolled her eyes. "Lucinda won't stay angry with you. She'll understand you weren't trying to hurt her. Or him, whichever one he is. It's the empire trying to do that. You have no control over them. Don't take their guilt on yourself."

Miranda nodded slowly. "I'll try not to, Mama."

She led them into the music room. Queen Marguerite was waiting, along with a dozen courtiers. Surreptitious glances and chatter behind fluttering fans indicated the courtiers knew something unusual had occurred and were making wild guesses as to its nature.

Alexander ignored them and sat beside his mother. Gillian, unoffended, sat where she could watch him watching her sister. Miranda sat at the pianoforte with her head bowed and her hands in her lap for almost a minute, long enough for the courtiers to grow restive, and then leaned forward and attacked the keyboard with a ferocity that astonished them.

Alexander had heard Sunderman's *Elegy in D Minor* at his father's funeral and at his grandfather's, but it had not then been a blade carving into his soul. He raised watering eyes to the cherubs floating across the sky-blue ceiling. He had never been fond of their gambols; today they seemed more than ever inappropriate.

He had not cried at either funeral. He had loved his grandfather dearly, and would never have shamed the old man by indulging in such unseemly behaviour. Later, at his father's funeral, he had been too conflicted for tears. Anger, disgust, and relief had won out over grief. But now grief flooded through him and threatened to unman him.

His mother sobbed into her handkerchief. He reached out and pulled her towards him. She turned to him and wept on his shoulder. And to his surprise, he found that in giving comfort he, too, was comforted.

If ten-year-old Eddie had not demanded to go to Thule to watch the tournament, would Lucinda have felt premonitions of danger across such a vast distance? However it was, she was there on the sidelines, with chill fingers crawling down her spine. Her edginess infected Eddie: after exchanging cross words with him three times in half an hour, she left him with the other watching children and found a quiet vantage point across the valley from the throng of cheering spectators.

By noon on the second day, the effort of piercing the billowing smoke and distorting waves of magical energy was exhausting her mind's eye, but vultures' talons gripped her. She abandoned the Fire Eaters, following Jean's lighthouse beacon and René's diamond-hard brilliance. After the midday meal, she dragged Hildur away from the playing field, silencing her protests with "René's in danger."

For the next three hours, the two women kept up a constant scan of the arena, with Hildur providing running commentary on the state of play. Lucinda closed her physical eyes and let her mind's eye travel a complete circuit of the valley, seeing the four participating warlocks only as bright stars among constellations of dimmer ones. On the edge, a fifth point of brilliance flickered, as if hiding behind a cluster of dimmer lights.

Lucinda jabbed Hildur and pointed. "Who's that?"

The fifth bright spot and two dimmer lights were converging on René. Hildur disappeared in a blast of flame.

Lucinda yelled, *Little brother, watch out*, and followed, arriving in time to witness Hildur throwing herself between René and the combined fire of three savage attacks.

In the Thule healers' hall, René cradled his wife's shrouded body in his arms, murmuring, "Hildur, come back. I need you. I love you."

He had never said that to her before. He'd known better than to lie to a warlock, but he hadn't known his own mind. What an idiot he'd been. It was a wonder she still talked to him.

The senior earth witch touched his arm. Her voice was very gentle. "She can't hear you. We've done all we can for her, but it's not enough."

"She's not dying. I won't let her." He closed his eyes, willing himself to sink into that blackness he'd been frantic to escape from, so many years ago.

The witch's finger dug into his arm. Her voice became sharp, urgent. "Stop that. You'll lose yourself, too. You don't know—"

"I've been there before." The witch gasped and let go.

The door flew open. Eydis Johansdottir, Hildur's mother, charged in, screaming. "It's that wretched Frank's fault. Let go of her, you—"

He lifted sightless eyes. She blanched. Some part of him, not yet drowned in the cold dark, delivered a quenching command. "Shut up and get out."

The earth witch shoved the stunned air witch through the door. "And stay out."

René sank further into the darkness, purging himself of all emotion other than love for his wife. Anger would do them no good there. Hundreds of miles away, Alexander cancelled the evening's entertainment. Courtiers and servants scrambled aside as he paced the halls in a murderous rage.

Closer at hand, Lucinda, too, was engulfed in anger: Jean's, René's, the Fire Eaters', Mjöllnir's, her own. The tournament was in shambles. Outside the healer's hall, two old, angry men kept watch. The Empire's assassins were dead, the warlock at Lucinda's hands, the other two fire wizards at René's.

Jean, is Eydis right? Is this René's fault?

No, my love. René is not responsible for the Empire's actions, and Hildur is a warrior. She would have flung herself in harm's way for anyone here. Take heart, my love; if you had not strengthened her shields by training her to summon the lightning, she surely would be dead.

Small comfort, that. Lucinda traded the healer's hall for solitude on a black sand beach. Unlike that Danish king who ordered the incoming tide to retreat, her feet did not get wet. The water boiled away in an immense, towering cloud of steam. She sensed René's return to the world of the living, and knew that Hildur would survive, but her anger fed on his and did not abate. The foreshore was baked dry and the sun had dipped below the northern horizon and risen again after the short night before reason returned and the world ceased to be tinged in shades of red.

She had nothing to say to René. Nothing needed to be said. He had promised Sorceress Lorraine he would not seek revenge on the emperor. He was bound by that promise. Lucinda was not.

Paul and the Enchantress

Gillian did not often ask for a Fire Guild escort through the tunnels to Airvale, even though the Fire Warlock had said they'd be happy to accommodate her whenever she wanted, but for several days the feeling had been growing that she needed to see her sister. She was too familiar with magic to ignore the quivering sense of anticipation, although she didn't yet know what it meant.

She had picked a good day to come. With wind whipping her hair into tangles and driving rain-heavy clouds at a breakneck pace across the sky, it was a day only a member of the Air Guild could enjoy, a day when anything could happen, miracles and horrors both. Her first papa, Enchanter Oliver, would have loved it. Papa Sven, if he had been here, would have been scowling at the sky, dreading a soaking.

Miranda, air witch though she was, didn't appear much happier. With her head bowed and a dark cloak pulled tight around her, she looked as solid as an earth witch. As light as a plumb bob.

Gillian started to call, but hesitated. Just because she felt as light as drifting leaves didn't mean Miranda was having a good day. If she had come out to this isolated dune seeking solitude, what right did Gillian have to bother her?

But Miranda had turned and seen her, and was waving in big sweeping circles that said, *Glad to see you, little sister.*

As Gillian bobbed along the top of the dune, a shaft of sunlight pushed through the clouds, turning Miranda's cloak from drab to ultramarine. She laughed.

Gillian stretched out her arms and opened her fingers to the wind as she ran. If she closed her eyes she could believe she had wings and feathers. Her feet had no purchase on the dune, but she was still moving forward. Miranda was shouting, but Gillian was too distracted to hear.

And then Miranda was on her, whirling her around. "You flew! I saw it! You flew!"

With blazing faces, they held hands and spun in circles, laughing and shouting. Miranda lost her footing and they tumbled together, sliding down the side of the dune and coming to rest in a tangled heap. Still laughing, they scrambled to their feet and brushed sand from each other's clothes. Miranda's joy faded.

"I'm sorry," she said.

Gillian's smile dimmed but didn't vanish. "For what? For being glad?"

Miranda wouldn't meet her eyes. "I tried. I really did."

"I know you did. How many times have I watched you out here trying to fly? And for what? To spend the rest of your life being miserable, hunched over musty old contracts and treaties?" Gillian caught a fold of Miranda's cloak and tugged her towards Airvale. "Come on. It's better this way. I like contract magic. You're too fine a musician to be wasted on the Guild Council."

They sang opera on the road into town, and talked music over a celebratory lunch, but all the while a question danced at the edge of Gillian's consciousness: was her new status a miracle, a horror, or both together?

***

The two girls stopped inside the door to the Air Enchanter's study. Without looking up, Enchanter Paul waved them closer. "What is it? I haven't much time today."

Neither girl moved. Miranda cleared her throat. "The Fire Warlock was right. I mean, about one of us being an enchantress."

Paul looked up, smiling. "My dear Miranda." He started to rise. "That's excellent—"

"Not Miranda," Gillian said. "Me. I flew."

Paul's smile vanished. He sank back into his chair. Gillian's lips tightened. Seconds ticked past.

Paul said, "Were there any witnesses? Sometimes a strong wind and flapping cloak can make even a mundane imagine the wind has blown them about."

"I saw her," Miranda said. "She flew. You shouldn't be surprised. Your mind's eye should have told you months ago her talent had gotten stronger than mine."

Paul's shoulders sagged. "You may yet be an enchantress. I have been hoping—"

"I haven't. I'm a musician. I hated the prospect of spending every day for the next fifty years working on treaties. Gillian's better at that than I am, anyway."

"Impossible," Paul snapped. He focused on Gillian. "You will, of course, return to the guild school immediately—"

"I won't."

"Don't contradict me, young lady. Or interrupt. You have wasted far too much time over the past five years indulging in idle mischief in the Fortress. If you are to be useful in the Guild Council you must resume your formal education at once, and begin making up for lost time, particularly on contract magic."

"Except for the music, I can already work all the air magic Miranda can."

"Usually better," Miranda said.

"And Mama has been teaching me contract magic."

"Your mother," Paul said, "is not a recognised authority on that subject."

"She should be."

"I warned you not to contradict me. Professor Beecham is a recognised authority, and he has done an excellent job of tutoring your sister."

"If you don't want Gillian wasting time—" Miranda enunciated each word distinctly. "—then don't force her to listen to that misogynistic bore. I enchant my pen to write down everything he says, then keep my eyes fixed on the paper and dream about music while he rants about wasting his time teaching girls. Mama already covered everything he pretends to teach more than a year ago."

Paul was scowling at both of them now. "You've never said anything like this to me before."

"I don't like to argue. Gillian does. If you make her take lessons from Professor Beecham, the results won't be pretty. I'd almost feel sorry for him if he weren't such a louse."

Paul slammed a hand on his desk. "Your attitude is intolerable. I expected this from your sister, not from you."

"This is beside the point," Gillian snapped. "I'll have time later to study contract magic in depth. The communication spells are more urgent."

A vein pulsed in Paul's temple. "Contract magic is the Guild Council's primary concern, and we are short-staffed. We have no time for anything else."

"But it doesn't have to be that way. The contract and treaty responsibilities could have been spread out across the whole guild if the Great Coven had done a better job of planning. We can fix that when we reforge the Air Office."

"Enough," Paul roared. "I will not tolerate any nonsense about changes to the Air Office, especially not from an untutored girl."

"You will. You need my help."

"Begone! I will talk to your parents about your education. And your manners."

"You do that," Gillian said. The two girls marched out onto the veranda with their heads held high, and didn't look back.

The servant who ushered Enchanter Paul into Alexander's private audience chamber retreated, closing the door behind him.

"Thank you for coming so promptly," Alexander said. "We are concerned about the succession to the Air Office, now that Lady Gillian has developed into an enchantress, and Lady Miranda has not. You may speak freely here. We shall not be overheard."

The wary look that had settled on Paul's face at the mention of the succession eased a little, but did not vanish. "Thank you, Your Majesty. I, too, am concerned about the succession. Years ago, when the other officeholders insisted that one of those two children must be my successor, I was aghast that timing should be their primary concern. Since we've seen that neither girl is fit for the office, I am sure you will agree we must wait until an enchanter appears."

Alexander considered this. "What, in your opinion, makes Enchantress Gillian unfit?"

"You spend much of your leisure time in her company, Your Majesty. I'm sure you already know her rather well. Forgive me for stating the obvious, Sire, but traits we value in friends may not be traits that would serve well in high office."

"Understood. And yes, we already have an opinion of her character. We are asking for yours."

"Very well. Her most outstanding character flaw is her disdain for formal education." The king gave him an incredulous stare, but didn't interrupt. Paul said, "Her refusal to return to the Air Guild School after only one term was unacceptable. I was shocked—shocked, sir!—that Master Sven, a mage, would indulge such irresponsible behaviour. I have been given assurances that he and Irene have had her tutored privately in the responsible use of air magic, but indulgent parents cannot provide the same objective assessments and discipline as the professional staff at the school. Her parents' mollycoddling has allowed her to become wilful, obdurate, undisciplined, and disrespectful of her elders. Nor can they have instilled any sense of duty."

"No sense of duty... We gather, then, you are unaware that from the age of seven, at Warlock Quicksilver's request, she has been steeling herself to be useful during the Fire Office reforging by voluntarily subjecting herself to increasingly longer periods of time underground."

"No, I am aware of that, but do not believe it is possible for any air talent to endure that monstrous chamber for long."

"Gillian can now spend an entire day there without undue stress."

Paul gaped. "Are you serious?"

"Quite."

Paul recovered his aplomb. "If she can spend hours underground, then she is clearly not pure Air Guild."

"We did not imagine she was."

"That alone must be a disqualification."

"Having discussed the issue with our advisors, and having read a number of biographies ourself, we agree with Warlock Quicksilver's view that guild purity is not a desirable trait in an officeholder, as it too often encourages rigidity and narrow-mindedness." Paul flushed, but the king didn't give him an opportunity to retort. "What have you done, Your Wisdom, to remedy what you consider your granddaughter's inadequate education?"

Paul's flush deepened. "Very little, I admit. The office's demands are constant, and without her nearby in Airvale, I have spent little time with her. Whenever I do, she displays a most unbecoming antagonism towards me, rejecting all suggestions I offer for self-improvement."

"That is unfortunate, but you have brought her disdain on yourself."

Paul's head snapped back and he began sputtering, but Alexander silenced him with a cool stare.

"The other officeholders are pleased with her respectful demeanour. They—men and women with many years' experience exploring the intricacies of human behaviour—warned you repeatedly not to favour one grandchild over the other, but you still continue to do so. You have paid the younger child so little heed you are unaware that at the age of sixteen she is already drawing attention for the quality of her spellcraft. This, sir, is not what we expect of an officeholder or a mage."

Paul paled. He stared mutely at Alexander.

Alexander said, "What you denigrate as obstinacy, the other officeholders commend as firmness of purpose and resistance to fashion and manipulation. They are relieved she is an enchantress, as they are united in their opinion that she, and not Lady Miranda, has an officeholder's temperament and the likelihood of another, better-qualified candidate appearing in less than half a century is extremely low. The fire and water mages are enthusiastic about her. The earth mages agree that she'll do. Yours, sir, is the only voice against her. You must overcome this wilful blindness. You must treat her with the respect she deserves, and begin training her as your successor."

Paul's face was colourless. In a low, rough voice, he said, "I knew you enjoyed my granddaughter's company, Sire, but I had not credited the rumours you were courting her. Am I to understand that you intend to replace all Frankish officials who do not please you, and install your favourites to do your bidding?"

"We believe you understand very little, sir, outside of contracts and trade. You just contradicted yourself. Is she biddable, or not? Since you do not understand, let us be blunt. The crux of the problem is not your successor. The crux of the problem is your unwillingness to face the black magic spell protecting the lock on your office. But the Air Office must be unlocked while the Locksmith is still in her prime."

"I do not accept that. Let me remind you, Sire, I have never agreed with the other officeholders that the Air Office required 'fixing.' It has served us very well for a thousand years. Yes, it does have flaws, but they are minor flaws we can live with—have lived with. Can continue to live with."

Alexander closed his eyes and breathed deeply, reviewing the arguments, pro and con. There was no point in repeating them; Paul had heard them all, many times over. "Your view on this matter is at odds with our other advisors."

"Who speak with inadequate knowledge of the Air Office. Given the radical experimentation being tried on the other offices, it seems to me imperative that at least one pillar of stability survive."

"We disagree. This bone has been in contention for far too long, and we will not let it continue. We regret that this ordeal should be forced on you unwillingly, but the lock was not our doing. You, sir, must face it. You cannot avoid it."

A spark lit in Paul's eye. "I can. I could retire—"

Alexander slammed a fist down on the arm of his chair, and sprang to his feet, shouting. "And let Enchantress Gillian face it instead? Your own granddaughter. How dare you!"

Paul was on his feet, too, backing away and stammering. "No, no, I didn't think... I didn't mean..."

"Don't lie to us, sir." Alexander stalked to the window, breathing hard.

"I didn't think...Please, Your Majesty, I still find it difficult to imagine an Air Enchantress. I would never force such a burden on a woman."

The emerald tucked inside the king's shirt was quiet and cool. Whether or not it was true, Enchanter Paul believed what he said. Alexander clasped his hands together behind his back and took a deep breath, held it, then exhaled slowly. He repeated that several times. Sometimes he regretted his affinity for the Fire Guild. Giving in to rage would not soften this recalcitrant old man's resolve.

"It's an easy thing," Paul said, "to talk about someone else facing mutilation and possible death. You will never be faced with something so monstrous yourself."

"You have forgotten, sir, that we were unshielded on our foray to the palace during the Yule War." Alexander fought to lower his voice. "We apologize for shouting at you. That was unseemly of us. We will do what we can to make Enchantress Gillian's apprenticeship easier for you. We will ask the other mages to oversee her continued education. You need only be involved in matters relating to enchanter-level magic, and her apprenticeship will relieve you of the necessity of returning to the Fortress during the Fire Office reforging to move the corpus of Air Guild spells."

He took another deep, steadying breath before turning to face the enchanter. "We do not often order other Franks to risk their own lives, but sometimes we must. There is no one else to shift the burden to, nor would it be fair to do so, to someone younger, when being officeholder has given you decades beyond a man's normal life. We order you, Your Wisdom, to begin training Enchantress Gillian to become Air Enchantress, and to set a target year for reforging the Air Office."

The two men faced each other, both erect and rigid. Paul spoke through clenched teeth. "No, Sire, I will not. The Air Office is my domain. You do not have the authority to make me relinquish it." He turned away without receiving the king's permission to leave. "I will name her my apprentice for the Fire Office reforging, and when that's done I will revoke the authority. Good day, Your Majesty."

Nerves

"That isn't a good idea." Lucinda studied the young woman facing her across the kitchen table. Hildur had been on the thin side before the assassination attempt, and had lost twenty pounds in the days after. Her head sported a fuzz of red, but she disdained wigs or scarves. Above sunken cheeks, enormous, defiant eyes stared at Lucinda…but she detected fear in them, too. "You haven't recovered yet." Lucinda went on rolling out a piecrust. "Put on another fifteen pounds, and then maybe—maybe—we'll resume your training."

"That will take too long." Hildur massaged her arm, as if remembering the first time the lightning's power had flowed across it. "If you won't help me, I'll practice on my own."

"What?" Lucinda's head snapped up. "You can't do that." But Hildur was already in the fire. Lucinda yelled for René, and followed.

They converged on her in the caldera. Lucinda clamped a hand on Hildur's shoulder just as she drew on the volcanic forces. Even with Lucinda's intervention, it was a near thing. They carried her to the practice rom, laid her on the floor, and applied the standard treatments for heat stroke with a squad of gawking wizards gathered around while René lambasted her for stupidity.

Hildur wasn't listening. She came out of her daze, sat up, and stared at her hands in horror. "My magic. What's happened to it?"

René said, "Lucinda set her lock on you—the one that hides your magic from even yourself. That's what you get for being monumentally stupid."

She struggled to her feet, holding onto the table for support. "I have to be ready."

"Ready for what?"

"The Fire Office," Hildur said impatiently. "You have an enchantress now. What else are you waiting for?"

Lucinda bit her lip. No one outside the Fire Guild Council was to know they were waiting for the first hard frost—without cold air coming in the vents, the Forge would in truth get as hot as a forge—but no one outside the Fire Guild Council was to know that.

René said, "If you've recovered when the time comes, you'll help. If not, you'll stay put in the Fortress and I won't have to worry about you."

"How can I do what I need to do stuck in the Fortress?"

"How can you train Thule warlocks if you kill yourself?"

"My dear Hildur." Jean slid between the two shouting warlocks. "One must be hale and whole to summon the lightning. Anyone who is not, dies. Neither Lucinda nor I attempted summoning the lightning for more than five months after our ordeal. If we let you attempt it now, three months after yours, we would be guilty of negligent homicide, as well as bereft. The time will come when you will prove to us in other ways that you are healthy, and you may resume your training then."

Hildur's head drooped. "Yes, sir."

René said, "Lucinda will take the lock off if you promise not to be that stupid again."

Hildur glared, but said, carefully, "I promise I won't call down the lightning again until Lucinda or Quicksilver says I can."

René huffed. "That wasn't quite what I meant, but hey, it'll do." He put an arm around her shoulders and pulled her close. "Look, Hildur, I know being patient is hard, but—"

She shoved him away. "You know nothing. I am not a mundane housewife you can order around."

"Is this the thanks I get for saving your life?"

She spat out a stream of blistering Norse. He reddened. She flounced through a tunnel, slamming the door behind her.

Lucinda raised her eyebrows. René made a face. "I am not translating that."

A watching fire wizard snickered. "Guess you're sleeping in the dog house tonight."

René glowered.

Lucinda said. "Show's over, folks. Get back to work."

Slanting beams from the half-risen sun made diamonds in the dewy grass. Alexander strolled across the lawn. Wet shoes didn't dampen his enjoyment of the fine early-autumn morning.

A soprano voice called, "Alex!"

He turned, smiling, into the glare. "I hoped I would see you today."

"I'm not too early, am I?" Gillian asked. "I wanted to catch you before the hoards gathered."

"You and Miranda are always welcome, any hour of the day or night. I had been expecting you for days. I thought you would want to show me yourself that you can fly."

"I needed to get a little control over it first. I'm still learning how to land."

"Show me."

"I'll do better than that." She grabbed his wrist and pulled it around her shoulders, and wrapped her other arm around his waist. "Run with me."

"What? Are you—"

"Quiet. Just run." She gave him a hard shove.

They ran. Half-a-dozen steps later they were a foot over the lawn. They sailed a dozen yards, to within several feet of the balustrade marking the edge of the upper garden, and dropped sprawling on the wet grass.

"Oops," she said. "Sorry."

Alexander rolled to his feet, smiling, and offered her a hand up. They brushed dew off their clothes and turned to look back across the lawn. The dark band of green where their feet had disturbed the dew ended halfway across.

"Thank you," he said. "That was fun."

"It was, wasn't it? I'll take you higher when I get the knack of it better. I don't want to drop you from treetop height."

He laughed. "Well, no, that wouldn't be fun." He sobered. "I'm glad you're enjoying your new powers. I was afraid you might be angry at me for putting you in an unpleasant position. I'm sorry to have done so. I hadn't realised I was giving anyone the impression I was courting you. I should have known better."

"Oh, that." She shrugged. "Don't worry about it. No one who knows us well thinks that." She made a sweeping gesture taking in the ever-present guards and servants at a discreet distance. "We're not fooling them."

"Ah, but if we should be giving her a mistaken impression…"

"I doubt it." She tucked her hand into the crook of his arm and they strolled alongside the balustrade. "I'll tell her…Or maybe not…" She wrinkled her nose. "Sometimes a denial gives a rumour more weight than it deserves. I shouldn't worry if I were you. She knows you, too."

"Yes, but the rumour could have arisen because I've spent more time in your company than hers, lately."

"She's been avoiding you, you mean."

Alexander leaned on the balustrade, gazing out into the distance. "I haven't wanted to believe that. She has been quite busy this season, with one concert after another."

"And anything distracting her from her music is an imposition. But she might come around. She was ecstatic when I flew. Imagining herself as Air Enchantress was giving her ulcers. Without that pressure…"

Alexander turned to Gillian with a sardonic smile. "And being queen would be less pressure? You gave me notice that being queen is not a fairy tale happily-ever-after existence."

"If it weren't for that… I mean, the way she's been mooning over you…"

"Thank you. I think. I was half hoping you would say she didn't care two beans about me. That might almost be easier to bear, because I can't avoid my duties, even for her. I can't have a wife that isn't a queen, either… And what about you? Can you bear everything that will come with being the first Air Enchantress?"

"You mean, being Enchanter Paul's apprentice? That's what I thought you meant when you apologised for putting me in an unpleasant position."

"Yes, it isn't fair to ask a sixteen-year-old to be more adult than her ancient and childish grandfather, but we must. He considers your apprenticeship a temporary measure. We still hope to persuade him otherwise, but for Frankland's sake, we must ask you to put aside your justified resentment, and accede to his authority."

Gillian jerked her hand free and ran to the far end of the balustrade, where she stood with her fists balled and her back to him for several minutes. She returned with a stiff back and flashing eyes.

"Sometimes," she said, "I hate you. You're a master at forcing people to do things they don't want to do."

"You wouldn't be his apprentice if those who know you didn't believe you capable. It isn't a question of can you, but will you?"

She raised her chin and met his gaze. "I can, and I will, because my king orders me to. If my friend Alex had asked, I would have told him to bugger off."

Alexander winced. "Your language, Gillian."

"I have a talent for languages. I can say that in seven different ones. Want to hear?"

René staggered through forest on a frigid night with a quarter moon. His foot caught on an unseen root and he fell. He lay face down without moving.

René, my friend, do you remember me once prodding you with a foil and saying, 'You are dead'?

Yeah, Alex.

I say it again. You are dead.

I am. My legs are rubber. I don't have enough magic left to scorch paper and I don't know where I am. Where's the nearest tunnel?

A quarter mile to the southeast.

René groaned. Another ten yards would be torture. A quarter mile might as well be the moon. *Fine. I'll get up in a moment.*

He had a right to be tired. He and Alex had started the day with a pre-dawn race up the Fortress stairs, from the gate, past the ballroom, as far as the library. Then he'd spent most of the day with the Fire Eaters, a dozen of them at a time attacking him alone. Sometime during the day he had fenced with Alex, but he wasn't sure when. After dark Quicksilver had set him to drawing down the lightning, bolt after bolt in a barrage that left him deafened and blinded, even with the earplugs and dark spectacles.

They had stopped that when he missed his target three times in a row, and he admitted he was on the verge of losing control completely. Since then they had been playing this infernal game of tag, with warlocks skipping through the fire the length and breadth of Frankland, and the army's officers popping out of tunnels at random, shouting "Nyah, Nyah, can't catch me." That was more for Alex's benefit than his own, as everyone but Beorn and Quicksilver had their badges on, and tracking these apparent mundanes simultaneously had stretched Alex and Gillian's capacities to their limits.

The game had been fun for the first ten minutes. The last hour had been excruciating, but they couldn't stop. When the battle for Frankland began in earnest, the empire would grant them no recess.

René, you must move or you'll freeze.

"Relax, Alex. I've got him."

René blinked at Beorn bending over him. The big wizard gave him a hand, steadied him when he would have fallen over, and in a moment dropped him, warm and dry, into a chair in the Fortress kitchen. The other warlocks were already eating. Lucinda slid a plate of scrambled eggs and bacon in front of him. He attacked it with single-minded determination.

In his head he heard Alex telling the officers the exercise was over and thanking them for their participation. Shortly afterwards Alex emerged from the Forge and slid into the chair across from him.

René said, "Where's Gillian?"

"Asleep in the ballroom. She left some time ago. Said she had a pony sitting on her chest, which she thought wasn't bad for having been there twenty hours. We agreed it would be counter-productive for her to stay so long she would be afraid to come back."

"Unh. And you?"

"Tired. My eyes are full of sand and my head aches, but otherwise I'm fine."

The other warlocks finished and left, after congratulating them both on a successful exercise. René and Alex ate in silence. René was on his third bowl of porridge when Tom and Katie arrived on their way back from the Warren and its network of tunnels.

Alex said, "I did say you could go home."

Tom said, "We wanted to see for ourselves. Is it true Snorri's out of magic?"

René stretched out his arm on the table and tried to conjure a flame in his palm. Nothing appeared, not even a wisp of smoke. Tom and Katie came close, one on either side, to peer at his hand.

"That's it." René's throat tightened. "I'm cold ashes, and the night's not over."

"It's time," Katie said. Together, she and Tom snapped their wands up, and from point-blank range, poured jets of flame at their unshielded commander.

Unlocking

René flung himself backwards. His chair clattered across the flagstones. Alex yelled and grabbed for a sword that wasn't there. René scrabbled away, but couldn't escape the flames.

Tom said, "You're not burnt."

René froze.

Alex rounded the table with a kitchen knife in his hand, shouting, and planted himself between René and the two flame throwers. The flames died. The hammering in René's chest had an echo; he was hearing Alex's pulse, too.

Katie said, "That was payback for listening to the empire's lies and believing we'd ever turn traitor. As if! Mrs Rehsavvy told us he can absorb fire like she can, so we couldn't hurt him."

"Oh, hell." René sprawled across the floor, a mound of quivering jelly.

"Payback, too," Tom said, "for favouring water and earth wizards over us."

Beorn emerged from the fireplace. "Alex, relax. Put the knife down."

Alex didn't move, or relax his white-knuckled grip on the knife. "We do not understand."

"Years ago, one of the empire's wizards predicted Snorri's most trusted lieutenants would turn on him, and flame him when he was too exhausted to hold a shield. Jean and Lucinda and I have been worrying it ever since. Lucinda suggested running him ragged, so we could force the prediction to come true in a way that works for us."

Tom tapped René's boot with his wand. "And to remind this useless oaf that the empire will give him more firepower, free for the asking, if he does run out, so not to worry about that."

René thrust a hand into the kitchen fire. "I'd forgotten I could do that."

"Miss Underwood, Mr Russell..." Alex laid the knife on the table. "Consider yourselves fortunate we did not have a sword at hand."

"We're sorry, Your Majesty."

Beorn said, "They had to make it convincing or it wouldn't work."

"Convincing, hell," René said. "Nearly gave both of us heart attacks. They did fine. Firepower for the taking..." He pulled his hand from the fire, with a flame dancing on his palm. His grin was a tiger's bared teeth. "Gunther's so proud of being pure fire. Ass! I'm twice the wizard he'll ever be."

While the Reforging Coven trickled in, Lucinda surveyed the preparations in the Forge. She had already inspected the preparations, twice, the previous evening, and found everything in order, but inspecting them again was easier than reviewing what she had to do. The Earth Guild had strung screens across one end, partitioning a third of the room into two sections with cots, one with enough medical supplies for a small field hospital, and the other in shadows under the awning, for coven members to rest briefly, even nap if they could, when their expertise wasn't required. Also at that end, doors led to recently overhauled and expanded privies. If the next half hour proved too much for her weak stomach, they were within easy reach.

At the room's other end, soup pots bubbled over a low fire. On either side, buffet tables held platters of cold food. Tablecloths hid crates of additional supplies, enough to feed the entire coven for a week. Jean had not objected to Mrs Cole's insistence on providing more than he had asked for, but if they were still in this room a week after unlocking the Fire Office, Frankland would have ceased to exist.

In the middle section, the iron worktable and chairs stood under the awning. An array of magic mirrors stood across from them, under the clouds. The king and Gillian would be working there, surveying the battlefield and keeping René informed.

Close to the hospital partition, the coven gathered around a tight circle of chairs. Enchanter Paul, the last to arrive, studied the illusions with an expression of mild astonishment. The room now appeared to be a paved terrace surrounded by breeze-blown shrubbery and trees. The only wall still visible was the one supporting the awning.

Paul said, "Do you really expect me to be taken in by this illusion?"

"Taken in, no," Jean said. "Made comfortable enough to tolerate being underground for the time it takes Lucinda to unlock the office, yes."

Paul scowled at Lucinda. "Let's get this over with."

"Yes, sir," Lucinda said. "The Fire Office is so complicated that even once I find the lock, the smallest distraction could make me lose it, and I'd have to start again. Work any last-minute protection spells you want now, before I start looking for the lock."

Enchanter Paul growled, deep in his throat. "In other words, we will be in this ghastly chamber longer than I had expected. I do not appreciate that."

"Too frostbitten bad," Beorn said. "And if you don't like that, I'll say something you like even less."

Paul gave him a baleful stare. Lucinda rubbed sweaty palms on her skirt and cursed her churning stomach. She hadn't eaten breakfast this morning; she couldn't have kept it down.

She said, "The rest of you follow Sven. As soon as the office is unlocked and the healers have stabilised the injuries…" She stopped and blinked hard through watering eyes. "We'll call you back in and begin the teardown. We estimate the unlocking will be over in a half hour or less."

Sven held open the door leading to the Fire Warlock's study. "This way, please."

The non-essential Coven members left, most taking a surreptitious look at the four officeholders over their shoulders before they exited. Beorn glowered at them and chewed his moustache. The two earth fathers staying on hand for the unlocking, Martin and Pierre, retreated to the Forge's far end.

The king didn't move. "We will stay."

Jean sighed. "We have already discussed this, Your Majesty, several times. We cannot allow you to stay. We cannot guarantee your safety."

"The Fire Office's shields protect us."

"The Fire Office's shields may not hold when the lock is opened."

The two men's eyes met and held briefly, then the king turned to Lucinda with questions in his eyes.

"I'll manage, Your Majesty," she said. "I'm a warlock. I'll do my duty."

He nodded and walked through the door Sven still held open. Sven hesitated.

"What're you waiting for?" Beorn growled. "Move."

"Don't be an ass." Sven held out his hand. Beorn shook it. They stood for a long moment without moving, hands clasped, Sven's face working like he wanted to say more, before he let go and sprinted into the tunnel.

Sweat trickled down Lucinda's back. Not all of that was due to nerves. Years of intense firefights had heated the rock all around, and it was too warm for her comfort. She and Jean had done what they could to cool the room, and Eleanor had offered to help, but the Fortress's defences had thwarted their efforts. The heat might take years to dissipate. By the time they were done with the firepower needed for the reforging, it might take decades.

The spellcasting done, Lucinda, Jean, and the officeholders crowded together in the circle of chairs. Paul pushed his backwards, giving himself more room.

Lucinda said, "I need to pull threads of power from each of you and hold them ready, before I look for the lock. We need to be touching for me to do that."

Paul grumbled.

Eleanor said, "I don't care for it either, but I trust that the Locksmith knows what she's doing. We can tolerate tight quarters for half an hour."

Beorn said, "Don't drive Lucinda to distraction with your infernal fidgeting. The more you fidget, the longer it will take."

Paul shot him a look filled with venom, but held himself still, tense and rigid.

Lucinda didn't expect that to last. She closed her eyes and viewed the Tokens of Office with her mind's eye. Two shouted for her attention: the Fire Office on her left, the Air Office on her right. The other two, within reach across the circle, were more subdued. She drew lines of power— red, green, blue, and white—from the officeholders, and keeping a mental finger on them, touched her target with her mental flame. The tight ball of spells opened for her, as if the office itself knew it was damaged, and was begging her to unlock it.

She looked up. Beorn was hunched over, his elbows on his knees, his head down. Paul stared at the fading stars and breathed noisily through his mouth. The two witches were relaxed but alert, ready to provide the power needed when she called for it. Jean nodded encouragement at her.

She dove in. Even with the office's help, threading through the thicket of spells was a challenge, because she was on her own, with no help from the officeholder. She glanced up from time to time, and noted the sheen of sweat on Paul's face, the vein throbbing in his temple.

She had been searching for the lock for twenty minutes when Paul started twitching. She tensed, but he wasn't paying attention to her. His eyes were frantic, flicking across the ceiling, around the walls, back to the ceiling. Hunting for an exit. His thread of power was fraying.

Lucinda clinched her jaw and hurried. "Found it. Ready?"

"Ready," the officeholders echoed.

Frostbite. She wasn't ready. She'd never be ready for this.

The four lines of power became burning cables. Paul's head snapped down, but before he could react further, she shoved. With a blinding, deafening roar, the lock opened on the Air Office.

Further Argument is Fruitless

The lightning bolt shock of unlocking an office rolled over the Reforging Coven. The king charged through the door in the Fire Warlock's study to the tunnel leading to the Forge. Irene followed, still blinking away the flash's afterimage when she emerged into chaos.

Shouts battered her ears. The smell of blood filled her nostrils. Arturos, upright, filled her vision. Arturos? An instant later he vanished in a column of fire.

If not Arturos, then who...

Her eyes slid away from the bloody, mangled figure sprawled on the flagstones. What she had seen made no sense.

She almost walked into the circle of spattered blood. She stopped off-balance, fought to regain her footing and got blood on her shoes anyway, then thrust out an arm to block Gillian.

"Do not berate the Locksmith." The king's knife-edge voice cut through the clamour. "She acted on our direct order."

Mother Astrid whipped around and barked, "Explain yourself, young man."

"We will, madam," the king said. "But see to your patient first."

"Humph!" She gave him a scorching glare but bent over the injured man. While she and the two earth fathers bandaged him and began making what repairs they could, Irene began to make sense of the scene before her.

Enchanter Paul looked like a slaughterhouse carcass. Her eyes refused to stay focused on him. Lucinda sported a fixed stare. Her hands made futile brushing motions at her drenched gown. Nearly invisible blue flames danced over her and Quicksilver. Sorceress Eleanor appeared unharmed and unmoving, as if carved from ice. She stared, unblinking, at the king. The other members of the coven had spread out around the circle of gore, all blank with shock.

Beside her, Gillian was making choking noises behind the hands clamped over her mouth. The Earth Mother glanced at her and snapped, "Stop that. We have enough mess here, we don't need that, too." Gillian hiccupped and crept closer to her mother. Irene put an arm around her.

The healers lifted Enchanter Paul onto a stretcher. The two earth fathers carried him away. Mother Astrid sniffed, made an impatient gesture, and snapped her fingers. The gore disappeared. Irene breathed a deep sigh.

"He'll live," Mother Astrid said. "Now tell me, for God's sake, why?"

The king stood at parade rest, his spine straight and rigid, his chin up and slightly out. He drew in a deep breath, but before he could speak, Irene stepped forward and dropped into the deepest curtsey she could manage.

"Because otherwise it would someday have been Gillian lying there maimed and bleeding. Thank you, Sire, for sparing us that."

Gillian said, "I guess I don't have to work at ambidexterity any longer." Her voice shook. "Good thing; even I can't read what I write left-handed." She flashed a brilliant but short-lived smile at the king. "Thanks, Alex."

"You can't mean," Mother Astrid sputtered. "You can't believe...surely not... His own granddaughter?"

"His own granddaughter," the king said. "The enchantress whose spirit he tried to break by keeping her locked for hours in a tiny closet."

The colour drained from Mother Astrid's face. Quicksilver pushed a chair into place behind her. She sank into it. "I didn't know... No wonder you've been angry, Sven."

"Is that your reason, Your Majesty?" Sorceress Eleanor was thawing. Her colour was returning, but her eyes were still locked on the king.

"Yes," he said, "although I did not discuss this with either Enchantress Gillian or her parents. I had independently reached the conclusion that Enchanter Paul would never willingly submit to this trauma. We had no leverage to compel him to do so, and he had demonstrated that if we pushed him harder he would fight us with every weapon at his disposal, including but certainly not limited to insubordination, obstruction, and slander. The resulting strife would inflict further damage on the already fractured Air Guild and leave—in Master Duncan's quaint phrase—a right royal mess for his successor to clean up. A task that would be difficult, if not impossible, for even a guild head untainted by character assassination. We could not let him have his way. We became convinced that leaving the Air Office untouched after the other offices were reforged would be fatal to Frankland's long-term prospects. Do you doubt that?"

"No, not at all." Sorceress Eleanor nodded at Quicksilver and took the chair he offered her. "The Water Office is satisfied with your reasoning."

"I'm not," Mother Astrid said, "You should have talked it over with the other officeholders."

"Especially," Gillian said, "since we're not ready. We can't reforge the Air Office now. We don't know... He hasn't done the analysis. He wouldn't let me... It would be a disaster."

"You are correct, we are not ready," Quicksilver said. "Lucinda will relock the Air Office as is, with her new, non-lethal lock. Enchanter Paul will recover and continue being Air Enchanter, while you and Mistress Irene analyse the spells and lead the discussions on the necessary changes. When you determine we are ready, we will rebuild the Air Office."

Irene's heart sang. Between her relief over Gillian and this vote of confidence, she was as buoyant as a cloud. But Paul would still hold the Air Office. She came back to earth with a thud. Gillian displayed the same mix of delight, relief, and trepidation.

"Enchanter Paul won't give us access to the spells," she said.

The king and Quicksilver exchanged a long look. "He will," Quicksilver said. "Trust us."

Irene bit her lip, but said, "Of course, Your Wisdom."

He gave her a small smile, then turned to Mother Astrid. "Neither Lucinda nor René knew of the change in plans until this morning, but the king did discuss the problem and his solution with Arturos and me several months ago, and we advised him not to tell anyone else."

"What? That's outrageous!"

"Not at all. The Fire Warlock generally discusses security issues with as few as possible."

"Security issues? Jean, what are you talking about?"

"King Brendan has not conveyed that today's unlocking of the Air Office serves a dual purpose. Besides removing the decision from Enchanter Paul's hands, which we agreed would be the best course for Frankland, we have confounded the empire. As you are aware, the emperor has not believed our attempts to mislead him, and has his armies massed on our borders awaiting the Fire Office's unlocking. Warlock Arturos is even now demonstrating that he is strong and healthy, our defences are still intact, and they are making a serious mistake in attempting an invasion. While the emperor's attention has been focused on us, rebellion has erupted in the Empire's Eastern provinces."

"With some encouragement from us, I believe," Lucinda said.

"Quite so. The empire will now be forced to attend to those problems in the east and, we hope, the emperor's displeasure will create discord and vacancies in his armies' upper ranks. In two or three days, while the Empire's back is turned to us, we will unlock and reforge the Fire Office."

A shiver like a breath of wind through autumn leaves ran through the gathered coven.

"Well done, Your Wisdom," Sorceress Eleanor said. "Your Majesty."

"Now, that I can agree with," Mother Astrid said. "One old man maimed but alive is fair trade for giving our young talents a better fighting chance. The Earth Office accepts that logic."

The king acknowledged her with a half bow. "Thank you, Your Wisdom. When we leave this place, we will spread word that Enchanter Paul is an Air Guild hero for nobly sacrificing himself." The king's lip curled. "And that we will begin rebuilding the Air Office as soon as he has recovered. The revised plan will be the coven's secret."

René surveyed the Fortress from the central staircase. In the ballroom, the Fire Warlock was soothing the rattled residents, telling them the coven would begin work on the Air Office as soon as Enchanter Paul had regained his strength. In the suite for visiting royalty, the Queen Mother and Princess Sophie were at ease, reading while waiting for Alex to come and escort them home. And at the foot of his flight of stairs, a young woman waited with her hands on her hips and blazing eyes. René gulped. He'd never seen her angry before.

"Frost you, Snorri," Miranda said. "You and your Fire Eaters, too. Why did you send one of them to drag me out of bed and force me to come here?"

He grabbed her wrist. "Can't talk here. Too exposed." Flames rose. They walked into the Fire Warlock's study. "Look, Miranda—"

She wrenched her arm out of his grasp. "No, you look, Snorri.

I've never seen the spells—no one but Paul ever has—and I'm not an enchantress. I can't help reforge the Air Office."

"We're not doing the Air Office." He steered her, unresisting, towards a chair. "You'd better sit down."

As he explained, her eyes grew enormous. "Wow. Alex did that?"

"Yes. Well, him and Quicksilver. Mostly him, I guess." He hunched his shoulders. "I don't like Enchanter Paul, but he is your grandfather. I'm sorry, Miranda."

She flicked her wrist. "He brought it on himself. After all the hurt he's inflicted on Gillian and Mama, and even me, I'll not cry for him. But I still don't see what this has to do with dragging me here this morning."

"I didn't know until the last minute, and by then I'd already sent Carl to fetch you. I thought we were fighting the empire today, and you're the most important potential hostage, after Alex's mum and sister."

The spark in Miranda's eyes rekindled. "That's nonsense. And I can't abide that Forge for more than a quarter of a day. A full day and night inside the closed Fortress would be torture."

"The shutters aren't airtight. I didn't think—"

"You're right, you didn't think. Mrs Rehsavvy told us what it was like during the siege. Her description made my skin crawl."

"Well, would you rather be buried, frozen, or shunned?"

"I beg your pardon?"

"Fortress, Crystal Palace, or Warren. Those are the only places we can be sure you're safe."

"Why are you even concerned? I'm a musician. I'm not important."

"Miranda, don't be an ass. Your mum, your dad, and your sister are in the Reforging Coven. What would it do to them and the reforging if that sadist captured you? And Alex... If he goes berserk I'm in trouble."

She deflated. "Oh. But... Alex?"

René rolled his eyes. "What did you think? He's only asked you to marry him twice."

"That was years ago. We were children."

"You were fifteen the second time, as I recall. He was nineteen. I got married at nineteen."

"Oh, for... Go away." She sounded close to tears.

"Sorry." He went to the door, but stopped with it almost closed and stuck his head back in. "Buried, frozen, or shunned?"

In a very small voice, she said, "Shunned."

Alexander and Quicksilver stood together at the foot of Enchanter Paul's bed in the Warren, their faces impassive as they listened to him vent his anger. After the initial fury had washed over them—Paul was too weak to maintain the diatribe for long—Alexander interrupted.

"We regret the use of subterfuge, but you gave us no choice. You should perhaps consider your good fortune in avoiding the terror the other officeholders must have experienced in the hours and days before the unlocking of their offices."

Paul rasped, "Good fortune? You expect me to thank you for this butchery?"

"No, but you should be grateful for the Reforging Coven spreading the polite fiction that this was your choice. Your cowardice is our secret."

Paul's bloodless face was grey against the while pillowcase, his burning eyes providing the only colour. His mouth was a hard, lipless line.

Quicksilver said, "You have given Enchantress Gillian a limited delegation for reforging the Fire Office. You will now give her your full delegation until you are no longer under the Earth Guild's care, so that she may take your place in relocking the Air Office and dealing with any other problems that arise."

"You will also," Alexander said, "turn over to Countess Irene the transcriptions of the spells in the Air Office, the private journals you and your predecessors have kept, and any other material you have concerning those spells or the behaviour of the Air Office. Once the Fire Office has been reforged she and Enchantress Gillian will undertake the analysis you have neglected."

"I will not," Paul said. "I am still Air Enchanter, and I believe Frankland needs the stability of at least one untouched office. Nor can you convince me that wild girl won't destroy it completely."

"You, sir," Quicksilver said, "stand alone in your opinions, but the integrity of the offices is a serious matter, and an officeholder's opinion cannot be dismissed lightly. You will make your case for the Air Office's preservation to the Company of Mages, in opposition to the arguments for its reforging, which I and Sorcerer Charles will champion. I must warn you those arguments will include Lucinda's statement that on yesterday's unlocking, the Air Office seemed aware of its shortcomings and willing, eager even, to be unlocked.

"You will also base your arguments solely on the behaviour of the office. It will go ill for you if you cast aspersions on the character or abilities of either Countess Irene or Enchantress Gillian."

"The competence of the people involved is certainly pertinent to the discussion."

"If you slander Gillian or revoke her apprenticeship, we will destroy you." Alexander was trembling. He gripped the bedpost so hard his hand ached. "We will see you stripped of your office—"

"You can't."

"I have already assured His Majesty," Quicksilver said. "That with the agreement of the other three officeholders, the king may dismiss an officeholder for incompetence. It has been done before."

"And," Alexander said, "ejected from the Company of Mages. All of Frankland will hear the reasons why: your cowardice; your misjudgements of Countess Irene, Enchantress Winifred, and Enchantress Gillian; your unreasoned antipathy towards the commoners' hero, Master Sven; your gullibility and connivance at giving your son credit for Countess Irene's spellwork..."

Paul thrashed about, shaking a fist at Quicksilver. "He can't. The Company of Mages promised—"

"We will keep our promise." Quicksilver's tone was arctic. "Our agreement did not include King Brendan or Lady Miranda."

"Who respects her parents and her sister more than she respects her grandfather," Alexander said. "If you undermine Enchantress Gillian or withhold the required documents, you will spend your last years in disgrace and bitter isolation. You are already suffering the results of our displeasure; do not doubt we will do as we say."

"Further argument is fruitless," Quicksilver said. "We await the full delegation, sir."

The silence stretched out. Then with his eyes fixed on a spot on the ceiling, Enchanter Paul began tonelessly reciting the magic words.

Geoffrey Bullfinch, fire wizard, opened his eyes to cold blackness, and swore silently. The summons had jerked him out of a pleasant dream of dancing on the midsummer bonfire. He was tired of these frostbitten drills. They'd had one two days ago. That had been a shocker, feeling the magical blast from an office being unlocked, and then finding out it had been the Air Office and not the Fire Office. They hadn't even started taking the Air Office apart; what was the point of a drill now, other than disturbing his sleep? Worse, disturbing his wife's sleep. She could be nasty when roused too early.

He closed his eyes and snuggled closer to her warmth. They could drill without him, this once.

Five minutes later he shot out of bed and scrabbled in the dark for his trousers with the Fire Warlock's bass reverberating in his head. *YOU, GEOFFREY BULLFINCH, GET YOUR SORRY ARSE TO THE ASSEMBLY POINT NOW, BEFORE I TORCH IT.*

"What is it?" His wife said. "Light the lamp before you break something, you idiot."

"Got to go. Drill." His heart was pounding like he was in a duel with the emperor. "Drown those warlocks." He grabbed the rest of his clothes, flung a kiss at his wife, missing her mouth and brushing an eyelid instead, and thundered down the stairs with only one arm in his tunic.

He was still struggling with his clothes when he skidded, breathless, into the glass-ceilinged courtyard in the Warren serving as their assembly point, hard on the heels of two other grumbling latecomers. They froze in the tense silence of the already assembled Unconquered.

"I repeat, this is not a drill. The Battle for Frankland will begin soon." Snorri handed the latecomers their badges. "Don't forget, if you take your badge off, you're exposed, and today that can kill you. This is the real thing. The Locksmith is deep in the Fire Office spells, on her way to the lock. The coven will tear it down as soon as it's unlocked. There's food on the tables, grab something before you go. We've got some time; a few scouts will show up almost immediately, but it will be several hours before the defensive spells are all stripped, and before the empire can swing it's forces our way."

Someone said, "The Air Enchanter…"

"Enchantress Gillian is handling his spells. It's all covered. Anything else?"

The Unconquered exchanged worried glances, but no one spoke up. They'd covered all this in their drills, many times before.

Granddad Ernest said, "We all know what to do, sir."

"Right. Do it."

The Battle for Frankland Begins

Frankland's Unconquered hunched over their breakfasts in the Warren's Palm Courtyard. René frowned at a link of sausage. He needed to eat. He was hungry—he was always hungry—but food didn't interest him this morning.

This courtyard had seemed like a perfect meeting place, and he had agreed to it. One of the Warren's primary junctions, surrounding tunnels forked off to guildhalls in every city and major town in Frankland. The courtyard had room for everything they needed to fight a war. Buffet tables filled one end, cots and shelves of emergency medical supplies the other, all squeezed in between the potted trees.

Yet now that the day had come, the glass ceiling disturbed him. It felt too open; they were exposed, vulnerable. The Warren had its own formidable protections, but being outside the Fortress when its shutters closed, by his own free will, frightened him. He gritted his teeth and fought down the urge to run for home.

But first they had to get through the unlocking. Lucinda's weak stomach was giving him butterflies in his own usually cast-iron insides.

He watched the scene in the Forge through her eyes. Gillian was calm. Good. Enchanter Paul had done them a favour by letting the school staff lock her in a closet, but he couldn't blame her for hating the old man for it. If anybody had tried it on him, he would have burnt the school to the ground.

Beorn sat hunched over, unmoving. Sweat trickled into his beard.

René rubbed his nose and brushed at watering eyes. His throat was too tight; he couldn't swallow.

I'm ready, little brother.

He said, "Put your cups down. She's there."

The blast rolled over them. In the Warren, a pair of slow-reflexed wizards spilled coffee. In the Forge, blood flowed. The two earth fathers closed in, Pierre pushing Lucinda aside. Quicksilver, blood spattered, leaned back with his eyes closed, already at work tearing down the Fire Office. Gillian ran for the privy with her hand over her mouth.

Burn it, big sister, is he alive? Look at him.

I can't, little brother. I just can't.

Drown you! I have to know.

The door to the Fire Warlock's study flew open. Alex charged in. For a moment, René saw double, then he blocked Lucinda. Alex bent over Beorn. René got a good look, and jerked away from the connection. The Unconquered were watching him. He saw fear and pity, grief and horror. He couldn't bear it. He shut his eyes, blocking them all out.

Listen, little brother...

René relayed news. "Arturos survived. The Earth Guild won't let him die now." He blew his nose. "He lost an arm. We expected that. But his face... My God... You thought he was an ugly bastard before..."

He dared look through Alex's eyes again. The earth fathers lifted Beorn onto a stretcher and carried him behind the partition. Mother Astrid dispatched the gore. The coven took their places at the table, and joined Quicksilver in breaking down Frankland's defences.

"They've started the teardown. Get to work, people."

René bent over a map in the Paris Water Guildhall, surrounded by unnerved guild members, half of them still in bathrobes and rubbing sleep from their eyes. These witches and wizards understood weather magic and cowed miscreants, not invading armies. He was not enjoying frightening them.

"Keep up a steady drizzle," he said. "Empty the Seine if you have to. If you can drown any of the Empire's fire wizards on the riverbanks or bridges, that would be great, but don't go looking for them."

"Where's the Fire Warlock?" A querulous old wizard raised his voice. "It's not our job to fight the empire."

René glared but kept his voice soft. "I'm not saying it is. The full Fire Guild will be engaged. I'm not asking you to fight. All I'm asking for is help in keeping Paris from burning."

"It shouldn't be in danger of burning," the wizard shouted.

"Hush, Gerald," the ranking witch said. "Warlock Snorri explained why. I'll go over it again after he leaves, but he has work to do." She guided René towards the door, saying, "My brother is in the Unconquered. We'll do our share. Go."

Outside, he paused on the riverbank to check in with Alex, before going to the next guildhall on his list.

Any problems so far?

No. The evacuation of Blazes is proceeding apace. Most families with small children are already through the gates. They're too frightened to waste time arguing. Lots of consternation in the guildhalls, as we expected, but they're all taking our advice seriously.

Yeah, that was part of the point of the Guildhall Defence Project. Miranda?

Safe in the Warren. None of the potential hostages refused to go, once they understood why. Gillian says the teardown is going quickly. I can't tell. They all look half asleep to me.

They're not. They're ripping through it. Lucinda's keeping me informed on that side of things. Ignore them. Keep your eye on the empire.

I am. They're gathering on the border, planning a massed attack, as you predicted they would. And they're shifting the barrels of black powder closer.

Oh, joy.

The emperor is still in the east, trying to keep his forces there from panicking, but his threats are making them more agitated.

René snickered. *Surprise, surprise.*

That's it so far. I am a bit worried…

About?

With so much going on, will I miss the emperor's arrival?

Not likely.

Won't be long…

Shortly before noon word spread among the Unconquered: Get ready. They're at the spell the empire's been waiting for.

The Earth Guild spell channelling attacking armies towards the Fortress dissolved. The empire's sentinels, watching from the borders, relayed the news. General Strazsky, the empire's only senior officer who had reservations about this invasion, twitched, gulped, and issued the order to attack.

The more eager junior officers in his command were already in motion. With a dozen or so rapid jumps each, warlocks scattered squads of lower ranking fire wizards and their attached earth and air aides across Frankland's cities before moving on to their own assigned targets. Earth wizards had already been at work, for more than an hour, on tunnels designed to connect with Frankland's existing network.

The empire's water wizards—the despised underclass in the empire's current power structure—raised storm clouds and searched for fire wizards to drown. They didn't notice—or didn't bother pointing out to their superior officers, the arrogant bastards wouldn't have listened anyway—that they could not find a single member of Frankland's Fire Guild outside the Fortress higher than level two.

A column of flame rose in the royal palace's main courtyard. Screaming tourists scattered. A warlock emerged from the flames. Nearby, a fountain gurgled and stopped flowing. He ignored it, watching the running tourists with curled lip. Didn't they know their country was at war? The emperor was right—this campaign would be a stroll in the park. Their single fighting warlock was too soft to make a lightning strike in an arena as crowded as this one. And the proportion of wood in that palace was comical. These people knew nothing about war.

He was going to enjoy burning this silly excuse for a royal residence to the ground. He lifted his wand. The cobblestones beneath his feet split apart. He dropped. His yell was abruptly cut off as the water in the shaft closed over his head.

Above, the gap in the cobbles closed. The fountain resumed flowing. Nothing indicated a warlock had ever been in that courtyard. Under a nearby colonnade, a grinning water wizard and a grim earth wizard shook hands. Leagues away, Alexander had no time for more than a smile. The first man down was not a Frank.

At the water's edge, on the furthest northwest island in the Hebrides, two women grappled.

"You can't go," Katie panted. "I won't let you."

"You can't keep me," Hildur said. "Let go, drown you, or I'll torch you."

"You don't frighten me. You're not a lightning-wielder yet. You're the one frightened. I know you are."

"Damn right. I'm not a fool." Hildur drove an elbow, hard, into the other woman's midriff. Katie's grip loosened. Hildur broke free. She disappeared in a spurt of flame and reappeared a dozen yards away. "Tell him I'm sorry." She turned towards Thule and vanished.

"Burn you!" Katie kicked at a piece of driftwood and hurled it, burning, into the sea. With her fury spent, and the wind whipping her eyes to tears, she whispered, "Oh, Snorri, I'm so sorry," and turned back towards her post.

For the first time in a thousand years, Frankland had no Fire Office. The Fortress's shutters closed in anticipation of attack. Even muffled through layers of rock, the banging was loud enough that the Reforging Coven, with the exception of Jean and Sven, raised their heads and stared around them, wild-eyed.

"Everything is fine," Sven said. "We warned you this was coming."

How could he be so calm? Lucinda couldn't hold her coffee cup steady. She put it down and sat on her hands. There ought to be some notice taken, some acknowledgement of this momentous, soul-chilling event, but Jean and Sven had slipped from teardown to rebuild without pause, and the other members of the coven were settling down and flipping to the second page in their spellbooks.

Except for her. She'd lost her place. How could she concentrate when she was sick with fear for her family, her country, her little brother? They had already tried to kill him, and had nearly succeeded in killing Hildur. Fear evaporated in a surge of red heat. She breathed on the coals, stoking her fury. She would not give in to fear. Anger, a warlock's closest friend, would get her through this.

She found her place, and readied herself for her first spell.

A detailed map of Frankland hung on the wall in the Palm Courtyard. René paused before it to take stock, reviewing the current situation. Alex finished his summary of the hot spots.

You're holding out on me, Alex. What else is wrong?

There was an uncomfortable pause. *This news will hurt. Are you sure you want to know now?*

Frost you, Alex. You asked the Fire Warlock for help because people weren't telling you what you needed to know. I'm a warlock. I can take it, whatever it is.

Very well. Hildur has fled Frankland.

The news hit him like a kick in the gut. He put a hand on the map to steady himself. *Where?* But he already knew the answer.

Miss Underwood said she jumped towards Thule.

When?

A few minutes after the invasion started.

More than an hour ago. There was nothing he could do for her.

He was blind with grief and fury. *She wasn't back to full strength yet. She couldn't jump that far! And why? She would have been safe in the Fortress.*

Miss Underwood said she had made her grandfather a promise... René, are you still there?

Tell the Water Guild to look for her. Get them to send a message to the Water Guild in Thule.

Miss Underwood has already done so.

He had thought that if they lost Frankland, his future—what little there might be before the empire killed him—would be bleak and bitter. He had never imagined it might be so even if they won.

René, my friend... Remember your own promise to Sorceress Lorraine.

Right. Keep my temper. No revenge.

It wouldn't be fair to push his anger and pain out to Lucinda or Alex or Quicksilver. They all had their own parts to play in this ordeal. He forced himself to focus on the here and now. The few people in the courtyard at this hour had taken cover behind the columns. Anxious eyes peeked at him.

"Sorry," he said. "One bit of bad news. Overall, we're in good shape."

He left the courtyard and threaded through the maze to the Warren's library, a comfortable space that would let him turn himself into a cold fish. He could never hope to gain the control over his emotions that a member of the Water Guild could, but the techniques he had practiced with Sorcerer Charles and Sorceress Eleanor would let him dam them so that they would not overpower his intellect. For a time. The snag was that once the dam broke—as it had when he'd burnt Jimmy Ferguson—for a short interval he would be nothing but emotion.

He had meant to wait until Gunther arrived in Frankland to build the dam, but the news about Hildur had rocked him, and he needed it now. After ten minutes alone in a quiet corner of the library, he contacted Alex.

I'm ready.

Good. Gunther has arrived at the border. Just… Will your dam last long enough? If it doesn't… that will be just too damn bad.

General Strazky was not a man who frightened easily. He was not worried about surviving the war. He was worried about surviving the next five minutes with his emperor.

He couldn't blame Warlock Sturmmeister for being in a rage. The entire command structure had been boiling ever since Tuesday morning when those damned Franks had tricked them into exposing the extent of their preparations for this war. Sacrificing that useless enchanter must have been old Quicksilver's idea—both Arturos and Snorri were too soft to have planned something so clever—but when a toady air wizard had made the mistake of praising the move, saying it was an idea worthy of Emperor Sturmmeister himself, the man had gotten a face full of fire. This would have been fine as far as the general was concerned—the airhead deserved a punishment for his stupidity—but the emperor had had him dragged away and thrown into the dungeon untreated. Strazky fought down nausea.

The emperor had been in a better mood this morning, when it seemed they were poised to rout the eastern rebels, and then the Franks had thrown this new spanner in the works.

Strazky finished his report. The moment of silence that followed was more ominous than if the emperor had roared. The general and his three sweating aides stood at attention.

"Tell us," the emperor said through clenched teeth, "how Frankland's entire Fire Guild could disappear."

"We believe their Locksmith has used her lock for hiding magic talents—"

"Impossible. First, their officers need to know where they are, and second, our spies say she was in the Fortress when those wizards entered the tunnels and disappeared. They must still be in the tunnels."

"No, Sire," Strazky said. "Our men have been engaged in a number of serious firefights. The Frank's wizards are out in the open, in force. We simply cannot tell wizard from mundane until they throw fire." The compulsion to say 'I told you so' was nearly overwhelming. Strazky chewed the inside of his cheek. The emperor shouldn't have ignored his warnings that the Franks were more innovative than he gave them credit for. The rumour the Frank's enchanter had trained their king in using air spells had given Strazky sleepless nights. "We suspect their king is using air spells to transmit orders."

"A mundane." The emperor gave him a long, burning stare. "We expected Snorri to be under that witch's lock, but you should have noticed whenever he jumped through the fire or threw lightning."

"He hasn't yet. He's been in several firefights, but he doesn't need to call the lightning to punch through a level four's shields, and he must have travelled through the tunnels."

"Ah, yes, the tunnels. You haven't broken into their tunnels either." The roar Strazky had been expecting finally came. "Have you no good news for us? If we had time we would sack all of you. We will find this mongrel upstart ourselves, and when we are done with him, and his puppet king and stronghold are in our hands, then we will deal with you sorry lot of traitors, cowards, and incompetents. You make us ill, all of you. And you, Strazky, if you cannot show us dead Frankish wizards, we will see you drowned."

René, my friend, the emperor has issued orders for his men to stop hunting you. You are his sport.

René snickered. *He told me I wasn't worth his notice. Yeah, right.*

I expect it will not be long before he rescinds that order.

Sparks and noise like fireworks exploded across their shared bond. *What the hell was that?*

Ow, my head. That was notice that a foreign lightning thrower crossed into Frankland. And I'd been worried about missing it. Ha!

Alex, are you all right?

Don't worry about me, René. Take care for yourself.

Reinforcements

A jagged line of lightning strikes zigzagged across the Massif Central, leaving burning trees, scarred stone, or blackened corpses wherever it touched the ground. Leapfrogging wizards clashed, broke apart, and clashed again until finally the invaders fled, skipping back across the border.

René leaned against a tree trunk, panting. Two of Gunther's strikes had gotten close enough for his shields to become heavy draws on his reserves.

Should you go after them?

René snorted. If he hadn't built a barrier around his emotions, he would already have been over the border, hot on Gunther's tail, chasing the bastard down and making him pay for the damage he was doing to Frankland. For what he'd done to Hildur.

No. I don't know the territory, and they have their own traps. Besides, I need a breather, and I want to understand what happened before I face him again. Where's Ernest?

A few minutes later, René and Ernest were examining a blackened corpse, while René recounted the battle.

"I hit him dead-on, half-a-dozen times. I swear I did. Even Quicksilver would have suffered from a beating like that, but it didn't seem to bother Gunther at all. Every time I hit him, some other man went down. Like this one. He was a dozen yards away."

Ernest's eyes bulged, enhancing his resemblance to a startled rabbit—a dire rabbit, with vampire teeth and a rabid animal's aggressive stance. Someday, René hoped, he would find that funny.

Ernest said, "Describe the men with him, and where they stood."

René drew a diagram in the dirt with his wand. "Gunther was in the centre, here, with his communications aide. He had three earth wizards, two level fours and one five, in a triangle around him, yards away, plus a warlock. The rest—"

"Why the other warlock?"

"To help move all those people, so Gunther can save his power for the lightning. The rest in a circle, were mundanes. Could the earth wizards be holding shields for him?"

Ernest rubbed his nose. "That could explain it. And with them deflecting your strikes onto the poor souls in the outer circle, he could direct all his power to calling down the lightning."

"Pretty rotten deal for those mundanes."

That was not a fair fight.

Come on, Alex. Did you think it would be? If you can send your voice as far as his field headquarters, poke him a little. Make him lose his temper.

Alex breathed a laugh. *Yes. It will be a pleasure to point out to his staff how cowardly this tactic is.*

Ernest was still frowning over the diagram. "I'm sorry I didn't think of this."

René shuddered.

Ernest said, "Even if you didn't use it, we wouldn't have been taken by surprise."

"Don't be an ass. Nobody can think of everything. Just tell me how to beat it."

"That's easy. Don't aim for the emperor." Granddad Ernest, earth wizard, looked pained. "Aim for the earth wizards."

General Strazky and his staff were taking another beating.

"We jumped through the fire to Paris," Gunther snarled, "more than two dozen times, and never reached it. All we saw were god-forsaken mountains, nowhere near a useful target. Why?"

General Strazky said, "Apparently it is some variant of the earth spell in their Fire Office that directs threats towards the Fortress. It is deflecting you from your destination."

"How is it we did not know of this?"

The general spread his hands, palms up. "We expected there would be surprises. No one can think of everything."

"Fool. It is your job to think of these things. When this is over you shall pay for your incompetence."

Gillian surprised Alexander by handing him a glass of water. "You look hot."

"I am. Thank you."

"Roll up your sleeves."

He did. He loosened his collar, too, without taking his eyes off the mirrors. Four earth fathers had taken possession of the abandoned watchtower on Storm King's south-eastern flank.

René, look at this. Tell me what they're doing.

René watched through Alexander's eyes. *Frost me if I know.*

One earth father made the motions of swinging a sledgehammer. A dull thud followed, as much felt through Alexander's feet as heard through his ears. Among the Coven members not at work, heads popped up.

Got it, René said. *They're looking for weak spots. They did that during the siege, in the last war.*

I trust they did not find any?

No, but several skylights and vents were added since then. Still…they'd have to make a direct hit on one to find it.

And if they do?

The earth father swung again. Another thud pulsed through the rock.

We'll have to hope the Fortress's defences are rock solid.

Late in the afternoon, the game of Hunt the Warlock resumed, stitching another jagged line across Frankland's mountains. The game had no definite outcome other than René's jeers drove Gunther into such a towering rage that on his retreat to the empire's command post over the border, he torched the man reporting their forces in North Frankland were being trounced.

René, wolfing down a plate of cold ham in the Palm Courtyard, watched the sinking sun and fretted over the wasted mundane lives and his inability to break Gunther's protective triangle. He grabbed a roll and went looking for Ernest.

"I killed half his sacrificial lambs before getting a clear shot at a wizard," he said. "Gunther retreated after I killed an earth wizard, but he'll return with a full complement."

"He'll wear you out that way," Ernest said.

"Right. Can you tweak Father Pierre's diversion spell?"

Ernest chewed his lip. "Maybe. I'll have a go."

Lucinda watched Jean. They still had hours left, and he was already tired. He had taught them well, ensuring his protégés understood and were capable of recreating the Fire Guild spells. Given enough time, either Beorn, René, or Lucinda alone could rebuild the Fire Office without his help.

They didn't have that time. The empire's muffled hammer blows on the Fortress walls were a constant reminder of that. The three fire talents in the chamber—Jean, Sven, and Lucinda—had to do this as fast as they could, and neither she nor Sven could execute the spells as quickly as Jean could.

Of Frankland's four warlocks, René, they knew, would survive and be Fire Warlock. Beorn was in the healers' hands; they wouldn't let him die. That left her and Jean, and she would never call herself a warrior.

Lucinda watched Jean, and let worry feed her anger.

The Unconquered were doing well. None of their engagements needed Alexander's immediate attention. He scanned the empire's makeshift camp at the border. They were preparing for a secondary offensive strike at dawn tomorrow. If all went according to plan in Frankland, that strike would be too late to do the empire any good, but the activity still made his scalp prickle. Non-combatant sorceresses and enchantresses were delivering scores of low-ranking wizards. Worse, musketeers were emerging from their tunnels.

He had argued for providing their own forces with firearms, but had eventually been swayed by the argument that firearms would be too conspicuous, and defeat the purpose of the badge's lock spell. Armed with longbows, the Unconquered would blend in with and recruit help from the general population, and archery's quick fire, accuracy, and relative silence would compensate for the musket's greater range. He prayed the warlocks were right.

He turned his attention to the activity at the base of the Fortress. The growing stack of gunpowder barrels made his mouth go dry, but the invaders had not gotten close enough to begin sapping the walls. The

268

Fortress's own defences were supplemented by the inhabitants of Blazes who were neither in the Unconquered nor standing guard over children within the walls. The wizards tending the barrels were being harassed unmercifully.

Gillian said, "A legion of fireflies."

Alexander's spirits lifted. "Better than. These have real fire in their tails."

His satisfaction turned to terror as fireworks exploded in his head.

René, there's another warlock—a lightning thrower!

Who?

I don't know!

Frostbite. René stumbled as Alexander's panic over the new threat infected him. He jumped blindly to the nearest hilltop, taking himself out of the firefight.

Can't be another lightning thrower. The empire only has one.

I don't recognise him, but Hildur's there, and down—René, wait!

But René was already jumping through the fire. The flames died. Hildur sprawled, face down, on shingle. The warlock kneeling beside her grinned at him.

"Drown me if we've missed the fun," Mjöllnir said.

Katie was in the Palm Courtyard, ladling out stew, when Snorri arrived with Hildur in his arms. No one reacted; they were both still wearing their badges. Mjöllnir, badgeless, emerged right behind. Yelling wizards scattered.

"He's a friend," Snorri bellowed. "Hildur's grandfather. He's here to help." He laid Hildur down gently on a cot next to an earth witch tending a wounded earth wizard.

The healer said, "What happened to her?"

"Exhaustion. Drained all her magic."

The healer gave Mjöllnir a sharp glance, but turned back to the earth wizard. "I'll get to her in a minute."

"It's fine. She needs rest and food, that's all."

Katie hurried over with a brimming bowl. "The king said you were back. What took you so long?" Both warlocks turned scorching glares on her.

Mjöllnir said, "You wanted us to fall in the ocean a hundred miles out?

Had to make her rest and eat."

Snorri said, "You knew what she was doing and didn't tell me?"

"I didn't want to raise false hopes," Katie said. "I didn't think she'd make it."

Hildur's attempt to breathe fire left her coughing. "Wretched witch," she wheezed. "I'd never desert him. Never! You said you were my friend."

"Easy." Mjöllnir stroked the red hair with a gnarled hand. "Almost didn't make it. Days before you can make sparks." He dropped the equipment he was carrying beside the cot.

Snorri did a double take. "What did you bring a musket for?"

Mjöllnir shrugged. "She wanted it."

Snorri picked it up and handed it to Katie. "Here. Keep an eye on this." He gave her another glare. "And for God's sake don't let her out your sight while she can't hold a shield." He bent down and gave Hildur a brief but solid kiss. "All right, old man. You ready to make the emperor wish he'd never heard of calling down the lightning?"

Mjöllnir grunted. "Been ready sixty years."

Katie fed Hildur stew while the two warlocks threaded their way through the courtyard. When they had vanished into the tunnels, she turned to the earth witch. "Granny Martha, don't you get tired of men having all the fun?"

The rhythmic hammering was setting Alexander's teeth on edge, and it wasn't bothering him as much as it bothered Gillian. She cringed with every hammer strike. He counted seconds between strikes. The next one was—

The Forge rang like a bell. He clapped his hands over his ears. Gillian screamed. Chairs scraped on flagstones. Dropped china smashed. The coven were on their feet, shocked out of their trances. Mother Astrid swore, using language Alexander's mother would have been horrified he understood.

"What happened?" he said.

"They found a weak spot," Astrid said.

"We've lost half an hour's work," Sven said.

"If that happens again…" Eleanor said.

"It will," Quicksilver said. "You may count on it. Mother Astrid, what can—"

The hammer struck again. Everyone but Mother Astrid ducked their heads and clamped their hands over their ears, but couldn't block out the ringing.

"—the Earth Guild do?" Astrid said. "Let's see." She laid her hands flat on the stone wall. "Jerome, Martin, Pierre, help me."

The next hammer strike was not as loud. After several agonising minutes, the noise returned to the level of dull thuds. The four earth talents separated and returned to their places at the table or with the wounded. Gillian whimpered and clung to Alexander's arm.

Astrid said, "We've muffled the sound and strengthened the Fortress as well as we can without overtaxing ourselves."

"Tell me," Alexander said, "what strengthening the Fortress means."

"They won't break in quickly, but if they are allowed to keep hammering eventually they will."

"How soon?"

"Mid-morning, I'd say, unless something else goes wrong. If we finish before dawn, as we intended, we should be fine."

Quicksilver said, "Then let us continue."

Thunder rolled. A barrage of lightning lit the sky of a remote valley. René breathed a silent prayer of apology to the poor minion he was aiming for, and let fly. The strike hit. Mjöllnir took out a second of Gunther's earth wizard shield holders.

René had guarded himself well against rage, but his emotional dam collapsed under the weight of Mjöllnir's contagious glee. He pumped a fist in the air and shouted. "Show him, old man!"

Mjöllnir grinned and jumped closer to their target, dropping a few feet to the side of a farmer's shed. He raised his wand. A thrown rock hit his shoulder hard enough to crack bone. He clutched at it. His shields collapsed. Gunther's strike, aimed at René, quite by accident hit the shed a few feet away. That close, the discharge of power was enough to stop an unshielded man's heart.

René's joy turned to horror as Mjöllnir's brilliant torch flickered and went out. Rage turned his world crimson. He jumped to Mjöllnir's side, dropped his shields, and stole the fire from the burning shed, bellowing, "You'll pay for that, you frostbitten weasel."

As René let fly, Gunther vanished. Absorbed in relocating his target,

René never saw the danger. The air wizard's thrown knife sliced cleanly across his calf. He fell. In the Fortress, Lucinda screamed.

Failure

The agony in Lucinda's calf, matching the knife wound in René's leg, was supplanted by a stinging cheek. Sven, paler than usual, leaned towards her across the table, his hand outstretched. She gaped at him, too shocked to throw fire.

"Sven," Irene hissed. "You just slapped a warlock. A warlock."

The remaining colour left Sven's face, but his hand was steady. "I slapped a warlock, and I'll do it again the next time she screams. Pull yourself together, Lucinda. René's not dying. You know he'll be Fire Warlock when we're done."

Her heart screamed, *He needs me.* Her head knew he didn't. Sven was right. If she broke the circle now they would lose two hours work. Jean's head was down, his eyes closed, his hands clasped together. Tension showed in the set of his jaw, the tightness of his grip. He was hanging onto his place in the fabric of spells by sheer willpower.

Alexander was ashen, with a hand clamped around his own calf. He said, "The Unconquered are tending to him."

"I'm sorry," she said. "Go on."

Sven settled back into his chair and closed his eyes. Lucinda dripped tears onto her spellbook. She could not see; the phantom knife wound overpowered her senses.

Little brother?

Nice to know you feel for me. His voice, usually loud in her head, was faint and sluggish, with the barest hint of humour.

The pain stopped. Lucinda pushed her spellbook away and dropped her head onto her arms, shuddering with relief. *Of course I do, runt. Don't ever do that to me again.*

His voice was stronger now. *Right. If I die I should make it instantaneous. Exactly.*

For the first time in his life, Gunther was alone. There were no servants he could call, no other wizards, not even any mundane Franks on this mountain. He had lost his communications aide when Snorri had forced him to jump unprepared, and he couldn't find that location again. He had no idea where he was, where he had been, or how to return to somewhere civilised. His three attempts to return to his field headquarters had all deflected him to some random rocky wilderness.

If he didn't make contact with other Europan wizards soon, that mongrel cur would find him and finish him off. It wouldn't take much. He needed to rest and rebuild his reserves, but there was nowhere safe. He had, at best, one or maybe two lightning strikes left before he lost control. Snorri's better stamina enraged him. His better aim was salt rubbed in Gunther's wounded pride. And what had he done to that shed? Gunther couldn't fathom that at all.

Behind him, underbrush rattled. He whirled, his pulse pounding, but it was only some scurrying animal, not an arriving wizard. What was Snorri waiting for? The bastard was toying with him! He would never have believed it, but there was no other explanation.

Gunther jumped blindly through the fire onto another mountainside, above a village of sleeping mundanes. He torched the village from pure spite, and jumped again.

Paris was burning, and the South Frankland Army couldn't put it out. Even with the Water Guild draining the Seine, there had been too many hot spots, and some they had missed had ballooned into monsters in the tinder-dry city. Their fire wizards had done their best, but the fighting had raged for hours, and they had taken a beating. The Earth Guild threw dirt on the fires, smothering some, but it wasn't enough.

Granddad Ernest fingered his badge. "I'm sorry, Your Majesty, but we need help."

General Strazky chewed his moustache. They'd beaten Frankland's Fire Guild in one city. One! They should have taken a dozen by now. The spectacle of water wizards protecting fire wizards in a firefight had baffled him. He shook his head over the absurdity of it. The empire, with the mightiest collection of fire wizards in Europan history, had never beaten their water wizards into submission. Who would have thought those spineless Franks would?

The emperor would have nasty things to say about their lack of progress when they found him. If they found him, before Warlock Snorri did. An air wizard had re-established a communication link, but couldn't tell where the emperor was. For one brief, glorious instant Strazky considered abandoning him in the Frankish wilderness. He squashed that treasonous thought, but took a measure of grim satisfaction in acknowledging that Snorri was beating his emperor's butt.

Katie Underwood took in the scene in the Warren's courtyard in a glance: Snorri shuddering face down on a cot, Granny Martha tending to his leg, a ring of red-faced, silent wizards looking anywhere but at Snorri or each other.

Men. If they'd just give in and have a good cry, they'd feel better, but no… If it was her grandfather dead, she'd be bawling.

She trotted across the courtyard and shoved Carl Miller aside. "Snorri, I heard about Mjöllnir—" She got a good look at the slab of raw meat that was Snorri's leg and sat down hard on the floor. "Snorri, your shields… What happened?"

"I screwed up." He turned his face away from her and mumbled into his arms. "I broke a promise and we'll all pay for it. Oh, God, Quicksilver will be furious."

"What promise?"

"Sorceress Lorraine, years ago, made me promise not to seek revenge. To fight the war for Frankland's sake, and not let it get personal. But then Mjöllnir arrived and we attacked together and it felt so good to have that ass Gunther on the run that I lost my head and just pounded at him and then he killed Mjöllnir and I lost my temper and dropped my shields—"

"*All* your shields?"

"Yes."

"That was stupid."

"I know that! I wanted to show him I could absorb the fire and he couldn't, and didn't raise my shields fast enough. And now I'm finished and Mjöllnir's dead, and oh, God, what will I tell Hildur?"

Granny Martha paused in stitching his wound. "For starters, tell her he ought not to have been here fighting with you in the first place. The old man was sick."

Snorri's head jerked up. "What?"

"I couldn't tell what with when you passed through earlier, but I could tell he didn't have much strength left. He was pumped full of restorative potion to keep him on his feet, but it wouldn't have lasted long. I'm not surprised they got him."

"If I'd known that..." Snorri peered at Hildur sleeping in the next cot. "Burn it! All the more reason I shouldn't have lost my head."

The healer wrapped a bandage around the wound. "All done, but you're inches away from tearing it open again. Don't put any more weight on it than you have to." She handed him a cane. "Use this and if you give me any guff about looking like an old man, I'll box your ears. I'd tell you to stay off your feet for a few days, but I guess you wouldn't listen."

Snorri rolled and sat up. "Not tonight. But..." He dragged a sleeve across streaming eyes. "I don't know what to do. We took out the earth wizards that were holding his shields. Gunther's got his own shields against normal fire—none of you fire wizards could touch him yet—but he's vulnerable to a lightning thrower."

"So?" Katie said. "Get out there and—"

"I can't." Snorri slammed his fist against the cot's wooden frame. "Quicksilver and Mjöllnir would never let me forget that you have to be hale and whole to throw the lightning. If I do it now I'll kill myself, not hurt him."

The shuffling ring of wizards froze. They stared at Katie with bulging eyes. She swallowed. "Oh."

Snorri put his head down in his hands. "See? I failed."

"So now you're just an ordinary warlock?"

"Yes."

"But you've still got that water magic, whatever it is."

"Yes."

"Paris is burning. Douse it."

He went still with his head down and a two-handed white-knuckled grip on the cot's frame. "Right." He climbed to his feet, grimacing, and saluted. "Yes, ma'am."

Once he was gone, Katie shook Hildur's shoulder. "Wake up. It's time for that musket."

Lucinda watched Jean, and practiced the Water Guild's calming exercises. He noticed her attention, and smiled. His attempt at reassurance failed—his shoulders sagged, his head drooped, and the laugh lines around his eyes had become black crow's feet. He looked decrepit and long in the tooth. Was that a tremor in his hand? Maybe that was her imagination. His voice was still steady and robust.

If he began to sound like an old man, they were in trouble.

In the next two hours, they would be dealing with the Fire Guild's hardest spells, the ones for prioritising threats and drawing on Storm King's power. Lucinda risked another glance at the clock. Between one and three in the morning was not a good time for clear thinking on anyone's part.

Burn it, they should have done a better job of planning.

Nonsense. They had spent years planning this. There were no better options.

If Jean couldn't handle those spells—the ones at the heart of Frankland's defences—they would fall to her. Sven had the theory down cold, but two needed a warlock's power. She could do them, but they would take three or four times as long in her hands.

Irene threw a worried glance at Lucinda.

No, not at her. At someone behind her.

She glanced over her shoulder. Hazel stood a few feet behind, watching Jean. Lucinda's stomach dropped.

She shifted her weight forward, but Hazel put a hand on her shoulder, pressing her back into her chair. Hazel shook her head, and moved on cat's feet to stand within reach of Jean's right shoulder. She stretched out a finger for a feather's touch but snatched it back, flapping her hand in the air.

Lucinda reached across the table and brushed the back of his hand. Hot enough to cook with. How long had he been so hot? A sustained temperature rise isn't healthy, even for a warlock. She stole as much of the heat as she could without disturbing him. The tension in his face eased a trifle. Hazel nodded and retreated a few feet.

Lucinda leaned on the iron table. Cold iron? No longer. The room and everything in it were too hot for comfort. How much heat could she steal from him without overheating herself? They still had hours to go.

She measured the passage of time in the unbroken rhythm of the empire's hammering. She and Hazel watched Jean, and worried.

René, do you have any men you can spare to drive the invaders away from the Fortress?

What? No. Alex, the Fortress shouldn't need any help, as long as they haven't started moving the black powder.

We didn't consider the impacts of this infernal hammering. Watch.

René looked through Alexander's eyes. Gillian was absorbed in the scenes in the magic mirror, motionless except for one hand twisting a lock of hair around and around. The next hammer strike fell. Gillian flinched. The illusions flickered. The hand twisting her hair tightened and gave a hard yank.

Uh-oh.

You see? Every strike reminds her she's trapped underground. Countess Irene says we're still at least two hours away from moving the Air Guild spells. I don't know how much she can take.

I'll see what I can do.

T hree women clothed in black tried to make sense of a chaotic battle from the cover of a rock wall.

"Idiots," Katie said. "They're a herd of cats. Their attacks aren't doing any good. If they worked together they might be useful, but all they're doing is getting themselves hurt."

"Not true," Hildur said. "They're drawing the invaders' attention away from us, and keeping them from using the black powder. The invaders are wasting effort shielding those barrels from our firecats, and they cannot defeat the herd because it isn't a single attack. This must be what Quicksilver and Snorri had in mind when they refused to admit all the townsfolk into Frankland's Unconquered."

"I thought it was because they wouldn't obey orders."

"Even cats can be useful, catching vermin."

Granny Martha said, "Getting closer seems like a bad idea. We'll get burnt. Or stoned. Or something."

"Katie's shields will protect us from the flames. Yours will protect us from the rocks."

"Up to a point."

"They won't see us," Katie said. "That's what the badges do. I'm more worried about Fluffy. He'll smell us."

"Fluffy?"

"The Fire Warlock's pet lion."

"Lion?" The earth witch squawked. "You didn't warn me about a lion."

"He will not eat us," Hildur said. "If he notices us, you will distract him."

"I what? Now wait a minute—"

"You said the restorative potion you gave me would not last long. Stop wasting time." Hildur moved like a shadow, flowing over the rock wall and flitting across the moonlit ground. Katie followed. Martha plodded along behind, head swivelling in search of Fluffy. They waited for her in the shadow of a large boulder halfway to their target.

"I found the lion," she puffed. "We don't have to worry about him. He's hiding in his den. All the fire being thrown around has terrified the poor beastie."

"Good," Hildur said. "I don't want Arturos angry at me for hurting him."

"Are we close enough?"

"No." Hildur broke from cover and sprinted past a pair of wizards intent on burning each other. Martha sucked in her breath. The wizards ignored Hildur.

"You sure the emperor won't see us?" Martha said. "Where is he, anyway?"

"He's not here, that's all I know." Katie gave the earth witch a shove. "Stop stalling. Hildur's waiting."

In a few minutes they were crouched behind a closer boulder. "Close enough?" Katie said.

"For me, yes," Hildur said. "For you?"

"I think so." Katie edged into the open. "Give me a minute." She chewed on her lip and stared at the pyramid of barrels. The other two women waited.

Katie slid into the boulder's shadow. "Your idea ought to work. The powder's well protected against water and fire coming from outside a small, shielded circle. The shields will stop flaming arrows, but they haven't thought of this. Not that I can tell, anyway."

"We'll find out soon. And we will have only one chance." Hildur lay on the ground and crept into the open on her belly. Moving carefully, in no hurry, she brought her musket to bear, resting the gun barrel on a small rock. Soon she said, "Shields ready?"

"Mine are," Katie said.

"Mine too," Martha said.

"Good. Tell the king."

Katie fingered her badge. "Your Majesty, tell all of ours in the lion's field to run for cover."

What?

"The black powder is about to blow. No time to explain."

A moment later the firecats scattered. The emperor's forces guarding the powder were floundering, searching for targets, when the musket roared, followed an instant later by a much louder, more violent explosion.

End Game

Cups rattled in the practice room. Lamps flickered. Alexander gaped at the magic mirrors. Sorceress Eleanor paused in the middle of a spell. Someone yelped, "What was that?"

Quicksilver held up a hand. "Hush."

Eleanor stared at him blankly. "I've lost my place."

Irene leaned across the table and drew her pen down the page in Eleanor's spellbook.

"Oh, right. Sorry." Eleanor shook her head, and went on with her work.

The other coven members not engaged at that moment clustered behind Alexander and gawked at the mirror showing dying flames and a new crater in the field at the Fortress's base. Alexander watched a boulder at the crater's edge. With his heart in his mouth, he waited for movement that didn't come until long after the last stone had thudded back to earth. The rigid tension in his back and jaw didn't ease when two figures finally crept from the lee of the boulder and began digging into what now resembled a shallow grave.

When at last a moving arm emerged from the pile of rocks and dirt, he let out a great "Woof!" He hadn't realised he had been holding his breath. He rose, strolled across the room to the medical stores, poured himself a thimbleful of brandy, breathed in the fumes, and tossed the liquid down his throat. He contemplated the bottle for a moment, before re-corking it and returning to his station at the mirror. It displayed his friend's wife, grimy but unharmed, fighting free from the earth.

"Sorry it took so long," the earth witch said. "Just wanted to be sure nothing else was falling."

"Understood," Hildur said. "I was not eager to raise my head."

Katie, grinning, gave her a hand up. "That was better than the fireworks shows old Sunbeam used to put on. That'll teach those silly wizards that women can be dangerous, too, even when we're out of magic."

"I am a warlock," Hildur said. "I am always dangerous."

A t two thirty in the morning, Lucinda was out of the hunt, pacing the floor and gnawing her knuckles. Deep in the heart of the most complicated section, with Jean carrying the weight of one spell, Sven another, and Mother Astrid and Father Jerome weaving their own strand in the mesh, Jean checked. Lucinda tensed and stopped pacing.

"Mistress Irene," he said, "do you verify this wording?" He had already asked for verification several times, though less often than Sven. Irene had caught him in fewer mistakes than anyone else.

Lucinda resumed pacing. She could watch Jean and worry, watch the clock and panic, or watch the mirrors and rage at the wanton destruction they showed. She watched the mirrors.

Fifteen minutes later Jean checked again. On the third time, minutes later, Irene threw a worried glance at Lucinda. Hazel and Lucinda converged within arm's reach behind Jean's chair. The four spellcasters went on with their spellcraft, undisturbed. The other healers crept closer. The rest of the coven watched the mirrors or studied their spellbooks, oblivious to the healers' concern.

Jean finished that spell, and moved on to the spell making the Token of Office the conduit of Storm King's volcanic power; one of the few Sven, a mere level four, couldn't handle. After this spell, they would have a momentary respite. This was the hardest; Lucinda would take the next few and let Jean rest.

Jean scowled. The worry in Hazel's expression deepened. She ran her hand, an inch away from him, over his head and shoulders.

Looking for cooler spots? There wouldn't be any.

Lucinda went down on her knees on the floor, and reached for his hand with a feather-light touch. He acknowledged her presence with a frown and shake of the head. She dropped her hand. Hazel stood at his left shoulder, hand raised. They waited.

Jean grimaced. He glowed red hot. Hazel's worry changed to alarm. She reached for him. Lucinda pushed her hand away, and prayed.

Jean?

His eyes were clouded, dead. *Wait, love. One more stanza.*

Jerome finished his spell. Sven finished, and then Astrid. Jean finished his.

He turned blind eyes towards Lucinda. *So sorry, love.* His expression slackened, past relaxation and on into senility. He fell forwards. She grabbed him, twisting him away from hitting his head on the table, and they went down together. She pushed heat downwards, past the flagstones and into the Fortress's granite foot. Hazel dove after them and dragged him off Lucinda, wrapping her arms around his shoulders and laying her cheek against his temple, like a lover, and whispering to him.

Other healers crowded around. Father Jerome, a decrepit-looking nonagenarian, lifted Jean as if he weighed no more than a kitten, and carried him to a cot. Hazel walked alongside without taking her hands off Jean's temples. The rest of the Coven gathered around, staring.

Lucinda pulled on the edge of the table to get to her feet. Her vision was tinged in shades of red and black. She met Sven's horrified gaze across the table, and turned away. She wanted to run after the healers and sit at Jean's bedside, holding his hand, like a perfect wife. She wanted to bury her face in Mother Astrid's accommodating shoulder and weep. She wanted to jump onto the ramparts and fling lightning bolts at Gunther and his wizards.

She couldn't do any of those. If she did, Jean would never forgive her. She had to finish the reforging, and then she could seek revenge. Or weep.

"Take a ten minute break, people," Astrid said. "We all need it." She squeezed Lucinda's shoulders. "And you, don't argue. Wash your face, drink some water, and eat—some cheese and an apple. You need it. If you don't take a break, you'll make mistakes, and waste more than ten minutes." She steered Lucinda towards the buffet table, but the king blocked their path.

He said, "What happened? Warlock Snorri is frantic. What's wrong with Warlock Quicksilver?"

Mother Astrid said, "Cerebral haemorrhage."

"Bleeding in the brain?"

"Yes, Your Highness. The strain was too much. Several blood vessels burst, and flooded his skull. The pressure has done damage."

"The damage can be repaired, can't it? Shouldn't you be there with the other healers?"

283

Lucinda met the Earth Mother's glance with a shake of her head. Even if the healers could undo the damage now, it would happen again and again. He was dying, of overwork and extreme old age. The Earth Guild couldn't afford the effort they had been putting into keeping him alive. Once this was over, they would let him die. Drown the man! He would even argue it was the right thing to do.

Lucinda said, "He's in good hands. We need Mother Astrid here, for the spellwork."

Gillian said, "But without him…can we…?"

"Finish?" Lucinda said. "We have to." She locked eyes with Sven. "Sven and I can handle the rest. Right, Sven?"

Sven's Adam's apple bobbed but he nodded. "He made sure we can."

The work resumed. Gillian slipped into the circle around the iron table, her spellbook in hand, to move the spells from Sorceress Eleanor to the Fire Office. Alexander turned back to the mirrors. For a few minutes everything continued as it had, then without warning, the scenes in the mirror vanished. His horrified face stared back at him from three rectangles of silvered glass.

He spun. Gillian was hunched over, eyes screwed shut. The other Coven members at the table were unmoving, deep in their wizardly trances.

Gillian whimpered. He started towards her but Countess Irene stopped him with a raised hand, palm out. Had the transfer worked? Or had the spells collapsed? He couldn't tell. Mrs Rehsavvy smiled and gave him a thumbs up.

The next hammer strike fell.

Gillian flinched, tearing a page in her spellbook. Mrs Rehsavvy winced. No one else reacted overtly. He massaged his calf's phantom wound, matching the throbbing gash in René's leg.

Gillian left the table and stumbled towards him with blind eyes. He gathered her into his arms and she whimpered against his chest, trembling like a trapped hummingbird.

"You did it," he said. "Didn't you?"

"I almost…didn't," she whispered.

"Can you fix the mirrors?"

"What's wrong with them?" She jerked free and lurched towards them. "No. No." She dropped into a heap before the middle mirror and raked her hands through her hair. "Nooooo."

Alexander grabbed her hands and held them. "You're panicking. Slow down. Take a deep breath."

With her hands in his, she stared at the mirror. It clouded over, streaks of bright colours flashed across, then a burst of light like fireworks stung their eyes. She wrenched away from him, ran to the vent, and pressed her face against the metal grate, crying.

He ran after her. "Tell me what's wrong."

"Too much... I don't know... I never..."

"Shhh. Breathe."

Several deep breaths later she managed a coherent sentence. "Something in my head went poof."

"Beg your pardon, Sire." Father Pierre pushed past Alexander and murmured in her ear. Alexander returned to the mirrors. Sorceress Eleanor was frowning at them.

He asked, "Can you help?"

"Only if you can tell me where to look. I cannot sense trouble beforehand."

"Paris. London. Outside the Fortress."

"That's too vague. Where in Paris? The palace? A guildhall? The cathedral? Even the Fortress is too large. The gates? Atop the outer walls? Higher up? Where?"

In a few minutes they had settled on three viewpoints: the palace roof in Paris, a spot on the Fortress's western ramparts, and the watchtower the empire had claimed as its new field headquarters. He resumed his watch, but he was overtaxed. Had been for some time, but Gillian had been shoring him up. Without her help his head felt stuffed with cotton wool. His keen eyesight was eroding. His excellent hearing, fading. Half deaf and blind, he probed for hints of danger. Nothing. All he could do was watch the mirrors.

René, he is here.

Gunther?

Who else? An enchanter found him and carried him to the watchtower on Storm King's flank. With Sorceress Eleanor's help, I can watch him and the activity around the Fortress, but I can see nothing else. My friend, you are on your own.

An argument in the watchtower came to an abrupt end. An air wizard bolted. The empire's two remaining warlocks didn't notice his departure. They were stunned into silence by the sudden overwhelming sense of something vast and furious stirring to life.

General Strazky clamped a hand over his mouth and fought down the urge to whimper.

"That's impossible," the emperor whispered. "They needed days… How…"

The Fire Office's attention sharpened and focused on them. Strazky backed into the wall and bleated.

The map the emperor held disintegrated into flaming fragments. "Forget London. Only two things matter now: break into the Fortress, and kill that mongrel cur of a warlock. Whatever it takes, do it."

René leaned against a tunnel wall. The cool rough stone soothed his hot skin. Sweat-wet hair irritated him, but he couldn't be bothered brushing it out of his eyes. He would have sat on the floor, but he'd not get up again.

An earth wizard coughed at his elbow. "Sir?"

René peered at him. "What?"

"Granddad Ernest says the empire's earth wizards are trying to break the dam above Rubierre. A flood would destroy the whole town."

René groaned and pushed off from the wall. "On my way."

He emerged from the tunnels onto a hillside above the river. Wizards from all four guilds swarmed over the earthen dam and riverbanks, digging, fighting, and getting in each other's way. Unbadged Franks grappled with invaders. Despite the growing light René was blind, unable to tell friend from foe. Flying rocks, hailstones, howling winds, and every other nasty trick angry wizards could throw at each other added to the confusion. Even if he could have been sure which wizards were the empire's, he wouldn't have dared throw flame hard enough to punch through shields so near his own men.

He wanted to bellow, *Stop hiding and face me like men!* That wouldn't help and would make him look silly. He had a flash of sympathy, quickly suppressed, for the frustration Gunther had experienced hunting his elusive prey.

Granddad Ernest ran past. René lunged, grabbed a flying cloak, and yanked Ernest to a halt. "Are you nuts? What happened to your badge?"

Ernest leaned close, yelling to be heard over the wind. "Got ripped off. They've learned. The badges are the first things they're going for now."

"Oh, great."

"The dam will go soon. We need a sorcerer. We can't handle this much water ourselves."

Alex, did you hear?

Yes. Help is coming.

René said, "How soon?"

"Don't know. I want a look at it. Follow me."

René limped after the earth wizard along a narrow path toward a rocky outcrop.

"Frostbite," Ernest said. "It's about to go."

"If you say so." In the dim, pre-dawn light, René saw only an immense earthen wall.

René, it's a trap.

What?

They knew you would go there. They are trying to kill you.

Forget it, Alex. You relayed that Gunther said I was his prey.

That was hours ago. His last orders were to take any opportunity they have to kill you.

Gunther didn't know he'd been hobbled? René hooted.

It's not funny.

Sure it is, Alex, and the joke's on me. Gunther is—

The ground shook. Wizards froze. The wind dropped. The fleeting silence gave way to a roar as a jet of water broke through the dam. Defenders and invaders alike scattered, leaving René and Ernest alone on the outcrop, gawking. Other sections of the dam disintegrated. The valley echoed with the thunder of the rising water.

A churning, frothing wall of muddy water poured down the valley, carrying along trees, rocks, goats, and everything else in its path. The growing flood surged around the bend in the river and caromed off the canyon's far wall, hurtling towards the barriers the earth wizards had been hastily constructing. René watched in open-handed, slack-jawed stupefaction. Even when he had fallen into the immensity of the Atlantic Ocean, the water had seemed to him a passive thing. He had never imagined that the impersonal fury of the Fire Guild's mortal enemy could make a lightning-wielding warlock feel like a bumblebee.

The flow hit the barriers downstream and split, half diverted northwest towards open farmland, but half still surging towards the town. The water rose, coming within a dozen feet of their vantage point.

René, get out!

René reached for Ernest and called up the flames, but a plume of spray doused his fire. He damned himself for his curiosity. Lucinda would be pissed off if he drowned again.

That was René's last thought before an earth wizard's hurled rocks hit him.

The Seventy-Fifth Fire Warlock

Granddad Ernest's magic talents were more useful for planting trees and nurturing gardens than for tending the ill. He had a deft hand in applying first aid, extracting splinters, and setting broken bones, but a mundane with sufficient training could do those. He didn't have a healer's ability to diagnose subtle maladies with a simple touch. But when the rocks thudded into Snorri's back and skull, the jar travelled through the warlock's hand on his arm. His own skull resonated with the crack in Snorri's.

He caught the falling warlock and they teetered on the edge of the outcropping, but his wizardly instincts were sound; he had sent roots winding around the rocks below him before becoming conscious of the need. He was almost an earth father; no one would knock him off his feet, even with a blow to the head.

His pleasure in this small victory was short-lived. The enemy earth wizards sent the entire outcrop tumbling into the raging torrent.

The current grabbed them, ripped Snorri from his grip, and spun them around and head over heels until he had lost all sense of direction. He kicked, struggling to free himself from the rocks, long after the water had torn them free. He bobbed to the surface, was flung screaming towards the canyon wall, but an eddy caught him and threw him back in midstream before he hit.

Magic. Had to be. Some water wizard was looking out for him. He clung to that thought like a lifeline. If it wasn't true, he had no hope. He couldn't swim. He couldn't even float. Whenever he'd tried, he'd gone straight to the bottom as if he had weighted his pockets with stones.

He searched for Snorri, but couldn't find him. He couldn't have helped the warlock anyway, if he had found him.

The violence diminished as the canyon ended and the water spread out over the wide river valley. He was no longer being hurled towards rocks, but a torn-off roof smacked into him, breaking his arm above the elbow as it swirled past. He used what little magic he had left to turn his arm to stone, devoid of feeling.

His teeth chattered. He floated on his back, watching the sky lighten, and wondered if he would die of cold. It might be a relief, if Snorri was dead.

With the Earth Guild leading the spellcasting for the moment, Lucinda squinted at the mirrors. The Fortress's defences were failing. Two earth wizards were scaling the corner towers. The guard's arrows felled one, but the other, an earth father, confounded their senses and their shots went wild.

"Frostbite." Father Pierre slammed his fist against the wall. "If he reaches the second tier he could breach this strongroom."

"No way," Lucinda said. "We aren't there."

"The weak spot—the skylight they're hammering on—is. He's heading for that."

The hammer struck. Fine dust drifted down from a small crack high on the southern wall. A chorus of muffled curses sounded.

"That does it." Lucinda flung down her book of spells and rose. "I'll—"

Sven caught her arm. "You can't. You're needed here to put the lock on."

She snarled, "We can't let him—"

"I'll do it."

She sucked in a sharp breath. "Fine. Go."

"Sven!" Irene stretched out a hand but he was already running, out of reach.

Father Pierre followed. "Sven, careful. That man's dangerous."

Sven didn't slow. "And I'm not?"

"I didn't mean…" They disappeared into the tunnels.

Irene started after them. Mother Astrid grabbed her dress and yanked her back. "You. Sit. Let him be."

Irene sank back into her chair with eyes wide and fixed on the mirror. Lucinda would have told her not to watch, but there was no point. She wouldn't have listened to that advice either.

Lucinda closed her eyes, took a deep breath, and held it for the count of five before returning to her seat at the table. The emperor would pay dearly for his war. He wouldn't hurt her country, her home, her friends, and get away with it.

Flame roared across the wall. Sven, leaning over the parapet, swept another arc with his wand, searching for the earth wizard. A whisper, a suggestion of motion where there should have been none, warned him. He lurched to the right. A stone hit his left shoulder from behind, knocking him forward against the battlement. He twisted and fell. A shower of stones sailed through the gap where his head had been. He rolled, gasping as his shoulder hit stone, and flung an arc of flame across the top of the wall behind him. Someone howled.

How the devil had that demon earth wizard gotten up there?

He scrambled to his feet and sprinted for the cover of the guard tower. A stone hit him in the back and he fell through the door into Father Pierre's arms.

The earth wizard dragged him across the lintel. A guard slammed the door. More stones thudded against it.

"He's confusing our eyes," Father Pierre said. "Mind's eye, too, and he's fast. You'll never hit him by aiming for him."

"I hit him once." Sven staggered to his feet and rubbed his shoulder. "I can do it again."

"Not by aiming for him. Aim for where the stones come from."

"Yes! Follow the stones." Chagrin replaced excitement. "Right. The stones he's throwing at me."

Father Pierre lifted his hands, then dropped them. "I'll shield you as much as I can, but I don't have much magic left."

"Nobody does." Sven turned to the guard. "Hand me a torch."

The guard's eyes bugged out. "Sir?"

"I need light. It'll take all the magic I have left to kill this fiend. Hand me a torch."

Torch in hand, Sven turned back to Father Pierre. "Ready?"

Father Pierre nodded. Sven threw the door open and stepped out, Father Pierre a pace behind. A stone flew at Sven's head. He ducked, and raked the top of the wall with fire. More stones followed, and bounced off an invisible shield. The next jet of flame sailed higher, and further to the right.

The earth wizard screamed. The shower of stones became a torrent. A block the size of a horse's head crashed through the shield and clipped Sven's left shoulder. With his left arm hanging useless at an impossible angle, aware of nothing but pain and his target, Sven poured a steady stream of fire across the top of the wall. The wall collapsed. Sven and Father Pierre disappeared in a deluge of stones. The avalanche broke the guardroom door and cascaded across the floor, depositing at the horrified corporal's feet the earth wizard's blackened corpse.

Irene screamed, "Sven!" She surged to her feet, hitting the iron table a solid thump with her hip.

Mother Astrid snapped, "Sleep!"

Irene fell forward, sprawling across the table, sending spellbooks and coffee cups flying. Lucinda blinked at the fallen witch.

"We don't need her now," Astrid said. "I knew we shouldn't have put those mirrors so close."

"You've given her a nosebleed."

Astrid patted Irene's cheek. "Stop bleeding. Get back to work, Lucinda."

An air wizard found the Forge's chimney. Gunther and Strazsky poured a stream of flame through it. The stream cascaded across the buffet tables and leapt across the open space, hunting Lucinda. Flames billowed around her, climbed her skirts, and licked at her face. The coven scattered, yelling. Fire danced across the table, and over Irene. Her clothes caught, and her hair. Gillian screamed. Alexander yanked Irene from the table and rolled her across the floor, beating at the flames with his bare hands.

The floor shook. Cups rattled. The rumble of falling rocks drowned out the raised voices. Lucinda sucked in the flames.

The room stank of burned food and hair. As the injured and the healers bearing burn cloths sorted themselves out, Gillian's whimpered, "There's no air. No air!"

Mother Astrid's expression was grim. "I closed the chimney and all the vents. I'm sorry, dear, but we won't be here much longer."

The hammer struck. Dust and rock fragments showered them. Gillian's banshee wail raised the hairs on the back of Lucinda's neck. She followed Gillian's gaze. "Oh, dear God." The illusion of the lightening sky had disappeared. The room's ceiling showed a network of cracks radiating out from the southern wall.

Alexander left the still-sleeping wordsmith in Father Martin's hands, and hustled Gillian across the room, away from the cracks.

Mother Astrid stretched out a hand towards her. "I can put you to sleep—"

"No! Don't touch me! You won't bury me. I won't sleep underground, no, never!"

"Just trying to help."

"Do not be offended, madam," Alexander said. "She is not rational. She will apologize in due time."

The Earth Mother nodded and turned away. "Let's finish this."

As they worked, the crack in the ceiling grew large enough to fit a head through. On each successive hammer strike more rock fragments fell.

Gillian leaned against a silent vent. Her eyes were glazed. She'd scraped her knuckles and ruined her nails tearing at the metal grate. One hand plucked at her hair, yanking out one strand after another.

Lucinda dismissed her with a glance. "The full lock can wait. We'll redo it with the Air Guild later."

The hammer struck. More rocks fell. The hole was wide enough to let a person through.

Joining hands with Sorceress Eleanor and Mother Astrid, Lucinda drew strands of power from them to put the lock—the night's final spell—on the Fire Warlock's Token of Office.

The defensive capabilities of the Fire Office were fully functional once again. The office was awake, alert, and angry. Frankland needed a Fire Warlock to wield it, to finish the war, and René was unconscious, lost in the flood. Lucinda hadn't wanted this, but she didn't hesitate. She slipped the Token of Office on her finger.

Her mind's eye expanded to encompass the Fortress, the emperor and his forces, Frankland's defenders, the Rubierre flood, all of Frankland, and then shrank as the galvanised office focused on the emperor. Lava flowed through her veins as fury unlike anything she had ever experienced rolled through her.

The Fortress's defences came back to life. Fireworks blew climbing earth wizards away from the walls to smash on Storm King's flanks. Enchanters flying towards the upper tiers slammed into invisible walls and fell.

Lucinda soared like an air witch, rising through the hole in the ceiling.

Hands gripped Ernest. A woman's voice said, "Gotcha, luv." A boat nudged him. More hands grabbed him, pulled him over the side, and lowered him into the bilge.

Reggie Chandler, water wizard in the South Frankland army, bent over him. "All right?"

"Cold. Snorri?"

Reggie stripped off his coat and threw it over him. "Mabel's looking for him now."

The boat swung and bounced across the current. Ernest moaned. Boats didn't scare him, but he had no fondness for the nasty things, either. He preferred his feet on solid ground.

"Here's the other one," Mabel said.

The boat turned and rocked wildly. This was an improvement? He'd been cold in the water, but not seasick. Snorri, limp as a dead eel, landed on top of him, pushing his face into the bilge water. Reggie rolled Snorri off of him.

"How is he?" Ernest croaked.

"Alive. Just. He's not coming round."

"He got a bad knock on the head."

"That'd explain it."

An uprooted tree swept past, snagged Reggie, and dragged him overboard. Mabel screamed. Ernest's roots grabbed the tree and held on while the boat bucked and Mabel and Reggie fought with the tree. Ernest grabbed a thwart, pulled himself up one-handed, and wrapped more roots around Reggie. The water wizard clambered aboard. Ernest gave the tree a hard shove.

Reggie hunched on the seat, shuddering. "Thanks, mate."

Ernest leaned over the side and puked, then slid back down. "You're a water wizard. You can't drown, can you?"

"Sure I can. I'm all tapped out. I'm praying Mabel has enough magic to get us back to dock, or we're goners."

The boat jittered and bounced and thrust through the water like some wild, enchanted beast. Ernest caught glimpses of buildings sliding past. They were coming into the town. This hellish ride would be over soon.

"We all could've drowned," Mabel said, "but the Water Sorceress said fish 'em out. Especially that one." She nudged the inert warlock with her foot. "Friend of the Water Guild, she said."

Reggie winked at Ernest. "Imagine that."

Ernest shook his head, too dazed to reply. In the lawless past, an unconscious warlock in a boat with the Water Guild would soon have been a drowned warlock, with Ernest as a drowned witness. And they said nothing ever changed in Frankland.

Mabel said, "Why's he so important?"

Reggie said, "He's our next Fire Warlock."

She drove the last few yards in stunned silence. The boat slowed, thudded against something hard, made one final nausea-inducing lurch, and stopped. A pair of muddy wizards lifted Snorri, dropped him onto a stretcher, and trotted away. More hands reached for Ernest.

Reggie said, "All yours, mate. Take good care of 'em."

Gillian followed Mrs Rehsavvy, rising towards the breach.

Alexander shouted, "No," and lunged for the enchantress. He caught her in a flying tackle, clamping his arms around her legs.

"Alex, let go. I don't have enough magic for you, too. I have to get out."

"Not yet, you don't. Not now."

Lightning struck above them, momentarily blinding and deafening everyone in the chamber. When their vision cleared, a bonfire raged over the gap in the ceiling.

Gillian drifted back to earth. She settled into the king's arms, a featherweight, and whispered, "I could have been..."

"Yes. Soon. It will be over soon." One way or another, it would be over very soon. If the empire captured the Token of Office now... Alexander refused to consider that possibility.

Gillian said, "Mrs Rehsavvy?"

"She'll be fine," he said, with more confidence than he felt. "She'll have had all her shields raised."

Winifred Proven Right

Shields? Who needs shields?

The Fire Warlock stood on the ramparts in the centre of a blazing ball of light with miniature threads of lightning arcing from her fingertips, and laughed. With her expanded consciousness, Gunther was as clear as if he stood directly before her. His eyes bulged. He clawed at his cheeks, drawing blood.

"I hit her. I know I hit her. She should be dead."

"Fool." Her thunderous voice echoed off the mountain wall. "You are no match for me, and never will be."

She wrote a lock spell in the air with a lightning bolt for a pen.

Gunther called up the fire, but he couldn't outrun the Fire Warlock. She caught him and slammed her magic-hiding lock—a lock even she would never dare open—on the arrogant swine. And then gaped as two of his own wizards turned on him. An earth father hurled boulders. A sorcerer hit him face on with a raging torrent. The emperor was dead within seconds.

She shouldn't have been surprised.

The sorcerer got her next lock, then the regicidal earth wizard. The other level-five wizards fled, but the Fire Office had taken notice, and directed her attention to each in turn. Enchanters dropped from the sky, sorcerers drowned, earth fathers died as half-finished tunnels caved in, and her conscience said not one word.

Maybe later. Maybe never.

The worst threats eliminated, she threw locks on the enemy wizards, starting with the highest-ranking fire wizards and working her way down, and marvelled at how easy it was to find them, and to reach them across such distance. Why had she been afraid of this?

The war is over. Frankland won. The emperor is dead. The Fire Office is restored. Rejoice, Frankland's Unconquered!

The Fire Warlock's voice echoed in their heads. One pair in an untouched city danced a jig, but most of Snorri's exhausted army dropped where they stood, promising themselves a well-deserved celebration later.

Lucinda brought her attention back to the Fortress. The lowest tier was an ugly mess, but the Fortress still stood, and would stand for centuries to come. Deep gouges in the outer walls could be repaired. She could detect no structural damage in the inner storehouses, public rooms, and apartments. Even the hole punched through to the practice room could be mended.

Lifting her gaze from the foot of the curtain wall, still in deep shadow, Lucinda surveyed the upper tiers. The night's passing storm had dropped a layer of snow that sparkled in the rising sun's slanting rays. Light reflecting from the windows of the Fire Warlock's study made her eyes water. She closed them, and let her mind's eye soar.

Storm King's broken cone glowed gold against a cloudless blue sky. Gillian, almost invisible in a sky blue cloak, skipped along the rim of the volcano's caldera. Lucinda watched for a moment, pleased with the escapee's delight, before bringing her attention back to earth and her own situation.

Despite Jean's assertions that the Fire Office was a magical automaton governed by rules and devoid of emotion and personality, she had sometimes caught glimpses of something almost human. She had wondered how much it reflected its creator, Warlock Fortunatus. Now, with her consciousness expanded and supported by the rebuilt Fire Office, she was quite certain the offices absorbed something of their creators' essences, and Jean had given more of himself in forging the new Fire Office than Fortunatus had in the old. Traces of Jean's loving warmth enveloped her; his lighthouse beacon illuminated everything she viewed.

He had given enough of himself that the new Fire Office would surely be better behaved, helping Fire Warlocks control their tempers rather than inflaming them, reining in the worst excesses of the less competent ones, encouraging cooperation with the other guilds. The Scorching Times were behind them...for good.

Ernest huddled under a blanket in the Rubierre Earth Guildhall. He was dry and warm. His arm was in a sling. A cup of the healer's numbing draught eased the aches of his other injuries. Why did he still feel as if he'd been through a meat grinder?

It wasn't his own bruises that bothered him. He couldn't take his eyes off Snorri's left hand, where the index finger stuck out, bent backwards at an impossible angle. Why couldn't the healer have dealt with that? The overwhelmed and underpowered witch had set his own broken arm, but she had only tsked over Snorri before moving on to someone else in the queue of incoming wounded.

Katie Underwood had arrived shortly afterwards with Mother Brenda, called out of retirement for this crisis. The earth mother had her hands now on Snorri's head. Had had them there for a while. The fire witch had cured Ernest's hypothermia and was now wandering the hall, laying hands on other shivering refugees. But no one had yet bothered with Snorri's broken finger. Ernest tore his eyes away long enough to give the Rubierre healer a dark look, but his attention soon returned to the afflicted digit.

"He'll do," Mother Brenda said. "He'll come round in a minute or two." She moved her hands over Snorri's chest, his arm, then picked up his left hand and gently drew the injured finger back into its proper position.

Ernest's relief was so great he had to put a hand down to keep from toppling over. "Thank you."

Mother Brenda twinkled at him. "Oh, is that what was bothering you? I wondered. Don't worry, he'll be right as rain soon."

Snorri stirred, groaned, and opened his eyes.

Katie returned to Ernest's side. "God, Snorri, you look awful."

Ernest snickered. Fire witches weren't usually prone to understatement. The warlock sported a swollen lip, a lacerated ear, two blackening eyes, and other bruises darkening on all exposed skin. Ernest wondered if he looked as bad. He'd rather not have his wife scream at the sight of him.

Snorri rolled onto his side, shaking his head as if to clear it of fog, and pushed himself upright.

"Lie back down," Mother Brenda said. "I'm not done with you yet."

"Can't. No time. The war—"

"War's over," Ernest said.

Snorri's head snapped up. "Over?"

"The emperor's dead," Katie said. "We won."

"The Fire Office?"

"It's done. You were unconscious when the Fire Warlock ordered all the invaders to surrender."

Snorri's eyes grew wide and dark. "The Fire Warlock? Who?"

Ernest and Katie exchanged an uneasy glance. "Um," Katie said, "Mrs Rehsavvy."

"Noooo," Snorri howled. He lurched off the table, wrenched free of the cursing healer, and staggered towards the fireplace. Katie and Ernest reached for him.

"Hey, Snorri, calm down," Ernest said.

Snorri ignored them. He ducked into the fireplace and disappeared, dragging them with him.

Lucinda had never wanted to be Fire Warlock. When she had first learned she was a warlock, the idea had frightened her so much she had fainted. But as she had developed her powers under Jean's guidance, she had come to accept that she could handle it if necessary, and after Winifred's prediction before the Yule War, she had known that someday it would be.

With the Europan Empire in ruins and the authority of the Fire Office supporting her, she could be de facto empress. If the people of Europa objected to a female ruler, who could do anything about it? No one could take the Fire Office from her by anything short of deadly force. She could fix Europa's problems—some of them, anyway. She could stop those arrogant aristocrats from walking all over the common people. She could end several long running feuds once and for all. There were so many things she could fix.

If she lived long enough.

She scrubbed away an errant tear, then turned and dropped through the hole in the Forge's ceiling. The Reforging Coven formed a wide semicircle around her, staring, as she drifted towards them, but before anyone could muster the nerve to ask the questions they must be brimming with, a column of fire erupted. The warrior who had spent half his life training to be Fire Warlock appeared, with Ernest and Katie in tow.

Lucinda said, "You look awful."

René said, "You're glowing."

"Am I?" She spread her hands. They were no longer throwing off sparks and the light had faded, but yes, she radiated warm yellow.

"Lucinda, I'm—" René's voice cracked. He swallowed hard. "I'm so sorry."

"So am I, but what else can we do?" She wrenched the Token of Office from her finger and held it out to him. "Here."

For a moment he gaped, then strode forward and enveloped her in a tight hug.

"Umph!" She worked a hand free and shoved on his chest. "Take it, you fool, before I change my mind. Or don't you want it?"

He fumbled for the ring, one-handed, without letting go of her. "Hold still," she said, and pushed the ring onto his finger. He wrapped his arm around her again and shuddered. She braced against him. If he fell, they would both go down.

"I forgot," he mumbled.

"You didn't think we would reforge the Fire Office and not fix it so the Fire Warlock could retire?"

"Of course I knew you were going to. It just hadn't sunk in." His voice was thick. "When they said you were Fire Warlock... I thought... Nothing ever changes in Frankland, and Winifred said..."

"Winifred?" Ernest echoed.

Lucinda took pity on the bewildered, exhausted earth wizard. "Enchantress Winifred, years ago, predicted my reign as Fire Warlock would be the shortest ever. I proved the prophecy true, on my terms." She pushed René away and nodded at the clock. "Twenty-three minutes, start to finish. That's one for the record books."

The brilliance of René's grin outshone the glitter of his unshed tears. "Twenty-three minutes to bring down an empire. That's one record that's unlikely to ever fall."

She lookup up at him, dismayed. "It's your victory. I just finished it off. I don't want to steal your glory."

He kissed her forehead. "Don't be an ass, Lucinda. There's enough glory this morning for everyone."

Valhalla

The Reforging Coven and Frankland's Unconquered swarmed the buffet table. Corks popped. Glasses and cutlery clinked. René summoned the guards to join the impromptu feast, and in an hour's time the throng demolished the week's supplies Mrs Cole had laid in. Hugs, laughter, and tears were shared as freely as the wine and ale.

René would have been among them, shaking their hands and congratulating them on a job well done, as Alex was doing, but they had insisted, to Alex and Lucinda's undisguised relief, that he sit and rest his injured leg. He claimed a chair near the tunnel doors, propped the leg up, and let them bring him plate after plate of food, enough to satiate even a ravenous warlock. His vantage point let him speak to every witch, every wizard, and every guard, calling them by name as they trickled out, heading home proud of themselves and their guilds.

Mother Astrid, the first to leave, said, "I'm afraid our work's not done yet. The officeholders will need to visit Paris and London to reassure people that the war's over and there is still a Fire Warlock."

René groaned. "That makes sense, but I can barely hold my head up. And I should wash up before we go, so I don't embarrass the Fire Guild."

Mother Astrid surveyed him, taking in bruises, bandages, unkempt hair, scorched clothes, and streaks of ash. "No, let them see you as you are now. You're so young they won't believe you're the Fire Warlock unless you look like you been through a war. Let's show them you've been fighting for them." She laid a hand on his shoulder. His eyes brightened; his chin lifted. "And that you could fight another war, if need be."

Rene grinned. "Yes, ma'am. Thank you, ma'am."

At last the stragglers departed, leaving him alone with the one person he had been most anxious to see.

Hildur's footsteps echoed in the empty chamber. "You look…"

"Awful. I know. You look…gorgeous."

She snorted, but he meant it, despite her hollow cheeks, dark circles under her eyes, and the layer of grime coating her from head to foot. She had scrubbed her face and hands clean, but dried mud caked her hair. "You prefer brunettes to redheads?"

He flushed. "I didn't mean—"

"I know what you meant." She sank onto the floor and leaned against the chair his leg rested on, her cheek against his knee. "With the war over, will the Fire Office let you sleep?"

"The Fire Office would, but the other officeholders won't. There's too much cleanup work needed. And there's bringing home the dead…" His throat constricted. "You know about Mjöllnir."

"Yes."

Over the past hour his eyes had sought her out, over and over, but now his eyes wouldn't meet hers. What he had to say would hurt, but they both valued honesty too much to leave it unsaid. "It's my fault he's dead."

"Oh? How do you figure that?"

"I lost my head. He had Gunther pinned down, and we could have picked off everybody protecting him one by one, but I went in for the kill too soon and too fast, and it went pear-shaped."

"And you expect me to scold you for acting like a fire wizard?"

"If I hadn't, he'd still be alive."

"And very angry with you for cheating him."

He looked at her then. "Huh?"

"For an intelligent man, you sometimes can't see past your own nose." She reached for him, but checked. "I'd tweak yours if it didn't look broken and not healed yet. Is there any part of you that isn't bruised?"

"No. About Mjöllnir…"

Her eyes swam with tears. "He wouldn't have lived much longer, and he would have hated a shameful death in bed. This was his last opportunity to die a warrior's death. How else could he join the feast in Valhalla?"

René gawped at her. "Do you really believe in Valhalla?"

She flapped a hand at him. "Why do you ask that? It doesn't matter what I believe. He believed; that is enough. He made me promise, three years ago, to fetch him when the war began. I knew he would not return to Thule."

"And you didn't know if you could jump that far. That was... monumental. Stupendous. Idiotic. My God, woman, were you trying to prove you're the bravest warlock in Europa or the stupidest?"

She laughed. "Yes. Not the bravest. I was frightened."

He caught her hands and held them. "Of course you were. I knew that—I was just wrong about what you were afraid of. You should have told me."

"You would have worried."

"I was worried sick about you anyway. Don't ever scare me like that again."

She brought his hands to her lips and kissed his fingers. "I will do what I have to do."

"That's not what I said."

"I am a warlock. You knew that when you married me."

"And I love you for it, not despite it."

"Then you will have to put up with it."

His fingers tightened on hers. "I guess I will."

Later that morning, Alexander and René tromped through snow in a forest clearing. A squad of guards followed, carrying shovels and a stretcher.

René said, "Lucinda says we're close, but she's not sure exactly where."

Alexander said, "Can't the Fire Office find him?"

René said, "The Fire Office doesn't care about dead bodies. He's not a threat any longer."

A guard said, "There he is." A boot protruded from a heap of stones and mud.

"Careful, boys," the sergeant said. "Don't make him any uglier than he already is."

Alexander murmured, "Must we give him a warlock's funeral?"

"God, no," René said. "We'll send him back to Danzig. Let them decide what to do with him."

"Good."

They watched in silence for a bit as the guards dug. Then René said, "Life's funny, sometimes."

"Tell me."

"He went on and on about making me respect him, but the harder he tried, the less I did... And then, I spent all that time studying warfare, getting ready to outthink him, but when it came to it, it was a simple slugging match. I had some ideas during the preparations that the Unconquered used, but mostly it was them being innovative, not me."

Alexander gave him a quizzical look. "I disagree. You made one major innovation without which none of the others would have happened."

"I did?"

"You trusted them. All of them."

René lifted his head and stared into the distance. "I did. Didn't want to at first, but I didn't have a choice."

"Of course you did. You chose loyalty to Frankland over Fire Guild pride. You have treated all the Unconquered fairly, even when it angered the more narrow-minded members of the Fire Guild, and they love you for it."

René snorted. "Come on, Alex, they don't—"

"I am serious. When Emperor Sturmmeister was powerless, his men turned on him. When you were powerless, yours fished you out of the flood and set you back on your feet."

"They still needed a warlock."

"Not so. The war was over. Mrs Rehsavvy was Fire Warlock. They were taxed to their limits, but they went above and beyond themselves to save you. It would have been easier for them to simply stand aside and let you drown."

"Huh."

"For an arrogant, upstart mongrel cur, sometimes you underestimate yourself, my friend."

René's bemused expression faded into a grin. "That's Fire Warlock Mongrel Cur, Your Majesty, and don't you forget it."

Alexander returned the grin. "Of course not, Your Wisdom."

Turning their backs on the last Europan emperor, they walked through the fire to the Fortress, of one mind on the course to set for Frankland's future.

Miranda's pen raced across the page. She scratched out several lines, and began again. The stanza finished, she turned, reaching for her guitar. Alexander stood motionless in the music room's doorway.

"Oh!" She rose and bobbed a curtsey, hiding her dismay at his evident exhaustion.

He walked towards her, smiling. "I'm sorry, I didn't mean to startle you. Or interrupt, if you're in the grip of the muse."

"It's no matter. The song's done. Quicksilver asked me, months ago, to write something short to spread the news. I'll write a much longer ballad later, once Gillian shows me the details."

"Can she? She was distraught…"

"Father Jerome said there's no permanent damage. She'll be fine in a fortnight."

He laid his hands flat on her desk and leaned on them with his head down. "Oh, thank God."

She reached out to lay a hand on his arm, and snatched it back at the last instant, having recollected who he was. "You must be exhausted. You should—Alex! Your hands. What happened?"

He spread his bandaged fingers. "It's nothing. Minor burns. The Fire Office's shields for royalty haven't been rebuilt yet. That's tomorrow, if Mrs Rehsavvy and Master Sven are up to it."

"Oh, Alex." She threw protocol to the wind and caught his hands in hers. "I meant to tell you how grateful I am. Gillian told me you rescued Mama from the flames, but I didn't realise…" Her heartbeat was a snare drum in her ears. "I never thought you were in danger. But of course you would rescue her anyway. You're brave, and I know you'd do anything for Frankland. We'd be lost reforging the Air Office without her."

"It's true, we need her, but I wasn't thinking about that then."

"I know. You rescued her because you love her."

He reddened. She blinked at him. Her king, who could defang the most predatory female courtiers without losing his polite mask, blushing?

"No," he said. "I mean, I do love her, but all I was thinking at that moment was how devastated you would be if we lost her."

Some sliver of ice in her heart melted. She hadn't even known it existed. His keen eyes bore into her. For a moment the world seemed to stand still. Was he holding his breath?

He let out his breath in a rush. "Miranda, I love you."

"Alex," she whispered, "do you really mean it? I thought you wanted a witch for a queen, because that's what Frankland needs."

"Frankland be damned."

"Alex!"

His blush deepened. "I don't mean that. Your mother and Mrs

Rehsavvy are right—Frankland does need a witch for her queen, and I can't ever forget that. But I need something, too. I've tried to tell you before, but you didn't want to listen. I need…"

"What, Alex?"

He fumbled. "A…a wife I can trust, who isn't just another hanger-on who wants something from me. Who'll keep me company late at night after all the fawning courtiers have been shut out. Who'll call me Alex because she's my oldest friend. Who will fill the palace with music without worrying if the performance is good enough for a king, because of course it is, and anyway it's impossible to keep her from singing."

The corners of her mouth lifted. "Be warned, you can't silence a musician."

"I wouldn't want to." His hand tightened on hers. "Miranda, I've asked you this twice before. They say third time is the charm."

"They do say that."

"Miranda…"

The snare drum had become tympani. "Go on."

"Will you marry me?"

"Yes, Alex."

After that there was silence between them for a long time.

At sunset, a small band circled the stacked timber, squeezing together to make room on the small outcropping: Lucinda, René, Hildur, and the Fire Eaters. Plus Beorn, propped up between Hazel and Master Duncan. Mother Astrid had ordered him to stay in bed. He swore at her until she threw up her hands and walked away in a huff.

His face, never beautiful to start with, would now have frightened even Fluffy. His right ear was mangled, his right eye and part of his jaw missing. Too many other injured still waited for the Earth Guild's attention; they couldn't afford to regrow spares. The Fire Eaters gave him furtive, appalled glances, but Lucinda didn't flinch at the sight. In her mind's eye, she saw his bonfire, coming back to life from embers.

He didn't frighten her. Would never frighten her.

She nodded at Hildur. "Whenever you're ready."

Hildur stepped forward with a flaming wand, held it aloft for a moment, then thrust it into the pile of wood. The others followed suit, and Mjöllnir's funeral pyre roared to life. Scenes from his life played in the fire. Lucinda watched, mesmerised, until Hazel tugged at her arm. Beorn was sagging, swearing under his breath, and they were struggling to keep him upright. Lucinda grabbed him, and took the four of them through the fire, back to the hospital quarters in the Fortress.

"Sleep," Hazel ordered. Beorn's head rolled, the swearing stopped mid-word, and he snored.

"He'll be good until noon tomorrow. Get some sleep yourself, Lucinda."

Good advice, but despite her own weariness, she was not ready yet. She went out to the ramparts and watched the bonfire burn down, and the funeral party return to the Fortress. When the watching crowd had dispersed, she turned to go in.

On the patio by the ballroom, René and Hildur sat together, quite still, their arms around each other, heads turned towards the feeble glow of the burnt-out pyre. Their two flames merged into one steady, brilliant torch.

She gave them a wide berth, and paused at the door to the unlit music room. The king dozed in an armchair, facing the windows. In deep shadow, Miranda played something soft and restful on the spinet.

Lucinda moved on, casting an eye over the Fortress, and spied someone who needed her help. In another moment she was on the Matheson's balcony. Gillian's eyes and nose peeked out from an enormous bearskin.

"How is he?" Lucinda asked. "I heard a rumour…"

"In pain," Gillian said. "Not complaining, mind you, but it's obvious. Between him and Father Pierre they had so many broken bones… Father Martin did his best, but his magic gave out while he was setting the bones in Papa Sven's face, and some didn't set right. It'll be days before anyone has enough magic to try again, and by that time they'll have to re-break some bones to get them to move. Mama's afraid they can't ever put his face back together the way it was. She may not let them try, if it means they'll just hurt him again. I can't blame her."

"I'm so sorry."

The bearskin moved as if Gillian shrugged. "He's alive. It's a shame about his face, that gorgeous face, but he's not hard on the eyes even with things askew. Not like…"

"Right. Well. How's your mother taking it?"

"She's acting a bit punch drunk. She had a fit of giggles when Miranda said she wanted to be the first to congratulate the Damaged Duke."

"Damaged Duke? But he's not…"

"He will be, once Alex hears that Miranda started it. Self-fulfilling prophecy, you know."

"And what about you? You need to sleep."

Gillian pulled the bearskin tighter. "I can't go inside. I just can't."

"It's a clear night. It will be much colder before the night's over. You could get frostbite—uh, sorry, meant that literally—on your face."

"I don't know if I can ever sleep indoors again. I'd rather die of the cold."

Lucinda considered the angle where the walls met. "You won't have to. I can heat the walls enough to keep this corner warm for hours."

"Would you? That would be wonderful."

A short time later, the walls glowed cherry red. Gillian snuggled into the bedding Lucinda had dragged out for her and murmured sleepy thanks. Lucinda moved on, taking her time to reach the bedroom where they had taken Jean.

She stood outside his door with a lump in her throat. Even with the door closed she should have sensed his lighthouse beacon, but the beacon had dimmed, and would never again shine as bright. She opened the door and saw an old man with white hair and a spider's web of wrinkles.

He opened his eyes and smiled. His dark eyes, vivid and sparkling, still entranced her. The years and worries dropped away, and she lost herself in his joy at their accomplishment. He held out an arm. She nestled beside him with her head against his shoulder, and related all that had happened since he collapsed.

He listened to her recital without comment. When she had finished, he offered the only opinion, besides her own, that mattered:

"Well done, Your Wisdom. Well done."

The End